Destiny Revealed

Eleanor Tremayne

Scotoma Books Publishing—Hamilton,OH
ISBN: 978-1-7323245-0-3
Library of Congress Control Number: (pending)
Destiny Revealed | Tremayne, Eleanor
Available Formats: eBook | Paperback distribution

DEDICATED

I would like to dedicate Destiny Revealed to the universal literary geniuses that are my inspirational muses; my living compass.

CHAPTER 1

There are carpet makers,
Carpet layers, and even Carpet flyers.
But, the Carpetbagger, is the only one,
That will peddle your dreams
To escape any sorrow,
Or, will allow you to end,
The life you borrow.

Gabriella Girard Blair

Gabriella Girard Blair
March, 2010
Tybee Beach, Georgia

The cold ocean water begins to swallow me into its warm belly. It is not until I see the floating specks that resemble ashes—*Jake's ashes*—that *I* know where I am. Only now, this very minute, does it become clear to me that this will NOT be the day that I die.

Subconsciously, I ask, *"Is this my end?"* *No, of course, your journey doesn't end here. The response is clear. Death is just another path, one that we all must take. The gray rain curtain of this world rolls back, and all turns to silver glass, and then you see it. (JRR Tolkein.)*

At a distance, slightly distorted by the sea salt vision, my lighthouse begins to emerge. *My lighthouse, with its surrealistic beams, is slightly shrouded by billowing soft clouds.*

It invites me to a salacious slumber. *Come to me, Gabby. I will sweep your past into my safe abyss, like a reliable housekeeper.*

At first, there is a sense of relief, not fear that resonates through my veins. A voice from nowhere then reminds me *that this really is only a temporary escape; a momentary peace of mind.*

It is not until the hyperthermia begins to attack my hands, like a well routed wire, that I understand how real this is.

My legs and all remaining external extremities begin trembling, like a string puppet with no control.

Finally, when my eyes lose focus, and my sea water coated tongue becomes numb, I ask once again… *"Is now the time to relinquish all guilt or remorse for those unwise choices that lead me to desperate solutions?"*

Before I am able to mentally register what is happening, , a familiar voice from some unknown realm resonates everywhere and nowhere.

"Death? Why should I fear death? I AM, death is not. If death is, I am not. Why should I fear that which cannot exist, when I do?" (Epicurus)

Suddenly, not knowing why or how, my limp body; smelling like a sea urchin, is sitting on the grainy sand with an oversized beach blanket wrapped around my shoulders.

I have been right here before, during another lifetime. Yet, I cannot recall why, or when.

Not until my eyes begin to slightly focus, do I search around to see who rescued me from this restless ocean. Soon, it becomes clear that I am really all alone.

Slowly, beginning to return to normal, my senses reel in a clear message from my brain that a substantial amount of time has passed since I first stepped on this beach.

Why me? Why here? And what has just happened? There does not seem to be a rational explanation; yet, there is a nagging rush of urgency. Vaguely, I recall that there is somewhere I need to be. But where?

Next to me; in the sand where I am sitting, is a crumpled sweatshirt with a picture of the Eiffel Tower on the front. It has been half-hazardously thrown, as if it was a discarded memory; a reminder of what I want to forget.

It is so much more than just my pathetic life that I am escaping from…it is Molly's death! Beautiful, brilliant, aesthetic, avant-garde Molly.

How could you leave me like this? You were always my pillar of strength; the everlasting fire that rekindled my inner spirit. Never was there a moment that even distance could keep us apart. Our roots are forever intertwined among eternal remembrances.

Please, forgive me Molly for not being strong enough to sit through another eulogy that could not possibly do justice to your life. If I never attend, then are you really dead?

Maybe, there will come another time when I will be able to honor your memory, but today is not that day.

Gabby reaches inside the pocket of her denim jeans and finds the cell phone she has safely hidden before her short walk into the ocean. Caden has nearly blown up the phone, leaving more messages than she is capable of understanding, or retrieving.

Whatever direction she finally decides to take, Caden, must be included somehow. But, for now there is only one person that will help her find the answers…Sterling Powers.

Sterling will be able to sort out this mess, without making any judgements. I know instinctively what I must do, but will I have the courage to move forward?

First, I need to leave; NOW, without hesitating. One lesson that I have learned in years of therapy is that everything is expendable; and, that change is reliable.

Jake's journals, the ones I brought with me to the beach, will be the only significant item that I take when I depart from here.

Leaving my cell phone, my room key; even my sandals here on the beach will be just the proper amount of distraction. Before the searching begins and any questions can be asked, I will be far from Savannah.

Tomorrow, when I don't show up for the funeral service, and my personal belongings are eventually found here, all of this may finally make sense to me.

Maybe; just maybe, this will be the new beginning that I desperately need.

It is a necessary purging—a cleansing of the mind and spirit.

Eventually, even Jake's journals will have to be put to rest. But, for now, they continue to be my lifeline, my safety net—a thin thread that refuses to let me go.

Chapter 2

The empty stage, with languid ghosts, are moving me from the frightening unknown, to a realistic world with living phantoms.

Gabby Girard Blair

Gabby Girard Blair
March, 2010
Tybee Beach, Georgia

Traveling earlier today from the Savannah Airport to Tybee Beach, I passed a Best Buy store. It would be the fastest place to get a prepaid TracFone. The convenience of this type of phone is that it cannot be easily traced.

I do not want to hear how irrational my behavior is, or that I am merely experiencing a midlife crises. The only person that could ever understand how desperate I feel; at this very moment, is presently preoccupied in a cedar coffin. I need time to understand rationally what to do next.

The strip mall is where Best Buy is located. It is so busy that I am having difficulty finding a parking space. After circling around several times; finally, one space becomes available near the front door.

I am so rushed and nervous that I nearly leave the car barefoot. My sandals are still on the beach! Luckily, there are a pair of tennis shoes that I left in the car. While lacing the shoelaces, I realize that these are the only shoes that I now own.

Inside the store, I go directly to the section marked, Electronics. There is no difficulty finding the TracFone; advertising is everywhere.

When the clerk rings up the price for the phone, I automatically hand him my credit card. Then I realize the irony, and pull it back.

"I am sorry, but I would prefer paying cash."

The salesperson looks at me with that Cheshire Cat smile. He realizes at the same time as I do that paying for a Tracfone with a credit card is defeating whatever purpose I am attempting to achieve.

Although, initially, I am self-conscious about my purchase, once I return to the car, my composure has stabilized.

After all, this is my life I am escaping from. I am not some fictional character in an espionage novel.

It is time for this mission to get started. Thankful to 'old school' phone books, I still have all my most important contacts. Tonight, this will be indispensable.

"Sterling? It is Gabby...Gabby Blair."

I wait patiently for what seems like a very long time for a response, not even sure if this is still his private number. Eight years is since we last spoke last, is a lifetime.

But, Sterling is the only hope I now have of leaving Savannah quickly and without a trail. Finally, I hear his familiar voice.

"Gabby? Gabby Girard? **OH My God!** Are you alright? Where are you? I did hear about your friend, Molly, recently passing. I am so sorry."

His voice resonates echoes that stir many awkward, conflicting emotions. *"Why don't people just say dying anymore? Molly is dead. She will never pass through my life again. She is just...**Dead!"***

This is now more difficult than I originally thought it would be. Take a deep breath, Gabby. Focus. This is Sterling, he will understand your pain. When, finally my confident inner voice assures me it is safe to continue, I reply.

"Well, yes. As a matter of fact, this is why I am here right now; in Savannah, for Molly's funeral."

My voice begins to tremble uncontrollably, until once again the inner voice says loudly, *"Damn it, Gabby! I want to have some control here."*

"Baby, what is wrong?" His voice instantly removes any negative inhibitions. I feel him close to me. "Whatever you need ...Gabby, just tell me."

The tone of Sterling's voice is so calm and sincere that it reassures me that there is never anything that I couldn't share with him. He is my male version of Molly. There was never a time that he ever judged me, or turned me away.

"I thought that I could do this, Sterling, but I just can't. I was walking on the beach and suddenly...I am soaking wet on the sand; somehow, a mysterious towel is wrapped around me. I don't know how I got there or why I was in the water in the first place. Honestly, I think I am losing my mind. I just can't go back to Lexington, at least not right now."

For many years, Sterling and I had an intimate relationship that is complicated. At first it seemed like he was merely a multi-billionaire playboy trying to keep himself amused. But, as the years went by, it became clear that Sterling was much more an enigma than his outer shell portrayed. It was not until that unforgettable Halloween night, nine years ago, when Sterling Powers demonstrated an entirely different persona than his normal evasive self. Murray and Calhoun Jackson, brothers, chose to hijack my Bentley that night.

But, it was Murray, the psychopath that wanted to expand his modus operandi to include rape. I became his unwilling victim. There is no doubt that it was Sterling who saved my life when he arrived at the scene preventing Murray from killing me.

A bullet hit him an inch below his aorta. This is when I knew that I could count on Sterling forever.

It does not really matter where I go, as long as it is away from Savannah and Lexington. Sterling will know where it is safe!

"Are you alone in Savannah right now, Gabby?" Sterling asked quietly.

Caden Cassidy and I were nearly engaged forty-five years ago. But, there was no reason to reveal this to Sterling. Only Molly knew that we were currently cyber lovers.

Strangely, it was Molly's untimely death that led me back to Savannah, where Caden lives. We were planning on finally meeting again, for the first time in decades, while I was staying at Tybee Beach. Honestly, this entire unconventional relationship with Caden is something that even I have difficulty accepting.

"Yes. I am all alone. Well, at least physically alone. Recently it feels like I am sharing the inside of my skin with someone else," I said, knowing how nuts this must sound.

"Alright, Gabby. What you need to do right now is just listen to me, carefully. I am in Mexico, on business. Do you have a rental car?" Sterling asked, staying calm.

"Yes. I am in it right now, talking to you."

"Great! Then drive to Hilton Head. Go directly to the *Salty Dog Cafe*. You do know where that is, don't you? I recall you once said that you grew up near Hilton Head. And, this is important, Gabby. Is there anyone, like Alex that might report you missing to the police?" Sterling said this slowly, as if he was talking to a toddler.

"Alex is in Spain. He knows nothing, except that I am here for Molly's funeral. By tomorrow morning, however, some people will notice my absence. I was asked to say a few words during the ceremony. And, yes, I do know exactly where The *Salty Dog Cafe* is. But why do you want me to go there?" I asked, genuinely confused.

"Because, I am sending Thomas to pick you up. At this moment it is the only place I can think of that you both are familiar with. If I remember correctly, this is Spring break. It should be really crowded. It will be easier for you to blend in with the others. Just wait at the bar until you see Thomas. He will have the details where you will be traveling to next."

There was a slight pause as if Sterling was expecting me to

respond. But my mind was still in limbo. Whatever he told me to do, at this point I would not question.

"Hang on, Gabby, we will work this out together, and I will see you soon." Now, there was no doubt; Sterling's voice was fading away.

"Oh, just one more thing, Sterling. I bought a TracFone. I don't know if you will be able to reach me on it?" I said, with a sense of panic in my voice.

"Gabby! Gabby! You should know by now that I could find you even if you were on Mars. I will see you, soon."

And, the phone went dead.

The first thing that Sterling did; once he was off the phone with Gabby, was send an email to Alex that his wife was safe. He would let Gabby fill in the details later.

Alex's phone number and email were still stored in Sterling's data. He insisted Gabby give him that information just in case there was ever an emergency when they were together. This definitely qualified as an emergency!

Sterling could only imagine Alex's reaction once he got the message. But, even that would be better than getting a phone call from the Savannah Police Department. Or, even worse, learning through the news media…"Gabriella Blair; wife of renowned surgeon Alex Blair, is presumed drowned at Tybee Beach. Her husband is the prime suspect ."

CHAPTER 3

Beware of peddlers,
That offer you Fiddlers on the Roof.
Or chimney sweepers,
That will steal your heart
For pittance,
Leaving shallow, straw men,
To mend the empty spaces,
With their dirty shoelaces.
There are Liars on every corner.
Selling their love songs
To lonely maidens
That take refuge
In their Poets corners,
Praying for their wisdom.

Gabriella Girard

Gabby Girard
March, 2010
Hilton Head, South Carolina

To say that life is a challenge is an understatement. It took me an entire lifetime to recognize that learning to adapt and survive is vital in the process of natural selection.

My evolution began in Savannah, Georgia during the turbulent sixties. I contribute my hometown for being the place where my initiation into adulthood was nurtured .

Born Gabriella Girard on October 25, 1949, I witnessed more, and experienced more, than I ever imagined I could withstand. Being involved in extraordinary events, while only being quite ordinary, requires much tenacity.

Early in life is when I realized that *the consciousness of being deemed dead is next to the presumable unpleasantness of being so. In reality, one feels like his own ghost is unlawfully tenanting a defunct carcass. (Herman Melville)*

In fact, it was the tumultuous experience of the Vietnam War—its emotional fallout—that forced me to finally accept that any control of my future was limited. I had no real control.

When Jake Chevalier, the only man that I ever really loved, chose to marry someone else, his reasons were inconsequential. At seventeen years old, all it felt like was rejection.

That Jake had lost a leg in Cambodia, returned with a death certificate in his hand, and a shiny Purple Heart on his chest was impossible for me to accept.

The irrational choices that followed, and led me to that fateful New Year's Eve in 1967, was more than I could embrace at the moment. Later, maybe, at another time, I will be able to replay that scenario , and determine why it happened.

But, now at sixty years old, I am in search for an epiphany. One that, at the very least, will allow me to accept what I cannot change.

Why now do I feel the need; more than the desire, to abandon a comfortable, secure lifestyle, for the unknown, is impossible to explain? What I can acknowledge is that my life has never been predictable.

This short sixteen mile drive, from Tybee Island to Hilton Head, does not give me enough time to reflect.

Why am I so determined to risk my marriage; to pursue this obsession? Maybe, at least, that question will be answered.

At some time during our relationship, I must have told Sterling that I grew up in Savannah. That is most likely why he assumed I had visited the now quite famous *Salty Dog Cafe*. In reality, this popular hot spot never even opened until 1984; long after I left

Savannah.

As a teenager, I, of course, was familiar with the charm of Hilton Head Island. Its ability to retain the same natural, pristine seascapes that William Hilton saw from his ship; three hundred years earlier, is the main tourist attraction.

It was not until 1956, however, that the first resort was established. After that, it did not take long for Hilton Head to be recognized as the East Coast playground for the rich and famous.

When I married Alex Blair, in 1970, his parents were one of the most established, elite horse breeders in Kentucky. As a member of this prestigious family, I finally had the opportunity to visit Hilton Head Island.

This is where many golfing junkets were arranged. Alex would often join his golfing buddies for several days of tournaments, at these very popular links on Hilton Head Island.

On rare occasions, when I accompanied him, it was because all the wives were expected to "entertain" their husbands in the evenings. It was our wifely obligation.

Even then, *The Salty Dog Cafe* was considered too Avant-garde for this elite circle of friends that somehow now were a part of my permanent life. Soaking up the sun by the pool, hosting dinner parties at exclusive dining venues, and shopping at the pricey boutiques was why most of the wives attended.

A few ladies were also in tennis leagues, and extremely competitive. Those who were not, spent their afternoons at the spa, enjoying the resort's amenities; facials, massages, and manicures.

There was always an abundance of alcohol and other recreational drugs to keep everyone satisfied. Occasionally, a Cabana boy might offer a new type of excitement.

As I now approach The Sea Pines Plantation entry gate, it becomes quite obvious that Alex' friends are the same exclusive group of people that I avoided in high school.

It is strange how I ignored those similarities until right now. It does explain, at least, one reason why I can no longer imagine returning to this plastic, facade life that I live daily.

My psychologist, Dr. Laura, taught me to confront my demons while accepting responsibility for keeping them close. This impromptu hiatus will test how perfectly honest I am without blaming Alex, Jake; even Caden, for my mental instability.

The odyssey that I am embarking on will allow me to finally take responsibility for the new direction that I must go. Once I become in control of my own destiny, many answers will be resolved.

It is becoming clear to me that *death by suffocation is much more likely to happen to me than death by water, like Ophelia.*

Escaping the 'phonies' is actually much easier than facing the anxieties that clearly contribute to my recurring nightmares.

Several years ago I was the victim of a brutal rape that has been impossible to relinquish. That traumatic event lead me to open a **Death Box** that was left for me by Jake Chevalier at his funeral in 2001. The same Jake Chevalier that broke our engagement…and my heart!

Thirty four years later; finally, he acknowledged how deep our love was—with the contents in this **DEATH BOX.**

Jake's final request was that I complete a thirty day spectacular trip to Europe—with amazing gifts and personal journals intended to guide me through my remaining life—until we meet again, in the afterlife.

Then, when I returned from that trip, Molly—for some unknown reason encouraged me to reunite with my second lover; Caden Cassidy, whom I had not seen for nearly forty-one years. I can only presume that Molly had good intentions. Knowing,, even now how I love Jake , she must have thought that Caden could ease that loss.

Using the internet, texting and phone to communicate with Caden seemed like a safe alternative. Molly was also one of the few people to know that my marriage was a disaster.

When I told Dr. Laura, my therapist, that I was in contact with

Caden, she cautioned me not to become dependent on the past.

"Gabby. This relationship, even though you are not physically engaged, could cause you more pain than peace of mind. Keep a safe distance emotionally," she insisted.

It was also stressed that I was not ready to physically meet with Caden, regardless how confident I might feel.

Then today, when I arrived at Tybee Beach, preparing for Molly's funeral service I realized that I could not avoid meeting Caden. It first, seemed like a safer alternative to meet for drinks, in a public venue, before the funeral service. When I began to think rationally, the entire thought of meeting Caden, at all, did not seem wise. Nevertheless, whatever I decide about the future now, I do owe Caden an honest explanation . Meeting with him will just be another obstacle that I can have to learn to overcome.

All of these issues finally came together at this climatic event—the premature death of my childhood friend and female soulmate— Molly McGee. She is the only reason why I would ever agree to return to Savannah, Georgia.

In 1967, when I left, I vowed never to come back. And, I almost kept that promise!

If all this is not enough to be in search of a Houdini escape route, Jake Chevalier took elaborate measures before his passing. In two personalized journals—both dedicated to me—his primary intention was to prove that not only will we reunite after death, but that he is constantly with me, even now. He continues to be devoted ; even after his extinction on earth, to show me how we can overcome, our temporary intermission of love.

It is the secret of the world that all things subsist and do not die, but retire a little from sight and afterwards return again. (Ralph Waldo Emerson.)

Returning to Alex, as if that is even an option now, cannot happen without drastic changes. One thing that I am certain about, is that our current living arrangement is not only toxic, but also impossible to continue.

At last, I am relieved when I see the parking lot directing me to the restaurant. The Cape Cod blue building is affectionately known throughout the island; *The Salty Dog Café*, is very inviting.

At the front entrance wall, I am greeted with a hand painted image of a friendly Labrador wearing a bright yellow slick fisherman's rain cap. It is both amusing and friendly.

I request to sit on the outside deck, in the bar. In the dark, fire flies perform their native ritual dance near the wooded area that borders the cove. This bar is situated near the boat marina, which is another reason why it is always busy. There is an excellent view of the water and front entrance from my table.

When my 'Bloody Mary' arrives, I begin to relax for the first time all evening. To help the time go by, on the back page of the menu is the famous story of how this place got its name.

Apparently, as the legend has been told, John Braddock and his best friend, Jake, (*a rather sick ironic joke*)a Labrador retriever, were out fishing on his small boat when a massive sea storm; without warning, caused the boat to capsize.

Somehow, Jake courageously, after three days at sea, pulled his owner to safety. This was the exact place that John Braddock decided to immortalize Jake's heroic act by building a café in his honor.

It is a cute story that contributes to millions who annually visit; determined to not only eat at the café, but also shop at the souvenir store. This is where they can buy the famous *Salty Dog* merchandise, to wear in public, confirming their visit to the now famous café.

"Miss Gabby?" Thomas lightly touches my shoulder, but I am nevertheless, startled.

"I am so sorry, Thomas. Lately everything seems to make me nervous," I replied.

Thomas pulled up a chair and insisted that I finish my drink before we leave. "Please, Miss Gabby, take your time. There is no rush."

Thomas has been Sterling Powers personal driver for many years, even before we were together. He knows everything that happened in my past regarding Sterling and I.

"Thank you, Thomas, for meeting me here. Has Sterling given you any idea where I am going?" I ask quietly.

Thomas removes a large envelope from his jacket and hands it to me.

"This will outline the next twenty-four hours. You will receive further instructions when you arrive at the Hotel Coronado, sometime this evening," Thomas said.

For some reason, this news slightly overtakes me. I have never visited California and am rather confused why Sterling chose this destination. "Hotel Coronado? Is that the famous landmark in California?" I ask, obviously surprised.

"Yes, that is definitely the one. It is located in San Diego, the most southern part of California. Have you ever been there before?"

Thomas is attempting to make all this sound like a normal vacation. I am curious just how much Sterling shared with him about this trip. It could not be very much, since he didn't give me many details.

"No, Thomas, I have never had the opportunity to visit California. It just seems quite a distance." It was not up to me to question Sterling's logic, or to sound ungrateful.

"It will be approximately a five hour flight on Mr. Powers' private jet. It is being prepared at this moment at the Hilton Head Municipal Airport. I am certain it will be ready for takeoff by the time we get there." Thomas was careful not to sound as if he was rushing me.

As I stood up preparing to leave; before I could pay for my drink, Thomas left a fifty dollar bill on the tray. We, then, proceeded to the front entrance. Thomas follows closely behind me—almost like a body guard does.

"If you remain right here under the canopy, Miss Gabby, I will bring the town car around, immediately."

Before I can insist on walking, Thomas is gone. All the people coming or going appear happy, normal. I wonder if I ever was like them.

My thoughts are kindly interrupted when the town car arrives.

"Do you have any luggage that you want me to store in the trunk, Miss Gabby?"

I smile nervously; nodding 'no', as I try to relax on the supple leather backseat for the drive to the airport. Thomas doesn't appear surprised that I am traveling without any luggage, and I am not about to fabricate some illogical explanation.

According to my watch, it is currently 9:00 pm. That makes it only 6:00 pm in California. *Finally, going back in time. Something I always wished I could do,* I thought to myself. This would mean that the estimated time of arrival would be around midnight.

The illusions that were taking residence in my mind were now creating an interesting blend of anticipation, laced with speculation. A new beginning with the hope for healing was enough for me at this moment.

CHAPTER 4

Man can live about forty days without food, about three days without water, and about eight minutes without air, but only one second without hope.

Charles Darwin

Gabby, March, 2010
San Diego, California

The drive to the airport was dark and quiet. Thomas would never be the one to start a conversation with his passenger, and I was still trying to accept that I was really doing this.

Alex was still in Spain. He did not expect me home for a few days. Unless, of course, someone like Caden, or Gigi; Molly's life partner, reported me missing to the police, there should be nothing strange about my absence. Even if that should happen, I always intended to let Alex know where I was before any mayhem begins to take over.

There are just too many decisions to make at this moment. Once I have a chance to explain to Sterling what has been happening the last few years; especially with Jake's legacy, I know that he will provide me an unbiased solution. Tonight, on the beach, the overwhelming circumstances seem impossible to unravel.

As Thomas pulls off the highway onto the one way road toward the private jet hangers, immediately, Sterling's Boeing Business Jet 3 becomes visible.

On the wing; in a distinct font, are the silver initials, 'SP', inside an elaborate laurel wreath. The very first time I saw this spectacular airplane, I asked what the laurel wreath represented.

"You are an inquisitive creature, Miss Gabby. Most people just assume that it is an elaborate design for my initials," Sterling explained.

"Really, Sterling? Anyone who spends time with you would realize that nothing that you do is random." I can still recall how impressed he was with my response.

"Right again, Gabby. You really are quite observant. Most people who make an assumption about me, believe that it symbolizes the Olympic Games. However, what they usually do not know is that the laurel also represents victory. To me it is a reminder to never merely rest on my laurels. Always be prepared for competition." Sterling waited for my response.

"For some reason, Mr. Powers, you have never impressed me as anyone who would ever be satisfied with his own accomplishments," I responded, emphatically.

Thomas brought me back to the present when he opened the door and helped me toward the air stairs. "You have a safe flight, Miss Gabby. I guarantee that you will enjoy San Diego. Spring is the best time to visit." Thomas saluted as I began ascending to the main cabin. Once at the top of the stairs, I waved 'goodbye' to Thomas.

A flight attendant dressed in a dark purple skirt and blazer welcomed me. None of this crew is familiar, but, of course, it has been many years since I was a guest.

The last flight on this same plane was unforgettable. It was a short flight to New Orleans for the Erotica Halloween Extravaganza...the one that nearly cost me my life.

"Welcome, Ms. Blair. If you will follow me, I will lead you to the dining area." The attendant; whose name tag read, Pamela, said pleasantly.

This plane I recall is used for corporate travel and can accommodate, comfortably, up to twenty-five people. However, when Sterling used it privately, there was also a master bedroom available, a full bath, reception area and several dining room options.

On this flight there is a pilot, co-pilot, and two flight attendants. Once Pamela made sure that I was comfortable, with a glass of wine, both pilots came by to introduce themselves to me.

"Tonight's flight will be approximately five hours, Ms. Blair, and we are not expecting very much turbulence. It should be a smooth flight into San Diego. If you feel like getting a few hours of sleep after dinner, Pamela will prepare that cabin for you. Let us know if there is anything that you might need," Officer Miller recited perfectly; as he does, most likely every flight.

"Thank you. Everything looks perfect. I am leaving it all up to you, the experts," I said, really anxious to leave as soon as possible. *I am not sure why I feel the necessity to escape so strongly. I am fairly certain that no one, except maybe Caden, has noticed me missing, yet.*

Soon after takeoff, a rather tall, young gentleman with long pitch black hair, tied back into a sleek ponytail and a chef's apron, introduces himself.

"Good evening, Ms. Blair. My name is Chandler. I will be serving you this evening. Here is a menu for your dinner selection. I can also combine anything listed into a special entrée, if you prefer." He waited patiently for me to select. *Could Chandler be his real name? Maybe he changes it each month? How fun would that be?*

Food was the last thing on my mind during the past several hours. In fact, the last meal I remember eating must have been a bagel with cream cheese when I left Lexington early this morning.

"Would it be possible for you to make a chef's salad with perhaps some chicken?" I asked, not even sure if I could keep that down.

"Of course, that can easily be accommodated. Is there anything else that I can add for you, Ms. Blair?" Chandler graciously waited for me to dismiss him.

"Thank you, Chandler. And, maybe another Chardonnay? That is all. I won't be needing anything else."

Hopefully, the wine will put me to sleep. I find it rather amusing that everyone on this plane refers to me by my married name, while both Sterling and Thomas use my maiden name. Perhaps it is just another one of those oddities that I notice without any relevance.

After taking a few bites of my meal, I decide to stretch out on the reclining chair, rather than opting for the master bedroom. This is a reasonably short flight. Once my head touches a pillow, even on an airplane, I might not be able to wake up.

When my eyes close, my mind enters that vulnerable phase when *the current sweeps its own way through us, as the streets of a city are swept and flushed at night. It sweeps through our nerves and our blood, sweeping away the ashes of our days spent consciousness towards one form or other of excretion. This earth current actively sweeping through us is really the death activity busy in the service of life. (DH Lawrence)*

A disgusting sewage stench is coming from the pores of this creature from hell. His lizard tongue is licking my inner and outer body. The images of his greasy hands; his nails coated in slime, hold my naked breasts as I desperately twist my body like a contortionist, trying every angle to escape.

The slobbering saliva foaming from his mouth causes a wrenching vomit in the back of my throat that I cannot control.

Then, without warning, my face is in the mud and he is humping me with his male member; piercing my anus, feeling like a red hot iron until I sense a sudden relief when my wretched body is released. As the monster is being pulled away, I hear his low growling voice…"You are my Bitch, now. I will find you wherever you go. My semen is floating inside you. I own you. Never forget that."

When my eyes open, it is Pamela, the purple flight attendant that is restraining my hands and trying to talk as softly as possible to sedate whatever just occurred.

"Miss Gabby, you are okay? You are safe. Do you know where you are?" I hear her voice, but I cannot understand why she is concerned. I try to pull my hands free. Pamela gently releases her hold.

By this time, Chandler has also arrived, and both are still trying to determine what they should do next.

Then, like clips from a film reel, I begin to remember slowly what happened.

"Miss Gabby, you were screaming so intensely that I was afraid that you may be having a seizure. Do you recall any of this?" Pamela now has regained her professional demeanor.

"I am beginning to put the pieces slowly together. I apologize for such a frightening experience. But, I am alright now." I also try to convince myself, as well as the two flight attendants.

"We are approximately forty-five minutes from descending. Maybe a cup of camisole tea and a croissant will make you feel better?" Chandler says, without waiting for me to respond.

When the tea arrives, it definitely relaxes me. In the bathroom, I attempt to clean myself up as best as possible. I take advantage of the complimentary toiletries.

As I look in the mirror, I notice for the first time my sunken eyes surrounded by black circles. I hardly recognize myself. Before I can completely evaluate how terrible I truly look, there is a gentle tap on the door.

Pamela hands me a lovely Louis Vuitton apricot colored pants suit with a white linen button down blouse.

"There are also a pair of casual heels right outside the door. Please let me know if there is anything else that I can get for you, Miss Gabby."

Before I can even thank her, Pamela has left. I should have known. Sterling always made certain that I was taken care of and comfortable.

Thankfully, I have not gained any weight. This suit fits perfectly!

As far as the 'owl' eyes; for the time being, my Jackie O glasses will at least camouflage the worst part.

"We are approaching our final descend into the San Diego International Airport. Please make certain that your seat belt is secure. Welcome to Southern California, Ms. Blair," the pilot cheerfully announces.

I glance down at my watch. It is already set for West coast time, 12:08 am. I take a few deep breaths, cross myself, and say quietly, *I am within and without simultaneously; enchanted and repelled by the inexhaustible variety of life. (F Scott Fitzgerald.)*

CHAPTER 5

If you are going to love,
Love like the moon
It doesn't steal the night
It only unveils the
Beauty of the dark.

Isra Al-Thibeh

Sterling Powers: 1945-1970

On July 9, 1945, a total solar eclipse occurred at Wichita, Kansas. Just as the moon completely covered the sun, the earth became dark for nearly two and a half hours. While the Bailey's beads began to grow and merge into a crescent, the midwife was preparing a young mother for the crowning of her son's head to push through the birth canal with such a designed intensity that it appeared premeditated.

As long ago as the Dark Ages, people marveled at how the stars influence human nature. Astrologers claim that they are able to predict a person's future based on the alignment of planets and stars during birth. Solar and Lunar eclipses are another phenomena that influences fate.

The very idea that the universe for a short amount of time is out of balance; or like scientists might say is in an 'ascending and descending mode', creates an uncomfortable environment.

According to most astrologists, those who are born during a solar eclipse are at that moment experiencing the transformation of karma. Their lives are destined to reciprocate to the earth all the beneficial gifts the universe bestows to them when they take their first breath.

This is both a blessing and a curse. Forever, these 'eclipse babies' will experience tremendous opportunities to succeed, but they also have the obligation to recompense. Those who ignore this will be in constant turmoil between their inner and outer self.

Once, Celeste heard her son cry, for the first time, all the anxiety that had overcome her during the zealous hours of labor dissipated almost instantly.

"Your son, Celeste, is strong, healthy and with outstanding lungs," the midwife said, handing the swaddled child who barely fit into the receiving blanket, to the anxious new mother.

Celeste, immediately, looked into her son's eyes that resembled polished platinum, and declared that his name would be Sterling. The fact that her son was born during a total eclipse assured Celeste that Sterling was destined for great achievements in his future. Perhaps, even more significant, Sterling would restore balance in her life, similarly as the eclipse assures stability to the earth.

Celeste never allowed the fact that Sterling's father left her, soon after he discovered her pregnancy, to influence her positive energy. Her son would always be her first obligation.

Celeste considered Sterling a gift from God and when he was born during the solar eclipse it was a sign that they were both blessed.

Soon, after Sterling's birth, Celeste returned to Akron, Ohio, to live with her widowed father. Together, they would raise her son. Sterling became the center of their universe.

At an early age, it became obvious that Sterling was gifted. His ability to converse, compare and contrast; as well as offer analogies, by the age of four, was more than impressive.

It was, however, unclear how this intelligence would serve him or what his gift might be. That is, until high school.

At the age of thirteen, Sterling was already six feet tall. It seemed to Celeste that this occurred almost overnight. The doctor assured her that it was common for young boys to grow quickly and that he was definitely healthy.

Sterling was so preoccupied with his academics that he never took any interest in sports, except as an observer.

But, it was Sterling's Algebra teacher, Mr. Henry; also the assistant basketball coach, that finally convinced him to meet in the gym one afternoon.

"Sterling, I just want to see how well you throw the basketball. It won't be more than thirty minutes, max." Mr. Henry had been trying to get Sterling to the gym all semester, with no success. Finally, Sterling agreed, but for only thirty minutes. "Okay…Okay. Thirty minutes. What? You have a heavy date that you can't give me any more time?" Mr. Henry said, half joking.

"No heavy date, Mr. Henry, it's just that I have never been an athlete. If I'm going to make it to college, it is going to be on grades," Sterling said, seriously, and then added, "Not on any basketball court."

"I hear you, Sterling, but just humor me and give me thirty minutes of your precious time," Jacob Henry said with a wink.

Sterling often enjoyed looking back at that moment, as if it was when the stars lined up perfectly for him. After that time, his life would change more dramatically than he could ever imagine.

During those four years that Sterling attended St. Vincent-St. Mary Catholic High School in Akron, Ohio, the basketball team brought home state championship trophies every year.

At the same high school; years later, St. Mary's would produce an even greater basketball star, LeBron James.

On May 2, 1962, Sterling signed his intent to play basketball with the University of Kentucky. He was offered a full academic and basketball scholarship. It was the best of both worlds.

Sterling pursued his business degree while continuing to impress professional agents who were searching for new talent.

In his senior year of college, Sterling was approached by an agent from the Kentucky Colonels that offered him $413,000 a year with a

$20,000 signing bonus. Sterling never even hesitated. He knew that this would be a life changing opportunity for his family.

During 1968-1970; while on the team, the Colonel's had the highest winning percentage of any other franchise.

Sterling was quite content with his contract and the team until Paul Mason, his agent, made him an offer that was difficult to ignore.

"Listen Sterling, you have had a great career here with the Colonels, but there is a new NBA team starting in Cleveland called the Cavaliers. They are willing to pay nearly double your salary. More importantly, you need to consider realistically how long those knees will last. This is a great opportunity that I strongly urge you to take."

As Mason predicted, Sterling only had a few more good years on the court. Financially, he had first taken care of his family, and then invested, or saved, the remaining majority of his earnings. While most of his teammates were living luxuriously, Sterling was quite content with a simple standard of life.

Once again the stars were lining up in a majestic pattern that would provide Sterling with another 'once in a lifetime' economic opportunity.

Brian Tucker, a fellow teammate, who was also considering retirement, one afternoon at lunch, shared with Sterling a business proposal that was highly confidential.

"I am going to let you in on a very lucrative investment opportunity, Sterling. All that I ask is if you decline the offer, you mention it to no one else." Brian was definitely serious.

"Well, you know me Brian, I am not the kind to throw away money and I have managed to stay away from all the glitz. If this offer is legitimate, then you know my word is good enough," Sterling replied, quietly.

That afternoon was the next phase in Sterling Powers amazing life. Both he and Brian invested in a variety of unknown stocks in a secluded area known as Silicon Valley. A very keen financial investor, eventually, made each of these two men multi-billionaires.

CHAPTER 6

Clocks slay time...time is dead as long as it is being clicked off by little wheels; only when the clock stops does time come to life.

William Faulkner

Sterling Powers 1970-2010
Lexington, Kentucky
San Diego, California

The same year that Sterling signed with the Cavaliers, fate would once again intervene.

One of the team players, Jonathan Smith, invited Sterling to the Kentucky Derby. His father happened to be the official Veterinarian for one of the horses entered in this legendary race. An added bonus was a wedding reception touted as the most spectacular event of the year.

Sterling, naturally, never knew then that the stunning bride, Gabriella Girard, would someday cross his path again. At that moment, he was just impressed with the magnificent details that lived up to all the hype.

Prior to meeting Gabriella Girard Blair; nearly twenty years later, Sterling was preoccupied...experimenting with life. His newly acquired wealth was both a gift and a curse. There were no longer restrictions of any kind on what he could pursue.

Eventually, he knew that he would find the perfect business where he could use his entrepreneurial skills. But, now it was time to enjoy exploring what the world had to offer.

There was never a shortage of women that were eager to entertain the debonair, wealthy playboy. Sterling was beyond the average good-looking man. He had an aura that followed him like a glowing shadow. The pitch black hair; accentuated with sparkling pewter eyes, was mesmerizing.

But, Sterling's truly outstanding feature was his ability to be authentic. Anyone listening to him speak felt the sincerity and sense of truth in his voice. His ability to capture the attention of any audience was charismatic.

Sterling's only flaw was a sexual appetite that he could never entirely satisfy. Naturally, this created many problems with his relationships. There was also no preference for male or female partners. Regardless of gender, a monogamous relationship was impossible to maintain.

On a trip to New York in the mid-seventies, Sterling became fascinated with Marina Abramovik—the 'grandmother of performance art'. The relationship between her and her audience experimented with how the body accepts the limitations of the mind.

During one performance at the Museum of Modern Art in New York, Sterling witnessed how Marina placed seventy-two various objects on a table. Some of these props were items of pleasure and some items could result in pain. For six hours, the audience was invited to use any of those objects on her exposed naked breasts.

As the performance continued, the audience seemed to become more aggressive. People, at times, would inflict a moderate amount of pain; then watch her reaction.

Although Sterling did not participate in this experimental exhibition, he could not ignore a degree of pleasure in watching. This would later lead him to explore the private sex clubs.

First, it was the voyeurism that gave him pleasure. Soon, however, Sterling recognized that his desire to participate in these rituals was an outlet, allowing him to function more productively in his everyday life.

Much of this changed when he met Gabby. His first impression of her was like taking a deep breath after a summer shower. All the impurities from the air were removed. She was the fresh oxygen that he needed in his life, and he embraced all she had to offer.

Sterling found it refreshing how Gabby was genuinely impressed with all the new opportunities that he offered her; both sexually and aesthetically, when in reality, it was she that provided Sterling with a new perspective. What was once considered blasé and common, now became unique and challenging.

Their relationship for so many years was mysteriously perfect. He never felt the obligation to justify anything that he did. And, she never expected him to be exclusive. It was a 'laissez-faire' bond that never disappointed either one of them.

Not until that doomed Halloween evening in New Orleans where Sterling first introduced Gabby to an exclusive sexual club experience. He should have known that this was beyond her comfort level. However, what followed, after they left was nothing that he could have ever predicted or prevented.

Although he continued to replay those events internally, attempting to alter the outcome, the brutal truth was that he failed to protect her from that vile rape.

Nothing would ever be the same between them again!

After her recovery, Sterling learned that Gabby went abroad for nearly a month by herself. Nobody seemed to know what prompted that decision. Or, if they knew, nobody was revealing it.

When Gabby returned from Europe, the few times they met for lunch or cocktails, she was a different person; distant, preoccupied, a distorted caricature of the once ethereal creature he was originally enchanted by.

When he received the phone call this evening from Gabby, she sounded desperate. Sterling could not imagine what happened to make her decide spontaneously to contact him after all this time.

Whatever the problem was, he vowed to never let her down, again. The responsibility that Sterling felt toward Gabby was

31

unconditional. Regardless of the situation, making sure she was safe was the main priority. That is the least he could do.

Once he arrived in San Diego, there would be plenty of time to work on possible solutions to any problems that Gabby was facing. Sterling looked forward to a pleasant reunion, in spite of the circumstances.

If her flight arrives on time, Gabby would be at The Hotel Coronado by one o'clock in the morning. He would not disturb her until the early afternoon. That should allow her an appropriate amount of time to become acclimated to the new time zone.

Sterling had instructed his personal assistant to reschedule any meetings for next week. The only time he was to be contacted was for an emergency.

Those who worked for Sterling only remember one other time he ever gave those instructions; that was two years ago, when he was informed that his mother was dying.

Then, Sterling vanished from the face of the earth for ten days before reappearing. When he returned, he made it very clear that he did not want to ever explain where he went. And, no one ever asked.

CHAPTER 7

He stepped down, trying not to look long at her, as if she were the sun, yet he saw her like the sun, even without looking.

Leo Tolstoy

Sterling and Gabby
March 2010
San Diego, California

Hotel Del Coronado was built in 1888 by Elisha Babcock and H. L. Story. Situated on the Pacific Ocean, the sea side resort was intended to be an impressive alternative to a busy environment. The combined, carefree luxury beckoned guests to relax, reflect, and reminisce.

In the early morning; before sunrise, the magnificent great dame hotel; with its red dome roof, invited Gabby to enter a peaceful oasis—a refuge from a distorted milieu.

Once the limousine stopped, and the driver opened her door, Gabby was greeted by an elderly gentleman with a very warm smile and strong hand.

"An early good morning, Ms. Girard, and welcome to the Hotel Del Coronado. My name is Charles, and I will be your personal butler while spending time with us."

Charles continued to hold my hand, guiding me up the short stairs into the lobby.

Once inside, we passed the front desk and continued to the elevators down the corridor.

Charles, thankfully, did not ask if I had any luggage. Inside the elevator, a designated key was required to make the elevator operate.

"Is this your first visit to San Diego, Ms. Girard?" Charles asked, politely.

"Yes, it is my first visit to California to be specific," I said, glad that we had reached our floor. I was not in the mood for small talk, but I also tried not to be rude.

When the elevator opened, we were directly in the suite. Charles walked ahead of me, adjusting the lights with a remote control. As the soft lights turned on, the drapes opened and the wall of windows revealed a patio with the ocean and beach directly below my living room.

"Later this morning, after you have sufficiently rested, you may want to have your brunch on the patio. There is always a welcoming breeze and, sometimes, the Dolphins will be at a short distance frolicking in the surf," Charles said in a pleasant tone.

It was far too much for me to absorb at the moment. Thankfully, Charles showed me briefly where the kitchen was and then directly to the bedroom.

Charles must have sensed how exhausted I was when he briefly said, "Good night," and led himself out of the room.

The gigantic bed, with six fluffy pillows, was already turned down for me. The only energy that I had left was to quickly remove my clothes and slip into the crisp cotton nightgown left on the bed.

Once my head felt the feather pillow, my eyes closed. The ocean's peaceful rhythm that could be heard through the slightly ajar glass door, serenaded me. Falling asleep was no problem, now!

There is that fleeting moment when you are between asleep and awake, when you don't know the difference between reality and fantasy, when—for just that one moment—you feel with your entire soul that the dream is reality and it really happened. (James Baldwin).

The sun block drapes made it even more tempting to ignore the necessity of waking and...remembering why I was here. A few moments of silence passed before I made any attempt to rise.

As my eyes began to focus and my mind awakened, I notice there was a clock on the bed stand that appeared to indicate that it was three o'clock. *Was that morning or afternoon? Perhaps more importantly, what day is this?*

Once the questions began to fill my brain, it was enough to urge me to find the answers.

Pulling open the drapes, the brilliant California sun assures me that it is early afternoon. Then, a slight tapping at the bedroom door reminds me where I am.

"Ms. Girard, it is Charles. Is it alright if I place your coffee on the patio? I will be back shortly to take your brunch order, if that suits you?" Charles waited, patiently, for a response.

"Yes, Charles, I will be out in a few moments. Thank you," I answered, politely.

In the bathroom, a white terry robe with a gold Del Coronado emblem sewn on the pocket was hanging conveniently behind the door.

Quickly, I wash my face and brush my teeth, throw my hair up in a ponytail; then, reach for my sun glasses. Thankfully, they are still on the dresser where I left them when I arrived early this morning.

As Charles promised, my coffee is in a silver plated server, sitting on a round glass table. A lovely small bouquet of red roses also greeted me.

But, it is beyond the clear glass door that my eyes fixate on the blue Pacific Ocean. Before I sit down on the inviting rattan chair, it is the children chasing the waves, dogs fetching Frisbee's and couples walking hand in hand that captures my attention. Everything appears exactly like an advertisement for a perfect seaside vacation.

Just as I begin to pour my coffee, there is an uncanny sense that someone is walking toward me from behind. Before I can react, a familiar voice breaks the silence.

"Gabby! It is wonderful to see you!" Sterling leans down to give me an innocent, light kiss on the cheek, as he takes the seat directly opposite me. Once I can see him, and feel his warm presence, I cannot hold back the tears.

"Sterling, forgive me for calling you and disrupting your life."

Sterling is up and holding me in his arms, stroking my head before I can say another word.

"And, who else would you call, my Gabby? That was always my promise to you. From the first day we met. Do you not remember?" Sterling whispers in my ear.

For just that short moment, anything and everything that ever happened to me evaporated. It did not matter that it would soon return; it was only NOW that mattered.

Chapter 8

Mother Nature will shake your shoulders gently, and remind you if you choose to stop caring what other people think of you and instead care what you think of you, you will experience a new era of your life you never dreamed possible.

Donna Ashworth

Sterling and Gabby
March, 2010
San Diego, California

"You know that I will do whatever I can to help you, Gabby. But, it is imperative that you tell me everything that has happened since we last met," Sterling said, with conviction. "I will never judge you or even attempt to solve all your problems. Together, we have been through so much that trust is the one thing I can guarantee. You must trust me, Gabby."

Sterling wanted to make certain that I knew his limitations.

"Trust me, Gabby." Those were Jake's words all over again. Although I truly wanted to trust Sterling, I am reminded of an ancient African warning to never trust a naked man that needs a shirt. Sterling may not even recognize that he needs a shirt.

I, too, may have had that problem early in life, but it is now time to place the past where it belongs.

To be perfectly honest, Sterling has been the only man who I could trust. Listening to him now gives me a sense that he knows how I feel. The confusion, insecurities, and recent losses of loved ones is overwhelming. Explaining my relationship with Jake and Caden to

Sterling will be a wrenching experience, yet I agree that he must be told everything if I expect him to help.

"There is only one other matter that we must discuss. I notified Alex that you were safe. However, he deserves to know where you are and why you are here. After that, whatever happens, the two of you must decide. Are you willing to talk to him, Gabby?"

Facing Alex will be unpleasant, but not impossible. I do agree that I owe him an explanation. Actually, it is Caden; not Alex, that I am the most nervous to talk with, or about.

Caden will be the one having difficulty understanding why I didn't confide in him. And, of course, there is also that little detail; Caden doesn't even know who Sterling is.

"I planned on contacting Alex today; however, he is still in Spain. I believe he is scheduled to return home tomorrow. I will let him know that I need some time by myself. Since this was not a mutual decision, I can predict that he will not be pleased. Nevertheless, as long as the Blair name is protected, Alex will not totally object," I said, feeling common sense returning after a temporary absence.

"Once we are able to resolve these issues, I thought that you might enjoy spending some time in Mexico. By any chance, do you have your passport?"

Sterling now sounded like he had successfully negotiated a business venture.

"As a matter of fact I do have my passport. For some coincidence I never removed it from my purse when I arrived home from Europe." Slowly, I am gaining my composure.

"As I mentioned to you when you called, I was in Cabo San Lucas closing a business arrangement with some Mexican entrepreneurs who have similar visions as I. It is an exciting opportunity to combine a lucrative transaction, while assisting the local community."

Sterling sounded enthusiastic about this.

Leaving the United States permanently, or even Lexington, never entered my mind. But, the idea of spending some time in Mexico actually sounded inviting.

Charles reappeared with a bunch menu, just as Sterling stood up from the table.

"Good afternoon, Mr. Powers. Will you be joining Ms. Girard for brunch?" Charles asked.

"No, but thank you, Charles. It is good seeing you again," Sterling answered, then turned back toward me.

"I know that you will be well taken care of Gabby under Charles' watch," Sterling said, sincerely.

"I will give you a call later this evening, for supper. That should give you enough time to digest all that we discussed. Oh, and one more thing, there are several outfits in the bedroom closet for you. I hope that they are to your liking. They should be sufficient until you have an opportunity to go shopping. "

Sterling was out the door before I could say another word.

It was less than twenty-four hours and Sterling somehow managed to have covered all the basics, including an assortment of clothes that I could wear.

There was no doubt why Sterling was so very successful. I envied how organized his mind was. But, then again, I also knew that he had some dark places in that brilliant mind that occasionally caused him to experience demons, similar to mine. Sterling just had better control at managing them.

Finally, being alone once again, I can no longer avoid contacting Caden.

When I enter his number into the Tracfone, and hear the ringing tone, I instinctively end the call. Texting is a better option. This will avoid answering any questions.

Caden, it is Gabby. I just wanted to let you know that I am safe, but no longer in Savannah. Once I am settled, I will contact you again.

Gabby

I pushed (Send)

There really was not anymore that could be said at this moment. It may sound sarcastic, but I thought that my text was more considerate than Caden's sudden exit that New Year's Eve in 1967.

My focus now needs to be on how to move away from this pernicious past and embrace the future. Allowing Sterling to have a major role in this catharsis process will be like staging a traditional Greek tragedy, with me taking the lead role. I can only hope that my fate will be better than Medea's.

CHAPTER 9

God turns you from one feeling to another and teaches by means of opposites, so that you will have two wings to fly, not one.

Jalaluddin Rumi

Caden Cassidy
March, 2010
Savannah, Georgia

Molly's funeral was a traditional Irish wake. The service itself was filled with grief, several emotional eulogies, and a touching video that Gigi somehow was able to produce—in spite of her obvious mourning.

The video and still photographs depicted Molly as a precocious child, through high school. Most of them included Gabby, also. This made her absence even more noticeable.

After the service, everyone moved to the Olde Pink House, a Savannah landmark restaurant, where Gigi had reserved a banquet room to celebrate Molly's life. There was a local band that played both Irish tunes and modern rock.

Gigi and her brother, Pierre, assured those attending that it was Molly's last wishes that the grieving would end at the chapel. These next few hours were intended to remember the joyful spirit that Molly shared with so many people.

When I arrived at the 'wake', there were very few individuals that I recognized. Only some classmates, and distant relatives, that I remember from picnics with my family. Ironically, most of the guests flew from Paris to show their final respects to Molly and Gigi.

"I am confused why Molly insisted on having her final resting place be Savannah, rather than Paris. The best times of her life seemed to be spent in Paris, with you, Gigi," I asked, genuinely trying to find a logical reason.

Since Molly's tragic death was claimed by a local terrorist group, while she was meeting for drinks in a Paris club, Gigi explained that the decision to return to Savannah was based on previous conversations.

"Molly always believed that Savannah was her home. She had a love hate relationship with this city. But, one thing that she always acknowledged was how Savannah gave her the 'true grit' she needed to discover who she was.

The experiences, negative as well as positive, gave her the ability to become independent. Perhaps, the most important reason why she wanted to return was because it was here where her fondest memories with Gabby still live." Gigi was holding back tears, insisting that this was not the place to grieve.

Kaitlyn, my wife, never met Molly, but she knew that I named our pub after her. During that entire forty-one years that we have been married, Kaitlin never discovered, or suspected, any of the secrets that are hidden in *The Molly Pub*. It was the accolade for keeping my love for Gabby alive. I always believed then, as I still do now, that our destiny is to finally reunite, and never be apart again.

Gigi brought several of Molly's water color paintings to exhibit in the banquet room as a tribute to her life partner's artistic achievements.

After dinner, Pierre announced that most of Molly's art was being donated to Savannah's College of Art and Design, a nonprofit institution that opened in 1978. Molly visited the studio, located in Lacoste, France, and arranged to offer a seminar in Savannah—prior to the bombing in Paris that claimed her life.

"However, there are two very special oil paintings that Molly insisted be given to Caden Cassidy, a close high school friend,"

Pierre announced to the guests.

Hearing this, I nearly choked on the chicken I was eating. Why would Molly leave me any of her paintings? We hardly knew each other in school.

It was my parents, and her mother, that were good friends. Of course, Kaitlyn assumed that this was all logical, since we did name our pub after her.

When I was called up front to accept both paintings, they were wrapped in butcher paper to prevent any damage. The audience insisted that I reveal the art objects while I was on stage.

There was no choice but to accommodate the crowd. The first painting was an abstract self portrait of Molly that she must have completed soon after she arrived in Paris. It was an impressive rendition of how Molly saw herself at nineteen years old. Her red hair piled 'messy chic' on the top of her head, smiling as if she just discovered nirvana; she had!

The next one; about the same size, was one of Molly and Gabby with the Seine River in the background. Gigi explained that Molly captured this pose from a photograph during her last visit with Gabby.

Both ladies' eyes were sparkling and there was a sense of genuine love. The audience showed their appreciation with a loud applause.

It was the first time that I had seen Gabby in over forty-two years. Although this pictures was dated, I could not get over how little she had changed. *There she was, my Abby with a G. Would this be the closest I would ever come to her?*

When I returned to the table, Kaitlyn immediately asked me, "Why would Molly insist on leaving you a picture that included this other woman?" She whispered, quietly.

"I really have no idea, Kaitlyn. Maybe it was because we all knew each other in high school?" I answered her, with as much surprise as she asked.

I was anxious to leave the dinner as soon as politely possible. Two days of worry about Gabby's unexplainable absence has been exhausting. Although, realistically there was nothing more I could do—just being here now was impossible.

When I said my 'goodbyes' to Gigi, she pulled me aside and privately asked me, "What are we going to do about Gabby? I will only be here for two more days, and then Pierre and I are flying home to Paris," she said, very frustrated.

"I will check back with the police later tonight, or early tomorrow, and let you know. There must be a logical explanation that we are not aware of yet." Caden tried to assure Gigi. "Do you have any idea why Molly left me the self portrait picture?" I asked.

"Molly was planning on sending you that picture when you contacted her about reconnecting with Gabby. She wanted you to know that she would always be making sure that you never hurt Gabby, again. Kind of like her eyes were watching you." Gigi said, seriously.

"Well, Molly can rest in peace. If ever I am given a second chance with Gabby, I will never leave her," Caden replied on his way out the door.

The next morning, he left for the pub early with both of Molly's pictures. He was planning on hanging them in the bar; Molly's self-portrait at the entrance and the one with Gabby in his private office.

At almost the same time that Caden was going to call the police enquiring about Gabby; Devon, the Pub manager, escorted two police officers into his office.

They informed Caden that Gabby's personal belongings were found at Tybee beach, but, at the moment, there were no clues as to where she was.

"It sometimes takes days, or even weeks, for a body to resurface in the ocean, or to wash up on the beach," the older officer said, while jotting some notes on his pad.

"You don't really believe that she drowned, officer, do you?" Caden's face looked ashen.

"At this stage we must not rule anything out," Officer Daly said, without emotion.

After I answered more general questions about how Gabby and I knew one another, and when we last spoke, both officers seemed temporarily satisfied and let themselves out.

On my desk, they left their business card with a phone number that I was instructed to immediately call them if Gabby contacted me.

Suddenly, my phone began vibrating. I waited for the officers to be completely gone. There was a text message. It was from Gabby, but I did not recognize the phone number.

After I read the short text saying she was safe, I sent back, "Where the hell are you, Gabby?" There was no response.

CHAPTER 10

I know well what I am fleeing from, but not what I am in search of.

Michel de Montaigne

Gabby and Sterling
March, 2010
San Diego, California

It took actually several evenings before I could 'digest' Sterling's request. Sharing with him my past six years required me to discuss my entire life. In order to do justice to the relationships with Jake and Caden, required me to reminisce some very painful moments.

Sterling was extremely patient. And, although I was not anxious to reveal some of the secrets in my past life, talking to Alex the following afternoon was one obligation that I did not delay.

My second day in San Diego, Sterling provided me with a laptop computer that I could conference call with Alex. We both agreed that this would be a more personal approach than a phone call.

If Alex insisted on meeting with me; in California, Sterling already offered an alternative private venue. Somewhere that would be easier to talk about serious issues. Thankfully, it never progressed to that stage.

Sitting in front of the computer screen waiting for Alex to respond to my Skype call, felt awkward, until the screen revealed his familiar face.

For some reason, I never before noticed how gracefully Alex aged over the years. The silver streaks, naturally shining on his dark hair, are still attractive. His smile is as charming as always.

Anyone knowing us as a couple would be truly shocked to learn that we are no longer in love; Perhaps, never in love.

Now, after so many years, I can admit that losing Jake to Isabella and then Caden shortly after, led me to Alex; the most vulnerable point in my life. Alex was the shining prince who would save this damsel from all the wicked spells.

Unfortunately, Alex was never my...Prince. He was in search for someone like his mother. A wife that would obediently accept her duties and his infidelities. When it became clear that I was not that wife, it was too late. Neither of us intended to hurt the other. This is what I was counting on now.

Alex spoke first. "What the hell were you thinking, Gabby? Do you know that staging your own death is against the fucking law? This is a great homecoming. You are so lucky that your friend, Sterling Powers, has friends in high places, and also that he left messages for me, so that I knew what to tell the police!" Alex was not only angry—he was livid.

Wow! Holy Mother of Mary, this is not going well. I don't know right now if I should blame Sterling, or thank him.

After a few uncomfortable silent pauses, I looked directly into Alex's eyes and answered each question as honestly as I could. "Thanks for asking how I am," I said, sarcastically. "Molly's funeral was more than I could handle. I had some

strange things happen to me at Tybee Beach. I still cannot explain it. I had to leave." I was still shocked at how angry Alex was.

"Well, I know that you are not here...and I can say with confidence that you are no longer in Savannah. I remember how adamant you were about never returning to Savannah. So, where are you, Gabby? By the way, you look like shit!" That was a typical sympathetic response from my husband.

Alex's expression never changed. Maybe, now wasn't the time to let him know exactly what I wanted, but I did need some money. I could not expect Sterling to care for me, financially, forever. The man already had plenty of orphans to care for.

"I am currently in California with a friend. I need some time to work out my problems. I am not sure how much time?" I knew that all of this sounded vague.

"I can only presume that I must be one of those problems, Gabby. So, let's be honest. When you know where you will be, I will set up some generous funds for you. But, I also have a life, Gabby, and I do not intend to wait, indefinitely. We both are fairly sure how this will end. When YOU get there, let me know…not an email, or a text…on the fucking phone! Tell me to my face. Until that time, I will come up with something to keep the family name clean. After all of this mess, I hope you appreciate that I am still trying to be fair."

It was a shocking revelation that he was so willing to cooperate. But, then again, Alex is known for exploding like a loose cannon and then…spinning back around like nothing happened.

It was clear looking at Alex's expressions that he was finished with our meeting. Gabby knew well when Alex was ready for closure.

"Thank you, Alex, for taking a civilized approach to this difficult predicament," I said, wanting this 'face to face' meeting to end, quickly.

"I have never been the enemy, Gabby. I want the best for you, also. Let's just leave it at that, alright?"

I smiled, politely. Alex sounded as if he had just successfully completed a legal transaction. Why do all these powerful men sound similar? And then, the screen went black.

When I reached down to turn the power button off the computer, there was a sense of blended relief overshadowed with sadness. I did not expect Alex to fly to California and beg me to return. He was never like that.

But, the reality that he was so willing to move on; to let me go without a dispute, reconfirmed that our marriage had died long before this moment.

The following days; after my talk with Alex, just as he promised, there was a wire transfer of funds to a local bank.

The first item on my agenda was to buy a few essentials to get me through the next few weeks. Not really knowing where Sterling was planning on taking me in Mexico, I kept everything simple and washable. The remainder of my extra time was spent walking on the beach, just steps outside of my temporary home; TheHotel Del Coronado suite.

At the nearby deli, I picked up a few doggie treats for some of the local 'fur babies' that adopted me on my beach walks. I didn't want to believe that those dogs, that I shared many secrets with, and helped me search for various sea treasures, were only there for the daily treats.

Then; one day, Max, the name I gave to the sleek silver Weimaraner ran just past me to a young surfer who was about to get into the water. But, Max would not stop barking; insisting that the surfer first walk to where I was on the beach.

"Forgive me if Enya was any trouble the last few days. I had to go to LA and my roommates never lock the garden gate when they leave," the young surfer said, throwing a Frisbee in the water for Enya to fetch.

"There is nothing to apologize for. Max…I mean Enya, and a few other dogs were just keeping me company during my stay at the Hotel Coronado," I said, pointing to where it was.

Gabby was just relieved that the dog had an owner. She would have hated to leave her on the beach, but couldn't ask Sterling to adopt a dog when she had already disrupted his life quite nicely.

Enya, and his surfer friend, walked away toward the ocean, while Gabby found a comfortable place on her beach towel to examine the seashells she collected.

Enya was a fascinating name. I remember in Ireland a famous singer named Enya. For several months I would listen to her CD's. They always were comforting.

Once the sunset began its horizon descent, the sky finger paints with the imagination of an innocent child. This is when a peaceful surge of energy rekindles my desire to complete this strange journey.

Returning to my room; a bit sandy, standing on the balcony, the natural vision of the seascape fades away. Charles has no trouble finding me, slightly melancholy, appreciating the final glimpse of the sun sinking into the water.

"Forgive me, Miss Gabby, for disturbing you, but Mr. Powers has requested that you join him at the 1500 Ocean Restaurant. That is if you are ready to discuss what you 'digested'? Forgive me, but I am reading this directly from Mr. Powers' notes. I hope that you can understand what he means?" Charles seemed perplexed, staring at the card.

"It is fine, Charles. I most definitely understand. Please let Mr. Powers know that I will be honored to join him," Gabby answered.

She was now ready to share with Sterling as much as possible about both Jake and Caden. There was also that minor detail, about him contacting Alex. She was curious as to why he had not mentioned that previously.

"Oh, Charles…where is this restaurant located?" Gabby was just able to catch Charles' attention before he closed the door.

"It is right here in this hotel. When you are ready, just push this button on the outside of the elevator and I will meet you in the lobby. Is 9:00 o'clock a good time for you, Miss Gabby?" Charles asked before exiting.

"Nine will be ideal. Thank you, Charles."

Gabby was grateful that she had the common sense to find the perfect 'little black dress' at the boutique located next door. Tonight, she would be dressed appropriately, all in black, reflecting the constant mourning condition that she has been experiencing lately.

And, while I am in this macabre mood, I would really like to know why Sterling always uses Charles to deliver his messages. Why couldn't he just text, or call me; or even stop…by himself? I suppose this must be his normal method of communicating with people, but it seems very impersonal to me.

50

Details like these forced me to realize that my relationship with Sterling was, now, on an entirely different level than it was nine years ago. I should not expect anything more.

Maybe, this would be the perfect time—before my dinner meeting with Sterling—to read what words of wisdom Jake has to say.

Was it just a little bizarre that a dead man's words were the only words that I paid attention to…whenever I felt alone?

For several days; since I arrived at San Diego, those journals remained on the nightstand, near my bed, left unopened. Now, randomly flipping through the pages not yet read, I saw the ominous title—MOLLY'S DEATH. My hands began to shake. *How could Jake possibly know about Molly's death? He died years before her. And, why didn't I see this when I was at Tybee Beach? I glanced at my watch. Was there enough time now to read this? No. It would have to wait. Sterling has been patient enough. It is time for me to open the relic bags filled with painful memories and allow fresh air to expose them.*

CHAPTER 11

Journeys end in lovers meetings.

   William Shakespeare

   Gabby and Sterling
   March, 2010
   San Diego, CA.

Sterling decided to use a small conference room located in the 1500 Ocean Restaurant. His instructions to the staff was to add plenty of atmosphere, colorful floral with twinkling mood lights accompanied by serene music.

   "What I want this room to look like when I return this evening is a Garden of Eden, without that nasty snake," Sterling told the restaurant manager, who was amused at the allusion. "Oh...I almost forgot the most important detail," Sterling said, instantly turning around. "We will need the utmost privacy. Please make certain that there are no interruptions during our meal. This simply means that, after the order is taken, I expect the servers to come in and out quietly and discreetly. No chit-chatting, please." Sterling's voice was pleasant, but serious.

   "Perfectly clear, Mr. Powers. This must be a very important client. I personally assure you that everything will be to your satisfaction." The manager bowed, and was gone within seconds.

   Sterling walked to the veranda that looked out toward the vast open sea. He took out a Cuban cigar, one that he always carries with him.

   As soon as Sterling sat down at the empty table, a young lady with extremely long legs and a very short skirt, bent over with her exposed cleavage and lit his cigar. A second attractive cocktail waitress delivered him a Bombay martini with three olives.

"Good evening, Mr. Powers. Is there anything else that I might get for you?" asked the fire lighter. This young hostess could easily be Sterling's granddaughter, yet she was obviously sexually interested in him.

Sterling gave her that slight smile; the one that drives women, of all ages, wild. He kindly dismissed her without even hesitating.

What Sterling really wanted to tell her was that flirting with older men; especially him, would never end well. But, he was sure that this naïve beauty could never begin to understand how complicated life can be. Instead of a lecture, Sterling placed a one hundred dollar bill in her hand. It worked every time he wanted to be alone. Except, for once, when an attractive young woman made him a proposition at The Four Seasons Hotel in Chicago.

It just happened that she was an expensive paid escort. At that time when he handed her a one hundred dollar bill she showed him how offended she was by slapping him in the face. Apparently, the one hundred dollars was below her pay grade.

There were still a few hours before his meeting with Gabby. Sterling began to surmise the best tactics to use to make her realize that there is no escaping the past. Once she is able to accept that it is the past, the easier it will be for her to move forward.

Sterling knew how difficult this was to achieve. Whenever he tried to escape the fatality that memory branded to his brain, the immense sadness would create a darkness impossible to penetrate. What Sterling did learn was that crumpling that memory; like a no longer needed scrap of paper, has a habit of resurfacing and reincarnating. Memories are frozen dreams that never melt!

There was something about the past causing Gabby to panic. He would try to make her understand that the past is needed for learning…not repeating. It has already vanished. Sterling was determined to teach her that there are too many emotional, conflicting interests in life to ignore the present. If he could accomplish this, it would be a lesson that they both could appreciate.

Although he was not a psychologist, Sterling recognized a desperate situation. But; then again, Gabby had a psychologist and for some strange reason she still called him anyway. There was no doubt that the rape caused her severe emotional damage. That would never completely be erased. But, Sterling was certain that this was only the surface problem. There were many alcoves still hidden. Hopefully, tonight would reveal some of those secrets—beginning the healing process.

By 8:45 pm, Sterling entered the private salon to inspect how everything appeared. Moving around the oversized room, he was impressed by the vast number of greenery, as well as aromatic floral arrangements, both hanging and draped around the inside pergolas.

The round dining table was in the center of the room, perfectly situated away from any roaming eyes, in the main dining area. There was a pleasant, relaxing and intimate ambiance created by a fine selection of serene music from various orchestra selections.

It would appear to anyone who saw this staged event that it was an elaborate setting for, perhaps, an engagement proposal. This made Sterling silently chuckle to himself as he waited for his guest of honor.

Over the many years that he and Gabriella had shared public and intimate moments, there was never a time when either felt the need to share their past or inquire about their future.

For Sterling, that is what made their relationship last. Now, that he is about to enter unchartered territories, he knew how important it would be to remain neutral.

Hidden in the back of his consciousness, Sterling could not rid himself of an uncomfortable feeling that, once, Gabby's issues became evident, he would also be part owner of that revelation.

Thankfully, Sterling no longer had time to dwell on this. Gabby was being escorted to the table by Charles. From a distance, the candlelight softness captured the California sun-kissed strands in Gabby's dark, chestnut layered hair.

Sterling could not help but recall the first time he witnessed this very same nervous young bride clutching the arm of an elderly gentleman—leading her to her future husband. Even now, at sixty years old, he admired how stunning Gabby still was.

As she approached the table, he stood up; all seven feet. When Sterling walked to Gabby, he took her hand, thanked Charles, and continued to escort her to their table, himself.

"You look amazing, Gabby. It is a miracle what a few days on a California beach can do, isn't it?" Sterling said, as he gently pulled her hair to the side of her neck, and kissed her on the cheek.

"I am not certain about miracles lately, but there is no doubt that being here is providing me with a sense of balance that I thought I lost," Gabby said, gratefully.

"Well, that is a beginning in any healing process." Sterling's response was to the point. Then, almost on cue, as if he needed to complete his thought, he returned to the dinner plans.

"This menu is quite extensive; however, if there is anything not on the menu that you want, I guarantee that they will accommodate," Sterling said, pleasantly.

Gabby reviewed the choices with little enthusiasm. Food, lately, was not a priority. She settled on Cajun salmon, with a small dinner salad.

During the meal, there was mostly small talk. Sterling shared with Gabby his latest business venture. He explained that the various bars throughout the Mexican Rivera included sports memorabilia, similar to the famous Hard Rock Café's emphasis on music. The exception is that their memorabilia is auctioned off several times a year. A substantial amount of the revenue goes to several local families and children's charities.

It fascinated Gabby; as well as impressed her, how generous

Sterling always is. But, never in the past did she recall him ever being this enthusiastic about anything before.

It was a lovely dinner…without any pressure. And, then, Sterling ordered after dinner drinks, looked solemnly into Gabby's eyes, piercing through all the layers of gauze that she used to suppress painful intrusions.

"Perhaps a Sambuca?" Sterling suggested in a more casual tone. He patiently waited for her response.

Aware that she has been avoiding the purpose for this dinner, Gabby remained aloof, intentionally. She reminded Sterling of a child who is caught raiding the cookie jar. As a distraction, she plays with the remains of the Tiramisu with her fork.

Gabby's poignant green eyes, then meet Sterling's, in a delightful staring contest that ends when they both start laughing at the same time.

Once they both gain their composure again, Sterling says, "Sambuca is an excellent choice. The anise will definitely contribute to the 'digesting' ordeal." Sterling was trying his best possible strategies to make light of this situation.

Gabby's reaction to simple questions were always amusing. Those spontaneous, serendipitous moments even now are still charming.

Once the two white Sambuca's arrived at the table, Sterling insisted on lighting the traditional flame that celebrates three floating coffee beans in each of their drinks. Only this time there were four coffee beans.

"Do you recall, Gabby, what the coffee beans represent?" Sterling asked, holding the lighter in his hand.

"As I recollect, the three coffee beans symbolize health, happiness and prosperity. But, I do not know why there is a fourth coffee bean?" Gabby was curious to hear what Sterling was conjuring.

"Very good 'grasshopper'." *He obviously is in a playful mood, I thought. The term 'grasshopper' is an allusion to a popular 1970 television series called, 'Kung Fu'. In that show, a young Shaolin monk is tutored by a wiser, but blind teacher.*

Sterling often referred to himself as my mentor. I was the naïve 'grasshopper' being taught how to survive by a much stronger warrior. That image was not too far removed from the truth.

I bowed my head reverently.

"But, Wise One, there are four coffee beans in our Sambuca's. What does that last bean represent?"

It was actually fun role playing once again with Sterling. He knew just how to reduce the tension and anxiety that I was anticipating.

Sterling reached across the table, gently stroked the back of my hand, while never taking his eyes off mine.

"That final coffee bean, Gabby, is the destiny that you and I— notice that I include myself—have been searching for our entire lives." Sterling then lit the flame. "Let tonight be the beginning of a new, less complicated, life for us both."

With those final words, we simultaneously took a small sip of the Sambuca. *I was finally prepared to let the catharsis begin.*

CHAPTER 12

Does such a thing as 'the fatal flaw,' that showy dark crack, running down the middle of a life, exist outside literature? I used to think it didn't. Now I think it does. And I think that mine is this: a morbid longing for the picturesque at all costs.

Donna Tartt,
The Secret History

Gabby and Sterling,
 March 2010
San Diego, California

As I recall from my philosophical studies, Aristotle, in his extreme wisdom, was the first one to identify catharsis as a method to release emotional tension, which was caused often by repressed memories.

Restored, normal intellectual balance may be achieved through discussion, art, music and writing. Exploring these effective techniques, eventually, prepares one for a healing process that restores the psyche to its original state of mind.

Sharing with Sterling my undying love and devotion for Jake Chevalier was not as difficult as I anticipated. But, once I mentioned the **DEATH BOX**, Sterling began to listen intensely.

"So, Gabby, what I am understanding is that this **DEATH BOX** that you inherited from Jake; at his eulogy, was the same box that you gave him on December 31, 1967, and the last time you saw him alive?"

How is it possible that this is also the same catastrophic day in my life. Gabby has no idea what happened to me on this date, and this was not the time to tell her. There may never be a time to tell her.

I could tell that Sterling was mentally recording all of these details.

"Yes." I shook my head to emphasize the response.

"But, by this time, Caden and I had just moved in together. We were still going to college at Georgetown University. When Caden witnessed Jake and me embracing, through the outside window of our apartment; he assumed that I was going to go back with Jake. So, it was not only the last time I saw Jake, it was also the last time I ever saw Caden." I paused, trying to regain my composure.

Sterling leaned closer to me and asked the very same question that Caden's Aunt Selena asked me a few days later.

"Would you? I mean would you have left Caden to be with Jake, Gabby?"

Once again, I could not honestly answer that question.

Sterling realized that this discussion was continuing to get intense. He suggested that we leave the public restaurant, even though we were in an exclusive room.

"Would you feel more comfortable if we went somewhere more private, Gabby?"

But, before I could respond, he removed an embroidered linen handkerchief from his suit jacket and lightly patted my cheeks, which by this time, were moist and flushed.

It was almost exactly the same thing that he did the first time we met. My mind was flashing back to when he said, "Whenever you are with me, Gabby, there is absolutely NOTHING that I will allow to harm you. That is my promise to you."

This was the reason why I now turned to Sterling, when I did not know what to do next. If there was ever a time I needed him to fulfill that vow, it was now. My interior monologues are more frequent with no control.

At this very moment, I am Anis Nin writing that reality doesn't impress me. I only believe in intoxication, in ecstasy, and when ordinary life shackles me, I escape one way or the other. No more walls.

Once Sterling noticed that Gabby's eyes appeared unresponsive and glassy, he didn't wait for Gabby to answer.

Sterling took control. His arm around her waist, he began to lead her out through a restricted exit. Within minutes, they were on the elevator moving to the penthouse floor.

This is where my room is located; only when the door opened, it was not my room. Gabby was trying to gain back some self-control.

Although very similar to mine, this room is so much larger. The sitting room has a large glass dome that resembles one I visited in an observatory. Only here the moon and stars can be witnesses to our folly.

Finally, I asked, pensively, "Are our rooms on the same floor, Sterling?"

Without immediately responding, Sterling lead me in a half circle to a locked door. When he inserted his key, it revealed my bedroom. I looked at Sterling totally confused.

"I apologize for not telling you earlier that your room was part of my penthouse. But, I can assure you that this was not done to make you feel uncomfortable or to suggest anything inappropriate. This was the most convenient and available solution, at the moment." Sterling waited for Gabby's reaction.

"I am certainly not in any position to question your motives, Sterling. It was I that reached out to you." Gabby reached for his hand as a friendly gesture.

"There has never been anyone, Sterling, that I have trusted like you. Shall we continue our little tête-à-tête?" Being in a more relaxed atmosphere, Gabby was confident now that she could continue without any other interruptions.

Although revealing that she and Caden were currently romantically involved through the Internet, it was still awkward. She also emphasized that they had not even seen each other physically for forty-three years. Sterling now could no longer remain silent.

"Do you really believe that rekindling your relationship with an ex-lover will make you happy? Isn't Caden still married, Gabby?

And, have you reconciled your enduring love for Jake? You just briefly expressed how important his journals to you are. If there is no logical validity to Jake's theory about an eternal union, how will you resolve your emotional attachment to him?" Sterling was finally beginning to understand the depth of Gabby's emotional crevice.

"Now, can you understand what a hot mess I am? My life has been in limbo since Jake left me. And, I do not mean since he died; I mean my entire life. Now that I am sixty, there is still no resolution ."

I knew that all of this sounded more like a best-selling romantic novel than a true story. Luckily, Sterling knew me well enough to understand that it is not in my nature to embellish the facts.

"Are you familiar with the works of Kahlil Gibran, Gabby?" Sterling interjected, before I continued.

"Absolutely! During graduate school in Georgetown, I took a class that entirely focused on Gibran's literary contributions that revolutionized the humanities. He was a genius. "The Prophet" still resonates in my scarred soul, Sterling," I said with passion.

"Well then, Grasshopper, remember that *'your pain is the breaking of the shell that encloses your understanding. Even though; as the stone of the fruit must break, that it's heart may stand in the sun, so must you know pain?" (Kahlil Gibran)*

Sterling paused, to watch Gabby's reaction.

"And, could you keep your heart in wonder at the daily miracles of your life; your pain would not seem less wondrous than your joy, and you would accept the seasons of your heart, even as you have always accepted the seasons that pass over your fields." (Kahlil Gibran).

When Gabby completed the quote that Sterling had started, they both took a long breath.

Gabby broke the silence. "That was certainly simple. If I had known that Kahlil Gibran had all the answers to my pathetic life, I wouldn't have wasted your time, Sterling." She said with a slightly sarcastic tone.

At that astute observation, both Gabby and Sterling began

laughing at the absurdity of what life throws our way.

Once they both gained back their composure, Sterling was the first to finally admit that, "Unfortunately, knowing the philosophical answers, and applying what they mean in a practical form is never quite that easy."Sterling responded.

With that prophetic observation, Gabby removed her shoes, and found a comfortable spot on the overstuffed couch. This was when she remembered that she hadn't told Sterling any of the details about Tybee Beach that lead to this unexpected reunion.

"Before this evening entirely ends, and the moon goes to sleep, wherever moons disappear, I must share with you, Sterling, Jake's latest journal entry and how I was mysteriously dragged out of the Atlantic Ocean a few days ago," Gabby said, still fascinated with the glass dome above her head.

"Definitely. This is important, Gabby. Hold that thought, while I open a bottle of Opus One to celebrate the progress that we are making tonight."

Sterling walked toward the refrigerator bar, removed the wine — often referred to as the ambrosia of gods. In less than five minutes, he returned to discover Gabby curled up sleeping in a classic embryo position. He carefully placed the wine bottle and crystal glasses down; walked toward the locked door, and opened it.

With Gabby's head leaning comfortably on his chest, Sterling scooped up her body, careful not to disturb her. He could sense that temporarily, she relinquished all the spirits that were controlling her every movement. Gently, he carried her into the adjoining bedroom.

Methodically, he removed her black dress, unsnapped the bra, and pulled down the silk underwear. Once Gabby was completely naked, Sterling situated her perfectly on the huge bed. Remembering how Gabby always slept with her feet extended past the top sheet, he arranged the bedding, accordingly.

Turning away, for just a second, he briefly returned to caress her long hair, and kiss her forehead. As she lay there in peace, Sterling recited on the way out: *Sleep, dear troubled soul. The death of each day's life, sore labourds' bath, Balm of hurt minds, great nature's second course, Chief nourisher in life's feasts. (William Shakespeare)*

CHAPTER 13

The best and most beautiful things in the world cannot be seen or even touched; they must be felt by the heart.

Helen Keller

Gabby
March, 2010
San Diego, California

At the station, I am standing on the platform waiting for my train to arrive, or leave, I am not certain which. A young girl; maybe sixteen, walks towards me with a collection of dandelions.

"Good evening lovely lady. May I inquire as to what brings you to platform 67?" This mystery girl smiles at me with a familiar grin.

"I really cannot say why I am here. It does seem like I have been on this platform before, at another time." Gabby looks around to see if there are any familiar landmarks that will jog her memory.

Without realizing it, the young girl has decorated the crown of Gabby's head with yellow and white dandelions from her bouquet.

"Were you ever told the significance of the dandelions, sad lady?" The girl continued to frolic, pleasantly.

"I am not sure that there is any meaning to the dandelions. They are not even included in the Etymology of Garden flowers. And, I do take offense of you calling me sad." I answered the girl who did not appear to be seriously paying attention until, suddenly, she stopped her twirling and moved as close as possible to me without touching.

"I would have you know that dandelions have been recognized as important flora since the medieval era. Today, it represents those who have

survived all obstacles. The dandelion is further known as providing intelligence, when needed.

And, this special white dandelion is yours to blow. The seeds will spread wherever they are needed to grant your special wish." Once the girl had finished with her message, she turned and began walking to another platform.

"Wait...please? Who sent you here and what train is mine?" I asked, almost in a tone of panic.

The girl was by this time almost to the end of the platform, turned and waved.

"You, Gabby. It was you that sent me here many years ago. Do not worry about the train. There will be many more for you to board if you miss this one. Keep making those wishes on the dandelions, they are everywhere."

Before I could understand all that just happened, she was gone.

And...I began moving my body in different directions on the oversized bed, attempting to find that place where, once again, I could return to the dream that I just had. But, it had vanished.

Time seemed to also vanish. For some reason, there were no clocks in this room. I reached over to the nightstand to check the time on my cell phone. It was just barely 6:00 o'clock a.m.

As I began to rise from the bed, I realized that I was completely nude. The last time I slept without clothes was when I was with Sterling, ten years ago.

STERLING...he must have brought me to bed last night. Hopefully, I did not do or say anything too outrageous. But, then Sterling has seen me from all angles and after revealing some very private secrets last night, there was not much left to feel embarrassed about.

My head was slightly aching; probably from the Sambuca. There must have been several that I consumed. It is rare for me to have a hangover, since rarely do I ever drink, anymore.

I threw on my terry cloth robe and went into the kitchen. In the fridge, thankfully, there was a bottle of orange juice that I emptied in five seconds.

Yes, this is definitely a hangover. What happened last night after we came back to Sterling's room? Nothing intimate—I am sure of that! Sterling doesn't play those sick games…at least not with me.

And, if we did have sex, he would still be in my bed. He hated when I left his Penthouse before having breakfast. He said it was like faking an orgasm. According to Sterling, I needed to stay the entire evening to appreciate the entire experience.

Returning to bed for a few more hours, I decided that would be the most effective remedy for, at least, the hangover part. As I began to push the remote that controlled the kitchen light, I noticed on the counter a dainty crystal vase that was holding a collection of small flowers.

When I moved closer to get a good look at what they were, it finally dawned on me that they were all dandelions.

This was an odd choice to decorate any room with? But, wait a minute, these cannot possibly be the same dandelions that were in my dream…or, could they be?

Why would anyone leave weeds…oh…sorry, the mystery girl reminded me that dandelions have a significant symbolism. What exactly did she say they represent? Something about being a misunderstood flower.

Well, I can relate to that description. If it weren't for Jake, I would have been called a wallflower. I wonder if the wallflower is a relative of dandelions.

Later, once I am fully awake, I will research on Google what the meaning is. Until then, this wallflower is going back to sleep.

CHAPTER 14

What lies behind you and what lies in front of you, pales in comparison to what lies inside of you.

Ralph Waldo Emerson

Gabby and Sterling
March, 2010
San Diego, California

"The laws of probability offers a theory that it is possible to have many different outcomes as you make changes to your original choices.

Along with this idea, is what Jake believed was a parallel universe. That would explain why my repeating dream is always at a train station.

Although I cannot recall all the details, the girl that greets me is always the same, only at different ages. I know that this somehow is related to my desire to change the track that I am currently on. It also seems to support what Jake was doing when he sent me on a parallel trip to Europe, after his death.

Those detailed, comprehensive journals that he left me are meant to be my spiritual guidebook.

To make it easier for me to comprehend, Jake explained that this parallel theory is part of the 'daughter universe' concept. It is all still based on laws of probability; however, his explanation is that every choice made has multiple opportunities to be revised. There is a range of universes where those choices may be altered. For example, using my train dream explains that just because I married Alex would not prevent me from boarding a different 'train' that would unite me with Jake. In fact, you might even say that the journal would be my boarding pass to that new life."

Gabby watched Sterling's reaction to this complex explanation. It was difficult to expect him to accept this interpretation of life when she was not completely convinced herself.

"Those are some very challenging ideas that could be interpreted as desperate wishes from a dying man," answered Sterling, hoping not to offend Gabby.

"I agree with you. And, this was also my first impression when he introduced me to this abstraction. But, Sterling, the people that I met in various countries that Jake knew, also seemed to support this theory. And, there is no rational explanation for what happened to me at Tybee Beach."

"That actually might be a good place to begin a lucid discussion," Sterling suggested.

He stood up from the lounge chair on the balcony and adjusted the umbrella. The afternoon sun had shifted so that Gabby's face looked like a shadow silhouette.

"Do you remember why you decided to go swimming at Tybee Beach in the late afternoon on an early spring day when the water temperature cannot be more than thirty degrees?" Sterling was careful that his voice did not sound like he was interrogating Gabby. Yet, it was important for her to remember what her motivation was on that day.

Gabby looked startled at hearing that question. Adjusting the chaise lounge to a forty degree angle, she somehow believed it would allow her to think about that question clearly. Silently, she contemplated how to respond.

It has now been five days since she left Tybee Beach; yet, there was a definite sense that time was elapsing slower here.

"That is a very interesting question, Sterling. I never really took the time to think about why I was in the ocean. I don't know if I can give you an honest answer, even now."

Gabby closed her eyes for a few moments as if the answers would somehow manage to appear from her subconscious.

First, there were dark specks floating on the waves.

"What I do recall is a desperate need to get to the beach as soon as I arrived at my hotel room. There was almost a gravitational pull...like a need for me as close as possible to the Tybee Lighthouse.

Then, the only thing that I remember is being soaking wet, sitting on an old tree stump, with an oversized towel wrapped around my shivering body." Gabby was determined not to allow herself to cry.

"Okay. I can understand how that must have been terrifying. But, it is possible that once you were safely out of the ocean, someone gave you a towel and left without you recalling? After all, everything is fairly vague relating how you even got in the ocean initially."

Sterling's voice was clear, but Gabby's mind was now in flashback mode.

"Years ago, when we were in high school, Jake was a lifeguard at this beach. One day, while surfing, an undercurrent pulled me down into the sand and I could not surface.

When Jake noticed that I was in trouble, he found me tangled among the seaweed. If it was not for him, I would have drowned that day. That is exactly what it felt like this time.

Black ashes surrounding me in the water was the last image before all went blank. When I gained consciousness, I was all by myself; yet I never felt alone." Gabby's voice was nearly a whisper.

Everything was now finally out. Was she trying to end her life that night? Did Jake somehow find a way to crossover from the afterlife to save her, even though death may have reunited them?

Gabby may never have the answers to those haunting questions. What she did hope was to possibly reconcile those daunting questions in a way that the answers were no longer necessary.

Once again, Gabby could feel herself resorting to the words of her literary saviors. Their universal truth assured her that there was never only one answer to all her questions.

Candide once wanted to kill himself a hundred times, but somehow was still in love with life. This ridiculous weakness is perhaps one of our more stupid melancholy propensities...for is there anything more stupid than to be eager to continue to carry a burden when anyone else would gladly throw away? Or, to loathe ones very being, and yet to hold it fast? To fondle the snake that devours us until he eats our hearts away? (Voltaire)

Gabby's thoughts were interrupted by Sterling's voice that sounded like an echo.

"I believe you are ready now, Gabby, to start the cleansing process. You may have difficulty understanding this , but it was not that long ago when I was in a very familiar mental state as you are at this moment."

Sterling finally sat down—after pacing several minutes on the balcony. It was emotionally heart-wrenching to listen to Gabby's confessions.

How do psychologists and priests ever do this without feeling helpless? Sterling was determined to keep a rational focus, knowing too well what the alternative was.

"Eventually, when the time seems right, I might share some of the ways that I have learned to cope with my nightmares. But, for now, you will have to let me guide you the only way I know how. It all starts tomorrow morning when we leave for Ensenada, Mexico."

Gabby knew little about Mexico. It would be like entering a new and unknown world where she hoped that the end would really be the beginning.

CHAPTER 15

Freedom is what we do from what is done to us.

Jean Paul Sartre

Sterling and Gabby
March, 2010
Ensenada, Mexico

One hundred twenty-five kilometers south of San Diego, on the Baja California peninsula, is a city that the locals call, "The Cinderella of the Pacifica."

Traveling, by car, to Ensenada requires us to cross the border into Tijuana from San Ysidro, California. The many years that I have known Sterling, there has never been a time that I saw him drive a car. He always had a driver in a limo or Town Car. There was no reason to believe that this would be any different today.

Charles informed me, this morning, that Sterling would meet me in the main hotel lobby. At that time, nothing seemed out of the ordinary. That is, until the car attendant escorted me; travel bag in hand, to the roundabout front entrance.

There seated in a canary yellow Humvee, with an Indiana Jones safari hat and Ray Ban aviator sunglasses, was Sterling Powers. I thought, for sure, he was incognito for some covert espionage assignment. Except that the color of this SUV screamed, "LOOK AT ME, EVERYONE."

"Buenos Diaz Muy Bonita Senorita," Sterling said charmingly, but with a heavy English accent.

"Do you mind if I ask you where you found this flashy vehicle? I never even thought you knew how to drive?" Gabby asked, genuinely amused.

"All in good time," was all he offered.

Once inside, Gabby noticed that the supple black leather passenger's seat was more like a captain's chair or recliner. The outer appearance of this 'tank' did not prepare her for the inside luxuries.

The windows were tinted to prevent people from looking in, and there was a climate control for comfort in each compartment.

And, the center console was actually a coffee maker. In the rear area, there was a fully equipped bar, just like in a Limo.

"What do you think of these wheels, Gabby?" Sterling sounded like a teenager with his first car.

"WOW! This is very impressive, Mr. Powers. But, do you really know how to drive it?"

Sterling lowered his sunglasses just enough to make eye contact with Gabby. "There are so many hidden talents that I have that you will never know." He said, with a smirk. Then, reached over the console to test that my seatbelt was secure.

"Am I going to have to worry that you are a speed racer in this mega tank?" I asked.

"That is one problem you can check off your concern list. Once we cross the border, there is no breaking any Mexican laws. We will be the perfect model Americans."

His once playful tone was now very serious.

"There are so many horror stories of wealthy Americans making stupid choices that they later regretted. I do not intend to be one of them."

Sterling explained to me on the short drive into San Ysidro that I was soon to eyewitness some of the worst ravages of poverty in the country. I was not naïve to impoverishment. The Blair Foundation sponsored many destitute countries.

"It is more obvious at the border towns, but I am not going to sugar coat any of this. There is a severe epidemic in this country. To ignore it is to support it," Sterling said.

"Then, why are we going here, if it is a futile cause? Don't forget, Sterling, that for many years, I worked for the Blair Charities that contributed millions of dollars around the world. Why is this country any different?"

My voice was abrasive and defensive. The men in my life never gave me credit for my ability to resolve any difficult problems. Yet, all the years that I represented the Blair family at various political forums, it required me to keep up to date with international economics.

"I never was implying that you weren't active in many organized charities, Gabby." Sterling reached over to pat my knee, as a peaceful gesture, but it felt more like patronizing.

Sterling could sense the tension from this topic, so he took advantage of playing his trump card to move forward.

"Maybe you forgot, Sweetheart, it was one of those charities that brought us together, in the first place." His eyes never left the road.

Before Gabby had an opportunity to answer him back with some clever response, she noticed the sign that read:

"Welcome to Mexico."

As Sterling turned the corner, the traffic came to a total stop. Now, Gabby had a clear view of the horrific indigence surrounding her.

Women and children roaming the busy streets barely clothed. Some with no shoes. Some with no feet. Some with no arms.

It was, also, impossible to ignore the cardboard houses sitting on soft dirt a few miles ahead of them. Some had tin roofs; none had water or electricity. Most were no larger than a utility box.

Gabby sat silent, while more of the hardship appeared; like those slides in an old fashioned view master. When you got tired of one disc, there was always another one to keep you entertained.

But, now, all the disks had various images of dearth, impoverishment, and starvation. Gabby wanted to find the reel that would instantly change all this pain.

73

Sterling noticed how helpless Gabby felt. The color of her face looked pale, as she nervously moved around to find some recourse.

He knew it was imperative to make her understand that pity is not a helpful solution. The beggars on the street were not receiving any donations. Like pimps in the background, any money collected went to their 'sponsors'.

"Regardless of how tempting it might be, Gabby, do not open your window, and try not to make eye contact with any of these people." Sterling's voice was stoical.

"Are you seriously asking me to ignore this obvious desperation? How can you be that callous?"

Gabby could not believe that Sterling could say this to her. She began to search in her purse for anything of value to give to one of the children.

Immediately, when Sterling realized what Gabby was doing, he auto-locked her windows and doors. In a very stern and firm voice, he said, "There is nothing that you can do right now to help any of these people..."

Before he could finish his last words, a light complexioned girl placed her tiny open palm on Gabby's passenger window to get her attention.

The child's hollow, dead eyes made Gabby fully aware of her presence. From either the hot sun, tears, or maybe both, the child's face was streaked like a lifeless portrait that 'Death' carries in his pocket.

This was when Gabby placed the palm of her hand on the inside part of the window. She, then, briefly closed her eyes. Although she knew that the girl on the opposite side of this window could not physically touch her, Gabby felt that the child could sense through the glass; her heart sending vibes of love and hope.

The only similar grief that Gabby had ever experienced was on her first visit to 'The Wailing Wall' in Jerusalem, many years ago. Now, there was a similar desire to scream as a way to release the inner torture that was overtaking her body.

But, instead, ringing in her ears was the same mournful cries that she heard at 'The Wall of Tears'. Then, Gabby opened her eyes, and her voice returned. But, the child had vanished.

The traffic finally started moving, but Sterling waited until they were on the coastal road to Ensenada before he said anything further to Gabby.

It was difficult to tell how upset she was with him. Although Sterling realized that experiencing Mexico in this barbaric way might seem cruel, he needed Gabby to understand his commitment to these people who had no voice of their own.

Regardless what Gabby was feeling, Sterling knew from his own experiences that this cruel awareness would help heal her own sorrow, eventually!

"I apologize for making you witness all the ugliness of this country before you could witness the beauty," Sterling said, gently.

Gabby heard him, but she was non responsive. Perhaps, she made a horrible mistake coming here with him.

What was she possibly thinking? What was he possibly thinking? What other new surprises would he expose her to?

"Gabby…will you, at least, talk to me about what just happened?"

"Yes, I think I will. Why are we here? And, what do you expect from me, if I am going to be in the center of all this poverty?"

As soon as the words came out of her mouth, Gabby regretted sounding like a spoiled American.

"I promise you that things will get better. I cannot promise you that there will not be other places where people are hungry and homeless. That is why I am here. To help in any way, financially and through personal interaction. You will make your own choices on what path you want to take. I will only provide you with various directions." Sterling felt satisfied that he honestly shared with Gabby all that he could, at this moment.

Gabby continued to stare out at the white beaches leading to the wide ocean. Somewhere, she knew that the answers that she needed were near the sea.

At least, at this moment, it appeared like the vast openness offered many opportunities to find those answers. No longer could she ignore her responsibilities.

Chapter 16

Your visions will become clear only when you can look into your own heart. Who looks outside dreams; who looks inside awakes.

C. G. Jung

Gabby and Sterling
March, 2010
Ensenada, Mexico

Sterling pulled off the toll road highway that led us through an archway with the words, 'Puerto Nuevo', colorfully inscribed.

In the 1950's it was nothing more than any other small Mexican fishing village. Today, there are over thirty restaurants and shops.

"We are going to stop here, Gabby, for some famous Mexican lobster, a Margarita and my favorite dessert, flan. It will give us an opportunity to highlight your stay in Ensenada."

Sterling was hoping that this short visit would erase, at least, some of the stigma Gabby saw earlier in Tijuana.

"That sounds like a good plan. I really apologize for sounding ungrateful back at the border. I think that once I know what to expect, I will be easier to get along with." Gabby was almost back to her normal self.

"Well, I don't really ever remember you being easy to live with, but any change is an improvement," Sterling said in his typical half joking tone.

Gabby looked back at him defensively as they both exited the SUV, simultaneously.

Once outside, she said, aggravated, "And when was I ever

difficult?"

Sterling wisely decided to ignore the bait and lead the way, instead, into the crowded dining area.

Gabby recalled how Sterling avoided being among crowds, especially in dining areas. She was curious how he was going to deal with this situation.

"Hola, Senor Powers. Welcome back to Puerto Nuevo." The middle-aged man dressed in a white linen shirt greeted Sterling.

Although there were more than ten customers in front of us, we were led directly to a table facing the ocean. The waiter placed two reserved signs on the tables behind and next to us. It was clear that Sterling's phobia of crowds still existed. This was not the time, I decided, to address that issue.

We both ordered a Margarita and decided on the Nuevo—which translates to Newport lobster dinner. It was prepared in a deep fried butter recipe served with salsa, beans, rice and homemade tortillas.

I knew, at the time, that a full lobster would be too much for me to finish, but Sterling insisted that I take any leftovers with me for a midnight snack, later.

Being frugal, in the past, was never something that Sterling practiced. I wasn't yet sure what contributed to this personality change, but I was curious what other new traits would surface.

"Ensenada is where I have been working lately since it is centrally located to major cities that I am currently invested with. You will recognize that Ensenada is larger than Puerto Nuevo, and offers more variety in social events, while still maintaining a strong Mexican tradition."

"Where do I actually fit into this plan?" I asked, politely.

"Nowhere and everywhere. I want you to take your time to acclimate at your pace. Once you find your comfort zone, we can discuss the next step. Does this sound reasonable, Gabby?" Sterling was determined to give her as much space and time as necessary.

"I intend to go into this arrangement with an open mind and

avoid making judgments. It really will be another world that I hope to embrace," Gabby sincerely said, although she wasn't sure just how much she truly believed that.

Before we continued on our journey to Ensenada, Sterling gave me some insight to what his latest obsession was.

Apparently, the investors that he is working with established a nonprofit charity to raise funds for local homes, schools and clinics. Included, is a work study program with practical skills they can use in their community.

One such example was solar lighting. The investors bought a solar lighting factory in Ensenada and transferred a skeleton of American workers. Now they would be able to train a group of unskilled Mexican laborers practical skills that they could use, immediately.

Not only did the factory hire over three hundred local workers, but once the city officials realized solar lighting was more lucrative than electricity, they began the process of replacing the existing lighting.

"This is a win-win situation for everyone, Gabby. We were even able to train some of the more motivated local men the basic skills of running their own solar lighting factory. Now, they too are part of the solution. Within two years, we were able to revamp the cardboard villages into residential neighborhoods." The pride in Sterling's voice was unmistakable.

Gabby could not refrain from her excitement at what endless opportunities there could be. This was so vastly more realistic than anything that she ever experienced with The Blair Foundation. This was a hands-on experience with concrete improvements.

"Can you understand, now, why I couldn't let you support the street children? Most are peddling goods for merchants that will confiscate all the money they earn during the day. We are trying to provide an alternative life style, but it takes time," Sterling said, determined to make Gabby appreciate the severity of the situation.

"Well, yes! This does make everything more obvious. But, you should have told me this before, Sterling.   I hope that my contribution; whatever it will be, may generate a worthy change."

It was the first time that I was not preoccupied with what was happening in my own life. There was a great surge of relief that flowed through my body. Having a purpose made me anxious to get to my destination. For the first time that I can remember, my life was going to be meaningful.

CHAPTER 17

Slavery is such an atrocious debasement of human nature, that it's very extirpation, if not performed with solicitous care, may sometimes open a source of serious evil.
Benjamin Franklin

Maggie Mendoza
San Diego, California
October 31, 2001

Halloween night, 2001 Gabriella Girard Blair was randomly kidnapped and brutally raped in Lexington, Kentucky.

Two thousand miles away; on the same night, Maggie Mendoza, sixteen years old, was abducted by a sex trafficking gang in San Diego. The odds that these two women would ever cross paths was one in six million.

Maggie Mendoza was anxiously looking forward to her junior year of high school, for many months. This was going to be the year that a very shy, introverted, wall flower was finally going to have an opportunity to bloom into a brilliant sunflower.

Selecting performing arts as an elective was an opportunity for Maggie to explore the acting world. Watching actors bringing stories to life, on stage, was fascinating. Whenever she had the opportunity to even see community theatre, Maggie went.

Several years ago; when Maggie was a freshman, her English teacher, Mrs. Rose, arranged several field trips to 'The Old Globe Theater' at Balboa Park in San Diego. Maggie was spellbound by everything that theater had to offer, from its history to the wide range of classical and contemporary performances.

There were the Shakespeare plays; Renaissance music and period costumed actors, performing outside the theater before the show even began.

The very first production that Maggie saw was, *Romeo and Juliet* . For months, Maggie memorized most of Juliet's lines. But, the lines that she related to the most were, "Tis but thy name that is my enemy: Thou art thyself, though, not a Montague. What's Montague? It is not hand, nor foot, nor arm, nor face, or any other part belonging to a man. Oh, be some other name! What is a name? That which we call a rose, by any other name would smell as sweet, So Romeo would, were he not Romeo call'd…"

Why can't people just see me beyond my name and brown skin? Even Mama and Papa want me to be always with their Mexican friends. I am so much more than just Maggie Mendoza! I am Juliet Montague. I am Scarlet O'Hara! I am Christine, in the Phantom of the Opera, and Eponine in Le Miserables! The stage is where I will discover who I really am.

This was Maggie's mantra. And, although, taking a real acting class would definitely challenge her comfort zone, it was the only way that she knew how to escape from all of the stereotypes surrounding her.

Until now, Maggie chose to isolate herself from most social groups in school. Some, even, labeled her a loner, although she did have a few close friends.

Maria Sanchez and Juanita Juarez both lived in her neighborhood. The three girls knew each other since they were in elementary school. All of them were from very strict Hispanic families.

Nearly twenty years ago, Maggie's father, Joaquin, and two other men all left their homes in Pueblo, a small Mexican village. Their dream was to live in the United States of America, where anything is possible. Owning his restaurant, El Gato Gordo fulfilled Joaquin's dream, but that wasn't Maggie's dream.

There were times that Maggie, sometimes, worried what would happen if Joaquin, an illegal alien, was discovered. Margaret,

Maggie's mother, was born in America—she was certain of this—but, how would they live if her father was deported?

Maggie's maternal grandmother lived in San Jose, but she knew nothing about her father's family. She presumed that Joaquin's illegal status was the main reason why her parents insisted that she only have Mexican friends.

At times, Maggie would, sometimes, briefly remember when her father worked as a laborer on an artichoke farm in Castroville, Northern California.

She wasn't sure why this kept creeping into her mind. Maybe it had something to do with that evening; many years ago, in the middle of the night, when her family was forced to leave their home.

Nobody ever explained why, or even discussed this, ever again. But, suddenly, Maggie was in a new place...San Diego.

Those early years were very vague. Living in a crowded, small apartment with other people, she didn't know, was all that Maggie could recall. It was not a bad arrangement, just uncomfortable.

Then, one day; somehow, all this changed. The Mendoza's managed to lease a small vacant restaurant downtown near the Gas Lamp Quarter District. Originally, this was known as the 'New Town' area, back in 1868.

Ironically, this was in contrast to the 'Old Town' area which has most of the historical Spanish architecture. Another oddity is that The Gas Lamp district did not typically have any Mexican restaurants.

Maggie still recalls her mother, father and two other ladies cooking, in a very small kitchen, authentic Mexican meals to strangers.

Soon, the small 'hole-in-the-wall' eatery, although located near fish markets and continental cuisine, became so busy that the Mendoza's began looking for a larger establishment. With the financial assistance from Margaret's uncle it soon became possible.

They found the perfect location across from the Casa de Estudillo, the home of Don José Antonio de Estudillo, a Spanish aristocrat. Later, this landmark became a sanctuary for women and children during the American occupation in 1846.

Joaquin was convinced that God intended him to select this respected location for his El Gato Gordo Restaurant. And, he was right! From opening day, every day, the restaurant was busy. Not only with regular customers but also those visiting San Diego. When the take out business became so busy, Joaquin needed to hire four new cooks just for take out on the weekends

The first item that went into the restaurant was a small; but noticeable, Lady of Guadeloupe, statue. Joaquin built a small alcove in the wall for the religious icon, located in the waiting area. It was how he expressed his thanks for being blessed.

This new Mexican Restaurant was soon known for its handmade tortillas, traditional menudo and Christmas tamales that became a local favorite throughout the city. Within the first year, the Mendoza's made enough money to pay back their original loan and purchase a home.

When people would ask how Joaquin named the restaurant, he explained that it was in honor of a very stout calico cat that the family adopted, mainly, because he was a great mouse hunter.

The English translation of El Gato Gordo means fat cat. Joaquin even had a painting in the main dining room of El Gato Gordo wearing a Mexican sombrero and a chef's apron.

The Mendoza's never became wealthy, but for the past few years, their life was comfortable. Maggie was five years old when her family, finally, was able to move from their small apartment into a pleasant neighborhood.

Even then, Maggie's parents always reminded her to be friends with only her own 'kind'. That rule isolated her from other students and limited her social activities.

This year, however, was going to be different. This year, Maggie was going to be noticed. How dramatically her life would change, forever, could never have been predicted.

The turning point came when Mrs. Garcia, the drama teacher, announced that the fall production this year would be, *Cat on the Hot Tin Roof*, by Tennessee Williams. After class one day, Maggie was asked to remain for a few minutes.

"Are you familiar with this play, Maggie? Because, if not, I would like you to read it entirely this weekend and try out on Monday for the lead female role," Mrs. Garcia said, handing a copy of the script to Maggie. Mrs. Garcia was very familiar with Maggie's love for theater.

Mrs. Rose, Maggie's former English teacher, raved about her favorite student. "All this girl needs," Mrs. Rose insisted, "is a chance. I can see her as your protégé, Sonia. Maggie has amazing acting potential. You will enjoy watching her aspire."

After a few weeks of class, Sonia understood why Mrs. Rose was so impressed. "When you get on stage Monday, I want you to convince me that you are Maggie, the cat."

Mrs. Garcia waited a moment for a reaction.

Maggie began to thumb through the pages of the play. Then she noticed that Elizabeth Taylor was the original "Maggie" in the movie version with Paul Newman.

"Is her name really Maggie, like mine?" she asked, confused.

"Well, her real name is Margaret, but everyone refers to her as Maggie. You will understand why once you start reading the script," Mrs. Garcia said, closing the classroom door behind her.

"But, I do not look like Elizabeth Taylor," Maggie's voice sounded nervous.

"And, I don't want you to be Elizabeth Taylor. I have been watching you in class. You have a natural born talent to act. Rely on that to find your own voice." Mrs. Garcia walked out toward the teacher's parking lot with her arm around Maggie. "Have a great weekend!"

That was the last Maggie heard. Once she was alone, Maggie was flying higher than any kite that she had ever seen.

This is it! A role that I can play where people will not see me as Maggie Mendoza, the Mexican girl whose father owns a Mexican restaurant, but as Maggie, the actress!

All weekend, Maggie searched for secret places to study her lines, without interruption. She did not want anyone to know about her audition…not just yet.

"Gato Gordo, where do you hide when you want to be alone? And, while you are it, can you tell me what it is like being a cat?"

Maggie looked into the mysterious eyes of the orange colored feline that was purring, contentedly, on the window seat. "I wonder how long you would last on a hot tin roof?" she said, petting him affectionately.

At last, Maggie wandered into the back yard. Hanging from the limb of the large oak tree was an old rope that Maggie would use to hoist herself up to reach the crude tree house that Joaquin built for her the first year they moved into this neighborhood .

I wonder if I can still climb up this rope? It would be the perfect place to prepare for my audition, Maggie thought to herself.

Within three minutes, she managed to reach the top and squeeze through the entrance. It looked like it was safe. Actually, there was more space inside than she remembered.

"Okay Melpomene, muse of tragedy, it is time for your gift of inspiration; whatever it may be, to help channel the true spirit of Maggie, the cat." This was said like a solemn prayer to the famous Greek goddess.

After several hours of dedicated rehearsing, Maggie felt that she could not only deliver all her lines perfectly, but that she had melded with the character.

In spite of her confidence, Maggie still decided not to tell anyone about the play until she definitely had the part. This would avoid any confrontation with her parents. Once she got the part she would tell them that she was now committed ; just in case they objected.

Monday after school when Maggie arrived at the theatre, there were seven other girls prepared to try out for the main role, of Maggie. Nervous, she decided to wait in the dressing room until it was her turn. Maggie knew what she must accomplish and wanted no distractions.

Once on stage, there was only a single chair in the center with a spotlight shining directly on it. Maggie walked over slowly and took her seat. It was impossible from the stage to see anyone who was in the audience. Then, someone behind the curtain signaled that she could start with the monologue.

Maggie stood up from the chair and, in a perfect southern drawl, began.

"Brick, I'm not good. I don't know why people have to pretend to be good, nobody's good." Maggie moved around the stage following after her invisible husband, Brick. The expressive tone of her voice; her body swaying forward and backward, showing control. After a brief, but emphatic pause, she continued.

"The rich or the well to do can afford to respect moral patterns, conventional moral patterns, but I could never afford to..." she stops and points her finger directly at invisible Brick, *"yeah, but I'm honest! Give me credit for just that will you, please? Born poor, raised poor; expect to die poor, unless I manage to get us something out of what 'Big Daddy' leaves when he dies of cancer! But, Brick?!"... Maggie is now on her knees, arms stretched out around an invisible leg..."Skipper is dead! I'm alive!"...She stands and turns around now, with both her arms over her head in victory..."Maggie, the cat is alive! I am alive, alive! I am alive!"*

Maggie stood silently; her head bent down, eyes toward the stage floor. Then, Mrs. Garcia motioned for the stage lights to come on. The audience, including all the cast members that had been selected—or rejected—were speechless!

At last, they all began cheering. But, it was one particular senior who yelled loudly from the back of the theater, "Bravo! Maggie, the cat is a tiger! Bravo." That caught Maggie's attention.

Kyle Montgomery was someone Maggie admired, but always at a distance. Certainly, he was way out of her league. That was until she discovered that Kyle Montgomery; her most enthusiastic fan, would be Brick Politt her disturbed husband during the four scheduled performances.

This was the very first time in her life that Maggie Mendoza felt proud of who she was, and terrified to be performing with such a gorgeous leading man. All the confidence that she gained she was now questioning again.

The next day, when the official cast list was posted outside the theater door, Maggie approached Mrs. Garcia privately about her anxiety. "I don't know if you chose the best leading actress for this play, Mrs. Garcia. I just mean that performing the monologue by myself on stage is just so much different than…" Maggie hesitated…"what I mean is…I don't think that I am good enough to play opposite Kyle."

Mrs. Garcia put her arms around Maggie, and looked squarely into her eyes. "Now, you listen to me real well, Maggie Mendoza, because I am only going to tell you this once. You are the most talented actress that I have EVER had as a student, and I have been teaching for forty years. So, please never insult me again by suggesting that I don't know how to cast a play. Do we understand each other now?"

"Yes, Mrs. Garcia. I will manage to make you proud of me." Maggie would merely need to remove any romantic notions from her mind when thinking of Kyle. Whatever happened on stage was role playing. Whenever her mind would wander, Maggie glanced down at her mustard seed necklace that Mrs Garcia gave her on the first day of rehearsal .

"Whenever you doubt yourself Maggie, just focus on this mustard seed charm. Notice how it is safely protected in this clear case." Mrs. Garcia showed it to Maggie before placing it around her neck.

" Do you know Maggie the story of the mustard seed?"

Maggie had no idea what power this little seed could provide, but if Mrs. Garcia wanted her to wear it she would wear it. Mrs. Garcia then put in her hand a small card that explained the significance of the mustard seed.

"Whenever you get a chance Maggie, read this short explanation about how the mustard seed will provide you with the strength you need, even if you don't think you have any."

When Mrs. Garcia left and before the theater crew or actors arrived, Maggie took a seat in the front row near the stage. On the card, she began reading the words to herself.

"The kingdom of heaven is like a mustard seed, which a man took and planted in his field. Though it is the smallest of all seeds, yet when it grows, it is the largest of garden plants, and becomes a tree, so the birds come and perch on its branches.(Matthew 13.31-32)

Maggie felt honored that Mrs. Garcia had such faith in her. But, she was sure that she would always remain as small as this mustard seed.

Maggie could never have predicted the tsunami that was following so close behind her. Once it landed, Maggie's Destiny would take many different paths. It would be nine years before she could finally, once again, be on the proper course.

CHAPTER 18

Great minds have purpose, others have wishes. Little minds are tamed and subdued by misfortunes; but, great minds rise above them

Washington Irvine

Maggie Mendoza
October 31, 2001
San Diego, California

According to the US State Department, six hundred to eight hundred thousand people are abducted across international borders, every year. Eighty percent are young girls. Maggie Mendoza was a perfect target for these well-organized predators.

Perpetrators begin by learning everything possible about their potential victim. Cynthia; a girl that Maggie barely knew, made it her priority to become close friends with her.

First, Cynthia started to sit with Maggie, at lunch. Then, she started complementing everything Maggie did—especially her dramatic talents. Whenever Cynthia had the chance, she would be with Maggie. It never seemed strange to her that Cynthia would never invite Maggie to her house. Maggie just assumed that Cynthia's parents did not like strangers, just like her parents. In spite of this after a few weeks, they became inseparable.

Other members of the sex trafficking group learned that Joaquin did not have his green card. This meant if he reported his daughter missing, he could be deported. This was enough for them to begin their strategy.

Once Maggie told her parents that she had the lead role in the school theater production, she was surprised how supportive they were. Joaquin and Margaret were hoping that the play would consume most of her free time. They did not like Cynthia being around Maggie so much and, with all of the rehearsals, they seemed to get their wish.

Cynthia was the authentic actor. She had managed to transport many young girls to various cities…even to Asia. Although Cynthia appeared to be only seventeen years old, she was, in fact, nearing thirty.

She was an expert at abducting; without a trace of course, and got paid extremely well for her job. This operation would be easy. It was scheduled for Halloween night. The perfect excuse for wearing masks.

The final production of *Cat on the Hot Tin Roof* was performed on October 30, the night before Halloween. The cast agreed that it would be ideal to have their final cast party the next evening, on Halloween.

Each member would come as a character from their favorite play, and everyone must wear a mask. To make certain that the party would not be crashed, Jessica Adams; who played Maggie's sister-in-law, during the play, volunteered to host the party. She would text a secret word, ahead of time, to each of the guests. This, hopefully, would avoid any party crashers.

At eight o'clock on Halloween night, Maggie was ready to leave the house to celebrate. The play was a success, Maggie bonded with a new group of friends and even Kyle seemed impressed with her acting. Maybe…just maybe, there was a little magic in that mustered seed after all.

Maggie was dressed; of course, as Juliet, from Shakespeare's famous play, *The Tragedy of Romeo and Juliet*. Once her mask was on, she looked at herself in the full length mirror in her bedroom. She was exactly like Maggie always imagined her favorite heroine would look like, if she could jump off the pages of the play. Mrs.

Garcia had loaned Maggie the costume, and she was the perfect Juliet.

Joaquin asked Maggie to stop by El Gato Gordo so that he could say, 'goodbye' before the party and take a few photos. This was also the first time that her parents allowed her to attend any friend's home this late in the evening.

"Papa, I am leaving for the party," Maggie said, trying not to draw attention from the dining guests.

"Papa, please...hurry. I don't want to miss my bus."

Maggie said whispering.

Her father rushed to the waiting area and asked a waiter to take their picture together. Joaquin , then, blew his only daughter a kiss as he rushed back to the kitchen. His fingers signaling the number twelve, reminding Maggie her curfew. She waved back, acknowledging the time.

By now, there were only a few young children in costume, left on the streets with their parents. There was Batman holding Sleeping Beauty's hand and Harry Potter chasing behind Dora, the Explorer.

A traditional witch was comparing her candy with Darth Vader's sack of goodies. It was a normal, typical Halloween evening.

The bus stop; where Maggie needed to go, was only two more blocks. She was relieved because her costume was rather heavy. Hopefully, one of the cast members, maybe even Kyle, would be willing to take her home, afterwards. She really did not look forward to riding the city bus—late at night. There were always odd looking men that creeped her out.

Several busses passed by, without stopping. Maggie got up from the bench to check the posted time schedule, when a dark blue van pulled up next to her.

"Hey, Maggie...want a ride to the party?" Cynthia asked her.

Maggie couldn't see the girl's face because of the mask. But, she was dressed like Belle from *Beauty and the Beast*. For just a short second, Maggie hesitated. But, then, she recognized the voice. It was

Cynthia and the person driving must be her date to the party. There was no need to bother verifying the secret word. Cynthia must be going with one of the cast members.

"Okay, thanks! This is so much better than riding the bus."

Maggie picked up her long dress and 'Belle' opened the side door so that she could get in. Cynthia slid in close to Maggie; placed a rag saturated with chloroform over her nose and mouth, then duct tape around her hands.

The next day, Maggie woke up in a strange room with five other girls ranging from twelve to eighteen. All were naked, or nothing more than a bra and panties. Some were handcuffed to a post.

CHAPTER 19

Do not be afraid; our fate cannot be taken from us; it is a gift.
  Dante Alighieri

Maggie Mendoza
and Charlie
November, 2002
Chicago, Illinois

Maggie had no idea where she was or how long she had been here. There were a total of seven girls—all sitting on a cold asphalt floor. It was so quiet that it felt like a death chamber. Maggie could almost hear the beating of hearts closing in on her.

"Does anyone know where we are?" She finally asked, realizing for the first time that her hands and feet were bound together.

A girl sitting next to her, with her back leaning on the wall, began to scoot closer.

"They brought you in last night. Probably drugged like the rest of us. Someone with a gun comes in about every hour and randomly takes two or three girls at a time. We never see them again. My name is Charlie. I have been here for three days...I think."

Charlie was older than Maggie, but she was not sure how much older. On her right arm was a red spiral tattoo. The single bare light bulb hanging loosely from the ceiling distorted Maggie's vision; or maybe, it was staring at that spiral tattoo on Charlie's arm that made Maggie's head start spinning.

"It takes a few days to feel like you are back to normal, well...at least as normal as you can be in this shit hole."

Charlie knew exactly how this new girl felt. Everyone here came

94

in the same way. Spaced out, black smudges on their face and hands and no clothes. They all looked like grease monkeys. And then, they disappeared.

Maggie must have dozed off; for a short time, because when she opened her eyes again, her head was on Charlie's shoulder. As soon as she noticed it, she bolted back up.

"You're okay. I know it doesn't seem that way now, but 'this too shall pass'. Funny, isn't it, how times like this makes you remember the weirdest shit?"

Maggie was not sure how to react to Charlie. She was the only one in the room talking, and either she was doing it because she was stronger than the rest of them, or she was just fucking nuts.

"That Biblical passage is from Acts 2:21, don't even ask me why I know this, but anyway, it is either Peter or Joel…Hell, I don't remember which one, but anyway, one of them said, *'And it shall come that everyone who calls on the name of the Lord shall be saved. For in Mount Zion and Jerusalem, there shall be those who escape, as the Lord has said, and among the survivors are those whom the Lord calls'.*"

Was this really said to make Maggie feel better, or was Charlie just the soundboard of a raving lunatic locked in this room for too long.

"I know…I know…I can tell by the look on your face that you think I am just some kind of Jesus freak preaching the Bible, but really, this is the only thing I know from the Bible. It was something that my grandmother used to tell me when things got really bad at home. What is your name anyway, honey?"

Charlie's eyes were grass green and when she got excited there was a thin yellow circle around the pupils that looked like halos.

"Maggie…my name is Maggie Mendoza, and I have no idea what is happening, but I do believe in Jesus and you are right, we are survivors."

She then remembered the mustard seed necklace that she always wore.

"Can you see if I still have my necklace on? It's not worth anything to anyone but me." Maggie said, not feeling it around her neck.

Charlie scooted as close as she could. "You mean the one with the strange seed inside the plastic bubble? Yeah, it's there. But, don't expect it to survive once those goons get their hands on you." Charlie said.

"Do you think that you can take it off of me? I don't care about the chain. You can just break that. I just want the seed."

Maggie was hoping that she could just find someplace to hide it.

Once it was off her neck, Charlie told Maggie that the only safe place was in her mouth.

"I am not sure if there is any way this little mustard seed will survive, but the only chance you have is maybe under your tongue."

Once Charlie heard the story about the mustard seed she told Maggie she would do what she could to help her keep it.

Neither one of these young women knew what would be next, but they vowed to work together to find a way out of this place. It gave Maggie hope. Just knowing that she had a friend would be enough to get her through this, regardless how difficult it could become.

Soon, Maggie and Charlie would experience the most traumatic journey of their short lives.

For now, Maggie was curious to find out how Charlie got here. She explained that a young couple stopped by her sunglasses kiosk, located inside the mall that she worked at, almost every day for two weeks.

The money she earned helped pay for an apartment that she and three other girls were renting at Berkeley. All of them moved out of the university's dorms their senior year when they could no longer afford the cost. Charlie was a political science major.

"It doesn't sound like a really practical major I know, but I already have a job once I graduate, in Sacramento, the Governor's office. It's only a Legislative Page, but I am hoping in time that it will develop into something greater... Anyway, this couple told me that I should consider being a model.

They kept coming back into the store trying to convince me that they were agents. They even offered me free head shots; a professional photo shoot portfolio, and a guarantee that they could get me a signed contract with a major model agency in Hollywood.

I never considered myself pretty enough to be a model, but they kept saying it was all about the lens of the camera. And, I could quit this minimum paying job, finish college and save money for the first time in my life. So…stupid. I believed them, and look at me now?"

What caught Maggie's immediate attention was that Charlie must have been abducted in Northern California, and she was at the very end of Southern California.

Why were we all brought together and are we even still in California?

When Maggie told Charlie how old she was and where she lived, this also made Charlie skeptical. The only similarity was that they were both young women. Not knowing how long they were going to be kept here was only one concern. The most terrifying question was, why? And, what were they expected to do before their captors would release them?

Just as the two girls were pondering these questions, three men entered the room, stood in front of them, wearing black hoods over their faces with no shirts and only bikini briefs.

One cut the tape off of Maggie's feet and then pulled her up with his hand. Maggie quickly placed the mustard seed under her tongue as Charlie advised.

The other man already had Charlie by the arms dragging her out the door. Both girls were then released to another room—by themselves.

This room had two chairs and a queen size bed. Maggie's 'escort' forced her into the seat and began to give her directions.

"You are now here to make money for Mama san. In a few minutes, another girl will demonstrate how to make money. Watch her carefully. She is your mentor. She will teach you how to give blow jobs and how to have sex with two men at one time. Each day you will both learn something new and then you will go out and make money."

The masked man could sense Maggie's disgust and noticed how she was moving nervously around in the chair.

That was when he yanked back her hair, took a revolver out of his back pocket and rammed it into Maggie's mouth. Somehow the mustard seed never fell out.

"If you don't cooperate like a good girl, I will blow your brains all over this room. Now, show me respect and that you understand."

Maggie's entire body was trembling.

Sweat was running down her face. *This, too, will pass. I believe in Jesus and I am a survivor. I am alive! Maggie, the cat lives!* Then, she was able to nod her head, 'yes', with the revolver still in her mouth.

A few seconds later, the hooded man must have been finally satisfied that she was ready to participate. He, slowly, removed the revolver from Maggie's mouth. She didn't move a muscle.

I've got guts to die. What I want to know is do I have the guts to live? (Cat on the Hot Tin Roof). Those words repeated themselves in Maggie's head while she watched the sex act play out in front of her.

When the two hooded men left Charlie and Maggie alone to watch and learn, Charlie grabbed Maggie's hand.

"But, Charlie, I'm a virgin. What am I going to do? They may as well just put that gun back in my mouth and pull the trigger," she whispered, hoping that nobody heard her.

"Whenever you think you can't take it any longer, think about that mustard seed and this." Charlie pointed to the tattoo on her right arm. "The spiral will lead you to the inner soul…it represents rebirth, and connection with nature. Focus on this. It will help you to retain hope and balance."

Maggie closed her eyes and painted the mental image in her mind. Even if everything that Charlie said about the spiral was not true, it was all she had at this moment.

"It's going to be fine, Maggie. Just watch what I do, and think of something else. Let your mind escape, even if your body can't. WE WILL GET OUT OF HERE, I promise you this."

Charlie's life before college wasn't this bad, but she did know girls who 'turned tricks'; prostituted, just to get out of the projects. Their survival stories would be her playbook. This is a nightmare with a black hole somewhere, and she was determined to find it.

After that first night, when Maggie horrified, watched hours of the live sexual 'teaching' instructions, the two young women were finally isolated from the others, permanently.

Charlie forced Maggie to listen to her. She knew what would happen to Maggie if her clients weren't satisfied. These piranhas would eat her slowly and painfully.

"We are being kept alive to make money for this gang. They expect us to do whatever it takes. But, we can set a few limits that they don't need to know. First, never let any of these 'johns' kiss you. Always use mouth wash when you are finished sucking their dicks. Most of the time, motels will have those small bottles, or even shampoo will work. And…when you are down there with his nasty penis in your mouth, start counting to yourself. One to thirty, stop, stroke, lick. That's what they paid for, and no more. Understand, Maggie?"

It was not the blow jobs that Maggie was worried about. That was disgusting, but it was the intercourse that blew her mind. Just the thought of a stranger inserting his penis into her virgin vagina, or her anus, made Maggie want to vomit.

"Well, the first time will hurt like hell, Maggie. There is no way to avoid that. But, there are some men out there that will pay extra to fuck a virgin, and you are a rare commodity. From what I have heard, from some of my 'hooker' friends, is that the only good thing about being a virgin is it doesn't last long the first time. The 'Johns' get freaked out about all the blood, even if they are the cause of it."

Unfortunately, for Maggie, the first time was not that easy. She was taken by an overweight Asian man that insisted on four more intercourses with her after she bled the first time.

The only positive outcome from that experience was she no longer had any more pain. The three days following the loss of her virginity there was no sex. The pimps wanted to make sure that the bleeding had stopped. Nothing worse than customers complaining about blood during oral sex.

When Maggie was finally allowed to be with other girls during her 'recovery' time, the first thing she asked Charley was why she chose that spiral tattoo on her arm. Just like Charlie told her earlier, it was that spiral tattoo that helped Maggie survive her first intercourse experience.

"I have been so worried about you the last three days, I couldn't think of almost anything else. And, now, you ask me about my tattoo? You are a strange one, Maggie Mendoza."

Charlie wanted to laugh at how absurd Maggie's question was, but, this was not the time to laugh at anything.

Maggie didn't even respond to her question. She just stared at her like a patient child waiting to hear a bed night story…something…anything…that would make her feel better.

"Okay…well, after high school, by some miracle, I received a scholarship to the University at Berkeley. My first boyfriend suggested that we get tattoos. I told him that I would only do it if it was something special, small and unobtrusive. He suggested the red spiral because people believe that the spiral makes you calmer and the curve is the cyclical power of nature and potential."

Once that tattoo was on her body, Charlie believed that it was a shield protecting her from eminent danger. When she was abducted, it was the spiral that gave her the power to stay strong. But, Charlie also knew that it would take more than just the spiral, or a mustard seed, to get them free.

"When we get out of here, I want to get a tattoo just like yours, Charlie," Maggie finally said.

"You need your very own symbol, Maggie. One that represents how special you are. I will find you one, I promise ."

Charlie felt that regardless how horrific this place was, God had a purpose for bringing Maggie into her life, even for a short time. She would never replace the little sister that she lost but, maybe Charlie could protect this new little sister.

One thing that Charlie was certain of is that freedom was only possible if they both started to seriously look for escape routes; bathroom windows, or open fields they could hide in.

Maggie was reminded to always pick up anything that had the name of the motel that they were taken to. It wasn't much evidence, but it was at least something.

Finally, they both agreed that whoever had the chance to escape first should take it.

"I don't think I could ever leave you behind, Charlie." Maggie said tearfully.

"Well you will just need to get strength from that mustard seed that you have protecting all these months. Because it is the only chance we might have to save each other."

Charlie explained that once either one of them were free, she could return for the other one with the police.

Whenever Maggie became depressed, Charlie would remind her, *"Aut inveniam viam aut faciam," translated from the Punic Language and said by Hannibal when he was told by the generals that it was impossible to cross the Alps by elephants, means "I shall either find a way or make one."*

After two months, two hundred different men, performing oral copulation, and sexual intercourse on her, Maggie knew that she would have to find some escape route. She was reaching the limit of her tolerance.

"If Hannibal was able to cross the Alps, Maggie, we will be able to get out of here. We just need to be persistent and keep the faith," Charlie said emphatically.

When the wolves become silent and only the moon howls,

Charlie's instincts alerted her that change was coming soon. The first sign was when the pimps, for no logical reason, decided to make Maggie and Charlie a sex team. That meant they would travel together to the same motels, private parties, and sometimes orgy clubs.

When customers wanted to buy a ménage trois, it was Molly and Charlie that went. Maybe, this was merely a coincidence or just maybe, it was God working in his miraculous ways.

Charlie tried convincing this to Maggie by reminding her that God was preparing them for an exodus, just like he did for the Jewish people in Egypt.

Whenever the pimps would drop the women off for work, Charlie would preach *the founding myth of Israel that explains how the Israelites were delivered from slavery.*

During one of the rendezvous locations, on the two month anniversary of her abduction, Charlie finally recognized that they were in Chicago.

This happened one day when they were returning from a six hour job, exhausted. It was the 'L' train that stopped at Memorial Hospital, and Charlie recognized it immediately.

"Maggie…we are in Chicago. I used to live close to here before I was accepted at the University of Berkeley. How the hell did they get us this far?" Charlie said, amazed at this discovery.

"Are you sure, Charlie? If you are right, when we escape, we at least know where to go safely." Maggie sounded excited for the first time.

"I don't know, Maggie? These pimps don't let us go sightseeing. They rarely even let us out of their sights. Do you have any suggestions?" Charlie wanted to find an escape route as desperately as Maggie did. But, if they were caught, the hell they were living now, would seem like paradise. This was a major sex trafficking operation, and all the girls were considered a valuable commodity.

"Listen to me, Maggie. We need to be perfectly sure that one of us can get away. If we don't make it, and get caught, these morons could start removing body parts from us. I have seen what pimps do to their 'property' that escape... you really don't want to ever come back here." Charlie was downright serious now.

"There must be a way out of this inferno. Now that we know where we are, there is at least hope," Maggie said.

Regardless what Charlie told Maggie, she knew that the escape needed to be soon, or they may as well kill her.

And then it happened. Something bizarre, like being in different states of consciousness at the same time. Maggie and Charlie both felt it. They were in a transcendental stage, rising above the muddy murk towards enlightenment.

The next evening, they were taken to a shabby motel on the east side of Chicago. Charlie knew that they were close to Egger woods.

In her past life, family and friends would have picnics at the park. Charlie remembered riding her bike through that wooded area the night that Amy, her little sister, was hit by a drunk driver.

The hospital they took Amy to was close by. Although Amy never recovered and died hours later, this same place, filled with sad memories, could be the best chance so far for Charlie to escape.

In the van, before she got out, she whispered to Maggie. "Once we are done here, keep the two goons occupied for just a few minutes. I am going to go for it tonight."

Maggie had no chance to find out the details or ask questions. They were walking to the front door of the motel.

Today, everything was different. Usually, when Maggie and Charlie arrive at the room, they know what to expect. This time, however, the Pimp told them that this 'John' wanted to watch the two of them have sex together before they did their threesome.

There was no time to object, or explain, to the pimp that they never did this before; the 'John' was already inside, waiting.

Once the money was exchanged for the girls, the pimp went over the rules explaining that there was a time limit. For some unknown reason, the girls were, then, left alone.

The usual routine is the pimp remains in the bathroom, or a connecting room, to be in control if anything wrong goes down. But, this time he was really gone. They were all alone.

The lesbian routine was new territory. Maggie and Charlie never did this before and really were not sure what to do. But, since Charlie definitely had more sexual experience than Maggie, she took control.

Charlie started by undressing Maggie, and fondling her breasts. While dancing seductively in front of her, and the 'John'. Finally, after a few minutes, she made Maggie sit on the chair, preparing her for a lap dance.

Charlie had just started her routine when the 'John's' cell phone started beeping. It was the signal he was waiting for.

He, then, walked over to Maggie and put his hand across her mouth. Charlie started pushing him away, saying that he didn't pay enough to rough handle either one of them. He, then, showed both of them a Chicago Police Badge. "Girls, this is a sting operation. If you cooperate with me nobody will be hurt," Officer Brady whispered. He needed to make certain that the area had been secured before any of them could leave the motel room.

Charlie and Maggie were in a state of shock. They put their skimpy clothes back on, and sat on the bed without moving or talking.

When Brady got the signal that the pimps had been handcuffed and in custody, he, then, led the girls to the unmarked police car; the one that he originally arrived in. Charlie was the first one to explain how both of them were kidnapped, in different places, in California and brought here.

Maggie was still clinging to Charlie, not really sure if she was yet free. The officer gave Charlie his jacket from the back seat, and another officer brought over a blanket to wrap around Maggie.

"You do understand that I will need to take you both in and book you for prostitution. Right?!"

Neither one of the girls objected. Being in the city jail could not be any worse than where they were for the last two months.

"Once we arrive at the station, I will see if there are any missing persons reports on the two of you. If you really were kidnapped, we will also need to keep you in protective custody while the prosecutors prepare for trial. Unfortunately, this could be a very long process."

Brady was sympathetic with what the girls experienced, but he was also determined to put away these scum bags for more than a few days. He and his officers had been working on this sex trafficking ring for two years. Any witnesses that he could find would need to remain safe until a trial date was set.

Just as the girls said, the data bank revealed that both Charlie and Maggie were missing for sixty days. In the waiting room, Maggie nearly collapsed from stomach pains. They were so painful that theParamedics were called. After a brief examination It was determined that Maggie needed to be rushed to the hospital for internal bleeding.

Tests indicated that due to excessive sexual intercourse at the age of sixteen, she needed a complete hysterectomy, as soon as possible. Maggie would never be able to have children. She also noticed that her mustard seed was no longer anywhere.

Once Maggie recovered from surgery, she was told that her father, Joaquin, was deported to Mexico two months ago. He lived for twenty years in the United States. El Gato Gordo was closed down. Her mother, Margaret, was still in San Diego, but was planning on following Joaquin back to Mexico.

At seventeen, Maggie felt desperate and alone. Her physical recovery seemed normal, but she never expected to ever live normally again.

CHAPTER 20

It is a mistake to look too far ahead. The chain of destiny can only be grasped one link at a time.
Winston Churchill

Maggie Mendoza
May, 2002
New York City, New York

It took six months for the prosecuting attorneys to accumulate enough evidence on the sex traffic predators. Even then, some of the accomplices walked away or plea bargained down to a minor offense.

Charlie and Maggie were placed in separate witness protection programs located in different states. They never saw each other after Maggie was rushed to the hospital.

The prosecution was careful that the defense attorneys could not claim that the young ladies' testimonies were corroborated.

Although the girls never met again after the trial, Detective Brady gave Maggie the mustard seed Charlie was able to retrieve before Maggie was rushed into surgery.

"Charlie thought that you might want to have this." Brady was not sure of the significance but he promised it would be delivered.

Maggie was also allowed to send a letter to Charlie through her attorney. He warned her that anything she wrote might be read by censors. The prosecuting attorneys needed to be certain that the girls were not discussing anything about their abduction. Maggie assured them that they could read whatever she wrote.

Dear Charlie,

I will never forget you. If you were not with me during that time in hell, I would have killed myself. You gave me hope and made me strong. I only wish that we could have been friends under different circumstances. I will be watching for your name on the election ballot. Wait a minute, I don't even know your last name? That's okay…I will know that it is you.

Love,

Your little sister forever!

Maggie Mendoza.

P.S I still can't believe you were able to save my mustard seed!

Since Maggie was a minor, she was placed with a family in New York. Lisa and Jim Hancock were retired police officers that worked with the witness protection team and children services to provide a safe environment. Maggie was home taught, but also worked part time at a book store.

Manhattan was entirely different from the West coast, but she easily adapted to the large crowds. This was where she could easily disappear. The easiest way for her to accomplish this was to consider herself a character in a new script, and she was the leading lady.

Each day, Maggie created her own scene, setting and dialogue. This fantasy world allowed her to temporarily forget about the past.

One day, before going to work in Manhattan, Lisa handed Maggie a letter addressed to her.

My dearest Maggie,

I have no idea where you are. I sent this to Officer Brady, asking him to deliver it to you, after receiving your letter.

You are right. I will always love you like a sister. Never feel that you are alone. It may take a long time, but I do believe we will meet again. Oh, and by the way, if you ever do decide to get a tattoo, the perfect one for you is a swallow. Symbolically, the swallow represents returning home. It will also bring you everlasting love and loyalty. Did you know that when swallows mate it is forever! I pray that you will finally find, peace, loyalty and everlasting love. Listen to your big sister!

Love,

Maggie held the letter close to her heart. She wished that, somehow, Charlie was here with her—now. But, her letter would, at least, be her dream catcher. It would keep her on track, it would help her move forward. Maggie placed the letter in the journal that she always carried with her.

Most afternoons, the commuter train was the most direct route from downtown Manhattan to Queens, but today there was a delay.

Maggie patiently walked over to platform 67, where the train was now scheduled to arrive in twenty minutes. As she turned around to verify that it was the right platform, an attractive lady, with long chestnut colored hair and a warm smile, asked Maggie if she knew where she was going.

"Well, I am hoping that this train is going to Queens, but it is difficult to be sure since the monitor keeps changing," Maggie said...her voice slightly frustrated.

"Nothing to worry about, Maggie. Whatever train that you take will always return you to the right place," the lady said kindly, tapping Maggie's shoulder.

"Do we know each other? You do look familiar, but I can't place where we met." Maggie looked rather confused.

"Actually, I do believe it was at another train station, not too long ago. You handed me some dandelions to take with me."

"Dandelions? Oh, you must be mistaking me for someone else. Why would I give you dandelions?" Maggie said...totally surprised.

"It doesn't really matter if you remember," the odd lady answered. "Because I brought the dandelions back to you. They are going to be more important for you, now, than they are for me."

Before Maggie could determine what the lady meant by that remark, a huge burst of steam—from nowhere—filled the station...and the mystery lady vanished.

The next thing that Maggie remembered was the screeching sound of the breaks bringing the train to a sudden stop. It jolted her enough that she had to hold on to the seat for balance.

On her lap was her daily journal. When Maggie opened it to write a few words, pressed inside the pages were three dandelions, still fresh with seeds intact.

Chapter 21

Out of suffering have emerged the strongest souls; the most massive characters are seared with scars.
Kahlil Gibran

Sterling and Gabby
April, 2010
Ensenada, Mexico

La Mansion Ensenada ocean front estate is fourteen thousand square feet, six bedrooms, seven bathrooms, and can accommodate twenty-five guests. When Sterling isn't renting the entire estate, it is open to the public. However, in the past year, he has been the exclusive resident.

Entering through the guarded gate immediately made me feel that I was entering a private island, with the amazing Pacific Ocean welcoming me back from an ugly journey.

Sterling and I were greeted, as we exited the car, by the estate's entire staff who welcomed us into the vast reception area.

"Welcome home, Mr. Sterling. On the veranda, you will find several bottles of wine, including a chilled Chardonnay. Please let us know if we can bring you any appetizers or tapas."

"Muchas Gracias, Alejandra. This is my very good Amiga Gabriella Girard. She will be our guest for some time. Could you please prepare the junior suite on the West Wing for her," Sterling said, politely.

Alejandra walked toward me, extended her hand and said in perfect English, "Welcome, Mrs. Girard to La Mansion. Our staff is dedicated to making your entire stay as comfortable as possible. You will have a maid on duty, twenty-four hours for anything you may need or desire. Please, never hesitate to let us know how we can assist you."

"Gracias Alejandra, and please call me, Gabby."

I decided not to correct her about my maiden name, since Sterling continues to refer to me this way.

Once Alejandra had left, I could clearly see the breathtaking view and courtyard below. There was even a helicopter on the landing pad, I presumed if needed.

A part of me felt that this extravagant lifestyle seemed in total defiance of Sterling's dedication to help those struggling, only three miles past the mansion's gate. But, I thought it best not to share that opinion at this time.

"May I pour you a glass of wine, Gabby? All these wines are local. Ensenada is Mexico's response to Napa Valley. One afternoon, I will introduce you to the fantastic wine country," Sterling said, handing me a frosted wine glass with chilled Chardonnay. "Every year, in just a few months, Ensenada hosts a summer wine festival that is internationally recognized. My foundation sponsors many of the events. I hope that you will decide to remain here so that I can share this tremendously entertaining time of the year," Sterling said, enthusiastically. He raised his wine glass, looked directly at Gabby and said, "Now, at last, we are starting the beginning of our new chapter, a 'Great Story' that no one has ever read—one that goes on forever—in which every chapter is better than the one before."

Sterling, then, walked slowly over to where I was sitting and gently tapped my glass, making this an official toast. "Oh, I guess I better give credit to where I stole those words from…" he started to say.

Gabby quickly interrupted him before he could finish. "CS Lewis. 'The Last Battle'. It was the seventh and final novel in 'The Narnia Collection'. Actually, a very appropriate choice, considering the circumstances," Gabby said confidently, while taking a sip of the refreshing, slightly buttery Chardonnay. The rich full bodied flavors of vanilla, butter, and even caramel from the oak, were beginning to effectively refresh her spirit.

"Smart ass. I keep totally forgetting that you are a literary freak. Do you still have those moments where quotes meld with your own experiences?"

Sterling was taunting me. That one flaw in his perfect personality was flashing back at me with beacon lights; he hated losing and always wanted to be admired.

Whenever I felt the urge to correct him, or perhaps offer another perspective, I would find the appropriate literary quote to support my position. It drove him mad. As intelligent as Sterling is; he is brilliant, I was always able to compete with him.

"Of course, I do darling, but it is now under control. It only surfaces when something obviously needs to be addressed."

I was praying that this was true, although, I never really had control when those quotes would purge forward.

The friendly bantering between us was something that I missed. It had been a long time since I felt this comfortable without any pressure. Sterling was always someone that listened to me...really listened to me.

Even before Molly's death, it was getting more difficult to accept that Caden and I would ever be able to meet again. And when the opportunity finally came, after forty-three years, why didn't I take it? Was it really because of Molly's eulogy and Jake's journals? Or is it a premeditated fear that everyone I have ever loved leaves me? I suppose that this is why I am here—to finally answer those questions.

"Perhaps after supper, or tomorrow morning, you might like to take a walk around the grounds. There are some spectacular flower gardens and rather unusual plants that are indigenous to this climate." Sterling could not hide his enthusiasm. He was excited to share all of this with someone who would appreciate this same new experience.

"I would like that. But, if you don't mind, I would rather pass on dinner tonight and just spend the evening relaxing. Maybe, take a warm bath and go to bed early," I replied, trying not to yawn.

"Of course, that is completely understandable. The entire purpose coming here is to take time to reflect and adjust. But, don't forget to let Alejandra know if you get hungry. You still have that lobster from Puerto Nuevo," he said, taking a sip of the Merlot wine and lighting a cigar.

I rose from my chair, walked slowly toward Sterling and gave him a warm embrace. He gently kissed my cheek as we parted.

"Is 9:00 am a good time for breakfast in the morning for you, Gabby?" he asked, just before I exited through the bedeviled glass French doors.

"That will be perfect. I will set my phone alarm. Will I need a road map to find the dining room?" I asked.

"Just set your GPS on your smart phone. It never fails," Sterling said with a crooked smile, just tempting me to respond. But, there would be many more days to play mind games.

The room that Sterling selected for me was larger than the Penthouse at The Del Coronado. But, this time no adjoining rooms. There was a small extra bedroom across the living room that I soon discovered belonged to my maid, Marisol.

Marisol's English was not as clear as Alejandra's, but it was easily understood. She assured me that all I needed to do was use the intercom in my bedroom at night and she would be there to assist.

I could not imagine ever having to call her in the middle of the night for a glass of water or any other request. Nevertheless, Marisol was determined to please .

It was obvious that being employed at La Mansion, she believed, was a gift from God. If this job kept her off the streets, then, maybe, the luxurious lifestyle that I was criticizing earlier, really does have a redeeming purpose.

Being on the West side, my balcony had a view of the ocean as well as the city. What caught my attention immediately was the lighthouse, a short distance from the cliffs with its welcoming beams.

I walked inside to my bedroom, removed the journal that I had avoided reading since arriving to California, and went back outside.

Sitting comfortably on the extended lounge chair, I hesitated opening the book. As my fingers caressed the engraved initials, I began to realize that what Jake and I really experienced , in the scheme of life, was the purest relationship possible.

We never had to deal with any daily obstacles or realistic situations. And, when we did, it was a disaster.

Years later, Jake compensated his decisions by determining that we could continue to share experiences together, although physically separated.

But, was it enough to last a lifetime? Could knowing that we would once again be together in the afterlife be worth sacrificing my present life?

Jake, the challenge for me is, when others penetrate through the bubble, that isolates us, how do I know what to do?

I now opened the journal to where I bookmarked my last reading. In the center of the binding was a perfectly preserved dandelion. It appeared to be pressed between two pieces of shiny wax. I had no idea how, or when, it was placed there.

Trying not to be distracted by this odd phenomenon, my eyes focused on the new entry.

When the daily obligations of life are finally ready to sleep, and the innocence permeates for a short time, there is a sound not of silence, but a sound of answers. Listen to the whispering waves and you can hear the true heartbeat of life.

We are surrounded by a gentleness that will restore internal peace once we recognize and acknowledge that our mentors' words is what unlocks life's mysteries. Do not deny or ignore the past.

Embrace the words that came before you, and recast them to show you new roads, invisible to those who cannot feel their true ancestors.

Gabby, you and I know where truth abides. Inhale the air, allow the elixir to heal your scars. Release the imagination, and miracles will make the impossible real. Inhale the future, exhale the past.

Once again, I placed the red ribbon with the miniature silver bell on the page, precisely where I stopped reading for the evening. Before closing the journal, for some unknown reason, I carefully repositioned the dandelion in the same place on the next page.

For a short time before returning inside, I tried to comprehend what I just read. This entry was labeled, "Molly's Death."

Unfortunately, it did not really address her death, or did it? Was it my expectations that Jake, somehow, had the answers to why she died? Or was he revealing to me the best method to close the door that Death opens?

"Miss Gabby, I have brought you a warm serape to keep the cool ocean breeze off of your bare shoulders." Marisol secured the Mexican shawl comfortably around my arms. "I will prepare the bath for you, now. No more than fifteen minutes, I promise." Marisol scurried toward the bathroom.

Recalling Sterling's toast about the future and Jake's inspirational words that resonated now, my mind created many images for me to ponder.

However, the most appropriate one for now came from the lines spoken by Scarlett O'Hara, in *Gone With the Wind*. "After all tomorrow is another day."

CHAPTER 22

You become. It takes a long time. That's why it happens to people who break easily, or have sharp edges, or have to be carefully kept. Generally, by the time you are 'real', most of your hair has been loved off, and your eyes drop out, and you get loose in the joints and very shabby. But these things don't matter at all, because once you are 'real'; you can't be ugly, except to people who don't understand.

Velveteen Rabbit
by Margery Williams

Sophia Santos
Margaret Santos Mendoza
1967-2001
California

On December 31, 1967, in San Francisco, California, Margaret Santos was born to a first generation family from Seville, Spain. Her father, Carlos Santos, was a district manager for the city of San Francisco his entire life.

Sofia Santos enjoyed being a stay home mother, until her daughter, Margaret, was old enough to be in school all day. That was when Sofia opened her own local bakery. From day one, it was a successful enterprise.

Located downtown, near the busy commercial business center, *Mama Sofia's Madrid Bakery* was known for its delicious selections, reasonable prices, and quaint ambiance.

Morning, noon, or even in the evening, the hot steamy, buttery vapors that cling to your tongue and fill your imagination with the taste of honey, almonds, and powdered sugar, are accentuated by the outside window tempting patrons to taste a variety of macaroons, such as strawberry pistachio and gin. Then there were also crepes, and seven different croissants.

But, during the holidays, Sofia needed to hire nearly seven additional employees to help bake and serve the most popular specialities, like Turron, a delicious candy bar of Moorish origin that contains chocolate, raisins, rum, and whiskey.

The truffles came in many different flavors. Specialties like Polvoron, and short bread cookies, known for its variety of vanilla, cinnamon, lemon flavor were some of the most requested orders. Next was Marzipan; a pastry blend of almonds, egg yolks, and butter, in holiday shapes and figurines. All of these pastries promoted the holiday spirit.

And, then there was Pestinos, a dough sensation, flavored with aniseed or sesame seed, and fried in olive oil. The bakery was such a success that what started as a hobby, flourished into a local obsession.

For all practical purposes, the Santos were a normal family. But, Sophia also liked to gently tease her only daughter, Margaret, about the day she was born.

"My beloved, Margaret, you could not even wait just ten more minutes to be born. Always in a hurry. You could have been a celebrity. You could have been...The New Year Baby!"

Margaret had heard this story so often that she would just ignore it. Not really caring what the superstition claims about babies born on New Year's Day; those babies will forever be lucky, but those who are born before the clock strikes twelve will forever live a regretful life.

Margaret refused to ever believe those tales. Until, she met Joaquin Mendoza, at age sixteen. Because Joaquin was three years older than Margaret, her parents forbid her to see him.

In the summer of 1984, tired of sneaking out to meet Joaquin,

Margaret eloped one evening with him. In Castroville, California, there were relatives that would help the young lovers begin their life together.

Margaret's parents, after three months, located their daughter who was now five months pregnant. After many tears and threats, Sofia convinced her husband to give their only daughter permission to marry, not wanting to have a "bastard" grandchild.

When the only job that Joaquin could get was as a day laborer picking artichokes, Margaret's parents tried to convince their daughter to return home.

But, once, Margaret Sofia, was born on December 9, 1984 everyone forgot all of the earlier tribulations . Her parents agreed to call her Maggie to avoid any confusion with her mother. Sofia also approved of the distinction.

"It is important that Maggie have her own identity; her own chance at life." Sofia said, trying not to express the disappointment she felt toward her daughter.

The broken fences that appeared to be permanently destroyed now were beginning to mend. Carlos and Sofia even offered their daughter and Joaquin to return to San Francisco, where they could all help to raise their grandchild. But, Joaquin was far too proud to ever agree to such an arrangement.

"It may not appear at this moment that we have very much Margaret, but I promise you that one day soon your parents will be proud that you married me." Joaquin said, with confidence.

Unfortunately, the first few years were extremely difficult for the Mendoza's . Joaquin's wages barely paid for food. Even living with his relatives became more difficult daily. Maggie was growing quickly, and even Joaquin began doubting if there would ever be an opportunity to keep his promise to Margaret..

One evening the household was alerted that the immigration department was conducting a local raid and all undocumented workers, if found, would be deported immediately to Mexico.

Although, at the time this just appeared to be another obstacle, the Mendozas were going to be given an unexpected opportunity.

This was the first time Margaret ever knew that her husband was an illegal immigrant. With the small amount of money that Sofia secretly sent monthly, Margaret was able to save enough for an emergency exodus, just like this.

Now was the time to pack their meager belongings in their old jeep and move as far south as possible. Maggie was only five years old when they left Castroville in the middle of the night.

When Margaret phoned her mother from San Diego, with no place to go, it was her father, Carlos Santos that gave her the address of his brother, who agreed to take the family in temporarily. When she told Joaquin, he was not pleased, but soon realized it was their only choice.

Within six months, Margaret was able to find a job as a receptionist in a dental office. Joaquin eventually was able to convince Margaret's Uncle to reluctantly invest a small amount of money in a local Mexican restaurant, that was for lease in Old Town San Diego.

Prior to this investment, the Mendoza's rented a small shop near the San Diego Wharf, or gaslight district, where he, Margaret, and two other women worked fifteen hours a day.

When El Gato Gordo opened its doors for the first time in 1992, in Old Town, it only took them six months to repay the loan Margaret's Uncle gave them, and one year later to purchase their first home.

Margaret finally believed that whatever curse she was born with had now passed. She could never imagine that the worst moment in her life was lurking in the shadows.

Margaret and Joaquin were perhaps over protective of their daughter, Maggie. Neither of them wanted her to experience the hardships that they had endured. Joaquin was determined that Maggie would be given the opportunity to graduate from college and pursue any profession that she desired. That is the least he could promise his only child. To assure this, for the past fifteen years, Joaquin saved enough money to guarantee that this would happen.

On Halloween, 2001, when Maggie did not return home from the cast party by midnight, her curfew, Joaquin knew that something was not right. Maggie would never ignore her curfew; if there was a reason to be late, she would always call.

Before the Mendoza's decided to notify the police that Maggie was missing, Joaquin needed to consider the risk this might cause if he was required to show citizenship papers. Living so close to the Mexican border meant that there was always a greater chance of being asked by ICE (US Immigration and Customs enforcement).

"Are you out of your mind, Joaquin? This is our daughter…this is Maggie. We can't ignore that she is missing." Margaret was nearly hysterical with fear.

"She has no boyfriends. There is nobody that she might be serious enough to run away with. She could be in an accident dying somewhere ." Margarita screamed.

Joaquin needed to calm her down and think rationally.

" Margaret. How do you know that Maggie doesn't have a boyfriend?"

"Maggie is not like we were, Joaquin. I would know if she had a boyfriend. This is fucking serious, and I am calling the police," Margaret said, disgusted. She was beginning to dial 911 on her cell phone.

"Hang up NOW, Margaret! You don't know what you're doing," Joaquin demanded, raising his voice to her like he never had in eighteen years.

But, it was too late. The emergency operator was already taking down all the vital information. In less than twenty-four hours, Maggie Mendoza was included in every data bank for missing children throughout the country.

And, after twenty-four years of living in the United States, Joaquin Mendoza was identified as an illegal alien and deported to his hometown Pueblo, Mexico.

Forty-four days after Margaret notified the police that her daughter was missing, she received a call that Maggie, was in Chicago. Immediately, Margaret booked a flight and the next day, she was reunited with her only daughter at Chicago Memorial Hospital where Maggie was recovering from a hysterectomy.

The police, then, informed Margaret that Maggie would need to remain in protective custody until the trial was over.

"Mrs. Mendoza, here is the phone number for a new organization that sponsors victims of sex trafficking…like Maggie. You should contact them, immediately. I have been told that they are phenomenal."

The social worker handed Margaret a card with the Celeste Powers Foundation folder.

All that Margaret really wanted to do was take her daughter home and care for her. But, after listening to everything that Maggie had experienced, Margaret had to admit that she needed professional help.

When Margaret returned home, she had made the decision to sign over the El Gato Gordo restaurant to her Uncle. He had agreed to sell her home and send her the proceeds, once she was established permanently.

Now, Margaret, a legal American citizen, found herself living in a foreign country, without her daughter, and a husband who felt he was a failure.

When The Celeste Powers foundation learned about Maggie Mendoza's circumstances they arranged for Joaquin to meet his wife in Ensenada, Mexico. They also provided them with food and shelter, during the entire time Maggie was in protective custody before the trial.

Once the trial was over; a year later, the Mendoza's were once again reunited with their daughter. All three of them attended counseling to help them resume a normal life once again.

Sterling Powers immediately took a personal interest in Maggie Mendoza's case once he realized they had much in common. She was a free spirit with a desire to achieve greatness and overcome obstacles, until that fateful night.

Maggie's abduction occurred on the same night that Gabby had been raped and he nearly died from the gunshot wound while trying to save her life.

When Maggie was settled in Ensenada, Sterling decided to visit her. He was determined to give her every chance possible to resume her life. Sterling knew how life changing this experience was for such a young girl. When the family entered his office the first thing he wanted to do was make them feel comfortable.

" Good afternoon Maggie, my name is Sterling Powers."

It was important that he make Maggie trust him from their first encounter. If she felt intimidated they would never move forward.

"This foundation that has been helping you, is named after my mother, Celeste." Sterling's voice was gentle and reassuring.

Maggie sat quietly staring at a tapestry hanging over the desk. It was the image of a unicorn being hunted by a group of nobleman. While Maggie heard Sterling's voice it sounded as if he was far away in the tapestry. Sterling noticed her fixation.

"Are you familiar with *The Hunt of the Unicorn?* The original can be seen in The Cloisters of New York and is dated 1495-1505."

There did not seem to be any reaction. Maggie continued to be absorbed with the images.

"A group of nobleman and hunters are pursuing the mythical Unicorn that is usually identified as Christ, or a virgin." Sterling noticed that when he said the word *virgin* Maggie twitched; tilted her head nervously.

"In mythology most interpret any animal with a single horn as a creature that can only be tamed by a...devoted lover." Sterling intentionally avoided using the word virgin again.

While Maggie began to interpret what this stranger was saying, all that she could remember was how she was hunted by similar ruthless hunters. It was a memory she was reluctant to share with anyone. The future she once envisioned for herself was now drained into a vulgar swamp. She had no idea what she would do any longer.

It was time for Sterling to change the subject to a more pleasant prospect. He would get right to the point, hoping this would work.

"I would like to offer you, Maggie, an opportunity to complete a college degree in any subject that you choose, and you never have to leave Ensenada or your parents, unless of course, you decide to. Does this interest you at all?"

Sterling stood up behind his desk, walked slowly to took a seat next to Maggie, trying not to intimidate her by his size.

Maggie thought for a few moments. Although she really did not expect anything to really evolve of this, she was willing to play the game. After all, isn't everything really just a game?

"Do you mean that I could be home taught, like when I got my high school degree in New York with the Hancock's?" Maggie asked in a very low, slow voice. No reason to act excited.

There was something about this young girl that Sterling believed resembled Gabby Girard. And it wasn't her appearance. Her hair was the color of fire, varied shades of red; whereas, Gabby's was chestnut, laced with honey.

But, both of them had the most intriguing green colored eyes that could penetrate through steel, if needed, or in this case, Sterling.

"Yes, Maggie. Just like home schooling, but you would attend classes in our new academy, downtown. It is limited to only ten students, so depending on what major you select, you would be tutored, basically, by yourself or at the maximum with two other students. And, we provide transportation there and back. What do you think? Does that appeal to you?" Sterling asked, his voice now more mellow.

"Could I major in Theater? I have always loved to read and write.

Not sure how practical it is, but I guess that I could worry about that later."

Maggie never made eye contact with Sterling. When she did answer him, it was robotic, lifeless. Sterling was just another talking head.

"Then, Theater it is. I will set up the program and ask Mia, our academic advisor, to contact you in a few weeks."

Sterling reached out to touch Maggie's hand; then stopped suddenly, waiting for her to extend it, voluntarily. He remembered being told that sexually abused women felt threatened, if touched.

Just before feeling Sterling's hand, Maggie finally made eye contact. What she saw; in his eyes, was something she thought she would never see again; Sterling was genuine. He was giving her an invitation to return to a world that she thought was lost forever.

This was just like Charlie predicted it would be, in her letter. As soon as she felt his hand, Maggie knew that this was real; this was safe.

Theatre? I wish that Gabby could meet Maggie one day. Even the with the difference in hair color she physically resembled a younger version of Gabby. And…she wants to major in a field that Gabby studied, or as close to Literature as possible. Unfortunately, after I failed to protect Gabby, as I promised, I doubt that Maggie will ever have that opportunity. The odds now would be one in six million.

CHAPTER 23

It's never the differences between people that surprise us. It's the things that, against all odds, we have in common.
House Rules
  Jodi Picoult

Sterling and Gabby
May, 2010
Ensenada, Mexico

La Mansion was much more than an opulent personal residence, converted to an exclusive hotel. Behind the gated entrance, guests could explore the secret gardens that led to mysterious caverns. Eventually, a cobblestone path would lead to a secluded beach. Gabby often found herself sitting for hours looking at the waves, ebbing in and out. And, each sea shell she found was another story for her to imagine.

As fascinating as it was to discover unique sculptures, water fountains and an inviting gazebo, it was the grand library inside that fascinated Gabby the most.

"I believe that there are over five thousand books in this room, although I have never taken the time to personally count them," Alejandra explained.

"Is there a catalogue or file folder that identifies where these books are located?" Gabby asked, in awe.

Alejandra led her guest to an antique desk that housed a very modern computer. Gabby learned that all the books were organized by genre, and most located on this main floor..

The upper level was reserved for rare books and limited first editions. To see those, she would need to request a key.

Gabby could easily spend several years stretched out on the inviting leather couches, and comfortable overstuffed chairs, engrossed in Dostoyevsky, Faulkner and even an occasional Hemingway. However, today she would focus on reviewing some Sociology theories.

At Georgetown, Gabby became fascinated how Psychology, Philosophy and Anthropology were various, and different, threads that created the background for all the literature that she studied.

This elaborate tapestry that she wove became the foundation in her life. And, apparently Jake had a similar experience. That is clearly reflected in the journals that he wrote for her. Gabby now depended on those journals for answers.

If I am going to commit myself to help improve the living conditions of these Mexican people, I must learn who they really are.

It was not long before she located a book that discussed the theory of social stratification. In layman terms, it was studying the various social classes and complex categories that society creates ;often to prevent the lower class from ever obtaining a desirable lifestyle.

Gabby already discussed with Alejandra and Marisol the opportunity to visit with them after hours at La Mansion. Once she was able to learn more about each of these ladies, from different backgrounds, Gabby could begin to approach the best methods to help them.

It would be important to discuss this plan with Sterling before she moved forward. Unfortunately, he had been away from La Mansion for several days. However, Alejandra mentioned, just this morning, that he was in the study reviewing several contracts.

Many years ago, when Sterling and I shared an intimate relationship, there was never any discussions focusing on business. Now, I wonder if he still considers me merely a legitimate interruption from his busy schedule. This platonic relationship, now, is new territory. Learning where my boundaries are is still a work in progress.

Sterling was sitting behind a massive desk that had stacks of documents covering the surface. When I walked in and sat down across from him, I took a few minutes to admire how he was able to always stay focused on whatever his project was at the time.

Sterling's dark hair was strategically highlighted with natural silver. Just enough to make him look debonair. Even the tortoise framed reading glasses added just the right amount of interest. I was never sure why Sterling never married. Perhaps there will be a more convenient time later when he will share that with me.

"Good morning, Sterling. I was hoping that, maybe, I could discuss with you some strategies on what my role may be in your foundation." Gabby said rather quietly, trying not to disturb him.

"Good. I am really adept at multitasking, so you talk, I listen, and then we can review all the options," Sterling responded without ever taking his eyes off the document.

"Okay, well…I would like to do some observations on different social classes to determine what I can do to help them. Alejandra and Marisol have agreed to let me start with them, and then they will introduce me to others." Gabby's voice was eager.

"So, you basically plan on stalking people? Is that a good way to get right to the point?"

Sterling knew how Gabby would react, and he was going to see how far he could go, before she exploded at him.

"Excuse me? I am not stalking anybody. What I am doing is what you suggested; become familiar with the culture and traditions."

Gabby was now becoming slightly agitated, yet still under control.

"You are absolutely right. A better word to use is dissect. Like an alien from space."

This time Sterling looked directly at Gabby. Her vibrant sea foam green eyes were now expanding. If he was able to stare at them long enough, he could see the volcano erupt.

"What do you mean dissecting? Becoming friends with people is the first level of trust. Once I am able to establish trust, I can offer them ways to improve their lives."

Gabby was still trying to maintain control of her temper.

"I suppose, maybe, it never crossed your mind that to single out these loyal ladies, who dedicate their lives to keeping us happy, may make them just a little uncomfortable when you make them feel that they are inferior to us."

Sterling knew that this last remark would send Gabby over the edge.

"You, Mr. Powers, are a hypocrite. And, I think maybe I made a terrible judgment error when..."

Sterling realized that Gabby was now standing, nearly in tears as she headed toward the door. With long strides, he was easily able to get there first. His hands on her shoulder, he said, with a big grin, "When did this Gatito Salvaje ever become so touchy? All I was doing was throwing a little catnip in your cage."

Gabby looked up at him, wiping her tears away, before answering.

"If you mess around with this wild kitty, she just might leave some scratches in some uncomfortable places...I can't believe you made me this angry, Sterling."

But, Gabby also couldn't help but slightly laugh when Sterling made a cat's claw gesture.

"I think your ideas are fantastic. If everybody was willing to really know these wonderful people, like you are suggesting, we could solve their problems quickly. By the way, how did you know what I called you? I didn't think you knew Spanish?"

"There are a few words I remember from my high school Spanish class. That was of course in another century," Gabby answered, now much more civil.

"While we are discussing past centuries, have you made that phone call to your internet friend, Caden? Was that his name?"

Sterling was careful not to make Gabby angry again.

"No. I have been eluding him. I know that this is just cowardly of me. I will make plans the next few days to let him know where I am. Maybe, by then, my life will at least be moving in a, somewhat, forward direction," Gabby said, reluctantly.

"For all the years I have known you, Gabby Girard, the word 'cowardly' never comes to mind. Maybe, a little spontaneous, or even eccentric, but never cowardly."

Sterling paused waiting for this to register with Gabby.

"I don't know if I should consider you my defender or my critic?" She said, while playfully jabbing him with her finger.

"Definitely your defender, Gabby! After all, you have always been my 'Dulcinea', and I, your Don Quixote, fighting those pesky windmills," Sterling said, only half joking.

Gabriella Girard Blair was the best one person, other than his mother, that he felt a bond with, beyond obligation, since s Gisselle. It was almost like an enigmatic dedication that he never could fully understand.

"I will let you know how my visits go next week. Are you still going to Cabo on Friday?" Gabby asked.

"Yes, but only four days. After the Wine Festival, here in July, I will take you with me to Cabo. I want you to meet the teachers at the academy. They might also inspire you. And, then later to Todos Santos to meet a special friend of mine. That is all I am going to reveal, so don't even ask?"

Sterling knew that this would drive Gabby crazy. But, he wanted her to meet Maggie Mendoza without any preconceived ideas. They really deserved to discover each other without any bias.

Gabby could not imagine who Sterling wanted her to meet, unless it was her replacement. But, then again maybe her imagination was working overtime. There were too many other immediate issues at the moment to dwell on who Sterling May be enchanted with now.

The following few days, I became anxious to begin my field study with Alejandra and then later Marisol. On Saturday, I was invited to visit the Espinoza's residence.

Jaime, the limo driver, agreed to take me on a tour of Ensenada, as well as drive me to each ladies' house.

"There really is nothing exciting to see here in Ensenada," Jaime said, trying to discourage me from wasting my time.

"That is because you, Jaime, have lived here forever. To me everything is new and exciting," Gabby insisted.

Jaime just shrugged his shoulders. Mr. Powers paid him to drive his guests, and if this gringa Senora wanted to take a tour of Ensenada, he would accommodate.

Alejandra lived reasonably close to both La Mansion, and the center of town. When I arrived at her home, I first noticed the solid block wall surrounding her residence. It resembled a fortress. But, once the front gate door opened, there was a lovely courtyard with a garden, and sitting area.

"Welcome Senora Gabby," Alejandra warmly greeted me at the front door.

"Come…come inside. I have prepared some regional appetizers and wine from our local vineyard."

I followed Alejandra into a very bright dining room. The wall of windows allowed the natural light from the sun to enter unobstructed. The home was nicely decorated with paintings from local artists and authentic traditional furniture that Alejandra proudly told me she brought here from Oaxaca.

Throughout the house, there were tables and cabinets made from a honey colored rustic wood that was embellished with copper and mesquite. This, and the leather couches, provided a warm, welcoming ambiance.

"Your home is very inviting, Alejandra. Thank you so very much for agreeing to share your personal life with me. What I really hope is that I can understand better the Mexican culture from a personal point of view. I hope that doesn't sound too invasive."

After Sterling's sarcastic remarks earlier, I was careful to be as diplomatic as possible, yet also honest.

"It is very flattering to have anyone take interest in our family's daily lives. Honestly, we are so busy surviving that, at times, we are so consumed with our normal routine, that we never think about how or why. Assuring that our children's lives become better than ours, never leaves any time to think too much about the process."

Not only was Alejandra eloquent when she spoke, she was also impressively elegant. Being small in stature; maybe five feet tall, did not prevent her from projecting a total sense of confidence. Alejandra just has a natural gift of finesse that everyone respects.

Contributing to this poise, Alejandra's long shiny black hair is always neatly coiffed in a French braided bun with never a single strand out of place. Her almond shaped, coffee colored dark brown eyes are so inviting that it makes even strangers comfortable.

Perhaps, the most impressive feature is how fluently Alejandra speaks English with an excellent command of the language. There are natural born Americans that I know who are not as intelligent, or intellectual, as this epitome of grace.

The round table that we sat down at, had on the back, carvings of various sea creatures: turtles, fish, mermaid, dolphins, sea shells and whales. All are painted in vibrant colors, representing the ocean close by.

Although I offer to help with the serving, Alejandra insists that, as her guest, I remain seated.

"That is a tradition in our household. We warmly welcome you to a relaxing meal with no expectations," Alejandra declared, as she brought various fried beef, chicken and pork empanadas to the table.

Next was homemade corn tamales, and cheese quesadillas. This was served with ice chilled Chardonnay. And for dessert, was a plate of trade traditional Mexican candies, and pastries..

During the afternoon, Alejandra proudly showed me pictures of her three children, two boys, Miguel, age twelve and Antonio, eight. Her only daughter, Veronica, would be turning fifteen years old in July.

"In our culture, when our daughters reach the age of fifteen, it marks their passage to womanhood. We celebrate this with a...'Quinceanera'. This is a major party where we give thanks to God for his blessings.

The young girl is then presented to the society as a young lady. She honors her parents, godparents, grandparents, and community for all their contributions. In extremely wealthy families, that celebration could be several days. For us, it will begin after Catholic Mass in the morning, and end sometime by dawn the following day," Alejandra said, proudly.

"In America, some families celebrate a sweet sixteen party, but I think that tradition is beginning to fade away," Gabby added.

"Although progress is inevitable, I believe that tradition helps reinforce the new generation, and strengthens families," Alejandra noted.

When it was time for me to leave, I felt like a distant relative who had returned home from an extended absence.

Alejandra updated me on where her husband worked at the steel factory, and that they had only one car because private school for three children was costly. Therefore, at the end of her shift, she boarded the community bus home.

"Senora Gabby, it is very important for you to realize that we thank God daily for our privileged life. My family is aware that many people are suffering within a few miles from us. We could be in that situation at any time. Senor Powers is our guiding light. Without his organization, we all would suffer," Alejandra said, leading me out to the car that was waiting.

On my way back to La Mansion, I was beginning to understand how respected Sterling was in this city, and very likely, throughout the country.

This was another side of him I was not familiar with. Now, I was even more curious to learn how these changes evolved. There were just so many transformations since we last were together, that

Sterling was no longer the same, at many levels.

It was several days later that Marisol, although reluctantly, finally agreed that I could visit her on Saturday. I emphasized several times that whatever we discussed would never jeopardize her job at La Mansion. Perhaps it was Alejandra who assured her that talking with me was not threatening. Whatever it was, I was thankful to spend some time with her.

The drive to Marisol's apartment was the opposite direction from where Alejandra lived. We were now on the outskirts of Ensenada.

Finally, Jaime pulled up to what looked like a warehouse building with individual doors spaced a few feet apart. Before I could ask him which door was Marisol's, I saw her approaching the car.

Jaime suggested that I text him when we were finished, and he would come back for me.

Once we reached the third door from the front, I was surprised how compact the space was, and yet, pleasantly furnished. It was nothing like Alejandra's home, but Marisol took pride in her modest living quarters.

"Senora Gabby, I have chilled some fresh fruit and some cheese enchiladas for lunch. Please, sit down here and we will enjoy each other's company."

Marisol pointed to the table that was already set with a nice crotchet white tablecloth.

In the living room there was one couch facing a small television. But, what captured my attention was a very elaborately carved wooden altar.

This showcased several crosses, religious statues and candles. In the center was a sterling silver frame with a picture of a small, light complexioned child. Her long dark curls framed the most hypnotic blue violet eyes that I had ever seen.

Just as I was about to move closer, because something about this child seemed familiar, Marisol was ready to serve the meal.

"Your home is very pleasant Marisol. Do you live here with your daughter?" I asked, casually.

Marisol hesitated for a second and then said, "After we eat and visit, I will introduce you to my Fatima. She is not far from here."

Marisol, then, explained how she was hired at La Mansion five years ago. In her own words, "It was a gift from God."

Prior to this job, she worked in a sweat factory making T shirts for tourists in Tijuana. She was living in the cardboard village when she moved to Ensenada. A friend told her about a new Padre that was going to help the poor.

"I was really just living on the streets begging for food, because the factory did not pay enough for Fatima and me to live. Until that one day when an American angel brought us to a shelter. Later, I learned it was The Powers Foundation. They are dedicated to rescuing as many street people as they can. The institute downtown would then prepare us to apply for suitable jobs. This apartment was built and furnished by the foundation. Senor Sterling Powers is referred to as our Messiah," Marisol said, then crossed herself.

Marisol was speaking with much more difficulty here than at La Mansion. At times, she would just stop, as if something was distracting her, and then continue without realizing the gap in time. Obviously; at work, she was able to modify this speech impediment when needed. She also avoided talking much at work.

After nearly an hour visiting, I helped Marisol wrap the remaining fruit and enchiladas in some foil that I presumed she brought from work, since she removed it from her employee bag earlier.

I was told that whenever there was any food leftover at the hotel, the employees were encouraged to take it home. There was no doubt that the fruit and enchiladas would be Marisol's meal for the next few evenings. I hoped that my leftover lobster that I never ate, was enjoyed by someone like Marisol.

Then, unexpectedly, without, going into any details, Marisol reached for her black shawl, placed a small vase with scissors in her tote bag, and waved at me to follow her.

"The walk to meet Fatima is only about fifteen minutes. I think you will enjoy seeing the spring flowers that are blooming," Marisol spoke so softly that it almost sounded like she was talking to herself.

Along the way, a few stray dogs followed us, hoping for some treats. It reminded me of the ones in San Diego, but much thinner. I wished that I had something for them. When they realized that there were no treats, they chose another path to follow.

The soft dirt and gravel road that we were walking on went up a slight hill. At the top, I noticed that there was a quaint chapel. Marisol entered first, crossing herself with holy water, genuflecting at the altar, and immediately moving toward the alcove with votive candles.

"This is where the statue of Our Lady of Guadalupe, with her arms outstretched, welcomes all visitors," Marisol whispered.

I watched intensely at every movement she made. It was not yet clear why we were here. After we both kneeled for a short time, all she said was, "Follow me, Senora Gabby. We are almost there."

My first thoughts were that perhaps Fatima was a nun, or worked in some way with the church. Perhaps the photo was one of her as a child, but now she was an adult. I suppose this mystery was soon to be solved.

When the side door opened, and we exited the inner chapel, from the rear, surprisingly there was a rather large cemetery. Marisol headed directly to the left side where a white gate separated the main grave sites. I followed, not really knowing what to expect.

Once inside the perimeter, I took a seat on the stone bench watching what Marisol would do next. Immediately, she kneeled down in front of a small headstone and began to pull the weeds from around the edges.

Once that was accomplished, she proceeded, toward the pink rose bushes, removed her scissors, and clipped just a few stems, of buds, that would fit in the miniature rainbow vase brought from home.

Next, she walked a few more feet, found the nearby hose and

filled the tiny vase with water. Then, almost methodically, Marisol carefully arranged the roses in the vase. Returning to the grave site, she fit the vase carefully in a metal holder above a small headstone.

After a few moments of speaking words in Spanish that I could not recognize, Marisol removed, from her bag, a colored photo similar to the one in her apartment, and handed it to me.

"Senora Gabby, this is where my Fatima now resides."

The Gravestone was very simple. It only had Fatima, with no last name, and her birth date March 31, 2001-April 10, 2011. She had only barely turned nine years old.

When I first met Marisol, I thought that she was in her early twenties. But, now all the suffering, pain and grief painted clearly on her face, she appeared much older.

But, It was when I could closely now see the photograph that my face became flushed. The tears from my eyes were burning with an unfamiliar pain. It took a great deal of control to avoid fainting at this moment. Fatima had only died a few days after I arrived to San Diego.

This innocent, angelic image, now staring at me, was the same child that reached for my hand in Tijuana, only a week ago. The dark tinted window was all that separated us from each other.

Like a sudden flashback I also remembered now, that this was the same child that appeared in my first dream at the railroad station, many years ago, when I was still with Caden. She was not even born yet.

Impossible! Maybe. But, sitting here right now, surrounded by death, there is no doubt in my mind that Fatima has a message for me. What that is, and why, I have no idea.

CHAPTER 24

Do not let the hero in your soul perish in lonely frustration for the life you deserved and have never been able to reach. The world you desire can be won. It exists…it is real…it is possible…it is yours.

Ayn Rand

Gabby Girard
May, 2010
Ensenada, Mexico

On my return to La Mansion, I felt totally empty. After my intense graveyard visit, I walked away with more questions than answers.

Jake's journals offered me a view of life through different lenses. Today, I was determined—it would be the day to arrange a call with Caden. But, in my current state of mind something could happen that I might regret.

Instead, I decided to reflect and examine why and how I could be seeing a dead child come alive; not only in my subconscious, but on the streets of Mexico.

Although Jake's journals are divided into sections that mostly reflect on past and present events, they also include how Jake internalized complex issues.

In addition, there are also some philosophical entries dealing with how the afterlife and the theory of parallelism might surface in my own present time.

I removed the red ribbon with the tiny bell, knotted at the end, from the section I last read about Molly's death.

The next page was titled, Supernatural Everyday Events. It was uncanny at times like this, that I felt Jake trying to comfort me, like only he could, when he was alive.

If you are now searching for answers to recent supernatural events that are making you feel uncomfortable, I can share with you a few of my own. They may not provide you with all of the answers, but, at the least, you will know that these experiences are not unique, nor are you able to control them.

Obviously by now, Gabby, you must at least understand how dedicated I have become to the theory of parallelism. The closer I move away from this life to the next, I find myself more certain that we have the ability to choose different platforms at different times in our lives.

These choices will not influence our previous ones. Without dwelling on all the scientific data that I have researched, I can reduce it to the idea that life has many versions of bubbles. Occasionally, we are able to attract a bubble from another universe, one that we might label death, and we discover that it interconnects with our bubble. Similar to a last minute decision to board a different train, than you originally intended.

By deciding to leave one destination does not impact any past trips, since you have already arrived.

At this point, immediately, I recall the dream I had when another girl, not Fatima, told me again that if I missed my train, there would be others for me to choose. Now, Jake is using the same analogy to explain his theory.

This idea of parallelism is a direct contrast to Nietzsche's Butterfly Effect that we discussed when I returned from Nam. Remember that it was Nietzsche who believed that if you were able to return to the past, and make different choices, they would result in negative consequences.

I believe that we have the opportunity to live various lives, including with those from our past, in a totally new environment.

Jake was insisting that our love for one another was so powerful that if we continued to remain connected, beyond the grave, ultimately, we would reunite. There was a time, once that this idea was appealing, however, more recently, with Caden Cassidy entering back into my world, there were no definite answers.

Regardless, I continued to reach out to Jake.

In many ways the presence of supernatural beings may be disturbing at times. If and when this happens to you, Gabby, there are some thoughts about this phenomenon that should put you at ease.

I will remind you of the insights provided by Edgar Allan Poe, in his poem Spirits from the Dead.

IThy soul shall find itself alone, Mid dark thoughts of the gray tombstone./ Not one of all the crowd, to pry Into thine hour of secrecy.

II

Be silent in that solitude, Which is not loneliness -for then The spirits of the dead who stood/ In life before thee are again/ In death around thee—and their will/ Shall overshadow thee: be still.

III

The night, tho' clear shall frown/And the stars shall look not down/ From their high thrones in the heaven,/ With lights like Hope to mortals given/But, their red orbs without beam/ To their weariness shall seem/As a burning and a fever/Which would cling to thee forever.

IV

Now are thoughts thou shall not banish/Now are visions ne're to vanish/From thy spirits shall thy pass/No more-like dew drop from the grass.

V

The breeze-- the breath of God—is still/--/And the mist upon the hill,/ Shadowy, Shadowy, yet unbroken,/ Is a symbol and a token--/How it hangs upon the trees,/A mystery of mysteries.

These words, I know you understand, illustrate how invasive you may feel if not aware of why the spirits seek the living.

Jake, often times in his journals, included literary examples to support or emphasize how much life mirrors fiction.

I wonder if he ever had moments like I do where words from literature overlap with moments that are being recreated? Not being able to personally speak to Jake about issues like this made me sad.

Nevertheless, I am confident that somewhere in these pages I will discover the reasons why Fatima is seeking me out.

Visitations, Gabby, from those who are deceased, are not meant to cause you fear. There are times, even now, as I am approaching death that I can still feel when you are disturbed; thirty-four years apart and this sensation is still strong.

When this happens, it is often followed by a child spirit visitation. Later, I discovered that because children are the purest form of innocence, what they offer is unconditional love and extended energy. Because their death is always untimely, they are willing to share with those who accept them, and escape, briefly, from their present grief.

Embrace their loving presence, Gabby, and know that the spirit's only intent is to comfort.

That journal entry ended unexpectedly. Once again there were not enough answers, and yet, paradoxically all the answers.

Before I decided to retire Jake's journal, for the evening, I noticed that at the end of the page was a very odd footnote symbol. It was a black stenciled serpent eating its own tail. When I looked at the bottom of the page, it explained that the illustration was an Uroboros, an Ancient Greek symbol.

This represents the continuity and immortality of the Natural Universe, where creation is born from destruction; Life out of Death. The note further explained that the serpent eats its own tail as a means toward an eternal cycle that renews itself.

The very last illustration, on this page, was a drawing of what I was using as a bookmark. Beneath the picture was an explanation.

"This red string, in the Japanese culture, represents the invisible one that everyone is born with. According to legend, when we find the person that matches our red string, we are destined to make history."

It was not yet clear to me why Jake felt the necessity to include these various symbols in the same section dealing with spiritual recognition.

Would the journals also include anything relevant about Caden? I know that he was aware that our relationship ended, and Jake's role in ending it.

If Jake had any thoughts about Caden, I chose not to search for them at this time. As most of his other messages seem to have a timely purpose, I am quite certain that eventually, Caden's influence on me will also be revealed.

CHAPTER 25

If we chose, we can live in a world of comforting illusion.
Noam Chomsky

Gabby Girard
May, 2010
Ensenada, Mexico

It is 2,423 miles between Savanna, Georgia and Ensenada, Mexico. There is also a three hour time differential. When I texted Caden asking him when it would be convenient to talk, I intentionally omitted where I have been the past few weeks.

It was a short, evasive message. Telling Caden that I was in Ensenada with Sterling Powers, because my deceased ex-lover saved me from drowning in the Atlantic Ocean, sounded so bizarre that even I had a difficult time believing it. Speaking to him by phone would allow me, at the very least, to explain the details personally.

It took several revisions to the text before, finally, I was satisfied. I also hoped that sending it now would allow me enough time difference, to gather my thoughts.

Caden, I know that it is only 5:00 am in Savannah, but I wanted to find a time when we could talk privately. Gabby

(Send)

Once the message was somewhere in cyberspace, I spent most of the evening tossing and turning, unable to sleep. Whenever my mind begins to enter that dream realm, where warped visions, are accompanied by a playlist of melodies, *A Midsummer's Night's Dream*, begins to weave itself into a spider web, known as the Phantom's Inn.

Not even *The Dream Police*, who begin to chip away inside my brain, will allow me to sweep away the shadows of my past.

Finally, I surrendered. Almost instinctively, I got out of bed, wandered into the small kitchen and quietly prepared myself a warm cup of milk with crumbled Mexican chocolate, cinnamon, vanilla and nutmeg.

Marisol continued to sleep in the maid's bedroom connected to my suite. Although it seemed like a totally unnecessary practice, I was told that it is an old tradition, similar to a Lady in Waiting. In many countries, the position has evolved into personal assistants, for the wealthy.

Alejandra privately shared with me that since Marisol lost her child so recently , from infectious intestinal parasites, she volunteers to spend her evenings at La Mansion.

Fatima's death was caused from drinking contaminated water for many years. Nobody recognized the symptoms until it was too late. Thankfully, her death was sudden and not painful for anyone, except Marisol.

It was not evident how long this arrangement with Marisol sleeping in the maid's quarters would last, but Alejandra was more concerned about Marisol's emotional health. If adjusting her hours to accommodate this evening ritual helps her, then Alejandra made sure it continues as long as needed.

After my visit with Marisol, I understood why Alejandra was so accommodating . The sleeping arrangements no longer seemed odd.

Finally, when I was told how Fatima died, I could only imagine how this tragedy affected her mother. I, also, never shared with anyone that I saw Fatima's spirit recently.It wasn't anything that they could say to me that would be of comfort. Better to keep this where all my other demons reside.

After a warm mug of cocoa; three hours later, just as I was beginning to fall into a deep sleep, I heard the notification on my text.

As I reached for the phone, my blurry eyes began to focus on the following text message:

What the FUCK is going on with you? How could you miss Molly's Eulogy? Hell, how could you just disappear without even letting me see you after all we have been through?

Before I could respond, there was another text that followed a few seconds later.

Okay...I am sorry for the language I used. I am giving you the benefit that there is a sane explanation. So, call me at twelve noon. I will be in my office where we can talk privately.

Caden

My first reaction was to remind him that forty-three years ago, he never gave me the same benefit of knowing when he left. I, also, debated about letting him know that I was in Mexico. Thankfully, one advantage with aging is knowing when to keep silent.

Once I began to answer his questions; in a text, both of us might lose our tempers. Much better to keep my response short.

Noon will be convenient for me, too. Looking forward to hearing your voice again. Gabby.

(Send)

I waited a few moments, but, thankfully, there was no further text. I, then, set the alarm to wake me up by 7 am. That should give me enough time to be able to run through the script in my head.

There were many roles that I could play with Caden, but in the end, the tragic heroine was more natural than I wanted to admit.

CHAPTER 26

Anxiety is love's greatest killer. It makes others feel as you might when a drowning man holds on to you. You want to save him, but you know he will strangle you with his panic.

Anais Nin

Caden Cassidy
May, 2010
Savannah, George

The adrenaline was running through my body in record speed. Faster than I ran my best track meet. It has taken her two months...two fucking months before she finally decides to call me? I thought she was dead, until she sent me that cryptic message from some phantom phone two days after Molly's funeral. I can't wait to hear what pathetic excuse she has created.

Caden, then, stopped his mind from over thinking. It has been forty-three years. Aunt Selena was right; that New Year's Eve, when he showed up, totally wasted at her house.

If he had only allowed Gabby to explain what happened that night, when he saw Jake leaving their apartment, both of their lives would be different today.

Caden knew that now, he, at least, needed to give her a chance to explain what happened without a preconceived judgment.

Every Friday, at noon, The Molly is packed with people celebrating TGIF. Today is no different. A few weeks ago, Devon hired a few more waiters; part time, to help out during the rush hour. This allowed Caden the privacy to slip away, into his office, and figure out this mess.

Only a few months ago, I was looking forward to finally being with Gabby. Now, I was not sure if that would ever be possible.

As soon as I opened the office door, before I could sit in my chair, the phone rang.

"Caden? Are you someplace that we can talk without interruptions?" Gabby asked.

"Yes, Gabby. No more excuses. I am waiting to hear where you have been?" Caden's voice was agitated.

Gabby explained what happened at Tybee Beach, and how she needed to get away from all the pressures that were suffocating her. She never intended for people to think that anything serious happened. All she needed was time to get her thoughts together.

"It never even occurred to you, that leaving all your belongings on the sand might make people imagine the worst..." Caden decided not to complete what he was saying, What he really wanted to know was what she was planning on doing now.

"And, Alex...how is he accepting all of this? Have you finally decided to leave him? And, where are you by the way ?"

Caden tried not to sound demanding, but there were so many blank pieces to this puzzle.

"I called an old friend who suggested that I spend some time in Mexico. He has an amazing charity and foundation that I will be helping him with."

Gabby knew that once she indicated that there was another man involved, Caden would draw conclusions.

"Can I just ask you, Gabby, after so many years, why didn't you turn to me for help? Why call someone in another country?" Caden was both hurt and angry.

"Have you forgotten about Kaitlyn? How would you explain me to her?" Gabby knew that this would lead to some serious decisions.

"I NEED to see you, Gabby. If that means leaving Kaitlyn, then I will have to tell her. We owe it to each other to either continue with what we had in Georgetown forty-three years ago, or end this relationship forever. Living in limbo is impossible."

Caden finally gave Gabby the ultimatum.

There were a few moments of silence. Caden first thought that Gabby hung up.

"You are right, Caden. I cannot deny that I still love you. I also do not know if it is enough, now. In July, I will be moving to Cabo San Lucas. That should give you enough time to decide if you can come for, at least, a visit," Gabby said, hopefully.

"That is all I ask. If we both discover that it is too late for us after that, we will know our fate was not to be together. Keep texting me. I will let you know what will happen next. And Gabby? I have never stopped loving you."

It was important for Caden to let her know this.

"Whatever happens, Caden, you are right, we will both know that we, at least, allowed each other one more chance; one that we never had years ago. And, you know I still love you, too." Gabby had not said those words to anyone else for a very long time.

When the call was at last over, there was a complete sense of Nirvana. Caden had spent some time studying Buddhism, as a method to relieve his constant turmoil.

Since Buddhism is totally devoted to liberating suffering and ignorance, he became determined to find ways of enlightenment that would lead to Samsara, or rebirth. Gabby was his Nirvana. She would lead him to the ultimate level of happiness.

Finally, Caden was going to get the opportunity to allow fate a rerun at a long anticipated feature, showcasing his life. He has been playing these tapes for many years in his mind.

Coming to terms with why he was never able to totally love Kaitlyn was difficult. Although, he would take the major blame for continuing with a loveless marriage.

In reflection, there were many issues that surfaced over the years that contributed to his emotional unrest.

What attracted Caden to Kaitlyn during the early years; ironically, was how opposite she was to Gabby. If he could never be with the one woman he loved, he would find someone that could make him forget her.

Physically, emotionally and intellectually, Kaitlyn was the perfect choice. When he was first introduced to his future wife, Caden was drawn to her naturally platinum blonde, cascade hair. It was not only silky smooth to touch, but there was a radiance that was striking when light reflected from it.

Whereas, Gabby had chestnut, sable brown hair with sun kissed blonde highlights that reached her lower back, Kaitlyn appeared like a sophisticated model in comparison.

When Kaitlyn stood next to Caden, her five feet ten inches; mostly legs, reminded him of a graceful deer. Even when wearing heals, Gabby was barely five feet three inches.

But, the most obvious difference involved intellect. Kaitlyn was a brilliant business accountant; however, like you would imagine, she saw only black and white, where Gabby's life offered everyone a kaleidoscope of changing colors.

Everything that, at one time, attracted him to Kaitlyn was now driving him nuts. Suddenly, he began noticing how everything had to be in perfect order. The spice cabinet was organized by alphabet. Bed sheets, she insisted, must be pressed at the dry cleaners. And, the order of books on the shelves in their study, was determined by the size of the book, not by genre.

One day while he was searching for an Architect Digest book, he noticed that Kaitlyn had placed *Lady Chatterley's Lover*, by DH Lawrence, next to *Don Quixote*, by Manuel Cervantes. He was fairly confident that Kaitlyn had never heard of either books.

Gabby would have a good laugh at that. The two of them could then joke about how long Lady Chatterley and Don Quixote's relationship would last being that close to each other on the book shelf. Gabby's ability to create spontaneous, clever humor was something he truly missed.

When he mentioned how amusing placing those two books

together to Kaitlyn, she merely shrugged her shoulders.

Then, soon after the twins were born, Kaitlyn decided to change her hairstyle. The beautiful mental image of Kaitlyn as Lady Godiva now resembled the Dutch Boy on paint cans.

Then came the total transformation from the snug pencil skirts that hugged her body and accentuated her perfect hourglass figure. Now it was more like a milk bottle frame. Dresses that resembled flour sacks or bib overalls, with a stained apron, replaced tight jeans.

Thankfully, once the boys graduated from college and moved to Huntington Beach, California, to open their surf and tackle shop, Kaitlyn and Caden started moving in different directions. She became occupied with Canasta once a week, reading clubs, cooking lessons and church activities.

He continued to perform his husbandly sexual duties, once a week on Wednesday evenings, after dinner, before he took out the trash. If he didn't know better, he would swear that Kaitlyn had her clock set every week at the same time, for this ritual.

Having sex just became another chore that he did not have the desire or energy to argue about.

Around this time, he reached out to Molly, once he discovered that she was living in Paris. With her influence, he finally was able to contact Gabby. Caden's extra time, from that moment on, was spent at the Pub talking and texting, whenever possible, to Gabby, never knowing when they would physically meet again.

Then, Molly's untimely death opened the door for their first reunion in forty- three years.

His desire to be with Gabby never faded during his entire marriage. Not even when his wife, after thirty hours of labor, handed him two healthy sons. As he looked into their eyes, his only regret was that Gabby was not their mother.

Then, being that close to holding her in his arms once again vanished — the night Gabby disappeared from Tybee Beach.

NEVER AGAIN! When Gabby agrees to meet me in Mexico, I will

explain to Kaitlyn that she can have this house, the bar, and even most of the savings, but I will be on an extended vacation.

Chapter 27

For last year's words belong to last year's language/ And next year's words /await another voice/ And to make an end is to make/ A beginning.

TS Eliot

Seamus and Claudia Cassidy
Dublin, Ireland 1930
The Cassidy Curse

In 1930, Ireland had nearly three million people. Most of them lived in rural areas, in the countryside or country towns and villages. Dublin accounted for almost a half a million people.

Seamus Cassidy and his wife Claudia were living in a small apartment with two bedrooms, located over the oldest pub in Ireland—the Brazen Head.

Seamus was one of the lucky men in Ireland who worked for the Great Northern Railroad, like his father and grandfather. At a time when the majority of Irish men and women were living on the streets, or in the slum tenements, due to lack of work or below appropriate standard of living jobs, Seamus and Claudia were able to afford at least one child.

It took over five miscarriages in seven years before the Cassidy's only son, Aiden Cassidy, was born.

Although Seamus and Claudia were grateful that their son would continue the Cassidy lineage, Claudia was told that even one more pregnancy could kill her. It was devastating news! Fearing that he may be the cause for Claudia to die, Seamus decided to refrain from sex with his wife.

Working on the Railroad allowed Seamus to travel throughout Ireland. He took this opportunity to fulfill his sexual needs. Most of the time there was never any emotional attachment to the affair. That is, until Seamus in 1932 found himself needing to remain in Belfast for a few weeks, while the train was being serviced.

During this time, he regularly frequented his favorite pub, *Sir Moses Cellars*. For many locals, it was known as the 'Alibi', since the proprietor would confirm that all patrons only came in for a few pints, and NEVER 'moseyed' upstairs for recreational sex with the known prostitutes who rented the rooms in the hotel for their business.

Seamus never needed an alibi, since he was never in need to pay for sex. He was known to have a pleasing penis that could remain hard for hours. Most of the time, women were more than happy to assist a desperate husband that could never be sexually satisfied by his ailing wife.

During one visit to the Sir Moses Cellars, Sean, the owner was bragging to Seamus about the new entertainers he hired from Spain. They would take the stage during the band breaks, and play exotic Spanish music they called Andalusia. It included: "cante" singing, "baile" dance, "toque" guitar and "palmas" hand clapping.

This music accompanied the most passionate dance ever. It was originated by traveling gypsies, who named it Flamenco. Its origin is associated with these outcast cultures.

Sean was eager for Seamus to witness what he declared was the most sensuous woman alive...Collette.

"And does Collette have a last name?" Seamus was now quite curious to see firsthand what this siren was capable of.

"Collette is perfection! She needs no last name. Once you see her in perpetual motion, sometimes only inches away from you, Seamus, then you will understand," Sean said, wildly.

Seamus had heard stories about gypsies and their ability to seduce their victims, but most of this was folklore that he never believed.

But tonight, when he was seated at the front of the stage, Seamus was not prepared for what he would feel and see. When Collette appeared with two other men, playing guitars, she was dressed in a tight fitting red satin gown trimmed in black lace. The bodice was pulled down to her bare shoulders, revealing an inviting buxom, holding one red rose in its cleavage.

Once the stage lights went dark, the audience became quiet. When the spotlight came on again, directly on Collette, she was standing with her arms above her head, and the stemmed rose now between her teeth.

At the music's introduction, her hips began to slightly twist back and forth opposite her upper torso. The swaying of her body, the intense stomping of her feet, and her black eyes, as dark as Indian ink, began their seduction directly at Seamus.

It was fascinating to watch this dancer interpret the spellbinding music, occasionally using her canasta's, one in each hand, to accent her every move.

Without any warning, Collette jumped down from the stage and continued a private performance, the remainder of her dance, so close to Seamus, that he could feel the heat projecting from her body, and the sweat dripping from his forehead.

At the conclusion of this seductive performance, Collette replaced the rose stem in her breast while leaning her bust as close as possible in Seamus's face.

Without knowing what he should do next, or how to react, Seamus sat so still that he looked paralyzed. When Collette bent closer to his mouth, her piercing eyes looked directly into his, and she whispered in his ear, "Remove my rose with your teeth, Senor, porfavor."

Seamus obeyed the request, and Collette, playfully bit his earlobe. She, then, jumped back on the stage, among loud applause, bowed, and disappeared behind the black stage curtain.

From that moment on, Seamus attended three more evenings,

until he could no longer control his passion for Collette. He followed her immediately behind the stage curtain. When she saw him, Collette took his hand and led him to a very makeshift dressing room.

Once in private, Seamus held her in his arms. He could now smell and taste her body that continued to gyrate, until he removed her upper blouse and began to suck her breasts with a hunger that he had never felt before. He gently moved her body against the only solid wall in the room. Without hesitation, his head went directly to her vagina, which was now soaking wet. While his tongue began to explore the vulva, his teeth applied just enough pressure to her clitoris for Collette to moan with delight.

With her hands on his head, she continued to move it slightly enough, until Seamus could taste her juices fill his mouth. Once she climaxed, he revealed his swollen penis that eagerly moved into the now inviting vagina.

Seamus lifted Collette into the air, while her long legs wrapped around his torso and her arms holding his shoulders for balance. He, then, began to move in and out, at a first slow and steady rhythm, until, just like the sound of the Flamenco guitars serenading on stage, he thrust hard his penis one final time. He felt Collette and his sperm mingle in ecstasy.

Seamus, then, waited for his new lover to change. Outside of the Pub, he took long drags from his cigarette. *I have never in my entire life felt real passion until tonight. There are no words in any language that can describe this moment of pure uninhibited love that I now know.*

Once Collette met Seamus outside, he brought her back to the hotel where they continued their lovemaking well into dawn without ever stopping. When they both were completely satisfied, Seamus fell asleep with the woman he now knew he was destined to grow old with.

They were inseparable for the entire three weeks that Seamus was in Belfast. He could never bring himself to tell Collette about

Claudia.

When he needed to finally return to work, Seamus made certain that Collette would have enough money while he was gone.

Sean also assured him that Collette could rent a room on the other side of the brothel until he returned. At home, it became more difficult each day with Claudia. All he could think of was Collette. Finally, after three days he found an excuse to return to Belfast. He would tell Claudia that his train route was changed, requiring him to spend more time away from home.

It really didn't matter to him if she believed him or not. He only needed enough time to arrange his finances, so that his son would not have to move into one of the slum tenement projects. Aiden needed to be cared for.

Each time he returned to Collette, Seamus' love for his Spanish mistress became stronger. Neither of them could have enough sex. It was like they were both starving until they realized how good each other tasted.

After hours of making love, and multiple orgasms, Collette finally revealed that she had missed two of her periods. She had been afraid to tell Seamus.

"Afraid? You never need to be afraid to tell me anything, Collette. We will love and raise this child together, and however many others that God sends us," Seamus said with great joy.

Every three days, when he returned to Collette, the child that their love was making grew more and more.

Seamus would lay his head on Collette's stomach, and sing songs while he lovingly caressed the image that he could hear moving inside. He was so in love with both of them that he could barely wait for the birth.

"Are you sure, my love, that you are correct about when our love conceived this joyous gift," Seamus asked one night after they had made love.

"The doctor has said that I have two more months. But, I can feel the child wanting to come early to be held in your loving arms. Are you sure Seamus that I am not disgusting to make love with now? I am so hideously grotesque."

Collette said, having difficulty even moving off the bed, "Never say that again, Collette! Being inside of you, tasting what you prepare for me when my tongue licks you, every inch of you I love, now and forever."

Seamus never knew what happiness was, until he met Collette. He knew that this next time he returned to Claudia would be the last.

He rehearsed the exit plan in his mind for many months. Now, he would leave Claudia a note with a key to a safe deposit box. Inside, she would find her share of the money he earned.

Claudia was young enough to go back to work and even find someone else to marry. Someone, of course, that would not want children.

Seamus was confident that this was God's will and the money he left would be enough to care for both Claudia and Aiden when he was gone.

The following morning, he left the note on the breakfast table so that Claudia would not miss it. By noon, he had arrived at Belfast and was anxious to tell Collette that they would never be apart again.

When Sean saw Seamus coming into the bar, he knew that he would have to be the one to give him the news.

"Top of the day to you, Mr. Sean, and it is a most marvelous one. I would love to stay and discuss how marvelous, but I must first tell my lovely lady," Seamus said, anxiously racing up the stairs.

"Seamus! Come back down, man. We need to talk." Sean sounded frantic.

When Seamus ignored Sean and continued toward Collette's room, he found it was empty. Sean placed his hands on his friend's shoulders to calm him down.

"Collette is gone, Seamus. When she began having labor pains three days ago, we knew it was time for the baby. She was taken to the Belfast Hospital, where she delivered your baby girl. She named her Selena Cassidy, moments before she began to hemorrhage. They were unable to save her, Seamus," Sean said, trying to hold back tears.

Seamus must have lost consciousness for a few moments. He felt the room turn dark and the ceiling was spinning like a saucer above his head. Once Sean helped him downstairs and he was seated on the bar stool, he began to register in his mind what he was told.

"The child? My daughter? Where is she now?" Seamus asked, half dazed.

"The nuns in the local orphanage are caring for her. I was able to retrieve her birth certificate. Collette did name you the father." Sean handed Seamus the paper.

Without taking time to even read what it said, Seamus placed the certificate in his coat pocket, and went directly to the orphanage.

When he explained that he was here to claim his daughter, the nurse directed him to the Mother Superior's empty office.

While waiting for at least thirty minutes, Seamus could barely hold back his grief.

How could you God take the love of my life away from me, now? Now that I have waited forever for this moment.

He was interrupted when the nun arrived and sat down behind a very intimidating oak desk.

Mother Superior, for all practical purposes, was God's messenger. Perhaps she had the answers he needed. After a few minutes with no greeting, Seamus declared, "I am here to claim my daughter, Selena Cassidy, whose mother, Collette, died a few days ago."

After a few more awkward moments, the nun said, "Mr. Cassidy. I understand that Selena's mother was not your wife. As a matter of fact, your wife lives in Dublin. Is this correct, Sir." The nun's tone was aggressive.

Totally unprepared for such an interrogation, Seamus responded defensively, "My personal life is not your concern, Madam. Selena is my daughter," Seamus insisted.

"She may be your physical daughter, but that child's soul is my responsibility. And, she needs to be raised by a family that is dedicated to God."

Mother Superior closed the folder, and was about to exit the room, when Seamus took hold of her wrist.

"I will be outside in the waiting room. If my child is not brought to me in fifteen minutes, I will return with the constable." Seamus was gritting his teeth with such anger.

He released his grip, and the obviously upset nun pulled away, her eyes sending imaginary darts toward Seamus.

Within his time limit demand, however, his three day old daughter was safely in his hands. Even at such a young age, she was the image of her mother. When Sean looked into her eyes, it was Collette he saw.

Once outside of the hospital, without hesitating, and not wanting any further confrontations, Seamus boarded the last train to Dublin, with his daughter. The only remains of the eternal love that was taken from him.

On the train, he held Selena close to his chest, singing to her the songs he did while she was still in her mother's womb. The child must have recognized his voice, because Seamus insisted that she smiled at him before falling peacefully asleep.

Although several women looked at him curiously, when Selena was given a bottle, prepared by the hospital to travel, most people chose to ignore the two of them.

Arriving on time to Dublin, Seamus and Selena went directly home. Once in the apartment, without saying a word to Colleen, he walked to where she was sitting on the recliner, mending a pair of Aiden's socks. Seamus startled her, but she was silent.

Selena was wrapped carefully in a white fleece blanket with tiny pink sheep on the outside. Seamus handed his daughter directly to Colleen.

No explanation was given. Before Seamus left again, he noticed that the letter he had left was on the dining room table where he had left it, but now opened.

It would be three days before Seamus returned, once, to his wife, son and infant daughter. Never would he leave again; and no one asked where he went for those three days.

Whatever punishment fate chose for Seamus Cassidy, it would be known by every generation as the Cassidy Curse.

On New Year's Eve, 1967, three generations later, Caden Cassidy would be another victim.

CHAPTER 28

The biggest curse in life is not losing your love, but not being loved, by someone you love.

Kiran Joshi

The Cassidy Legacy Continued
Selena Cassidy
1940-1949
Dublin, Ireland

Colleen Cassidy raised Selena as her own daughter. She never showed the animosity that she felt toward Seamus to this innocent child. From the moment Selena's mouth sucked the milk that Colleen produced, she knew that God had given her another chance to be a mother.

When Selena was old enough to understand, Seamus told her about her biological mother. He wanted to make her aware that she was never an accident, but a wonderful gift. Nevertheless, Selena considered Colleen her mother.

Aiden, who was six years older than his half-sister, always felt obligated to protect her. Although he was never close to his father, Aiden was dedicated to his mother.

Several days before Aiden was going to propose marriage to a young woman named Shannon, both his parents became seriously ill with consumption. A disease that eats the lungs with bacteria without warning.

Although many countries by 1940 were able to control this stage of Tuberculosis, it was still a deadly infection in Dublin.

Shannon, Selena and Aiden all took turns trying to keep Seamus and Colleen comfortable. But, when it became impossible to care for them, Aiden insisted that his parents let him take them to the infirmary.

Everyone knew, by this time, that they were at the last stages before death. The end was soon approaching.

Seamus and Colleen died three days after being admitted to the hospital, twelve hours apart. Arranging the wake and burials were exhausting. Selena felt that suddenly she had been abandoned, with nothing left, and no one to love her.

But, Aiden promised Selena that when he and Shannon married, she would come with them and be part of their family, like always.

At twenty-three years old, Shannon gave birth to her only child, Megan Anne. Unfortunately, after the delivery, she was told that her uterus was removed to prevent a suspicious cancerous tumor from expanding.

Aiden was pleased with his daughter, although Shannon felt guilty that she would never be able to provide him a son.

Aiden continued to raise Selena as her father. But, she had a free, wild spirit much like her mother. That spirit, at times, would lead her to compromising situations.

By the age of eighteen, Selena informed; not asked, Aiden, that she had taken a job at a local pub, two blocks from the apartment.

Both agitated and concerned, Aiden did not want to see his sister in that environment. Nevertheless, since Megan's birth, there were additional expenses and his small paycheck from the foundry sometimes was just not enough.

The lifetime connections that the Cassidy's once had with the railroad no longer existed. There was new management and, when his father died, the link that perhaps could have influenced his job placement was now broken.

Selena would always give Aiden her evening tips, which amounted to more than her salary. This made her defiance to work at the Pub a little more tolerable to Aiden.

Then, one evening when Selena arrived early to work there was a new rock band setting up on stage. The Whiskey Wolfhound was a traveling band from Wales.

Daniel, the drummer, noticed Selena as soon as she entered the bar. And, when the spotlight shined on Daniel, while the band was tuning their instruments, their eyes met.

The first move was initiated by Daniel, but Selena instinctively knew just how to play this game. What she wasn't prepared for was how fast and smooth Daniel was. Days later, he was pledging his love publicly to her.

By the third day, none of the customers were surprised when the lead singer invited Selena on stage. When Daniel moved from his drum set directly to Selena, the couple looked like they might be mirror images of the opposite sex.

Both had shining ebony black hair; Selena's only a little longer than Daniels, and the cobalt blue eyes staring at each other were undeniably enchanting.

While the band started to play a romantic ballad, Daniel fell to one knee and proposed to Selena by putting a Cracker Jack ring on her finger.

"I promise you, lovey, soon, that ring will be a diamond with a solid gold band. Marry me, Selena. You are the love of my life!"

The crowd was going wild when Selena jumped into his arms and he carried her out the door. That was the night Selena lost her virginity. And, the following three nights were followed with uninhibited sex in more positions than Selena knew were possible. Then nothing.

By day four, Daniel was history. He left her a note explaining that the band needed to leave for Scotland, but once settled, he would send for her.

Three months later, Selena was pregnant and Daniel was only a bad dream.

Once Aiden found out, he insisted that Selena have an abortion.

"You have no choice, Selena. Even an abortion won't guarantee that our name won't be ruined. The chances of you ever marrying someone decent has now been destroyed." Aiden was pacing back and forth trying to make all of this disappear.

"This is my child that I am carrying, Aiden. I will find a way to deal with it. An abortion is not an option. And, by the way, our good name was muddied many years ago." Selena was now defensive.

Shannon finally interrupted. "Perhaps there is a solution that will make everyone happy. My cousin lives on Inchydoney Island, in West Cork. You, Megan, and I will stay there until the baby is born. On the birth certificate, you will use my name as the mother and Aiden as the father. When we return to Dublin, all three of us will raise 'our' child together." Shannon was the only one fairly calm.

"Are you insane, Shannon? We will bond with this child and then Selena will take it with her the first chance she can. Are you prepared for that heartbreak?" Aiden's voice was louder than usual.

"I am your sister, Aiden! I would never take the child away from you. You are a fine father. My child will need a fine father," Selena said, emotionally.

Aiden finally embraced Selena, who was now unable to control her tears. Shannon joined the two of them.

Two days later, Shannon, Megan and Selena arrived at Inchydoney. On April 9, 1949, Selena gave birth to an eight pound, eight ounce baby boy that she named Caden Seamus Cassidy.

"I like the name Caden, Selena. Does it have any significance?" Shannon asked, while rocking the baby in her arms.

"Caden means spirit of battle in Welsh. I wanted him to have something from his father. And, he will have the same spirit that all of us Cassidy's have to survive life." Selena was finally at peace knowing that her son's future was, for now, secure.

Was it another mere coincidence that, fifty-one years later, a dying man would plan a trip to Inchydoney for the love of his life, not knowing that Caden Cassidy would also fall desperately in love with that same woman?

CHAPTER 29

You are never too old to set another goal, or dream a new dream.
  C S Lewis

Gabby and Sterling
July, 2010
Ensenada, Mexico

Spending the past three months at La Mansion, Ensenada, was life changing. Not only had I moved to another country; light years away from the Midwest, but I made some major changes about my role on this earth.

Time allowed me to reflect, not only on my choices in life, but also Sterling's visions and desire to improve so many lives. I was more than impressed and eager to help.

Some epiphany was responsible for this dramatic transformation. The Sterling Powers I once knew lacked any emotional DNA, frequented private sex parties and enjoyed living on the edge. Now, this same man personified the image of a choir boy.

Perhaps, that was only the outer façade that Sterling was projecting. This mystery woman in Todos Santos might reveal a different persona. Ever since he mentioned her; several months ago, I subtly attempted to learn more about her.

Was she an exotic Mexican model that Sterling met on a fashion runway in Milan? Or, was she an international Mexican actress that captured his interest while he attended, as usual, the yearly Cannes Festival?

During these last months—whenever I could find a slight wiggle room into a private meeting—every time I mentioned his mysterious lady, Sterling was so evasive that I was beginning to imagine that this

Maggie creature was only a fantasy.

What I did find intriguing was how adamant Sterling was about me meeting her, whom I only knew by name. Even that fact was a result of a misnomer when I called her Maggie, the cat, after the tragic heroin in Truman Capote's award winning play, *Cat on the Hot Tin Roof.*

"Not even close, Gabby. Maggie Mendoza is much more like a Sphynx cat. She carries mysterious secrets from another world. And, like the Sphynx cat, her looks are somewhat intimidating. This hides her lively, imaginative and intriguing personality. Very much like another cat I was once very enamored with."

Sterling looked deep into Gabby's eyes waiting for a reaction.

Gabby recognized the look that Sterling was giving her. It was a melancholy daze into the past. She often had the same one when she would think of Jake.

To reduce the slight tension, Gabby said sarcastically, "Don't you remember the felines in the musical, *Cats,* adapted from TS Eliot's poems, *The Naming of Cats?* Some of us end up like Grizabella…ancient and tragic."

Sterling began to laugh. "First of all, my Gabby amour, we saw "Cats" together in London. And, I am not going to reveal any more about Maggie until you two meet," Sterling said, gesturing a goodbye sign.

As he departed, Gabby could hear him mumbling, "Grizabella! What a joke that is!"

Although Sterling and I lived together in La Mansion, most of the time he was traveling, or busy in meetings. Since we were more like roommates these days, it was rare to even share a meal.

This distance worked to both of our advantages. I enjoyed the independence, the freedom, and mostly, the peaceful solitude.

Alex and I spoke rarely. Mostly the talks dealt with financial transactions. He was able to weave a believable story that my extended absence was due to my obligations with charitable organizations, internationally. Not that far from the truth.

The first gala fundraiser that I participated in was the Fiestas de la Vendimis (Wine Harvest Festivals). The Valley de Guadalupe began these celebrations in 1970—forty years ago. This entire event has grown to an elaborate season that begins in late July and continues until the end of August.

This is much more than wine tasting parties. There are concerts, special dinners, and soirees…just to begin with. Usually, the various vineyards host different styles of food and entertainment. Tickets to these events range from affordable to astronomical.

Many international celebrities attend. Sterling, naturally, offers rooms to his guests in his villa that attend. They graciously donate, in return, large amounts of money to the foundation in appreciation for this hospitality.

Regressndo a la Vendemia was always a sold out activity. Guests participate and learn the wine harvesting process. Later, they celebrate the tasting of the wine with regional food served under the stars.

The foundation; months earlier, researched a variety of venues that offered unique events for their members. At Adobe Guadalupe Gala Dinner—at gourmet meals—guests would have the opportunity to taste premium and rare wines that later would be auctioned. The funds collected would be donated to The Celeste Powers Foundation.

I was amazed to learn how many different festivals were offered. At a very exclusive one, the vineyard provided their guests with the opportunity to blend their own wine choices with a renowned wine maker. This event, along with workshops from the School of Oenology and Gastronomy, was always requested.

All of the vineyards had spectacular outdoor dining with stunning views and great sunsets. In some cases, directly after dinner, guests were offered more wine with a variety of cheeses and fruits packed in a picnic basket to enjoy during the three hour concerts.

This year, *Liquid Blue*, a controversial band, that claims it has performed in forty-seven countries in Europe, was one of the bands booked for the wine festival. BC Jean, a former band member, went on to write music for Beyoncé, and later was signed by Clive Davis, for Sony records. The founder and lead vocalist, Scott Stephens, was a former pro Roller Derby skater with the Los Angeles Thunderbirds.

As Sterling promised, months before the festival began, he introduced me to many of the vineyards that he did business with. On one occasion, a few members from *The Liquid Blue Band* were following the same tour Sterling was taking me on. It was Layla Lox, the DJ who competes in pro surfing competitions when the band is off tour, who introduced herself to me first.

The first thing that came into my mind was the song, *Layla*, by Eric Clapton. That was also a nickname Sterling used to call me.

"Sterling tells me that you are a native from Savanna, Georgia?" Layla asked.

"That was many, many years ago. Have you ever played in Savanna?" I enquired, curiously, wondering why she would even be interested.

"As a matter of fact, I was just there a few weeks ago. A friend I met, when we were scheduled to play in LA at the Hollywood Bowl, told me when I was in Georgia—if close to Savanna—check out a super cool pub called, *The Molly*," Layla explained.

She kept staring at me, as if she wanted to say something else, but decided not to.

I knew that *The Molly* was owned by Caden. But, since I was never there, I decided it would be best to say nothing.

While Sterling and I were sipping our wine, looking over the veranda, discussing how busy the vineyards were going to be in the next few weeks, Layla walked over and pulled out a chair.

"Hey, I apologize for staring at you, earlier. It's just that I could not get over how much you looked like this girl in that pub," Layla said, confused.

Sterling also looked perplexed. He knew that I never returned to Savanna after I left in 1967. Even Molly's funeral was not enough to change my mind.

"Sorry, Layla, you must be confusing Gabby with someone else. She hasn't been home for forty-three years," Sterling interjected when he saw I was uncomfortable.

"Oh, no...she wasn't there. But, a painting of her with another girl with red hair is hanging in the owner's office. I swear that girl looks just like you...only younger," Layla emphasized.

"That is very odd," I said honestly, having no idea how a picture of Molly and me ended up in Caden's bar.

"They do say that we have doppelgänger's—mirror images of ourselves. That must be what this is." I offered the only excuse that sounded valid.

"Let's toast to that," Lyla said, raising her glass and gently clinking it to mine and Sterling's.

When she joined back with her friends, Sterling seemed preoccupied...like his mind had moved to another plateau. Finally, when I touched his hand lightly, he seemed to return.

"Sorry, Gabby. When you mentioned doppelgänger, I was just imagining an entirely different scenario. Is *The Molly* Caden's Pub that you mentioned before? How did your talk with him go, recently? If you think I am prying, I will understand," Sterling said, reasonably calm.

"Yes, *The Molly* is Caden's Pub, and no, you never pry. It has just been awhile since we had the opportunity to talk about personal issues. I told Caden that I would be in Todos Santos for a few months. We both agreed that if given the opportunity, we had to personally meet, since neither of us had any closure.

Maybe this time, whatever happens, we both will find peace," I said, waiting for a reaction.

"Are you sure that you want to meet with him, again? It has been many years. What can possibly be resolved now, after so many changes, in both of your lives?" Sterling said, soberly.

There it was! The old Sterling that I remember surfacing once more. I would never be able to explain to him how passionate Caden and I were at one time. His ability to distance himself, emotionally, from any relationship is what initially attracted me to him. He was the perfect iceman for the perfect ice queen.

"Now is the best time in both of our lives. I cannot even imagine any other solution. If Caden tells his wife, like he claims he will, and travels to Mexico to attempt a forty-three year reconciliation with me, I cannot ignore him, nor do I wish to. This is an unconditional condition," I said, earnestly.

Sterling looked at me with those brilliant, penetrating grey eyes that, at times like this, touch my soul.

"As I have told you, Gabby, I will always be here. And, what happened to you—to us—seven years ago, will NEVER happen again. If meeting with Caden reveals your destiny, then I totally approve. If it doesn't, we will deal with that as well," Sterling said, pouring the last drops of Merlot in both of our glasses.

"We will be leaving Cabo San Lucas in about one week. After a few days of luxury at one of the most spectacular resorts in Mexico, we will then drive to Todos Santos. It may be a rather difficult transition to what you are used to, but I guarantee Todos Santos offers such magic that I know you will make the adjustment easily."

Sterling was eager to share this rustic village with Gabby.

"I have left the best for last. Until we find a suitable house, I have made arrangements for you to check into *The Hotel California*. My good friend, Eleanor Rigby, is the proprietor and she is a sweetheart." Sterling seemed amused.

"Is this a joke? Checking into *Hotel California*? As I remember those lyrics by The Eagles, 'once you check in you can never check out', are quite ominous. But then, I guess Eleanor Rigby is a perfect example, isn't she? Really, Sterling, does Ruby Tuesday also live in this town?"

I was truly amazed how Sterling was able to sometimes create the most amusing stories.

"This is all that I am going to tell you for now, my Gabby Layla. Oh, but yes, Todos Santos, is also where Maggie lives. Maybe she is Rod Stewart's *Maggie*? Now we are onto something. Like that classic Christmas movie…you remember… the one with the island for Misfit toys. Maybe, this is a city where 'Rock' n 'Roll' vixens are immortalized and retire."

Sterling seemed very pleased with this explanation.

I even recall the very first time that he used the name, Gabby Layla…borrowed from Eric Clapton's hit song, Layla. It was the third time I agreed to spend the night with him at his Penthouse. I was still nervous about being an inadequate sex partner. Sterling could sense my inhibitions.

To make me laugh, he would sing the lyrics, Layla, 'you've got me on my knees, I'm begging you please won't you ease my worried mind'?"

Later, he also told me that Layla in Arabic meant, night.

I asked him why he associated me with 'night'. His answer was that night is when he felt the most alive, and the most afraid.

CHAPTER 30

A bridge of silver wings stretches from the dead ashes, of an unforgiving nightmare to the jeweled vision of a life started anew.
Aberjhani

The Cassidy Saga Continues
Dublin, Ireland 1954

Six years after Selena gave birth to Caden, the Cassidy family were still struggling financially. Even with Shannon, Aiden and Selena all working now, there was barely enough food every day.

Caden would tell his sister Megan, thirteen years old, grotesque stories right before dinner. He would describe in detail how chickens were beheaded and how baby calves, still in the mothers uterus, would be slaughtered for veal.

Whenever one of the adults caught him with his disgusting stories Caden would be punished.

"Where do you come up with these morbid tales, Caden? You are only six years old?" Shannon would say angrily.

"I have my friends, Mum. They have friends on farms. They all tell me these stories." Caden would say defensively.

The truth was Caden didn't care if he was punished. It was all worth it to eat Megan's portion of food. And, after a short time she declared that she was now a vegetarian.

Aiden knew that it was now up to him to find a financial solution before it would be too late for him and his family. When there was not enough food for his children, it was a dire situation.

Between 1848 and 1955 over six million adults and children left Ireland, because there were no jobs. Or the jobs available would not pay enough to feed a family.

2.5 million Irish citizens departed from Cobb county, Cork Ireland. The SS Adriatic, that sailed for The White Star Line had fliers in Dublin advertising low fairs for immigrants traveling to New York. The ship would depart in two weeks.

Several of the laborers that Aiden worked with, gathered at the local pub after work, one day. Waving an advertisement flier from The White Star Line, that Aiden recognized from the street, a young man was drawing attention to the center of the pub.

"This here flier, Gents, is our way out of poverty! It is our ticket to a new world! A world where we can raise our children knowing that their destiny will be anything that they want it to be! "

The crowds, mostly men, began to chant and cheer in unison. Ale flowing in every man's mugs.

"The White Star leaves two weeks from today. I am going to be on that ship! Who else will join me?" The young man yelled robustly.

The crowds roared again with approval. Although, Aiden knew that most of these men would never leave Dublin, this may be God's answer to his prayers.

Nobody, but Aiden knew that his mother, Claudia, never removed the money, her husband, Seamus left for her in the safe deposit box, the day he was going to abandon her for Collette. Since she was the only one that had a key to that box, the money was still there.

On her deathbed, Colleen placed in Aiden's hand that key. Nearly inaudible, her last words to her beloved son were, "When you think it is best, Aiden, use this money to provide for your family. You are now the Cassidy patriarch." A few seconds later she passed on to the heavens.

Aiden had been tempted on many occasions to open the safe deposit box and see just how much money there was. But every time, whatever the crises was at the moment , passed by, and there was no further need.

But, now, this opportunity might be exactly what would change all their lives forever.

The next morning, Aiden chose to visit the bank. He did not tell Shannon or anyone else. He also missed work, which he never did in thirteen years.

At the bank, the teller took him to the vault, removed the steel safe deposit box, and told Aiden that when he was finished, he should lock the box and meet her in the front.

Aiden crossed himself, and said a silent prayer. Once the box was opened he saw the money, in various denominations of bank notes. As Aiden nervously began to touch the money, he realized that only the top first five and last five notes were one pound.

The rest in between were all one hundred pounds. More than enough to pay passage for the entire family, and even plenty left to live on, until they could become established. They would not to be wealthy, but more importantly they would not be poor, like they were now.

Before Aiden locked the box, he took a moment to examine one of the hundred pound bank notes. He remembered in elementary school being taught that these twentieth century banknotes were designed by Sir John Lavery, from Belfast. The portrait of the women he chose to be on the one hundred note, was a women that he called Colleen.

Aiden found that quite appropriate since it was his mother that chose to save this treasure her entire life for him.

Before returning home, he stopped at the transatlantic telegraph office to send a message to his Uncle Garret, who lived in Georgia.

Will be arriving from Ireland with my family of four in two weeks (stop) Would be forever grateful for any assistance. (Stop) Financially stable at the moment, however may need accommodations in New York and transportation to Georgia. (Stop)

Your loving Nephew Aiden Cassidy

(Send)

Uncle Garret, was Colleen 's oldest brother, who left Ireland twenty years ago. Aiden had only met him once when he was about Caden's age, six years old. However, Colleen always kept in touch with him, and Garret often suggested that Colleen and the family join him.

According to his mother, Garret owned a small convenience store in a city called Savanna. Since his wife, Alana and he were never blessed with children, Garret was afraid that there would never be anyone to help him care for the business when he became old.

Hopefully he would still be receptive to seeing his family again, and hire Aiden to help in the store.

The final stop, Aiden made, was to the ocean liners office to purchase passage tickets. To be safe and thrifty, Aiden selected the most reasonable price. This required that they sleep in the steerage area.

The berths would be privately separated by curtains and the family would need to share bathroom facilities. Not the best accommodations, however, the most reasonable. And, it would only be seven days at sea. Not a bad trade off for a new life.

Returning home with all his good news, he was greeted by Shannon who handed him a telegraph message that had shortly arrived. Aiden put it aside, anxious to first share what he had procured for his family.

Once the children and Selena were gathered, Aiden began. First he held up his hand with the ocean liner tickets.

Caden was the first one to scream,

"Papa! You have bought tickets to the circus! When? When?"

Caden was jumping as high as he could trying to grab the tickets, until Aiden, sat the excited boy down and said,

"These tickets are even more exciting than the circus?"

Caden was still not sure that there was anything more exciting than a circus.

"These tickets are magic! Magic for all of us. They are going to change our monochrome world to technicolor."

Aiden waited for someone, anyone to respond.

Finally, when Selena asked if he had won a new television, he knew it was time to stop the game and let them know that they were leaving Ireland forever.

" Okay…since you are all such bad guessers, I will tell you. In two weeks we are all leaving from Cork on a large white steam liner for New York." Again he waited for a reaction.

"Do you mean, like a vacation to America? How can we afford that Aiden? Have you gone bonkers?" Shannon asked.

"No, my darl'in . Not a vacation…we are permanently moving to America."

Aiden said no longer able to control his enthusiasm.

Finally, everyone, that is everyone except Megan, began to dance with joy. When Aiden noticed that Megan was crying he stopped the celebration and took his daughter into his arms.

"Why the tears my Megan bear? America is the land of rainbows, and sunshine." Aiden began to wipe her tears.

"But Papa…I have no friends in America. I will need to leave everyone I know…And…And…I have a boyfriend." Megan finally confessed .

Immediately, Aiden's mind was in flashback mode. It was Selena all over again. He would not stand by and watch his daughter while she became pregnant and ruin her life. After taking a few deep breaths, in a very calm, but stern voice, Aiden told his daughter,

"You are only thirteen years old, Megan. I am the head of this family, and in two weeks you, will be on that ship with us traveling to America. Is that clear?"

Megan had never heard her father that serious. All she could do was shake her head, yes.

Caden's only recollection of that voyage was, throwing up three days at sea, and the Statue of Liberty as they sailed by to Ellis Island.

Being steerage passengers, his family had to wait for the other passengers to disembark, and then they boarded the ferry to Ellis Island.

In the Great Hall Registry they sat for three to five hours for medical instructions and exams. Then there were the legal inspections. Not until it was verified that there identity matched the ones on the ship were they allowed to leave the island to begin their new life.

Uncle Garret had arranged for the family to be met by a member from a local Catholic Parish. For three days they would stay in the dorms of the nunnery. After that, they would be taken to Grand Central Station to board a seventeen hour long train ride to Atlanta, Georgia. That is where Uncle Garret would met them.

Aiden had just enough money left to rent a nice house near the Cassidy Irish Deli, that his Uncle owned.

By the time Caden was ten years old, his sister Megan had died five years earlier ,at the age of eighteen, by a drunk driver.

Aiden and Shannon buried their only biological child in the Laurel Grove Cemetery , among lush magnolia trees, dogwood, and pine.

This was also the year that Uncle Garret died of a heart attack. He too, was buried in the same cemetery as Megan. Since Aiden's Aunt Alana had passed away the year before, Aiden now inherited the deli.

During the next several years the Cassidy's were joined by other Irish families. Some would travel together in groups and live, almost like Gypsies in trailers , until they were able to save enough money to buy a small business.

The majority of theses Irishmen decided that they did not want to work for anyone else ever again.

Because Savanna was a small community, Aiden and Shannon would offer the newly arrived Irish families the hospitality that Uncle Garret and Aunt Alana had shared with them.

One pleasant summer evening, while visiting with a newly arrived family from Ireland, Aiden inquired how the Sweeney's decided to make Savanna their home in America.

"Well, I'll tell you Aiden. It was a very scientific method. Five families, and only one child, Molly McGee, had decided to finally make the move to this grand USA. So, we asked Molly to place a red stick pin on a large US map.

We all agreed that wherever she placed it, that would be our destination. And, when she was done, Savanna, Georgia was our new hometown." Samuel said with a very pleasant smile.

"I would say, that Molly McGee was an excellent navigator."

Aiden added, handing Samuel a cold beer from the ice chest.

Since Megan's tragic death, Caden spent most of his time drawing pictures of buildings or making skyscrapers out of empty, bottles and tin cans. Shannon and Selena were afraid that this isolated behavior would affect him at school.

Miriam McGee and Shannon became close friends very quickly. Molly, Miriam's only daughter was the same age as Caden, twelve. And, since Miriam was a widow, Shannon would invite both of them for dinner at least once a week. She also, secretly hoped that Molly and Caden would be eventually more than just friends.

Molly would always bring with her a sketch pad to draw . Her art work was extremely sophisticated for her age. For that matter, Molly was much more mature than most twelve years old.

"I really believe sometimes that Molly has an old soul living somewhere in her body. Ever since her Dad was killed on duty as a police officer, when she was eight, Molly has taken the responsibility to be in charge. At times this is good, but I also wish she would have been a child longer."

Miriam shared this with Shannon one day when they were talking about their children starting high school.

As much as both mothers were hoping that their children would somehow be attracted to one another, fate had other plans in mind.

At twelve years old, Caden could not have any idea, how much Molly would help him with a young girl named Gabriella Girard on more than one occasion in his life.

CHAPTER 31

Absence is to love, what wind is to fire; it extinguishes the small, it inflames the great.

Rodger de Rabutin de Bussy

Gabby and Sterling
July, 2010
Cabo San Lucas, Mexico

The day we left La Mansion for Cabo San Lucas was definitely bitter sweet. I had become close friends with both Alejandra and Marisol. After three magnificent months, living in a world where sea shells and ocean replaced a constant longing for something intangible, I now struggled to leave.

There are times when I am convinced that my lacerated heart, will forever be bleeding. From nowhere, spaces separated by seconds, like prolonged intervals, once again remind me nostalgically, of an uncontrollable desire that was distinguished by a mere whisper of wind. And that is when I regret who I have become.

Then, from somewhere, inside my internal library, filled with an archive of cravings, repentance, and dreams, I hear, Rudyard Kipling remind me, *If you can keep your head when all about you/ are losing theirs and blaming it on you;/ If you trust yourself when all else doubt you/ But make allowance for their doubting too/ If you can wait and not be tired of waiting/ Or being lied about, don't deal in lies/ Or being hated and not give way to hating and...most importantly dream without allowing those dreams to be your master, then Gabriella you have achieved more than most scholars.*

When Sterling signals to me from a distance that Jaime is ready to take us to the airport, my momentary doubts return to the abyss.

Sterling reminds me that La Mansion has a helicopter pad, but he doubted that I would be excited with that choice. He was right! Even this, two hour flight, in his elegant private jet, makes me nervous.

Sterling holds my hand for both take off and landing. He remembers my anxiety. It is difficult for me to justify, after so many flights, why I should be this scared. But, his hand is comforting, and the view from the aircraft window is relaxing.

"Okay?" Sterling removes his hand slowly, hesitantly.

"Yes…Thank you, for remembering my paranoia."

I answer calmly, attempting my best to make light of this annoying problem.

We are sitting in this roomy lounge cabin, with a couch and several swivel chairs. Although, I remain seated during the entire flight next to the window, Sterling has already moved to another cabin; presumably one with a desk and computer.

There was at least once, that I recall making love, or maybe having sex is a better description, with Sterling in the bedroom on this plane. I believe it must have been a transatlantic flight, maybe to London.

It must have been the medication that Sterling gave me before the flight that relaxed me enough so that we were able to have sex without being terrified.

Sterling kept reminding me that, if he was ever going to die in a plane crash he would hope that the last thing he would remember was being inside of me.

He then lifted me in his arms, took me into the bedroom, where we remained the entire flight. I don't recall getting much sleep, however.

"We are going to fly in to the south, Gabby, so you can get an aerial view of the quite famous Cabo landmark, known as El Arco. It is a magnificent natural rock formation that signals the start of Land's End, where the Sea of Cortez meets the Pacific Ocean." Rick Miller, our pilot, was telling me from the speaker.

What I saw below was aquamarine crystal blue water with rugged cliffs and even some quiet looking coves, as Rick flew even closer inland.

There also appeared to be a highway, or corridor, as I later learned it was called, that stretched from south of San Jose del Cabo to Cabo San Lucas.

Although the waters of Los Cabo's have been frequented since 1535, when Cortes discovered the tranquil bay, he was also greeted by unsociable Indians, that forced him to quickly leave. But, shortly after World War II, a group from Southern California discovered a fisherman's Mecca.

Eventually, dignitaries, politicians and celebrities also found Cabo to be a fascinating, yet still private enough to disappear for a short time.

When our plane finally landed there was a town car waiting for us on the runway.

The drive to Cortez Pedregal, the resort that Sterling had reserved, was touted as the best in Cabo. There were other hotels that I could partially see from the highway, and of course several golf courses that looked impressive. However, thus far, nothing seemed that much better than Ensenada.

And then we pulled into the guarded gate entrance to Cortez Pedregal.

On the southernmost tip of Mexico's Baja California peninsula, the resort encompasses over twenty four acres of mountains, and ocean front access, to private secluded beaches, each offering the most breathtaking, unobstructed, views on the peninsula.

Nothing was visible until we passed several mountains on a curved road that lead to a stunning group of villas. They appeared to be jutting out from the rugged mountainside.

The custom designed features blended in with the natural environment so dramatically, that it was difficult to separate the architecture from the earths own design; where one begins, and one ends was impossible to distinguish.

Immediately, Caden came to mind. How thrilled he would be to see such a phenomenal construction. Perhaps one day, I would be able to share this with him.

When at last we parked in the circular driveway entrance, I could only presume that this was the lobby. But, when Sterling helped me out of the car, he said, "Do you think that you could get used to these digs, Gabby?"

My eyes must have said all that was flashing through my mind, because for the moment I was speechless. I should have known when Sterling said that this would be one of the hottest locations for an exotic escape, he would never exaggerate. There was no doubt why he referred to this as the Mexican Riviera.

"This can't possibly be where we are staying Sterling? This villa is larger than La Mansion."I said amazed.

"It is an interesting design, actually. This villa is separated by a bridge that connects to the other side. It allows me the ability to use the entire unit or share it with another resident.

You could say it is like adjoining rooms, but in this case, villas. When my associates come, the entire home is used, however, for our short stay, of a few weeks, the east wing is closed? I hope that fits your approval, madam?"

Sterling bowed as he lead me into the impressive palace.

As we walked in, there was our Personal Concierge, dressed in a white linen suit, greeting us.

Once upon a time, when I was much younger, there was a television series called Fantasy Island. In every episode, the enigmatic, Mr. Roark was there to greet his guests and promise them that all their secret dreams would come true on this Island.

Unfortunately, as I recall, due to the nature of the show, many of those dreams resulted into nightmares. I didn't need any more nightmares.

"Buenos Tardes , Senor Powers and Senora Girard. Welcome back to Cortez Pedregal. I have arranged in the veranda some cool cocktails and light snacks. It will give you a chance to review the exceptional amenities that this Villa and surrounding properties offer."

The host, whose name tag read, Marcos, was directing most of his speech to me, since it was evident that Sterling had been a frequent visitor.

"Gracias, Marcos. I will orientate Senora Gabby with all the details." Sterling said pleasantly but with authority.

Marcos, understood that his hospitality was no longer needed, and departed quietly.

The reception room that we were now in was a lanai. A roofed, open sided veranda that extended to an enormous balcony over looking an inviting ocean.

There was something alluring and enticing about how secluded we were from the outside world, and yet, somewhere there were people closely waiting for any request we had.

"I am still having a difficult time believing that this property is real. It is, as if I am, surrounded by an enchanting maze that is lifting me to a surreal level of ecstasy."

I said stretching out on the closest chaise lounge nearest to the glass wall.

Sterling handed me a Margarita, and took a seat next to me. It was the first time in three months that I noticed he was relaxing. It was certainly easy to imagine how perfect Sterling's life was, by his travels.

But, there has always been something disturbing about him that never surfaced completely.

Whenever it appears that he might be able to release the demons that follow him, a rigid wall prevents any intruders from entering.

Perhaps that is why now, we are mutually enjoying these several moments of silence. When the ocean breeze sounds like a mystical echo, playing celestial harps from Agatha, a legendary city at the earth's core, neither of us move.

This peaceful interlude continues for an unknown period of time. We Both appear to be meditating.

A Nineteen century French occultist removed the mythological stigma, to Agatha, and offered the first reliable study, of what he claimed, was a secret world. This is where all mans wisdom is accessible through revelations, that release truth and knowledge.

Although, Saint Yves' version, depicts this obscure world in the Himalayas, many modern philosophers, claim that this divulgence is, in fact guided by a Holy Spirit. If this is true, the Lands End may be offering that spirit an archetypal homeland.

Casually shifting his body so that the sun was no longer preventing him to watch me lounging peacefully, Sterling ended my esoteric fixation, when he began to inform me of the various amenities available in this villa.

"Now that you have fully emerged yourself Gabby, in the sensual attributes of Cortez Pedregal, I want you to enjoy all that it has to offer." Sterling said in a pleasant, relaxed tone.

"Honestly…I would be quite content remaining on this lounge, day and night. I am really not sure that this is the best place to have brought me, if you expected any form of business to take place. How does anyone ever get anything accomplished in this environment?" I asked in a mellow tone.

"There is no doubt that the Mexican culture, and specifically those people who live in this region , are much more relaxed than those of us from the states. But, what you will learn Gabby, is that your mind and body begin to sync into harmony. The results are always positive, as well as, innovative." Sterling said honestly.

This explanation might make sense, but at the moment all I wanted to do was inhale the serenity.

But, Sterling insisted that it was time for my informal tour. I was first taken to the west side of the balcony where a private beach offered guests a large fire pit and leather sling chairs to relax on when the sun went down.

Slightly further out, was a boardwalk that lead to an enclosed open deck with dining tables and chairs. It was as close to the ocean as one could get while dining and not be in the sea itself.

"Occasionally, if you toss pieces of bread from the deck, fish will entertain you by jumping in the air for more food and attention." Sterling added.

"There are five bedrooms in this villa. Each with a mini kitchen that provides guests with cold or warm drinks and a small fridge with ice and cold snacks. Any other food will be prepared at the main kitchen by a chef and staff available twenty four hours a day."

Then, Sterling gave me a fast tutorial on the computer to show me how to order meals, request a massage or indulge in the private spa facility.

Basically, any treatment or food I might want was at my command. Somehow hired help would pop in and out of the hallways when needed and disappear when not.

"You should also know, Gabby, that one of the most appealing feature of this villa is that it is remote and isolated, not only outside, but inside as well. There may be days that you see no one, unless of course you want to.

My desire to mingle with others, while I am here is rare. It may appear to you that I have become a recluse, and maybe I have, but this is what I need to do to function. I share this with you now, because, quite honestly, you are the only person who knows me inside and out."

Sterling said all of this more like a confession than an excuse.

"I am not really certain Sterling how much I really know you, but I will always respect the privacy you need. I don't think that there will be any problems with this arrangement." I said quite confident.

Sterling bent down and lightly kissed the top of my head, like I was his favorite pet, although I knew it was just his guarded method of showing affection.

"Oh…and if you decide you want to go downtown for some shopping or to enjoy the famous nightclubs Cabo has to offer, I will arrange a reliable escort. Just never leave the complex beyond the gate alone. On your nightstand in the bedroom I have left you a binder that may be of interest to you. If you get a chance in the next week, look it over and we will talk about what I want to do with it."

Sterling was out of the room, without saying another word.

I could only presume that the remainder of the day was mine exclusively.

Becoming familiar with my surroundings, was the first item on my agenda. Next, I was curious what Sterling left for me to read. Nothing that he had said previously led me to believe that his foundation was involved with any doctrines, yet, he did mention spiritual counseling , which has a reverend tone.

At this moment, I intend to take full advantage of the rare opportunity provided, in these spectacular surroundings.

This includes my constant soul searching, preparing for my meeting with Caden, and studying Jake's profound messages recorded in his journals.

Once I am able to recognize my predisposed state of mind, that fluctuates often between my past and present, this love triangle that holds Jake, Caden and I captive will at last release me from these shackles.

As esoteric as all this appears, once I close my eyes it will fade away leaving only my imagination.

CHAPTER 32

The greater the obstacle, the more glory in overcoming it.
  Moliere

  Gabby Flying Solo
  August, 2010
  Cabo San Lucas, Mexico

Most of my days were spent admiring the secluded beaches, hiking short distances to mountain sanctuaries, and learning how to inhale and exhale, these glorious surroundings.

The San Jose estuary is a marshy lagoon, surrounded by a desert and a strip of white sand that separates it from the Sea of Cortez. In contrast to the desert, there are lush shady palms, that are home to a most social bird, known as the Hooded Oriole.

Occasionally the Oriole can be seen sharing the hummingbird's nectar and flying very close to bird watchers.

During the early morning hikes, It is fascinating to watch the Great Blue Heron, keep company with the egrets wading through the marsh grass and reeds. When a flock of egrets settle in the trees, they look like newly fallen snow from a distance.

One afternoon, Felipe, the guide that Sterling insisted be with me at all times, took me to a replica of a Pericu dwelling. The Pericu's tribe, were the aboriginal inhabitants of this region.

They have been extinct since the late eighteenth century. However, Felipe says that in Todos Santos those who partake in the Black Magic rituals, claim that they have seen tribe members.

"What do you actually mean Felipe by Black Magic rituals? Is that really still taking place, here in Mexico?" I asked both amazed and shocked.

"Yeah…Yeah. It is everywhere, but mostly underground. Not far from here, in Catemaco, Veracruz, the entire town is inhabited by warlocks and witches. It is a well known tourist destination.

In March, the city holds its annual sorcery event which draws nearly five thousand visitors each year I believe that at one time Mr. Powers was there." Felipe said quite frankly.

"Really? You think that Mr. Powers has associated with the sorcerers? That is hard for me to accept. What would make you say this? Has he ever expressed an interest in the occult?" I asked, apprehensively.

"Perhaps it is time to get back to civilization. We can continue this discussion, maybe over a Margarita?" He said casually, but obviously wanting to evade this topic.

"That sounds like you are avoiding my questions. But, I am getting rather warm and thirsty."

I said, still hoping to get some definitive answers.

Felipe led me back to the jeep and suggested that we take a short ride into town, where he would share with me, in more detail, some of the most common rituals associated with Mexican folklore religion.

He added that this plays a significant role in the lives of many Mexican people, regardless of their social or economic backgrounds.

Since I was here to learn as much as possible about this culture, what Felipe was going to teach me would be imperative to my objective.

And, then there was also this fascinating idea, that Sterling might have once been associated with the macabre. Both, slightly disturbing , and yet quite alluring.

Considering his past involvement with private sexual entertainment, in many ways I should not be that surprised. However, there must be some valid reason why Sterling was drawn to black magic.

Downtown Cabo San Lucas is an interesting blend of Nuevo and rustic. Most of the bars during the daytime hours, serve lunch and dinner, until the evening entertainment begins, as late as eleven, and the party continues into the sunrise hours.

Places like Squid Row, The Giggling Marlin and Happy Ending, cater to a younger crowd, whose idea of enjoyment often leads to a regretful next day.

Felipe chose a safe haven, early this afternoon. Locanda Paola was an Italian fusion restaurant, that offered us some privacy.

Greeted by a Maitre'd, that Felipe obviously knew well; we were seated in a seclude area, although it was still early in the afternoon, and rather quiet. Only a few business people, who were finishing a late lunch were here.

" I hope that by revealing that Mr. Powers participated in some unorthodox rituals, many years ago, will not make you think any less of him, or of me for that matter." Felipe said in a low tone.

" Do not worry about Mr. Powers reputation with me, Felipe. He and I have been very close friends, (*intimate lovers I wanted to add, but thought it would be inappropriate*) for many years. We all have skeletons rattling in our closets that we prefer would stay locked ." I said earnestly.

"Exactly, Senora Gabby! And, not only was this so very long ago, I think as many as forty three years, but the circumstances surrounding his decision was also quite tragic."

Felipe replied while pursuing the quite lengthy menu.

I was taken back for a few moments when Felipe used the words tragic. Could whatever happened to Sterling forty three years ago be responsible for his emotional deficiency? I was eager to hear more about this from Felipe, but I would avoid being obvious. If in the conversation, he elaborates on this tragedy, I will try not to act surprised.

Felipe ordered a house speciality, called chicken fajita pizza, that we shared with a local bottle of Chianti.

" To fully understand why the occult is practiced often in my country, you must understand that there are many injustices, and impurities. This is a major reason why Santa Muerta is accepted." Felipe said honestly.

"I am unfamiliar with this Saint. Is she exclusively worshiped in Mexico?" I asked, confused.

Felipe shook his head and clarified that,

"Nuesto Senora de la Santa Muerte, her full name, translated in English means, Our Lady of Holy Death. She is the personification of death. Although most of her followers are from Mexico, many in the Southwestern United States are familiar with this deity. She is associated with healing, protection, and safe delivery to the afterlife.

Those people who have recently lost a loved one will often seek a Christ Doctor, also known as a Shaman. Salvador, a very well known Shaman, is who Mr. Powers found. I am not certain if the ritual was performed in Veracruz or in Todos Santos . The intention of both are to seek dead spirits, bringing them to life for a short period of time so that their loved ones could seek advise or be consoled.

I myself have participated in this Mayan custom several times, and it is exhausting as well as exhilarating." Felipe said intensely.

"And, Felipe, you say Mr. Powers participated also at least twice that you recall? "

Felipe shook his head yes.

"And, do you know what would make Mr. Powers wish to seek this Shaman?" I finally asked the inevitable question.

Felipe looked at me with deep sorrow in his eyes.

"Mr. Powers was seeking answers and peace. Both times he only wanted one more chance to hold these two women that he loved the most, and were taken from him unexpectedly.

Those of us who knew about these tragedies tried with all our hearts and souls to comfort this pitiful man, whose grief had left him shallow. It was truly painful to watch.

The rituals brought Mr. Powers back to the living world, but Santa Murrieta took pieces of his heart both times." Felipe was obviously

191

becoming emotional.

"Who were these two women in Mr. Powers life that he lost so tragically?" I asked sincerely.

" They were his Madre, (mother) seven years ago, and his esposa (wife) and unborn Bebe (baby) on New Year's Eve, 1967."

Felipe crossed himself and said, what I thought was a prayer very quietly.

Not only was I shocked, that Sterling Powers was once married and lost a child, but that he lost both of them on that same New Year's Eve when my life began evaporating. Could all of this really be only a coincidence? It was too much for me to digest at once. The only thing on my mind at this moment was a verse: He heals the broken hearted and binds up their wounds. Psalm 147:3.

CHAPTER 33

By my soul, I can neither eat, drink, nor sleep, what still worse, is love any woman in the world but her.
  Samuel Richardson

Gisselle Marcellas
 Sterling Powers,
Lexington, Kentucky
1967

Cacias, Portugal is a former fishing village that later became a popular resort to early twentieth century nobleman. Today it is a quaint, cosmopolitan town with pedestrian streets, fashionable shops and trendy restaurants.

On October 25, 1949, Bridget and Atillo Marcellas, welcomed their first and only child, Gisselle to their world.

Bridget owned a very popular clothing boutique, and Atillo, was a well respected attorney, who had offices in Lisbon and downtown Casias.

Leonora, Bridget's mother, had moved from Lisbon to help raise her granddaughter, Gisselle. Living with ano, (grandmother) resulted in Gisselle being home taught until the age of eight . By that time Leonora began to show early signs of dementia.

When Gisselle was enrolled in the all private girls academy at nine years old, she was so advanced in all subjects that the head mistress promoted her to the Basic third level of education which is for children ages twelve to fifteen. By the age of sixteen, Gisselle was attending Lisbon University.

As early as thirteen years old, Bridget introduced her daughter to the most exclusive fashions shows in the world. At the end of January and the middle of July, while school was at recess, Gisselle and Bridget would attend The Mercedes-Benz Fashion Week in Madrid.

With her long legs, slim frame, and exotic features, Gisselle was approached on several occasions by top model agents representing such companies as, Christian Dior, Ralph Lauren , and Calvin Klein. Each time, she was very flattered by the impressive offers, but graciously declined. She already had another agenda for her life.

When Ano Lenora passed away, too early in life, from Alzheimer's disease, Gisselle was determined to study the psychological methods available that could prevent this progressive neurocognitive disease.

Once she entered Lisbon University , Gisselle pursued the possibility of studying in the United States with a student visa. There she would major in clinical psychology.

It was not until her second year in college that she was awarded a scholarship to the University of Kentucky, in a city called Lexington. Neither her mother or father were thrilled about this news.

"I am sorry that the two people I love most in this world cannot be happy for me. This is my dream come true. I must pursue this dream." Gisselle insisted to her parents.

"It is not that we don't support you Gisselle. You are only seventeen years old. Why must you travel four thousand miles away to follow your dream?" Atillo pleaded with his daughter.

"It has always been my desire to study in America. Once I have my degree, I will return home, hopefully a more enlightened person. I know that in your heart, Papa this is also what you want for me."

Gisselle presented her closing argument eloquently.

Both Bridget and Atillo finally, although reluctantly, agreed to allow Gisselle to accept the scholarship to Kentucky University.

By July of 1967, Gisselle was unpacking her suitcase at the Sigma Lambda Beta Sorority House. Because she was entering as a second year international student, she was allowed, even at seventeen, to live in the sorority house.

Sigma Lambda Beta strives to become instrumental in providing all women the ability of empowerment. This year the funds raised from the annual fashion show would benefit local women's shelters.

Gisselle found it not only ironic, but amusing, that she traveled halfway across the world to get away from the haute couture fashion world, only to be asked to "strut her stuff" on a makeshift catwalk in front of a group of horny males, that would contribute donations to empower women.

"Doesn't anyone else on this committee find this parading in provocative costumes just a bit degrading?"

Gisselle brought this up at the latest meeting.

"We all know that this is new to you Gisselle, but let me assure you, that first of all this show is traditional. The Sorority has been hosting the fashion show for decades.

And, it is not only attended by men, it is also advertised thoroughly to all women in Lexington. Last year there were over two hundred people, and we raised $10,000." Annabelle Jackson, the Sorority President stated proudly.

Everyone in the room waited to hear if Gisselle would participate. There was no doubt that she would draw the most attention to the fundraiser. The Publicity Chairman, Riley Richardson was already planning on using Gisselle's photograph on all the posters.

Gisselle felt the pressure of being obligated to assist in this fundraising event.

"Very well, I agree to model the fashions that are donated, but, it will be my final approval of the items. No bikini's and no lingerie." Gisselle insisted.

Although there were a few sighs of disappointment, other Sorority Sisters agreed that there should be a standard of decency followed.

The fashion show committee decided that they would honor

Lady Duff Gordon, a pioneer icon, that initiated the seasonal and media driven presentations that are popular today.

The title of this year's fashion show would be "Love in a Mist" and feature well known traditional gowns, such as those inspired for **Gone with the Wind, The King and I, My Fair Lady,** and **Gigi.** These would all be authentic replicas donated by the Museum of Fashion in New York City.

They would also present modern evening gowns, wedding gowns, and appropriate cruising attire.

One week prior to the well publicized Sigma Lambda Beta "Love in the Mist" Annual Fashion Show, five hundred tickets at twenty dollars each had been sold. An all time record.

On campus this was the most anticipated event, besides football and basketball.

Everyone was anxious to see who the Portuguese Cover Girl was in person. Gisselle's photo on flyers and posters plastered everywhere, resulted in her dressing incognito during classes. Most of the time she would wear black rimmed glasses, oversized T shirts, and a baseball cap. Luckily the poster did not include her name.

Due to the unanticipated amount of tickets purchased, the committee had to move the original location on campus, to the Crystal Ballroom, at The Brown Hotel. On the day of the event there were no open seats available.

Sitting nearest the runway, with a group of University of Kentucky basketball players, was Sterling Powers, a senior this year. According to reliable sources, he was soon to be recruited to The Colonials pro basketball franchise.

This was really not Sterling's ideal way to spend a typical Saturday night. Since he rarely dated, most of his time was studying, or in the gym practicing. However, most of the team talked him into buying a ticket to this event and just sit back and enjoy the eye candy.

So, reluctantly Sterling agreed, mostly because he thought that the fundraiser was supporting a worthwhile cause.

Once everyone was seated, the lights dimmed and a spotlight focused on the emcee, a popular young Economic Professor, Joseph Campbell. After a few minutes of reading some historical background on the gowns in the first group, he introduced Abigail Prescott, who would be describing each gown that the models were wearing.

"In addition to having the privilege to view some priceless historical gowns from classic motion pictures, tonight as a bonus you will find sheets of paper in the center of each table. Listed are the names of ten gowns. The models for these gowns have agreed to accompany the person who wins the bid for the "Love in a Mist" event prize.

Each prize, as you will see on the form, ranges from lunches and dinners at exclusive, well known restaurants or gourmet picnic lunches followed by an evening at the theatre, Jazz Club, or two tickets for a sports event.

The starting bids are $100 for each prize. Once you choose which model and event you want to bid on, please insert the bid in the proper labeled box, with your bid, on the back table nearest the bar.

Thirty minutes after the conclusion of the fashion show, we will announce the winning bid. All ten gowns, worn by the models to be auctioned, will be on the runway before intermission, allowing everyone plenty of time to bid.

Bidding closes at the beginning of the second half of our show. Good luck to all who participate, and we hope you enjoy our show tonight."

Abigail finished her announcement, returned to her seat, and began describing the gowns.

Gisselle had reluctantly agreed to the silent auction, at the last moment when one of the Sorority Sisters came up with the "brilliant idea". The exception was, if Gisselle did not approve of the "date" the committee would refund the winners money.

"Sorry ladies, but if some sixty year-old codger wins the bid, or somebody that has a criminal record I refuse to go."

Gisselle said unequivocally. And, there was nobody that objected.

The University of Kentucky basketball squad all participated in the silent auction. Most knew immediately who the models were and made their bids before the last gown walked down the catwalk.

Sterling was the only one that refused to play the "ridiculous" game. And then his eyes fixated on the final model.

When Gisselle stepped out dressed in a gown from the hit musical, **Gigi**, Sterling was unable to take his eyes off her. She was at least five feet ten inches tall, with the darkest black ebony hair that flowed like cold molten lava, straight to the middle of her back.

What Sterling noticed first were her eyes, only for a brief moment. This mystery lady's eyes were that rarest color known as Heterochromia.

The left eye was a ice blue, while the right eye was lavender. Both eyes were staring at him this very moment with such heat that he could feel his body's temperature rise instantly.

Once she graciously turned and walked back on the runway, she briefly stopped, looked backward and their eyes locked at the same moment, and they were all alone.

The next thing that he remembers, is Abigail announcing intermission. Sterling grabbed the final bidding form that was left on their table and wrote an amount. When he rose to deposit the form in the box labeled number ten, his legs began to nervously twitch.

At the end of the evening, just as promised, the names of the winners and bid amounts were all announced.

Abigail finally read the results for the tenth box. Sterling was beginning to feel the beads of sweat forming above his lip.

" And the final winner for a picnic lunch, followed by an evening of Jazz, theater, or sports event, is won by...

CHAPTER 33

Fortunes a right whore: if she gives aught, she deals in small parcels,
That she may take away all at one swoop.
John Webster

Gisselle and Sterling
July, 1967
Lexington, Kentucky

Before Sterling could even comprehend what happened, all the guys
were doing a celebration dance, and jumping in circles around him.

Then Micheal started yelling,

" Man...You're the most lucky son of a bitch that I have ever
known."

Sterling was still in a daze. Everything surrounding him was
moving in slow motion. Then he flashed back to a few moments ago,
when Abigail announced the winner of the final prize.

"And... the winner is..." She looked totally shocked.

"Okay, the winner is our own model, Gisselle Marcellas, with a
bid of $1000."

When Gisselle, walked from the stage toward Abigail, she was
handed the envelope. The audience was still slightly confused. Then
Gisselle removed a pen from her small purse, and wrote something
on the envelope.

Now , dressed in a low cut, off the shoulder bodice, tight fitting
wedding gown, Gisselle glided over to Sterling and handed him the
envelope, before walking back upstage, behind the curtain.

The final thing that Sterling remembers, is the crowd behind him
cheering, just like when he is on the basketball courts.

"Gisselle," Abigail stopped her as she was going to the changing rooms.

"When did you have time during intermission to vote for yourself ?" Abigail asked, truly confused.

Gisselle, just smiled, like she knew how the canary was able to swallow the cat.

"I didn't." Was all she said, while she continued to remove her makeup.

Back outside the hotel, Sterling waited patiently, leaning casually on a lamp post, chewing nervously on a toothpick.

Minutes later, Gisselle was walking toward him in a trendy, London Fog trench coat. He spit out the toothpick and walked toward her. They both stopped, only inches from touching one another.

Sterling made the first move, by extending his right arm to shake her hand.

"I am so glad to finally meet you, Gisselle. My name is Sterling Powers." He said, finally relaxed and comfortable.

Gisselle accepted his extended hand, and drew herself as close as possible to his chest. With her spiked heels, she was just tall enough to reach his mouth. Without taking her eyes off of Sterling her tongue entered his mouth knowing exactly where it belonged.

"I just have one question, Mr. Powers. When you put my name in as the winner of the auction, how did you know that I would pick you?" Gisselle smiled coyly.

"I didn't know. But, the odds are always in my favor when I gamble." Sterling said confidently.

After, a few more moments of passionate kissing under the lamppost, not caring who saw them, they broke apart. Sterling did not want this to end, but he also wanted to learn more about this provocative young lady.

He decided to take Gisselle to an intimate bar around the corner from his apartment. Sterling had no way of knowing that Gisselle was only seventeen. He ordered a beer, and she ordered the only alcohol that she ever saw her father drink, a Bombay Martini with three olives.

The conversation was relaxed and friendly. Sterling explained that he was on a basketball scholarship, his senior year, majoring in economics with a minor in psychology. His dream job was running a nonprofit charitable organization.

Gisselle shared her obsession with psychology, and that her mother was an attorney, and that her father owned a very lucrative fashion boutique. Sterling thought that was odd, but ignored it.

However, after finishing her third martini, when Giselle attempted to stand up from the bar stool, the room began to spin. Sterling left eighty dollars on the bar, and began to lead Gisselle out, cautiously through the front door.

Once on the street, in the fresh air, Gisselle started to gain her composure. Then without any warning, she broke away, braced herself on a brick flower planter and began to heave. Sterling bent down next to her, pulled back her long hair, and wiped her drooling mouth with his linen handkerchief.

Thankfully, his apartment was the next block and one flight upstairs. Once inside, he went directly to the bedroom, removed her clothing, put a clean buttoned blue shirt on her, and laid her on the king sized bed.

Once he was satisfied that she was sleeping, Sterling brought from the kitchen a cold glass of water, and a wet face cloth to place on her neck.

The remainder of the night he sat vigil in a chair next to her, occasionally moving her hair away from her angelic face.

Finally, before he fell asleep, he took one final look at his guest. Her face, in the moonlight looked like it was polished alabaster, perfectly chiseled with cherubic features. He was not sure how, but he knew at that very moment, that Gisselle would be his wife and the mother of his children.

After that fateful evening, Sterling and Gisselle spent every free moment together. In October, they drove to Akron, Ohio where Sterling introduced Gisselle to the other "love of his life". Celeste was thrilled to see her son so happy. A few weeks later, for Celeste's birthday, he took her to see a rock concert, by a new group that called themselves, *Chicago*.

Once back at the apartment he gave Gisselle her birthday gift. When she opened it, she found a framed picture of a star map, that represented the solar system on the day they met. Below was a caricature drawing that, Sterling asked an artist friend to create. It was a picture of Gisselle on a balcony, looking down at Sterling on one knee yelling loudly "Will you marry me?"

And, Gisselle holding a large poster, with the words "Yes".

It took Gisselle a few moments to connect the dots. By that time Sterling opened up the Tiffany ring box, and put the three carat pear shaped diamond on her finger.

"Please, Gisselle. Say YES! I cannot live another day without you."

Gisselle said yes many times between many kisses. That night, the two never slept. Sterling could not stop making love to the only woman that made him complete.

Although, Gisselle was a virgin, after the initial rupture, she instinctively moved in a variety of sexual positions. Sterling could not have enough of her. The more she gave, the more he needed.

When he plunged himself deep inside of her, he no longer was alone, he was part of her. Celeste had never known how much of herself she was willing to give until this moment. Sterling became her reason to breathe, eat, and live. Never again would she need anyone, but him.

One week before the Thanksgiving holiday, Sterling and Gisselle found a local preacher in the Appalachian Mountains that married them. Gisselle was eighteen years old, madly in love, and two months pregnant. She did not tell Sterling until she could confirm it.

On December 7, 1967 Gisselle kept her early morning appointment with an OBGYN doctor that a Sorority Sister highly recommended. Three days later the doctor's office called the Sorority House and left a message that it was urgent that Gisselle immediately come to the hospital and meet with Dr. Porter.

Although, Gisselle followed the instructions she assumed that the news would just confirm her pregnancy. Once Gisselle arrived, the nurse led her directly into Dr. Porters office.

"Gisselle, I am Dr. Porter. Your OBGYN, Dr. Mason referred your case to me. I specialize in advanced stages of cancer."

"Excuse me, Dr. Porter, you must have the wrong patient. I am pregnant. I am certain of this. Did Dr. Mason provide you with my test results?"

Gisselle wanted to set all of this straight. All she wanted to know, was that her baby was healthy and when the due date would be. She was planning on surprising Sterling tonight with the news.

"Unfortunately, Gisselle, you are two months pregnant. But what the tests that Dr. Mason ran also confirmed was advanced stages of uterus cancer. It is beyond our ability to cure you. However, we can make you comfortable, with very little pain."

Gisselle heard nothing further. This doctor just told her she would die in a very short amount of time. There was nothing left. She had to leave Kentucky, NOW.

Without even returning to the House, Gisselle took a taxi directly to the CVG (Cincinnati/Northern Kentucky Airport) booked a direct flight to Portugal and was home by the following afternoon.

When Sterling could not find Gisselle, he nearly went crazy. They had decided not to move into his apartment until the semester was over.

When he went to the Sorority House, all that they could tell him was that she had a doctor's appointment. By that time Dr. Porter was unavailable until the following morning.

The next day, Sterling was at the hospital by six AM, the time he was told Dr. Porter arrived for hospital rounds.

When Dr. Porter reluctantly agreed to meet with Sterling he made it clear that he could not divulge any personal information that was client privileged.

Sterling presented him with the marriage certificate and demanded to know where his wife was.

"I am very sorry that you need to hear this news from me, but your wife has final stages of uterine cancer. But, where she went when she left this office yesterday, I have no idea."

Sterling had to control every muscle in his body, to prevent from strangling this obnoxious son of a bitch. But, he knew that this would not help him find Gisselle.

When he returned to his apartment, he began to reconstruct all the conversations that Gisselle and he had about her family. They were planning to visit next spring after classes were dismissed.

Sterling then contacted a close friend of his mother, who was an attorney. Perhaps he could locate Gisselle's father, who was a reputable attorney in Portugal.

Within three hours, Sterling knew the address where Gisselle lived and he had booked his flight for the following evening.

Sterling was not certain what he would do once he was reunited with Gisselle, but whatever her diagnosis was, however long they had left together, they would use every minute.

When Sterling arrived at the Marcellas home in Casias, Gisselle immediately ran into his arms, trembling uncontrollably.

"Please, Sterling don't hate me. I was protecting you. With me your life would be nothing but a burden during my final days." Giselle was gasping for air between words.

Sterling refused to let her go, until she finally regained some normalcy.

"Gisselle, you are my life. When your time nears, I will be with you until your last breath. And when you are gone, I will continue, but I will be a hollow man, and nobody will ever be able to fill the spaces that remain." Sterling lifted her in his arms and cradled her like a wounded creature .

Atillio and Bridget Marcellas welcomed their new son into their home. They knew that the following holiday weeks would require all of them to be strong for each other.

Although Giselle had suddenly lost a tremendous amount of weight, and she was fatigued, there was enough strength to participate in the traditional holiday gatherings, just for shorter durations.

Father Christmas, or Pai Natal brings gifts to children on Christmas Eve. Since there was no one in the Marcellas home that felt the spirit of this tradition, it was Gisselle who insisted that her parents and Sterling shop for gifts that would be donated to shelters and orphanages.

"For the sake of my unborn child, who will be with Jesus Christ before walking one day on this earth, I am begging you to forget the next few weeks about my illness and provide joy to those who have none." Gisselle said with conviction.

Being home during the holidays, and having Sterling near her, made accepting death not easier but, acceptable. Gisselle had a sense of inner peace and appreciation as she participated in the Missa do Galo, or translated, the Mass of the Rooster Service.

During this service, parishioners queue to kiss the image of baby Jesus. Later the entire family returns home for an elaborate turkey dinner, fried cookies, Lampreia de ovos, sugary egg yolks made into the shape of a fish.

There is something surrealistic about knowing that everything you experience now, will be your final time. Sterling some times needed to go on isolated walks in the nearby forest, and just find a place to sit and weep uncontrollably. He was not certain , once the end was here, how he could continue to live without Gisselle.

Three days after Christmas, after a visiting doctor did a house call, the family was alerted that the end could come at any moment. They should take this time to prepare for the passing.

Bridget and Atillo spent their days and hours praying at the church. In the evening, Sterling would take his walks and allow the Marcellas to spend whatever time they needed with their only daughter.

On New Year's Eve, 1967 at four o'clock in the afternoon, Gisselle asked Sterling to move into the bed with her.

"Oh, baby, I don't want to hurt you. I am so much larger and clumsy."

Sterling said, trying to keep his tears from flowing.

Gisselle, reached her hand out to him. "Do you really believe Sterling that there is anything that you could possibly do to hurt me now?" She said smiling.

Sterling then managed to lie as close as possible to his wife's frail body, that he worshiped as much as the very first night they made love.

"Do you know what my last dying wish is, my darling?" Gisselle whispered into Sterling's ear.

"It is to feel you one last time; to be one with me. I want to feel your juices flow through my body and heal all the pain that I have. Do you think that would maybe be possible?" Gisselle said softly.

Sterling then carefully rose from the bed, walked over to the door and locked it. When he returned to the bed, Gisselle spread her legs and Sterling entered her body for the very last time.

Together, they felt the fluids pass through one another. Gisselle, held on to her husband's arms for as long as possible. When Sterling felt her hand release him, he pulled himself out and kissed Gisselle on the mouth praying that his breath would somehow right this wrong. Her last words were,

"Live, and love again my darling. Celebrate us, and death will have lost this battle."

And, it was finally over. All that was left was a Wasteland, where *a woman drew her long black hair out tight/ And fiddled whisper music on those strings/And bats with baby faces in the violet light/ Whistled and beat their wings/And crawled head downward down a blackened wall/And upside down in air were towers/ Tolling reminiscent bells, that keep the hours/ And voices singing out of empty cisterns and exhausted wells.* TS Eliot

CHAPTER 34

Come back. Even as a shadow, even as a dream.
   Euripides

   Gabby and Sterling
   August, 2010
   Cabo San Lucas, Mexico

The two weeks that we spent at Cortez Pedregal, I saw Sterling twice. When he declared that he didn't want to "mingle" with people, while he was here, I never really took that to be literal.

My interpretation was, that our visits would be limited to an occasional meal together. But, no, Sterling was as invisible as a distant memory.

   After my lunch with Felipe, nearly a week ago, I could not stop thinking of Sterling's wife. And, perhaps as disturbing to me was the date that she died.

   I was trying to recall how much I revealed to Sterling about my relationship with Jake. I remember that on the evening that we met, September 10, 1989, Jake was still alive, and Alex and I had been married for twenty years.

   With all of these statistics running through my head, I could only surmise that if I spoke to Sterling at all about Jake it would have been only about our early years together, and maybe that he married Isabella. But, then again neither of us talked much about our past.

   After Jake's funeral in 2001, I must have shared my feelings with Sterling. But, there is no doubt that I never went into any details about Caden and I.

   If I would be able, to get Sterling to discuss his wife and child, it would be a major accomplishment. I already knew that Sterling and his mother were extremely close, and it makes sense now, since she is no longer alive, that he named the foundation, Celeste Powers.

During the twelve years that Sterling and I were lovers, there was an unspoken rule, that neither of us would divulge any personal information, unless we wanted to. It was also, clearly understood, that to avoid any emotional attachment; I would never expect Sterling to show any signs of empathy.

"If you want to pour your heart out Gabby, about how miserable you are with Alex, and how neglected you feel, I will be a good listening post. However, if you then expect me to offer you a solution, beyond sex, I will honestly tell you right now that it won't happen."

Sterling was very adamant about this condition.

During the entire relationship, through many years together, Sterling treated me with tremendous affection. I never felt a lack of attention, physically or emotionally. Although, love was never mentioned.

When we went our separate ways at the end of our tryst, there were no promises by either one of us, that we would ever meet again. No false promises ever made. The anticipation for our next rendezvous, made each moment together seem like the first.

At the very beginning, there was an invisible line that set the boundaries. And, because Sterling was extremely attentive when we were together, obviously capable financially to provide exotic and thrilling adventures, there was really nothing to complain about.

The lack of commitment, did not seem to be an unreasonable request, considering that we both were equally happy with this situation.

After the Halloween fiasco, nine years ago, it was I that chose to end the relationship. Mostly this was because now Jake's journals, that I acquired on my whirlwind, exotic trip through Europe. It is odd, but after that trip I felt more guilty pursuing the relationship with Sterling than cheating on my husband . When I made the decision to stop seeing Sterling, I was fairly sure, it would be nothing more to him than any other financial business transaction.

Eventually he would replace me with another companion. Not too much different than selecting another employee for his company.

We remained distant friends. Nevertheless, when I felt desperate on that beach on Tybee Island, I knew that I could still count on Sterling to save me.

The really unsolved puzzle, was how, after nine years of living our separate lives, did Sterling evolve from the Iceman, to a saint? Everyone that knows him recently, has referred to him as their Padre, Messiah, or Savior.

It is clear that Sterling has touched a vast amount of people with more than just financial assistance. The Mexican communities that I have visited, are careful not to reveal much, when asked how their lives have changed, but on several occasions, a few would share that their respect for Mr. Powers. Most conclude that this compassion is a result of his grief and agony. His ability to share their pain makes Sterling authentic.

However an outside billionaire has been able to bond with the Mexican community, is locked somewhere in Sterling's clandestine past.

I am beyond merely curious now, I am determined to learn what those secrets are. If Sterling has really changed this drastically, then anything that I can emulate gives me hope for realistic changes.

Perhaps, some of these answers will come to light once I complete reading the binder Sterling left me, when we arrived, at Cabo.

The Art of Repairing Lost Souls seems like quite an ambitious task. I imagine, that if anyone has practical answers to repairing souls , they must have a direct line to Jesus Christ.

Abstract powers, are only found in Marvel comic books. However, since Sterling did give it to me, out of courtesy, I will at least read through the handbook.

The introduction, explains that there are various lessons contributed by a number of different authorities. The objective is not to select one over another, but to take the resources from all and apply them to particular situations.

Thus far, everything said makes sense and avoids favoring one method over another.

The first section explains how The Stephen Ministries, began in St. Louis, Missouri, in 1975 . It is a one on one carrying ministry, that never promises answers ; rather the caregiver provides strategies to help the care receiver to find their own answers. It is also, a non profit Christian educational organization.

The footnote here states: *If you are a Christian and/or an atheist, agnostic, or any other group that opposes Christianity, understand that it is the practices in each section, that our editor chose to study, not the religion.* An interesting disclaimer.

As I continue to flip through the section, a brief history about St. Stephen was also included. He was one of seven deacons appointed by the Apostles to distribute food and charitable contributions to those in the community that were in desperate need.

This original pastoral activity in the modern era has expanded to assisting individuals in need of personal attention.

Once a relationship is established with a person who is grieving for various reasons, the counselor provides comfort offered by sharing passages from literature, psychological studies, and religious doctrines. The objective is to establish hope. A very powerful word.

Wow! Did Sterling really believe that I was capable of reaching out to people in this way? I wasn't even sure if I believed in hope any longer.

Regardless, I would at least now be able to tactfully bring up the loss of his wife and child, without sounding like I was prying.

It was still early enough to ask Felipe to take me downtown, to buy a few items for our drive to Todos Santos.

Sterling had said, the last time we spoke, that Todos Santos was charming, but it lacked many conventional items that resort towns have easy access to.

Since, according to my calendar, our departure day would be tomorrow, I didn't want to leave without some personal hygiene items.

Wearing makeup in this hot weather, was restricted to only gala events or personal private gatherings. Recently, I found it quite comforting just wearing my hair up in a ponytail, or perhaps in a neat bun, with sunscreen and sandals.

Quite a contrast from a more formal appearance in Lexington, when I would always run into friends or Alex' associates.

Checking my phone for messages, before going downtown, I noticed a text from Sterling, sent a few hours ago.

Good morning, Gabby. Hoping that you have enjoyed your stay at Cortez Pedregal, these past few weeks.

(Stop)

Meet me for a farewell dinner at eight. We will be dining waterfront with the barracudas, J/K

Sterling

His text did not state if we were dining alone or with company. I checked my watch, and it was now four o'clock , plenty of time to finish my errands.

The drive downtown was slower than usual, since many people were leaving work, eager to get home.

While sitting in traffic, on the way back to the Villa, a modern, fairly nice sized playhouse, with a flashing neon sign, identified as The Gisselle Theater, caught my attention.

"Felipe? does that Gisselle playhouse offer stage productions?"

I asked, fairly confident that I had never noticed it before.

" Yes, of course. At the moment, however, it is closed because the actors are in rehearsals. I believe that the name of the original play that will be debuting next month is called, "Moments of Silence" by Maggie Mendoza."

Felipe said, looking in the rear view mirror for my reaction

I was trying to recall why that name was familiar . Then, just like a lightning bolt I remembered. Maggie Mendoza was the lady Sterling briefly told me about. Was she really a playwright? Now that would be impressive. I just came straight out and asked Felipe,

"Isn't Maggie Mendoza a friend of Mr. Powers that lives in Todos Santos ?" I was obviously slightly confused.

"Si..si. Maggie lives half the time in Todos and half the time in Cabo. She works for the institute. Maggie is a drama teacher, writer, and director. And, the Gisselle theater was bought by Mr. Powers for her to produce plays in Cabo. It is very popular. It is great entertainment."

Sterling bought Maggie her own theater, to produce her own plays? I definitely, cannot wait to meet this new love interest in Sterling's life.

As the traffic began to start moving again, Felipe added one more detail.

"Oh, and Senora Gabby…The Gisselle theater…it is named in honor of Senor Powers' wife."

CHAPTER 35

There are as many worlds as there are kinds of days, and as an opal changes it's colors and it's fire to match the nature of a day, so do I.
John Steinbeck

Gabby and Sterling
August, 2010
Last night in Cabo

Maggie, Gisselle, Celeste. What did they all have that Sterling felt the need to assure their legacy? Was I even a slight bit jealous? Maybe. But, I could not imagine why. I was never in love with Sterling. I mean, I did love him, but not in love , like I was with Jake and Caden, and even at one time with Alex. So...what was it that bothered me about these women? Then, at last I figured it out.

It was not jealousy, at all. It was more a sense of inadequacy; a feeling of hurt. After twelve years of spending countless hours with this man, some extremely intimate moments, Sterling chose to never share with me that he was once married, at an early age, had an unborn child and that they both died.

I could perhaps rationally accept if that death had been recent. But when we were together, it had already been twenty years since he lost them.

And, who is this Maggie Mendoza. Her own original plays are being produced in a "temple of honor" that Sterling built for "Gisselle."

Maggie of course, I can only assume has been told all the details.

I took one last look in the mirror, and realized, maybe for the first time, that I was no longer young.

There were a few age spots that I tried to cover with makeup. My roots were dyed every five weeks. Even my body, that I attempted to keep in condition, was beginning to show the typical signs of wear and tear.

Hopefully the kind candlelight on the outside deck will hide all of these imperfections. I am finally old enough to understand how Blanche DuBois, in "A Streetcar Named Desire" felt when she said ," *I don't want realism. I want magic. Yes, yes magic."*

Sterling was already seated at the table on the wharf, pensively looking out to sea. When he saw me approaching he stood up, and greeted me with a friendly smile.

"So glad that you could join me, Miss Gabriella Girard. You look absolutely stunning." Sterling said pulling out my chair.

I had been thinking for days how I would approach the subject of Sterlings life "BG,"(before Gabby). Finally, I concluded just let the conversation flow naturally and see what consciousness stream we discover.

"Thank you, Sterling. It is so nice that we can have our final dinner, in Cabo, here together. And, this spot is perfect." I said trying to be as polite as possible.

Sterling, broke apart some chunks of bread, and offered me the first choice to feed the fish. When I looked confused, he then stood up, close to the edge of the deck with his hand extended in front of him and within seconds a fish, that must have been several feet in length, rose to the occasion. With great finesse, it grabbed the bread from Sterling's hand.

This caught me by such surprise that I screamed, and then started cheering.

"That was just so perfect Sterling. I had no idea when you originally told me , how large these fish are." I said amused.

"They are definitely great performers. We don't want to give them too much though, because then they will start begging, like a dog. Come here and you can give the next one to Charley." Sterling said amused.

Standing next to Sterling, it was so obvious, that he was at least, one foot taller than me. When he extended his arm out to the fish, his feet were still a good distance from the edge of the deck.

Guiding me to where he was standing, Sterling handed me some bread and said,

"Ready? Now don't move. Stand very still. The fish will do all the work."

"I am not so sure about this Sterling. What if…"

And, before I had a chance to finish my sentence the fish was up in the air and I was lunging into the water.

At the very last second, I could feel Sterling's arms around my waist, pulling me toward him.

Once I was safe on the deck once again, Sterling started laughing,

"You don't have to perform tricks for your dinner, Gabby. You are my guest."

It took me a few moments to gain my composure and sit back at the table.

"If you have any other fun activities planned, Mr. Powers, I would prefer dry land." I said, trying to control myself.

The remainder of the evening, ironically, we dined on fresh caught salmon, lobster and crab. Thankfully the portions were small and succulent.

For dessert, the waiter brought out a tray with a portable oven, and prepared at our table, cherries jubilee flambé, served over vanilla ice cream.

"Now, I am going to introduce you Gabby, to a very complex after dinner drink that I discovered on a remote island in France. It is called China China Amer Bigallet. I find it quite amusing that it's name is China yet originated in France."

Sterling then poured me a generous cordial. The taste was a strange orange flavor, from the Dutch colony of Curaçao. The oranges are blended with anise, cinchona, gentian, clove and a few other spices. The flavor is definitely original, and the alcohol an effective addictive.

The evening was relaxing. Perhaps too relaxing. That drink that Sterling poured me, gave me the confidence to comfortably test uncharted waters.

"Today, on the way home from downtown, Felipe pointed out to me The Gisselle Theatre. He mentioned that Maggie Mendoza was producing a play that she wrote. Is she the same Maggie that you are eager to introduce me to, Sterling?"

I attempted to sound as natural as possible.

Sterling was a slightly annoyed that Felipe was discussing Maggie with Gabby but, he answered without hesitating . She was indeed the same young lady, but that was all he was going to divulge. He appeared amused how, I was still trying to get more information about his elusive female acquaintance.

"Tomorrow we leave for Todos Santos , Gabby. It is a fifty mile drive, no more than ninety minutes. You will just need to be patient until then."

Sterling said sipping his drink calmly.

Then, out of nowhere, perhaps it was the alcohol, I just came right out and said,

"And, how many more years will it take before you tell me about your wife, Gisselle?"

As fast as those words uncontrollably rolled of my tongue, I wanted to rewind what I said.

The color in Sterling's face, even by candlelight, turned grotesquely red. I had never seen him outraged before. And, I could tell when I saw his clenched fist, that it was taking all his will power, to control his reaction.

Suddenly his fist came down like a hammer. I jumped afraid that he might slap me next. And, maybe I deserved it. But, rather than displaying any further anger, Sterling stood up and said,

"NEVER, ask me again about Gisselle. Do you understand?" It

was more a demand than a question.

I shook my head and answered "yes" then waited, as he walked back to the villa alone, without saying another word. Once he was out of sight, I realized how out of place I was.

After a few moments of crying, I decided that the best approach was no approach. Like a well played chess game, it would be Sterling's move next.

CHAPTER 36

When one door closes, another opens; but we often look so long and so regretfully at the closed door, that we do not see the one which has opened for us.

Alexander Graham Bell

Gabby and Sterling
August, 2010
Todos Santos, Mexico

Back at my room after dinner, I packed my belongings. It wasn't much, thankfully , that I managed to accumulate in the last few months. Next, I prepared for bed.

Once the China, China wore off, the reality of how stupid I was, began to surface. I was not sure how long, if ever, it would take for Sterling to forgive me.

There was no doubt that I crossed his tolerance boundary, and it was my inappropriate curiosity that lead Sterling to react defensively.

What was I thinking? This man's personal life, past, present, and future, is not my business .

When I finally put my head on the pillow, I took a last glance at my cell phone for messages. There was one unread text from Caden.

When you arrive to Todos Santos give me a call. No need to text. I am in California. Same time zone.

(Stop)

I wasn't sure at this very moment how I felt about Caden being this close. Maybe, it was just that my mind was preoccupied.

Tomorrow is yet, another new move. Ninety minutes in a car, with someone who probably now regrets he ever met me, is difficult. I decided to deal later with everything, in good time.

After, a thankful, uneventful slumber, when I did wake up, I made certain that Sterling would not have to wait for me, like normal. It was a new morning, with the potential for being a good day.

I was hoping that by now, Sterling was at least beyond the malevolent fury stage he demonstrated last night.

Gypsies, I am certain travel less than I have. This will be my third move in five months, and still I am uncertain how long I will remain in Mexico.

On normal travel days, I would look forward to the scenery and the light conversations that Sterling and I would partake in.

Today, anticipating the silent treatment, I brought with me a book that I found about Todos Santos. It would entertain me for the duration of the short trip if necessary.

At ten o'clock sharp I was sitting outside on the rocking chair waiting for Sterling. Almost, as if we had synchronized our watches, that familiar canary yellow Hummer, that I had not seen since Ensenada, reappeared in front of me.

With the engine still running, Sterling put the Tank in park, and within seconds opened the passenger door for me, and placed my luggage in the back; without saying one word. However, once in the car, he did ask,

"Are you ready for the next big adventure?"

It was a question that broke the ice, but his tone remained fairly cool. After a few moments, I decided to make the plunge, hoping it was not filled with alligators.

Since Sterling was wearing his aviator glasses, it was impossible to determine what mood he was in.

"I began to read the binder you left for me, *The Art of Repairing Lost Souls.*"

I waited for a reaction. Sterling seemed to be calculating his response strategically to avoid any other questions like last night.

When he did respond his tone was official.

"The study was organized by a close friend, who spent several years blending many reputable programs into one that we have just started to work with. The most important element that we discovered, is establishing a definite trust base.

Without that trust, those who need help the most will not benefit from anything."

Now , Sterling's voice became serious, and he never took his eyes off the road.

Although I would never dare vocalize my thoughts, I was wondering if Sterling would ever trust anyone enough to help them mend his soul?

Since it appeared that we had reached the end of our conversation, I decided to begin reading about Todos Santos.

The mission at Todos Santos was founded by Father Jaime Bravo in 1723. Located across the street, from the small town plaza. Inside the mission is the statue of The Virgin of Pilar. This is another name for The Virgin Mary, and Todos Santos celebrates her spirit in the November festival.

Once the government paved Highway 19 in the mid 1980's, tourists would visit often to experience a rustic, authentic Mexican village, far enough away from the stressful modern civilization and yet close enough to return when they had recovered .

Today, it is an artist Mecca. Throughout the town there are various studios and handcrafted items for sale. The recent addition of upscale restaurants and boutique hotels have added another dimension to this region.

The Hotel California, is a favorite stop for many visitors, although the proprietors claim there is no connection to the famous Eagle's song. Nevertheless, the town hosts The Festival de Cine and The Todos Santos Music Festival.

The two points that caught my attention was, the Art Colony, which I was certain Molly was spiritually leading me to , and The Hotel California that still gave me goosebumps.

I could only imagine at night, driving down this highway, with the shadows at a distance, and the wrestling warm wind, carrying the smell of colitis for miles. This could make anyone's eyes grow heavy.

In The Eagles lyrics there also is an allusion to mission bells. From what I just read, the mission is near this Hotel California. Another coincidence? Maybe, but, if Sterling's friend, Eleanor Rigby welcomes me with candles in her hand, I might begin to feel a bit uneasy.

"You do understand , that I can tell you just about anything about Todos Santos that you want to know, Gabby. I have been coming here for nearly forty three years." Sterling's voice was back to being mellow.

I am not a math wizard but, I know that forty three years was the year Gisselle died, and the same year that my world stood still, as well. If only there was a way that Sterling would break those brick walls he built around himself, we might be able to comfort one another.

But, after last nights disaster, it will have to be him to initiate that healing process.

"Okay. Well I haven't started to read yet about the surfing and beaches. How far away from the town are they?"

I asked, trying to keep the communication moving in a positive direction.

"I thought we might stop for a light lunch at one of the best beaches, on the way to Todos Santos. It will give you an opportunity to get a preview of the unabridged version of Baja."

Sterling said, pulling off of the main highway on a dirt road, with only a small sign that read kilo 66. There was no doubt that after a few minutes on this road, that we were off the grid and headed towards the ocean. For the next few miles any view beyond dirt clouds was impossible.

Then without notice Sterling pulled the Hummer off the dirt road and parked.

"Playa Cerritos is a world of it's own Gabby. I tried to book the

Hacienda Cerritos, up there on the hill." Sterling pointed to the beautiful hotel built on the cliff above the Pacific Ocean.

"It is where luxury and bucolic intersect, creating the most ideal getaway. I understand that each room is designed with original features. Personally, I have only stayed at The Presidential Penthouse North suite.

I was impressed with the outstanding views, and that the suite included its own library. Which I must say, has a good variety of reading material. Unfortunately even Sterling Powers at times gets outbid. Perhaps another time." Sterling was almost back to himself.

"Anyway, it has four pools, and two that are infinity. Each of the ten bedrooms also have their own fireplaces. When I inquired about renting the entire hacienda, because as you know, I prefer privacy, I was told that this week there was a celebrity wedding party.

So unless you want to crash the reception, you will need to be satisfied viewing it from here, for now."

When Sterling handed me his high power binoculars, I felt like a paparazzi, invading the privacy of some couple who believed that they were safe from prying eyes.

"Oh, Sterling, look…the Hacienda even has a helicopter pad." I said impressed, but not anxious to ever personally use it.

"You may have noticed that every property that I select has one. That is primarily due to many visitors wanting to protect their anonymity." Sterling shared with me.

" Really? Are you now moving around in the same circles as Bond, the infamous 'James Bond'?"

It was the first time all morning that Sterling relaxed enough to laugh, just slightly.

We then continued a short distance to The Cerritos Beach Club. Since it was a Sunday, there was a plywood stage on the beach, where various local musicians would play contemporary jazz and classic rock and roll.

Occasionally these bands would include their own original

music. CD's were available at the bar for sale. This was as commercial as The Beach Club got.

The bartenders, waiters, and even the busboys, were dressed in Day of the Dead costumes, or at the very least, they had skeleton faces, painted in white, with top hats on their heads.

Although The Day of the Dead is celebrated officially on October 31, it is meant to celebrate the spirits of those descended. Cerritos Beach Club extends that celebration to daily commemorations.

Sitting outside, on the sand with the ocean as our background, I could see surfers dropping into perfect barrels.

"I bet that you would never guess, Sterling, that at one time, I was able to get barreled just like those surfers are right now." I said reminiscing.

"Nothing that you ever do Gabby surprises me." Sterling waited to continue after the waiter took our food order and brought us both salted glasses and a pitcher of Margaritas.

" Being encapsulated by a wave, searching for safety as you spin uncontrollably, and looking for that light at the end of the tunnel, is what makes me maneuver each wave with just the right amount of finesse.

And, when time actually stands still, a transcendental feeling moves me to another stage in life." Sterling's silver grey eyes were now animated . If he hadn't been with me all morning, I would have thought he had smoked some weed.

"I had no idea that you surfed, Sterling. When was the last time you were on the waves?"

I wanted to say, that this is another example of what you never shared with me. But, again I knew better this time.

"Well, Gabby, I never remember you ever mentioning that you once surfed either."He replied almost defensively, before he continued."The last time, I was on a wave, was right here on this beach, Los Cerritos, probably a year ago. I have a surf board at the beach house near Todos Santos."

He said while pouring more Margaritas for us both.

"You are in super good shape, but, the last time I surfed was at Tybee Beach when I was sixteen…" Then suddenly I just stopped in mid thought.

"What is it Gabby?" Sterling said a little concerned.

"Nothing really, I just remembered that it was Jake that pulled me out of the water when I lost my board and got tangled with seaweed…And, it was exactly that same place, where I was sitting, dripping wet, with a towel wrapped around my shoulders, right before I phoned you, Sterling."

He looked at me solemnly.

"One reason why I brought you here Gabby, is because there is something mystical that will allow you not only to heal, but to experience guidance. If you are open minded to some of these rituals that are available, I can promise that you will become self-actualized." Sterling said with determination .

He may have finally discovered how to remove the negative karma that was slowly tearing Gabby to pieces.

This is when I had no choice but to allude to his own dilemma.

"And, have these methods helped you to achieve tranquility, Sterling?" I asked cautiously.

"I know that it is hard for you to accept Gabby after last night, and I am not yet ready to reveal everything to you, but, yes… I am closer each day to contentment ."

He looked genuinely in my eyes, and I finally felt that one brick had been removed from the torment wall.

CHAPTER 37

How come when mortals want things, their only option is to make a deal with Hell and sell their soul? Why can't they make deals with God in exchange for good behavior?

Richelle Mead

Gabby, Maggie, and Sterling
August, 2010
Todos Santos, Mexico

"Welcome, Gabby, to The Hotel California!" Said Eleanor Rigby with a warm embrace.

" And, Senor Sterling, muy amigo…it has been too long since our last meeting. I hope that your stay this time will last a bit longer?" Eleanor's embrace was very reserved with Sterling, whereas mine was a very natural cuddle, warm hug.

I could only surmise that she knew Sterling well enough, to realize that although not technically Haphephqbiac , he avoids personal touching in public almost always.

Eleanor Rigby was an interesting replica of what I imagined Paul McCartney envisioned when he wrote the lyrics to his well known song.

Our Eleanor was pleasantly "fluffy" but, definitely not obese. Although she had a double chin, and laughing wrinkles, her smile was pleasing, and inviting, with a jovial reaction. Immediately I felt that we had somehow been close friends at another time.

"I hope to remain here for as long as it takes to find a suitable house to rent for Gabby, as well as review the progress we are making with the academic programs and the humanity workshops." Sterling's answer was to the point, and nothing more.

"I know of several nice beach houses available in El Pescadero, not far from your casa. The best one that you may want to visit soon, is called Casa Azul. It is located at San Pedrito, with a private path directly to the beach."

Eleanor said, while searching for a current photo, in the counter drawer.

" I know exactly where this house is located. If it is the same one that I remember, I believe you will find it perfect, Gabby." Sterling said. But, when he turned to give her more details she was no longer there.

Gabby had strolled outside to the adjacent courtyard. That was where several talkative parrots greeted her. Some in cages and some sitting on the open beams.

In 1972, while Alex and I were still pretending that we loved each other, I accompanied him to Orlando, Florida for a surgeon conference that was being held at the newly opened Disney World.

While he was at meetings, I spent my free time at the amusement park. Although everywhere I went was magical, once I found the Enchanted Tiki Room, it became my favorite attraction. I visited it each day while we were there for the week.

The animated parrots were fascinating, but nothing as spectacular as the real ones I was now admiring. There were two Blue and Gold Macaws that were extremely intelligent.

They appeared to be talking to each other, then every once and awhile I could recognize real words being used, like "silly guests", or "pretty girl".

Then from nowhere, I heard someone say, "Hello down there my pretty. My name is Jake."

It was so clear that I actually jumped slightly into the air. That was when I noticed Sterling was standing directly behind me. Then I looked up at a tree branch, and perched above was a superior looking African Grey Parrot.

"I should have warned you about Jake. He is the biggest flirt. He also has the intelligence of at least a five year old child. You can just imagine what kind of pranks he can get into."

Sterling, took my hand and led me back into the lobby. I chose not to remind him about the other Jake in my life.

"By the way, not to frighten you, but you should know, that many people here, in Todos Santos, believe that the parrots that live in Hotel California are spirits of the dead returning to a place where other ghosts reside." Sterling was whispering this in my ear.

"Okay, you may have been right about the name of the hotel, and Eleanor, but I refuse to accept that I am going to be sleeping with ghosts." I answered Sterling back.

I was trying not to think about my brief encounter with Fatima at the Tijuana border, or the dream girl that made me the dandelion wreath, or even Jake's journal entry on spiritual revelations, but I kind of knew that it was going to be a very long night in this hotel. I was looking forward to checking out of the Hotel California, even before I officially checked in.

Eleanor handed me the keys to the only Penthouse room in the hotel, and Sterling acted as my Bell Boy. A rather interesting role for such a VIP.

"There are only eleven rooms in the hotel, and during the week, they are understaffed. Since I know where your room is, and you might have to wait for many hours for your luggage, I told Eleanor I would be your escort."

Sterling was leading the way to a very compact elevator, that barely fit us both, and the luggage.

When I opened the door to the suite, I noticed a king size bed, one single bed and a huge private patio with an excellent ocean view.

"In the early evening you will be able to hear the guitar players and maybe even the mariachis serenading."

Sterling walked out to the balcony which had several large chairs, patio table and chaise lounges . It was obvious that this outer area was used to entertain guests.

"Any reason for having the extra bed?" I asked curiously.

"Oh…yes, of course. It is for your personal ghost. Every room has one, so they won't disturb the guests at night." Sterling said seriously.

I picked up the nearest pillow and threw it at him. He of course, the basketball pro, had no problem catching the pillow in midair.

"Not funny, Sterling. By the way, where will you be staying? Since I have the Penthouse and the ghost has claims on the extra bed?" I asked coyly.

" I will be at my beach house. It is a few miles from here. Nothing elaborate. Three bedrooms, very quaint. Remember me saying that Todos Santos would be a drastic change from the other properties. For me, it is the perfect sanctuary. I come here as often as possible and stay as long as practical. I thought that this would be more comfortable for you for now.

It will give you the opportunity to explore the town and visit with the locals." Sterling walked out once again to the sunny patio.

I began to unpack my limited belongings and asked,

" How long do you think I will be here, before I am in my own house?"

" I have several people working on it. Maybe even by tomorrow afternoon, there will be a few properties for you to look at. And, I want to introduce you to the staff that operates The Celeste Powers Academy.

It is the prototype that we use in other cities. It has been operating successfully for the past eight years."

It was obvious that Sterling was proud of this accomplishment.

"Is the academy a private school? And, are all subjects taught?" I was now beginning to show genuine interest. I always regretted never having the opportunity to teach Literature in college. Maybe here I could fulfill that desire.

"Yes, and No. The academy is privately funded, but it is

accessible to any child from the age of eight to eighteen. They are required to stay in the dorms, but their parents are welcome to visit at any time.

We have found through our own learning process, that when students are offered traditional classroom structure, from eight in the morning, to three in the afternoon, their absences prevent their progress.

Lack of a proper diet also contributes to academic failure. Once we were able to control their living environment, offer them three nutritious meals a day, and safe housing , each student became successful. How many public schools can you think of that can meet our one hundred percent success results?"

Sterling took much pride in these statistics .

"How many students are living in the dorms, and how many teachers are on your staff?" I asked, impressed with those statistics.

This part of the foundation was particularly interesting to me.

"Currently, I believe there are about fifty students, more girls than boys. We have hired five local residents to manage the dormitory, and there are currently ten teachers. We recruited most from Mexico City, but there are two retired teachers from California that chose to join our team. "

Sterling continued to explain that once the students graduate from the Academy, they are offered the opportunity to become skilled laborers, or attend the University Academies in Cabo or Ensenada.

This was a very impressive undertaking that, Sterling had dedicated the last seven years of his life to.

"So, Gabby, are you prepared to visit some of these classes? I am hoping that with your extensive literature expertise, that you might enjoy preparing some curriculum for our Humanities Department."

Sterling finally stated what he was implying for several months.

"Well, I am sincerely honored that you believe that I somehow am capable of working on this ambitious undertaking, but I have never had any training as a teacher. My literature experience has always been as a student." I said reluctantly.

"But, that is exactly what we need. These students are excited about learning, and I know that you could make them excited about literature. I have seen how you take the classics, and make it relevant. There is nobody here that has that talent."

Sterling was using his best negotiating tactics to convince me to accept.

"I will carefully consider everything and once I have a chance to observe the classes, I will be in a better position to make a decision." I said tactfully.

" That sounds like a very wise choice . I have made dinner reservations at La Casita Tapas & Wine Bar. Because The Hotel California is so centrally located, we will be able to take a leisurely walk and have plenty of time. Will an hour be sufficient for you? I have a few things that I want to check out. Meeting downstairs in the lobby seems like the best place." Sterling was almost out the door, when I asked,

"What is the dress code at this restaurant?"

"Casual. Wear anything comfortable. Adios!"

And he was gone.

I planned on picking up a few resort style outfits while I was at Cabo, but spent most of my time enjoying the Villa. So, now, I hope my jeans, pastel gauze blouse, and a versatile jacket will be appropriate. Too late now to second guess.

I checked my cell phone, to make sure I was not late. Then walked past the elevator toward a lovely winding staircase, that looked like it belonged on the Casablanca movie set.

As I carefully maneuvered myself down one step at a time, I noticed several other people gathered around the patio bar.

Once in the lobby, I weaved through the small crowd, to where I recognized Sterling dressed in a mint linen shirt and cream colored linen pants. Perfectly matched as usual.

As I approached, I noticed him in a conversation with a young

Mexican girl, in her late twenties. Her long dark hair was perfectly styled in a French Braid with red ribbons interlaced that matched her scarlet red elegant dress.

When Sterling turned towards me, he guided me past a few others, and I was now only a few inches away from the lady in red.

"Gabriella Girard, I would like you to meet, Maggie Mendoza." He said, stepping back watching each women's reaction. He had been waiting for this reunion for nine years.

Our eyes met before our hands. When we touched it was as if an electric current was flowing from each of our bodies. Both of us, at the same time, could see the past, and future flash so fast that there was no chance to react.

Maggie Mendoza and Gabriella Girard, unconsciously, just shared a moment in a parallel universe.

CHAPTER 38

This must be what a parallel universe looks like. Everything looked the same but I suddenly felt like it wasn't. Like everything had been taken apart, brick by brick, flower bed by flower bed, and put back in the wrong order. Just like me.
    Jordanna Fraibergberg

Gabby, Maggie and Sterling
August, 2010
Todos Santos, Mexico

When Alice went through the looking glass, and then returned, was it really the same Alice? Sorcerers are somehow able to illuminate other worlds that invite fantasies to escape the subliminal and enter into a conscious twin existence.

For that very brief moment, I was my own ghost standing in front of myself, just like everything that Jake had spent months writing about, before his death. The elaborate reconstruction of a trip that should have been our honeymoon; the journal of enlightenment to help me understand the parallel universe, and the significance of the dandelions, representing both space time and time space. All became relevant in one split second.

The short walk to dinner was uneventful. There was a sense that neither Sterling, Maggie, nor I wanted to discuss the "shadow" life that surfaced. Neither were any of us prepared to invite the other into an imaginary existence that we all experienced.

At dinner, after a few glasses of wine, the conversation centered on common, yet safe subjects. Maggie shared her early theatre experiences, in high school, as Maggie the Cat in *Cat on the Hot Tin*

Roof.

I saw Sterling's eyebrow slightly raise, remembering when I alluded to that play a few weeks ago.

Without going into details, I mentioned that I had a Masters Degree in Literature, from Georgetown, but never had the opportunity to pursue a career with that degree.

"I would love to spend some evenings sharing with you how I have attempted to blend my interest in literature with the plays that I write."

Maggie said, obviously glad to speak with anyone who appreciated the arts.

"I noticed while I was in Cabo that you are producing an original play that you wrote. I would be thrilled to talk with you about how your inspiration leads to a finished work."

I said, pleased how the evening was progressing.

"Maggie and I have been good friends for the past nine years, and she is much more than a talented playwright. Maggie works with the Humanity department at the Academy.

Because of her, many of our students are now performing in professional theaters throughout Mexico and the United States." Sterling said, reaching for Maggie's hand.

He was sixty four years old, but, it was not yet clear what his relationship was with Maggie. I was not naïve enough to believe that age alone would be a deterrent, to either of them.

On the walk back to the hotel, it was still early, but even the bars were empty. Maggie had said earlier that Todos Santos is the complete antithesis to Cabo San Lucas.

"That is why most of us prefer to live here. The locals refer to Todos, as a true oasis. 'El Puebla Magico' is our nickname. That is also because of the underground river, beneath the desert. It is a miracle that we have so many luscious green areas, that sprout up from nowhere.

Perhaps in a few days you would like to visit the art galleries? We are known internationally for the art that is plentiful here."

Maggie was determined to help me acclimate comfortably. "I would definitely enjoy that." I said. Then I noticed the odd bubble necklace with a seed inside on Maggie's neck. It looked almost exactly like the one Molly gave me the last time I saw her in Paris. I can still here her telling me the story about the mustard seed that accompanied the necklace. On the day I learned about Molly's death, I removed it and never wore it again. I decided that this was not the time to share my story with Maggie .

Once Sterling and I bid farewell to Maggie, we returned to The Hotel California.

Although, Sterling's beach house was a few miles from the hotel, he suggested that we have a night cap at the hotel bar.

"Well? What did you think of Maggie?" Sterling came right out and asked.

It seemed like a loaded question. Not certain how to approach the subject, I chose the safe route.

"Maggie is charming. I enjoyed our dinner and conversation. Looking forward to visiting the galleries with her." I said, nonchalantly.

Sterling lit his cigar, and took a few sips of his Chivas Regal. He wouldn't take his eyes off of me. It wasn't uncomfortable; it was introspective.

"Okay, Sterling, you win. What is it that attracted you to Maggie?" I finally asked.

"I know that you saw what I did when you met her, didn't you? There is something about her that is very similar to you. She could be you, in another life, couldn't she? I mean, I know you had to recognize this. The way she talks, her hand gestures, the way she tilts her head to the side…"

"STOP, Sterling…Maggie and I are at least thirty years apart. We are from different generations…yes, there may be some similarities, but even those are only physical." I said emphatically. *Trying to ignore that mustard seed around her neck.*

" We don't need to discuss it tonight, but you and I, and I am sure Maggie also felt that connection. Not sure what it means, but I am certain that eventually there will be more revealed." Then out of nowhere, perhaps just to change the strange mood, Sterling asked, "Now that you are finally here, when can you expect a visit from Caden?"

There were times when I really wished Sterling would not always remember what I told him. This would be so much easier if we had not shared so many years of history together. I was not looking forward to explaining my past relationship to Caden.

It was not that I was embarrassed to admit being unfaithful to Alex, as much as it was how complex Sterling and my affair was. Once Caden was here I had no choice to tell him about Sterling .Caden remembered me as a naïve seventeen year old, that he taught to be a woman. And, Sterling showed me how to take advantage of that womanhood; enjoying every moment.

"I haven't even spent my first night here. Maybe tomorrow, or the next day, I will give him a call. I prefer having my own place before we make any plans."

"Sounds to me like you are making excuses. Are you having second thoughts about reuniting, Gabby?" Sterling got right to the point.

"Well, I think it is only natural for me to be nervous. The last time Caden saw me…I was younger than Maggie. I don't even know if I am the same person now that I was then."

Finally, I was confessing some of my doubts.

" Eleanor is going to make arrangements for me to meet with a Shaman. It is a rather lengthy ritual that takes all night. It has always provided me with answers to questions that seemed impossible. If you want to watch mine and later have your own, it might help you with these doubts."

Sterling said all this as if it was a common occurrence. I could not help remembering Caden and my experience with Esmeralda, the fortune teller from New York years ago. Too many of those predictions came true.

"You are really willing to let me be part of your cleansing? Are you sure, Sterling?"I asked, confused.

"It is time that I need to move on. And if my journey will help you do the same, then I will deal with it."

It was an interesting end to a very odd evening.

CHAPTER 39

Give sorrow words, the grief that does not speak knits up the o—er wrought heart and bids it break.
William Shakespeare

Sterling Powers
1989-2010

DAMN YOU Gabby Girard for managing to stir up Giselle's ashes after all these years. I was finally at the stage when my inner compass and my sorrow prism, divided into mirrors and doors, allowing the grief to reflect before it departs.

It was not that my thoughts of Gisselle were fading, but at least, finally now, I had the ability to reshape those thoughts into a form that was more comfortable.

No longer did I need to stare at the picture album, that Gisselle struggled to complete before her death; or what we would name our unborn son.

Eventually, I finally will distribute those ashes, where Giselle requested; in those places that are most significant to me. That is, if I ever can determine where those places are.

So many years ago, I can still recall saying,

"But, Gisselle don't you want to have your final resting place to be where you found the most happiness? Perhaps places near you home."

When I made this suggestion to Gisselle, it felt as if I was making funeral arrangements for a close friend, certainly not my young pregnant wife.

"That is why I am asking you to spread my ashes at places that bring *you* joy. Wherever you are I will also be nearby. Being with you has been the happiest I have ever been."

Then Gisselle's eye lids began to close. Each day she lost more energy, until there was none left.

Bridget and Atillo had requested that I would leave some of Gisselle's ashes with them; and naturally I agreed.

When I received my urn, they had selected a blue and purple metallic one that immediately reminded me of Gisselle's intoxicating eyes.

Returning home from Portugal, with my wife and son's ashes was a sobering experience. It was difficult for me to accept that one moment I could hold Gisselle close enough to feel her heartbeat and, then suddenly, there is nothing left but cinders.

When the opportunity finally came, the next year to sign with the Colonels Basketball franchise, I was grateful that all my attention would be focused on a sport, although there was nothing any longer that kept my interest.

After the first successful season finished, all the player agents negotiated higher salaries. The majority of what I earned was sent to my mother in Ohio; the remainder in a savings account, or my financial advisor, who invested it in the most lucrative companies.

Celeste Powers had spent whatever generous amount Sterling sent her on abused women's shelters and children's charities. El Niño's Magic Casa was Celeste's favorite.

She would organize clothing drives for most of the year, and then fly to Rosarito Beach, Mexico, for one week distributing the clothes and filling pantries with as much food as possible.

Sterling had no idea how much his mother's contribution improved the lives of the poor, until her death, on January 31, 2002. It was three months after Sterling had being shot in the deserted warehouse parking lot, attempting to save Gabby's life.

Sterling received a phone call from a close friend of his mothers informing him that Celeste had suffered a heart attack earlier that morning and was in critical condition at the hospital.

Akron, Ohio is about five hours on I-71 from Lexington, Kentucky. It took Sterling less than four. The next three days he never left his mother's side.

Celeste had just celebrated her eightieth birthday. She was in perfect health until four days ago, when she was found passed out in the front yard watering her vegetable garden. The Postman who discovered her, immediately called an ambulance, and Celeste was taken to Akron General Hospital.

During the three days that Sterling spent with his mother, she only gained consciousness twice. The second time, she told her son that in her bedroom he would find a cedar hope chest. Everything she had for him would be inside that chest. Two hours later Celeste passed on.

The day that he buried his mother, local television stations broadcast from Tijuana Mexico. Over one thousand people, both poor and wealthy, had made a shrine in the center of town with Celeste's picture in a polished silver frame.

Beneath her picture, were thousands of flowers, and hand drawn cards from children wanting to demonstrate their love for a woman they compared to Mother Theresa.

Sterling was in shock at how much these Mexican people loved and admired his mother. In the following days he learned about the several foundations that she had started with all the money that Sterling had sent her.

When he finally was able to begin clearing his mother's simple house, he remembered the hope chest. There inside were photographs of him and Celeste from birth to his college graduation. Inside an envelope marked **Sterling,** was a two page letter and a bracelet.

My Dearest Son,

From the moment I laid eyes on you, there was never a doubt that you would be a great man and achieve remarkable recognition. I have started a foundation that rescues women who have been sexually abused and a home for Mexican children where they will be educated. Once you experience, as I have, the desperate need in this country, I know that you will continue my passion.

I am aware of how you continue to grieve for Gisselle, and wish that there was something that I could do to reduce that pain. There is a card with the name of a Shaman that assures me that he can help. Please, so that I may Rest In Peace, seek out this medicine man, for my sake.

Finally, the bracelet that is included, actually is two in one. Currently they are braided together, but at the right time, and you will know when that is, the red rope will separate into two. You are to give the other one to the women that represents the second half of your soul.

This red string of faith determines who your soulmate will be. The Chinese believe it is your destiny and it begins when the gods tie an invisible red string around the ankle of a newborn child. When they meet the other half of that red string, they will fall in love, regardless of any circumstances that may attempt to prevent it from happening. Your eternal lover is still out there. Do not give up.

Your loving and devoted mother

Sterling had doubts that any silly red string, even one that had been fashionably designed as this one, could replace the love he still had for Gisselle. That fateful red string, may as well be burnt with her ashes.

Nevertheless, in honor of his mother's memory, the red eternity bracelet remained on his wrist. What really fascinated Sterling was the Shaman, Celeste knew. If this Medicine Man can truly release thirty five years of trepidation, he must seek him out.

For ten days after his mother's funeral, Sterling could not be found. It was as if he had evaporated from earth.

When he arrived at Todos Santos, Eleanor Rigby, had reserved his room, at The Hotel California even before he knew that he was going there.

"Your mother asked me months ago to keep a place open for you.

She was certain that eventually you would arrive." Eleanor shared with Sterling.

" Did Celeste ever have the opportunity to tell you about the Shaman and the cleansing ritual?"

Eleanor was not sure if Sterling had any idea of how extensive this ceremony could get.

" Honestly, all I understand is that the Shaman is able to connect spiritually the departed with those of us who are living. How this is achieved I have no idea." Sterling confessed.

"Then let me give you a condensed version of what you may expect. There are many different spiritual cleansing. One of the most respected Shamans that I know lives in the Yucatán, but he knew Celeste, and I am certain that he will travel here to Todos Santos for you."

Eleanor did not want Sterling to enter into this solemn ceremony clueless.

"If you have some extra time to spare, after you settle in, perhaps this evening? We will discuss all of this in detail. She handed Sterling the keys to the Penthouse suite, with simple directions.

Sterling was not sure what he had gotten into, but he always trusted his mother's instincts. If this Shaman is able to reduce even a small portion of the pain he is experiencing, then it didn't matter how unconventional it was, the end result was what mattered.

Thirty five years ago he lost Gisselle. Three months ago, he nearly lost Gabriella . It was only days ago his mother died. He had vowed to each of them that he would always protect them; but he failed.

If there wasn't anything that he could do in this world, maybe the spiritual world would offer him answers.

Eleanor Rigby was a fascinating woman, with no resemblance to the infamous character, from that well known song. This Eleanor Rigby, that worked at The Hotel California, had no rice to throw, and she certainly didn't appear to be lonely. She reminded me more of a caring grandmother, who kept herself busy, making homemade cookies, with leftover flour that frosted her hair.

That evening, after strolling through the center of town, and browsing through some interesting art galleries, I returned back to the hotel, where Eleanor greeted me with a tempting cigar and a bottle of Vintage Porto.

I immediately recognized the imported red wine, that is fortified with brandy and originates in Portugal. The same wine that Gisselle's father offered me when I was first introduced to him at Casias. I chose not to point out this memory to my gracious hostess.

" Follow me Senor into the private parlor where you can enjoy some wine and a superior cigar that I selected for this very evening."

Eleanor was about to reveal some details about the Shaman's ceremony and she wanted Sterling to be completely relaxed.

The cigar was top quality. Sterling recognized the well known raised gold lettering; the iconic COHIBA, the best cigar in the world. Eleanor definitely knew how to select a premium smoke. Once lit, Sterling could taste, after a few draws, a peppery blast with hints of cedar and leather.

"I could tell when you first walked in the door, that you were a man of distinction Senor Powers. I hope that what I am going to tell you about the Mayan sacred ceremonies will help you understand that the Healers and Priests are extremely serious at preserving their traditions.

The Shaman that will travel from the Yucatán, has been performing these rituals his entire life. By previewing with you the various methods, hopefully it will make it less foreign to you." Eleanor waited for a response.

"To be perfectly honest, Eleanor, I do have my doubts about how effective this will be. Nevertheless, in memory of "mi madre" I intend to be as open minded as possible." Sterling stated with certainty.

"That is all we can ask of you. Therefore, I will now begin by briefly telling you about the various ceremonies: *U Jamal Pixar is a specific ceremony to remember deceased relatives and loved ones. There are offerings of food and flowers placed on an altar among candles. Most often a beverage will be given to you that contains many different herbs, including peyote, mezcal, salvia divinorum, opium, cannabis, and coca.*

All of these in the proper dosage, with many other sacred liquids will provoke hallucinating effects. It is the Shaman's power to control and channel you to the spirits you are seeking.

The Limpia, or spiritual cleansing will then follow. This will remove all the negative emotions from your body and soul. After the Limpia, you may feel light, peaceful, and happy. The Shaman may ask you to remove your clothing and enter a sauna. He will then wrap you with various palm leaves soaked in sacred oils.

During these times, many who have participated, claim that their deceased loved ones will be visible and for a short time there will be a human form that they can feel, and touch. When the spirit returns to their other world it is usually a comforting departure.

Although the cleansing may be done in the future again, it is unlikely that the spirit will return, although messages may be sent through a Shaman."

I listened through the entire explanation. To abdicate myself to a "witch doctor" who would intoxicate me with some pretty powerful drugs was less than appealing.

What did perk my interest, was to have physical contact one final time. I had never heard that before from any spiritual leader. It may be that this is what I wanted to hear, but regardless, I was willing to partake in all the rest for that slight opportunity.

"Do you happen to know of anyone personally that has experienced a spiritual physical reunion with their departed?" I asked, although my decision was already made.

"Ten years ago, Sterling, I was able to meet with my deceased husband. It was because of our meeting that I could put him to rest and begin living again." Eleanor confided to me.

Three days later my ceremony began. The Shaman took me to the desert, where many of these ceremonies have been performed. He had several assistants to help prepare a wooden dry spa, in a nearby cave with a makeshift altar.

Everything was exactly like Eleanor had explained. When it was time for me to drink the prepared potion, it resembled a warm grog. I was pleasantly surprised how easy it was to swallow.

There was no residual after taste. Within a matter of thirty minutes I could feel the drugs start to take effect.

My body was beginning to slowly pull away from my mind. Soon my inner self was exposed with no body to shield it. I can hear from miles away crickets, and someone whistling a strange tune that is echoing in my ears.

The fire in the pit is now dancing above my head, crackling like twigs breaking. At a short distance the mountain opened up into a lit tunnel that was moving, toward me. Inside, surrounded by a kaleidoscopic prism, two women emerged, barefoot, all in white gliding in the air.

As I approached them, I could see that it was my mother, and my wife holding hands. Someone, from the outside, with a gigantic hand took mine and led me into the cave. We all sat down on some large rocks that felt like marshmallows.

I could hear the smells enter my pores, and it was soothing. My mother reached out, touching my head as she often did when I was a child, and I could taste the soft words when she said, "Sterling, do not fall into the grief abyss. Look deep into the universe, it will lead you to the truth"

Then I saw Gisselle hold me in her arms. She had one body and I saw another body floating. Then without even knowing when it happened, she rocked me in her arms, while the body on the marshmallow rock began breathing life back into a shallow being.

She never spoke, but I could see her mouthing my name. After what seemed like eternity, Gisselle picked up a single dandelion from the air, placed it in my hand.

"When you find its mate, you will find your life." I heard her whisper.

Our lips then met, for a very long moment. At last, I watched both of the women that I loved most in my life, fade into the cave that formed back into the ridged mountain.

It was not until late the following afternoon that I finally awoke. My head felt light, as if I was in a dream state. The Shaman placed a sarape Indian blanket around my shoulders.

"It was a successful trip you to the other side. For the next few days the afterglow will continue to make you feel exuberant.

There maybe even hours where you will feel visual distortions. Solid walls could appear to be breathing. During the ceremony, you experienced Synesthesia, when sensory perceptions become mixed. Do not be surprised if what you see may be interpreted by your mind as sounds.

For the next several days, Sterling, you must avoid any physical activities. You also might notice your heart rate increase. That will not last long. The hallucinations may also reoccur, but only in short intervals."

The Shaman wanted Sterling to be fully aware of all the after effects.

"Is there any chance that I will be visited again by my…apparitions?" Sterling did not want to identify Celeste or Gisselle by name.

"It is very unlikely that your mother or wife will return to you. However, the messages that they sent you, may be reinforced in other ways. After a cleansing, your spirit is more susceptible to accepting what they have communicated."

Sterling continued to remember the entire spiritual ceremony. He never wanted to forget how he felt.

As the years passed, Todos Santos continued to be Sterlings sanctuary. Although the Shaman was correct, he never did experience the physical contact with Celeste or Gisselle again, he continued to be reminded of their words.

Gabriella Girard, the one woman he had to distance himself from emotionally, was his albatross. There were times when he had to restrain himself from feeling anything more toward her, than a sex partner.

Whenever he would begin to feel the slightest urge to become closer, instinct reminded him to change the pace.

Sterling refused to ever allow himself the privilege to love again. Gabby for years was a perfect partner. She was able to enjoy their sexual experiences without requiring any commitment.

It was not until Sterling witnessed, that animal, Murray attacking Gabby that he realized how important she was to him. Enough to risk his life.

It was a calculated risk he took when she called him from Savannah in March. Sterling needed to make certain that he would never again feel the way he did that Halloween night.

The nine years they spent apart would help him remember that they could only be friends now. And, there was always that Caden Cassidy who would soon be here.

After years of unfortunate separation, they both now had their opportunity to revisit destiny and make it right.

Sterling knew if he was ever given that same possibility to feel Giselle again, he would, without a doubt take advantage of it.

CHAPTER 40

Every parting gives a foretaste of death, every reunion a hint of the resurrection.

Arthur Schopenhauer

Gabby and Caden
September, 2010
Todos Santos, Mexico

Todos Santos has a fascinating cultural landscape. At one time, in 1724, it was founded as a Mission. Later, it became known as a major sugar cane producer. Now, the history of this village is kept alive in a local museum, church, theatre , and many other historical sites.

The art studios were of particular interest to me. Many of the paintings featured the magnificent Sierra Laguna Mountains, or a secluded beach with cerulean waves that lead to a mermaids cave.

One photography shop, tucked away in an alley, off the main road had a sign outside the front door that read "Always leave room for the unexpected. Serendipity and Destiny are twin sisters." This was definitely a motto of how my life seems to be.

Without hesitating, I opened the front door, and heard a bamboo wind chime announce my arrival. Yet, no anxious salesperson rushed to greet me, only a sweet and sour, vanilla, blackberry aroma urging me to follow the scent to the back wall.

Here I found various photographs displayed, from mini portraits, to wall size hangings. Some were framed, others, included colorful borders. There were black and white, moody, dramatic noir, contrasted with vibrant colors to capture the landscape façade.

The gallery was laid out with free standing white walls, that showcased various photographic genres. There did not seem to be any specific reason why fashion, food, and landscape were grouped in the same family.

As I casually strolled around the artisan studio, an elaborate banner above the photographs stated: " **You're my serendipity. I wasn't looking for you. I wasn't expecting you. But I'm very lucky I met you."**

Below the sign were pictures of couples, walking in the rain, sharing a plate of spaghetti, throwing snowballs, holding hands sitting on a bench, riding on bikes, and standing in front of a giant Christmas tree at Rockefeller Center, New York.

I almost walked right past that last photograph, when I recognized that couple. My hand went over my mouth, to prevent any surprising sound from escaping, I just stood there paralyzed.

"Hola, Senora. I see you found our special traveling exhibit by the very well known and admired Photographer, Diane Arbus."

The salesperson seemed to be waiting for me to react, but I was still stunned to see Caden and I so young, and so many years ago, on our weekend trip to New York, the day after Thanksgiving.

And now...being displayed in a public gallery, on the other side of the planet.

" I can offer you this particular piece, for a great price." I could hear the young lady trying to make a sale.

When I finally was able to get my senses back, I explained briefly to her, that the picture was of someone I once knew. But, at this time I would not be interested in purchasing it.

There were just too many memories associated with that time in New York that I was not ready to deal with.

She pleasantly informed me that the same picture was also being sold as a Christmas card. When I opened the card it said: *You are the serendipity that I never knew existed. Merry Christmas.*

Not certain exactly why, but I left with that card, now knowing that I could no longer delay making plans to see Caden. Back in my room I sat outside where the sea breeze and sunshine allowed me to think clearly.

My over-thinking about Caden was not going to provide me with any definite solutions. If he is already in California, then he is expecting me to meet with him soon. It was now four o'clock . The phone began to ring on his end.

"Hello, Gabby. How is Cabo San Lucas? Is it as great as everyone says it is?" Caden's voice was exuberant.

"Cabo was…well, it was a typical resort town. A lot of tourists, drinking…you know. But, I am really too old for all that debauchery. Tell me about California. How did you manage to get away from the Pub?"

Gabby was trying to be pleasantly evasive.

"California…or should I be more specific, Huntington Beach, is quite nice. I mean, it definitely lives up to the hype it gets.

The boys are doing well, although they don't seem to be too concerned about anything but, NOW. I guess you would say, carpe diem." Caden seemed content.

" I came clean to Kaitlyn about needing to see you. It was not a pretty scene. She made a lot of threats, and broke down a few times. But, when it was finally over, I had such a great feeling of relief. It was like, the first time in years that I felt purged from a lie that has been lodged deep in my throat."

There was a peaceful tone in his voice. A sense of relief.

Gabby had no idea that Caden had actually taken permanent, drastic measures to alter his life. How would he feel when he actually saw her? How would she react when she saw him?

"Caden. Do you really think it was wise to burn all your bridges now? I am not the same Gabby that I was when you left me. Forty three years, Caden…"

Caden interrupted her before she could finish her thoughts.

"I wouldn't care if it was one hundred years Gabby…And, if you are worried about the physical attraction, well…I can guarantee you that I am certainly not the same as you might remember me, either. Whatever this gravitational pull is that draws us together refuses to back off."

Caden was determined to make Gabby understand that time for him also, stopped on that New Year's Eve 1967.

There was a short, uncomfortable pause, while neither of them said anything. Then Gabby interjected,

" I am going to send you a recent…like a few hours old, photo of me. You can send one of you, if you like. If not, I will understand. Anyway, then you can decide if you want to make the trip out here. It still may be a few weeks before I find a house here in Todos Santos, so you have plenty of time to reconsider. And, I am certain that Kaitlyn would take you back. It would seem just like another male midlife crises."

Gabby said hoping that Caden would be reasonable.

"Send the picture. I will do the same. It won't change anything. I knew that I loved you forty three years ago, and I know that I love you now. I can wait a couple of weeks, now that I know this is really going to happen." Caden still sounded optimistic.

"Watch for the picture to come through in about an hour. And, Caden…I do still remember how I loved you once. At the moment, all I can tell you is that I really want to feel that way again."

Gabby could sense, even this far away, that Caden's arms were wrapped around her, whispering, *My affections and wishes are unchanged, but one word from you will silence me on the subject forever* (Jane Austin).

"I promise you, Caden, that as soon as I am able to get my house, we will have our reunion. Until then, look at my photo, think seriously about what you want, and please just be honest, with me and with you."

Gabby's voice was beginning to sound like static. A few seconds later, the phone call ended. Sterling did warn her that the satellite reception in Todos Santos was not strong.

By six o'clock Gabby's picture clearly transmitted to Caden's iPhone messenger. He was anxious to see her, at last. She was standing outside of a building called Hotel California. That was a real trip. How was she able to manage that clever background? There had to be something significant about alluding to The Eagles most famous song of all time.

But, right now it wasn't those lyrics that he cared about. Gabby was wearing a traditional Mexican peasant blouse. It was black with colorful embroidered flowers on the sleeves and around the plunging neck. The sunlight from the back of her, made the matching black gauze pants, slightly see through. He could see the traces, just barely of her bikini panties . That was almost enough to cause an erection.

Caden then enlarged the photo on the screen, and looked at Gabby's emerald green eyes. Even in this photograph those eyes reminded him of a rainforest, after a spring shower, or the green reflection of grass that the early morning dew kisses.

Oh, how he remembered the way those eyes would sparkle, with just the right amount of zest, seducing him without saying a word.

Caden was pleased that even at the age of sixty one, Gabby's dark brown hair almost sable now, flowed way beyond her soldiers with just a hint of silver tendrils, strategically, spontaneously natural.

Oh my Gabby, you were definitely right. You do not look the same as you did at eighteen…No, you are like a wine made of montepulciano grape, that when it ages, it reveals the true earthy, fruits that tempt men relentlessly. I am finally ready to take a bite of that apple now, Gabby.

After I left Georgetown and arrived back home to Savanna, Georgia I was convinced that Gabby had somehow caused all my mental anxieties.

She was the black cat that crossed my path. The number thirteen that would somehow appear causing disaster each time. She was the albatross that I could not remove. There was only one way to put an end to this madness, and that is to confront her.

How that would happen, I was never sure, until a few years ago, when Aunt Selena was no longer capable of caring for herself, I moved her to Savannah . She stayed with Kaitlyn and I as long as possible. But, at the age of seventy four, Selena was showing serious signs of Alzheimer's disease. I found a caring facility and visited her every few days.

After three months Selena became critically ill. On the day that she passed, she finally told me that I was her only son. For some reason, I was not surprised, or alarmed. Selena and I were always extremely close, and this deathbed confession only validated what I presumed.

Selena also left me a small financial fortune. She was fortunate to have many inside connections to stock investments . Over the years the residuals received were placed in a trust fund in my name.

When I made the decision to leave Kaitlyn, that trust fund made it possible for me to now revisit my destiny.

Caden stepped outside of the surf shop, and asked Liam, the oldest twin, to take his picture with the ocean and the boardwalk in the background.

Caden took one last look before sending it to Gabby. Time had not been as good to him as it had been to her. All he could hope for now, was that she would remember how he used to be and that would be enough.

CHAPTER 41

There is only one kind of shock worse than the totally unexpected: the expected for which one refused to prepare.
Mary Renault

Gabby, Sterling, and Maggie
A platonic ménage trios
September, 2010
Todos Santos, Mexico

"I know that you will never believe this, but I would much rather be here helping you find a house, than attending a charity golf tournament in Pebble Beach this week." Sterling said rather annoyed.

"You can always join me, if you like. It would give you an opportunity to see the beautiful Monterey Peninsula and Carmel."

It was difficult for me to tell if Sterling was serious or sarcastic. But, for me, just the thought of a golf tournament, turned my stomach and left a disgusting taste in my mouth. It was the epitome of what I was escaping from.

"I thankfully decline that kind offer. There is plenty to do here. Although, Eleanor has been very accommodating, I really need to find my own humble 'casa'. Caden is just waiting for me to let him know when he can arrive." Gabby said reluctantly.

"That sounds like he has made some serious decisions in his life. Are you prepared to do the same, Gabby?"

I never knew if Sterling was genuinely concerned, or apprehensive.

"If you mean am I ready for a commitment, the answer is no. Or at least not yet. But, I am ready to revisit our past and decide if we have a future."

I was at least confident about this.

"Okay, babe. I am going to leave you in the trusted hands of Maggie Mendoza. You seem to have much in common, and I can tell you that Maggie has exquisite taste. Just check out my Beach House. She helped me find it and decorated it. You won't be disappointed. I will call you when I get back in town, and you can show me your new digs."

Before I could agree or object about Maggie being Sterling's Good House Ambassador, he was out the door, with his luggage bag draped over his shoulder.

Great! I really now had no choice but to trust that Maggie will find me the right place, and soon. Keeping Caden hanging will only make our meeting more difficult.

I unlocked my phone, strolled down the page, and opened the picture file Caden sent. Looking older, was expected. What was not expected, was my reaction.

Leaning against a giant surfboard, with a glimpse of the Pacific Ocean, I recognized first that smile. The one that I woke up to in the morning, and the one I looked forward to in the evenings, so many years ago.

Whatever Caden has been doing physically the last forty three years, kept his body in great shape. He could be the poster boy for a Viagra commercial.

He was still hot. But, a closer look, revealed that beyond those periwinkle blue eyes, there was an empty, vacant look. It lacked the arrogant, ambitious, confidence that was his passport to many unsuspecting young ladies. Caden now appeared as he was in search of something he lost. Something that would complete him.

It was Caden's inner eyes, the ones that penetrated my soul that very first evening, at the Frat party, that remained the same. Even now, they still continue to make my blood flow faster. He was the only man, who could ever make me forget about Jake, even for only a short time.

Was Esmeralda's prediction actually accurate? Could these words now prove to be true? I can still here her say,

"For the future, it would be wise to remember that opposites are two sides of the same coin. You will find that without your other side, there will be chaos."

Chaos I could deal with. It is the constant tornado, that refuses to stop plummeting my life, that is intolerable .

I was hoping now that my house hunting with Maggie , would be the start of a new future. She had arranged to show me first, her home, then Sterling's beach house.

"This should provide you with some visual examples. At the very least it will give you an idea of Mexican architecture, and a point of reference. There are three properties that have some similarities, yet they also allow you to add your own unique thumbprint. Just make mental notes, or you can use this notepad, to save your ideas." Maggie said pleasantly.

Sterling and Maggie's relationship was still very vague to me. The age difference was inconsequential. Perhaps it was even a reason for the attraction.

Recalling how important it was for Sterling to maintain an elusive attitude, Maggie may be the perfect choice.

She most definitely has the exotic features that he is drawn to. But, I am still anxious to see why Sterling is so impressed with this young lady.

We first drove to La Cachora North. This neighborhood, I was told, is a thirty minute walk, down a pleasant country lane, to the town center . Very convenient. And, within five minutes, from the doorstep, there is a white sandy beach. This two bedroom home sits on one acre of land. It is where Maggie lives.

"Mi Amiga, please come in and I will give you a grand tour of mi casa. This ground floor is where my guests stay. It has a generous sized bedroom, a personal sitting room, small convenience kitchen, and an outside thatched covered entertainment area. My parents visit often from Ensenada, and this is a perfect arrangement for us both." Maggie said with pride.

There are two staircases that both lead to the upper level. The first one is in the interior of the ground floor, allowing access to the main living area. The second staircase is on the opposite side, and can be used without disturbing any guests. Maggie added that this privacy feature is very accommodating.

The upstairs included the formal living area, kitchen and outdoor terrace. It is an unobstructed view of the ocean, and a mountain view from behind.

The wet bar, and hot tub were both inviting. But, what I really liked was the rooftop terrace, located up the spiral staircase. Here is where a lush tropical garden is situated, with a water fountain in the center. Winding around a rustic arbor is a trumpet vine; a deciduous climber with orange pink, trumpet shaped flowers.

In the center of this arbor, is an impressive, inviting, wood carved picnic table, with matching chairs. In the center of this table is an original glass wine decanter, in the shape of a carafe, positioned inside of a wrought iron holder.

On the opposite side of this arbor is a pergola filled with blue moon wisteria, that spreads throughout the arch and drapes over and wraps itself around the sides.

This is where two padded lounge chairs are positioned, beside several chairs with leather seats. It was as if I had stepped into a Home Decorating magazine.

Every item complimented the other, creating a warm welcoming ambience, with an amazing aroma from the many plants, staged strategically throughout this amazing garden.

" I do not ever remember seeing anything like this before. Did you personally design your entire home by yourself, Maggie? this area is just incredible. The entire layout of this house is perfect. How many years have you lived here?" I asked, definitely impressed.

" I really enjoyed the renovation of this house. Believe me, seven years ago, it was ready to be demolished. I have a good architect friend, that helped me with the blueprints, and within six months, I moved in.

I am going to make us some Margaritas, you get comfortable and we will talk about what you want your house to include."

Maggie walked over to the outside kitchen, while I continued to admire all the personal touches.

That was when my eyes found a most remarkable mosaic relief. It was an ethereal creature, resembling a fairy. The background included various shaped stars and moonbeams, and in her hand was a dandelion that she was blowing. The pollen appeared to be captured mid motion, with suspended crystals.

"I see that you found my masterpiece. My very best friend, Mia, is an artist. She paints portraits for tourists and then on her own time she likes to experiment. So…one day I told her how this strange young girl approached me on a train when I lived in New York…"

"I am sorry to interrupt, but this girl who you met at the train, did she give you anything?" I asked, knowing the answer before Maggie replied.

"Well, yes…she gave me…"

And at the same time we said in unison, "a dandelion ."

"How did you know this?"

Maggie asked, stunned.

That was when I shared with Maggie all my encounters with the dandelion child, as I was now starting to call her.

There were many other juxtapositions that we were beginning to discover this afternoon. After several Margaritas, and some open conversations, it became clear that our paths crossed for a purpose. My first thought was Jake's parallelism theory. But, it was too early in our bonding to share this.

"Do you want to know something even more intriguing?

Sterling's wife and unborn child died on December 31, 1967." Maggie said in an eerie tone.

Gabby was speechless. Why was all of this being revealed now? And, what does all of this mean? *The fact that I, Jake, Caden, and now Sterling suffered tragic losses on the exact same day must be significant.*

"What is also very tragic about Sterling's loss, is that Gisselle was only eighteen years old. They were only married a few months. Can you just imagine how horrible that was for him?"

As Maggie was saying all of this, Gabby began to realize that Sterling's wife and she were the same age.

"Sterling also mentioned to me Maggie, that he met you soon after his mother's passing. Would it be too personal if I asked you, what brought you and Sterling together?"

Gabby was hoping that she was not going to discover anything sinister.

"I don't generally share my life before Todos Santos, with anyone. But, it appears that we are not truly strangers. So, maybe once we know all the situations there will be a logical explanation." Maggie said quietly.

At the end of Maggie's terrifying sex trafficking experience, the two most relevant common denominators were discovered. The date she was kidnapped was also the same date that Gabby was raped, and that Sterling nearly died trying to save her life.

But, the most disturbing detail for Gabby was why they both were visited by the same child, who gave them similar messages.

"I really do not know if any of this information is going to help either one of us. But, I do feel like you and I are at least kindred spirits." Gabby said, totally drained.

We both agreed that the following day would be much more productive at house hunting. Today, we needed to let everything settle.

"Just one more thing, Maggie. You don't happen to know when Gisselle was born do you?"

I was curious to know this, since we were born the same year.

"Why yes, I do know, because it is on the burial urn that Sterling has in his bedroom. When I was designing that room, he reminded me to create an unobtrusive area to place his sacred urn. That was when I realized how young she was when Sterling lost her. The date she was born was, October 25, 1949-died December 31, 1967."

Once alone, I closed my eyes and at a distance could hear Jane Eyre's familiar voice, " *Returning I had to look before crossing the looking glass; my fascinating glance involuntary explored the depth it revealed. All looked colder and darker in that visionary hollow than in reality; and the strange little figure there gazing at me, with a white face and arms, specking the gloom and glittering eyes of fear moving, where all else was still, had the effect of a real spirit. I thought it like one of the tiny phantoms, half fairy, half imp...."*

Gisselle Powers and I shared the same Birthday.

CHAPTER 42

Than smoke and mist who better could appraise the kindred spirit of
an inner haze?
   Robert Frost

Gabby and Maggie
September, 2010
Todos Santos, Mexico

The next morning, as promised, Maggie gave me a glimpse of
Sterling's beach house.

   The house was designed by a friend, an avid surfer that Sterling
met at Cabo San Lucas. What interested him was that this concept
was "old school". Daniel Cerritos wanted to bring back the spirit of
the true beach house.

   It was designed to be a modern version of a 1960 concept when
the pretense of luxury could easily be sacrificed for simplistic
comfort. .

   "When Sterling and Daniel discussed the architectural design, all
Sterling insisted on was ocean views from every room, and Daniel
delivered. Unlike many of the other properties that Sterling owns,
this home has only two bedrooms intentionally. He wanted it to be
secluded, with no room for surprise visitors." Maggie explained.

   "How many other properties that Sterling owns have you visited,
Maggie?"

   I was now sincerely curious, but it almost sounded as if I was
examining a witness on trial.

   Maggie did not react immediately to my question. Instead, she
continued the tour of the house. I had to admit, that the interior

design was comfortable and yet elegant.

It featured all rustic Hacienda designs, from the Mexican floor tiles with intricate birds, to sunken bathtubs with whirlpools. In the open dining room, an ornate Mexican crafted chandelier provided an intimate impression.

The property seems much larger than only two bedrooms. Perhaps because of the open areas that allows guests to flow from one room to another with no barriers. The final surprise was an infinity pool with a fire pit, and an outdoor kitchen/grill, with even a brick pizzaria oven.

It was rather amusing to picture Sterling wearing a chefs hat and barbecuing. I never saw him even prepare toast and coffee for himself. So, the idea of no available domestic help was quite foreign to me.

"I am sure Gabby that you must be imagining that I was your replacement after that terrible ordeal you experienced. But, I assure you, Sterling has been like a father to me, not a lover."

Maggie didn't sound offended, but quite at ease with her response.

Whereas, I couldn't believe that Sterling shared with Maggie that we were once inamoratas . Referring to us as lovers is really stretching that relationship. I would use the word sex partners. Although that sounds cheap and crass.

"What exactly did Sterling tell you about our relationship?" I said blatantly.

Without responding verbally, Maggie approached me with open arms and we embraced. It was such an unexpected, and genuine reaction, that I felt like it was me being comforted by the daughter I never had. When we released each other, I noticed Maggie's eyes slightly tearing.

"Gabby, you should know by now that Sterling cares for you greatly. He would never say anything critical about your relationship. Most of what I know is by observing. When I was suffering greatly from being sexually abused, Sterling comforted me like no one else could. When he spoke of you, it was always with respect and love."

Maggie's voice expressed how sincere she felt. This strange bond, whatever it was seemed comforting and real.

Then, almost without any warning she turned her attention back to our original goal.

"I think that I have the perfect home for you, Gabby. If we go now, you can view it and if it is what you want I will contact the agent this afternoon and we can celebrate at The Hotel." Maggie said enthusiastically .

It was as if we both had just found our comfort zone.

So much had now been revealed that I never knew, that it made me appreciate the direction I was going.

It was most exciting to realize that for the very first time in my life I would be in a home of my choice, living the life that I want. Whether or not, that includes Caden, will totally depend on how much freedom I am willing to relinquish and share. There will be plenty of time for those decisions to be made.

CHAPTER 43

In human relationships, kindness and lies are worth a thousand truths.

Graham Greene

Sterling Powers Meets Alex Blair
September, 2010
Pebble Beach, California

Pebble Beach, California is more than a golf course, although it was named the best public links in America. It is also, a small, unincorporated town on the Monterey Peninsula.

Those who worship golf, go on a pilgrimage as often as possible to Spyglass Hill, which claims to get its inspiration from Treasure Island, and is known as one of the toughest courses in the world.

Jim Murray, *The Los Angeles* sports writer once said, "If it were human, Spyglass would have a knife in its teeth a patch on its eye, a ring in its ear, tobacco in its beard, and a blunderbuss in its hand."

Pebble Beach has hosted the US Open Championship, five times, and various charity golf tournaments throughout the year. But, it is also the captivating, alluring ocean landscape that draws various groups to select Pebble Beach for their private events.

When Sterling was invited to join the tournament this year, he thought it would be an opportunity to network with many other entrepreneurs who also support nonprofit organizations.

Another attraction to this tournament, included a four man team that would compete for a million dollar prize at the end of the five days. The winning team would split the prize money four ways.

The entire weekend focused on showcasing each charity. There were elaborate videos, graphic art displays, and brochures promoting each foundation. The final night was designated as a celebration for all the winning teams, with an elaborate dinner, entertainment and dancing to a live orchestra .

Sterling Powers never hesitated when opportunities, like this could contribute to more positive exposure for his charities. What he could never have predicted, was that Alex Blair, Gabby's husband, would also be attending this golf tournament, and as fate would have it, they would be on the same golf team.

When Sterling arrived at The Lodge at Pebble Beach, a five star hotel, his assistant, Daniel, went directly to the welcome booth. Once, Daniel retrieved the schedule of events, obtained a professional caddie, and the list of team members, he returned to the lobby, where he briefed Sterling.

The first reaction at seeing Alex Blair's name, caught Sterling off guard. He was at least thankful, that Gabby decided to remain at Todos Santos. The next thought , was that this may be a rather amusing, and intriguing five days.

What exactly was it about Alex Blair that led Gabby into my arms for twelve years? And, naturally the most fascinating question is, how much does Alex even know or care about our relationship.

In March, when Gabby called Sterling requesting his help, he knew that once the police discovered her belongings at Tybee Beach, and she was missing, the first suspect would be Alex. And, then there would be a media circus trying to determine where, and how, Gabriella Blair, wife of Alex Blair, multimillionaire, owner of Blair Ranch in Lexington , Kentucky disappeared.

There was also another small detail, that Gabby obviously ignored. Faking her own death, or pseudocide , can lead to criminal investigations and possibly arrests.

Gabby would not have access to any of her legal personal documents. Passports, drivers license, bank accounts would all be frozen until there was a viable conclusion.

An immediate red flag goes up when there is any suspicion that a person drowned, since this is a plausible reason for the absence of a body.

In nearly every case, when a wife is missing, the husband is a prime suspect. Obviously none of these issues ever crossed Gabby's mind. And, that is why Sterling took the initiative and, contacted Alex.

Once the Savannah Police Department, was convinced that there was no foul play Gabby was free to move about anywhere she chose.

Sterling insisted that Gabby contact Alex, but he never confessed to her, that he notified Alex the day Gabby left Savannah.

Now it seemed that he and Alex Blair, would finally be meeting face to face. Thankfully there would be no need for dueling pistols, since both of them were rejected by the same damsel.

During the meet and greet reception at the exclusive hotel, there were about sixty men ranging in ages from mid thirties to late seventies, and all of them were admiring the attractive young ladies serving drinks in provocative outfits.

Sterling found it amusing to watch how many of the guests, whose financial portfolios exceed several million dollars, were nearly groveling for a few hours of female attention.

After the happy hour was over, the tournament host requested that all golfers find their way to The Pebble Beach Room upstairs. This room could also be expanded to accommodate one hundred and fifty people for the final evening dinner dance. The outdoor tiled terrace, overlooks the 18th green of Pebble Beach Golf Links.

Once everyone was seated at their designated team tables, the tournament host began to review the tournament rules. Sterling waited until everyone at his table were seated. He was the final team member, to take his seat.

Sterling surmised that Alex Blair was close to the same age as he. Although, Gabby never mentioned anything about her husband, Sterling would have recognized him, even without the name tag.

This was an exceptionally impressive man. Sterling recognized how Alex subtly played the table. He also admired how he was able to be in control. Everyone seated in this room was successful at whatever business they represented, but Alex was not only the heir of a prestigious Kentucky horse ranch, he was also a well known heart surgeon.

Physically, there was an uncanny resemblance to the actor George Hamilton. Alex' self confidence, and charismatic nature drew attention from women of all ages.

So, what exactly was it about this man, that immediately struck Sterling as obnoxious? Even if he could answer that question, Sterling was determined to avoid any unpleasant confrontations. As far as he knew, Alex had no idea about him and Gabby.

After the formal introductions and the tee times were assigned, most of the guests began to move into the cigar bar. This was a good time for Sterling to mingle with other friends, and get away from Alex.

Everything seemed to be progressing nicely. Sterling spoke about his Celeste Foundation, and politely listened to those promoting their charities. This was exactly the reason why he decided to attend this golf tournament.

When Sterling briefly stepped over to the bar to refresh his bourbon, he felt a heavy hand touch his shoulder.

" Sterling Powers...I knew that name was familiar. I just now made the connection. You are the same gentleman that saved my wife's life years ago, during a car hijacking." Alex extended his hand to shake.

Sterling noticed that Alex did not mention the rape. He also never acknowledged that he and Gabby worked together on the Derby Charity at one time.

"That's right. It was many years ago. How is your wife?" Sterling asked cautiously.

Alex, slightly turned his back toward Sterling, reached for his drink from the bar and said, " I was just going to ask you the same question. How is Gabby? Did she come with you?"

Sterling tried not to act surprised, or overreact. There was no need to give Alex more information than he needed to know.

"Gabby is adapting. She has had a difficult time, but then I am sure you know that." Sterling answered as vague as possible.

"Well, if you know Gabby as well as I do, you will understand that she doesn't reveal much, and she often causes her own drama."

It was as if the two were playing tennis and the score was love. What he wanted to tell Alex was, if he really knew his wife, like he did, she would not be in Mexico right now. But, this was not the time or place to challenge Alex Blair.

" I am certain that when Gabby works out these issues she will be in contact with you." Sterling added.

This was a good time to stop the volley and avoid any further confrontations. As Sterling walked back to the original group he was talking to, he noticed a tall blonde, considerably younger than Alex, approach him with a passionate kiss, and a whisper in his ear.

Soon after, the two of them left the reception together. Whoever, this mystery woman was, Alex made no attempt to disguise their relationship.

The remainder of the week on the links were uneventful. Alex paired up with an executive from United Way, and Sterling was partners with a VP from The Last Wish Foundation.

Their team, was currently in the top three, contending for first place. It took the last hole to determine the winner. Alex ' final shot , in the last hole sealed their victory. There was much to celebrate. Each of the team members equally shared one million dollars for their charities.

At the Victory dinner, there was champagne flowing, commemorative music playing, and plenty of back patting. Ladies were dressed in designer gowns, each one trying to outshine the other, while every man wore almost the exact same tuxedo.

It was well past 2:00am, and several guests were still partying. Sterling was approached by several attractive young ladies. As usual, he spent the evening graciously entertaining each one. However, when the time came to say goodnight, he returned to his room alone.

The final event of this tournament was a lavish Sunday brunch and presentation of trophies to the various winners. Sterling intentionally arrived fashionably late, so that he would avoid sitting at the same table as Alex.

What the past five days revealed about his nemesis was that the man is obnoxious, self centered and annoying. Sterling observed how Alex appointed himself the leader of their team, ignored most suggestions and arrogantly voiced his opinion about racial and political issues that were usually avoided during such events.

It was Alex that approached Sterling in the hotel lobby while everyone was preparing for their departure.

"When you see Gabby again, let her know that the perp that raped her was released from the Georgia county jail a few days ago. Someone, apparently messed him up pretty well, breaking his nose and a few ribs. But, the prosecutor did not have enough evidence to try him for the rape charge, since Gabby was the only eye witness, and she wasn't available.

A private investigator that I hired, told me that the word on the streets is that he is running drugs in Mexico. He was also planning on getting even with the guy who resurfaced his face. I believe his last name is Cassidy . My informant said, that Mr. Cassidy left the state, but if this Perp finds him, they wont even be able to make dog food from what will be left of the body."Alex almost sounded pleased to share this news.

"I just thought, if Gabby is moving to Mexico, she may want to know that this Murray fugitive might be in her backyard. By the way Sterling, you look like you have recovered well after all these years." Alex said almost sarcastically.

Sterling had no intention of telling Gabby any of this information.

The odds of this Murray ever finding her at Todos Santos was impossible. But, not to take any chances, he would take the necessary precautions to avoid any further problems.

The image of Gabby coated in mud, with that animal humping her from the rear, has caused him many years of sleepless nights. And, he knew that Gabby was living with that nightmare daily.

Murray Jackson
San Diego, California
September, 2010

What nobody knew at this time, is that Murray was now living in San Diego, earning money as a Coyotaje, the Mexican term for human smuggling.

Migrants pay large amounts of money for safe passage across the border. What Murray soon realized was he could double dip and make twice the money, by including drug trafficking in his equation.

Now that he finally had a chance at making some real money, he could plan on moving to Tijuana where he could have a different bitch any day he wanted one.

His fucking brother, Calhoun, always messed with complicating shit, like that car jacking. The only good thing that he ever got from hijacking on that Halloween night, was when he had the best pussy ever. That bitch, Abby...no, her name was Gabby. She was Jake's bitch in high school, but now she's his bitch.

Working on the Mexican border is the sweetest gig he has ever had. And, when he traced that Gabby bitch to Ensenada, he was already to add her to the other Mexican cargo.

Once he got her across the border, he would take her to the small house, with a basement he rented. He already redesigned that basement with chains, and handcuffs, and other sex toys.

That was going to be Gabby's new home, at least until he got tired of banging her. Then he would move to Tijuana and she could just rot, in that hell hole.

The only problem was, that when he tracked Gabby to Ensenada, that bitch was already gone. Where the hell are you now Gabby? Daddy is on his way… so keep those legs spread for me…your daddy is mighty hungry.

CHAPTER 44

He simply felt that if he could carry away the vision of the spot of earth that she walked on, and the way the sky and sea enclosed it, the rest of the world might seem less empty.
   Edith Wharton

Sterling and Gabby
September, 2010
Todos Santos, Mexico

Before returning to Todos Santos, Sterling arranged to stay a few days at Carmel. From Pebble Beach it is a three mile coastal drive. Paul Pollock, no relation to the famous artist Paul Jackson Pollock, had a fascinating collection of sculptures that he designed.

When Sterling saw Maggie's mural with the enchanted fairy blowing on an elusive dandelion, he enquired why Mia, chose that design. His own mother had also alluded to the dandelion in her final letter to Sterling.

"I have a close friend that lives in Carmel, California. He is an artist but, he also believes in holistic medicine. While I was admiring his impressive herbal garden, he pointed out to me a dandelion bed.

I thought this very odd, since my experience with dandelions have always been negative. They are irritating weeds in my opinion. Then Paul was quick to inform me that as a healer and soothsayer, the dandelion is a Devine Design, capable of shedding light on hidden hopes.

More so, the various shades represent specific meanings: the yellow flower will provide clarity, intelligence, healing, growth and joy; whereas, the white puffball, offers purity, cleansing of the spirit and soul, as well as new beginnings. The green leaves and stems offers wholesomeness, growth and Mother Earth's comfort.

These are all the gifts I wanted Maggie to have with her in this new home, and new beginnings. It was my way to honor her as a survivor."

So impressed with Mia's artistic expression, that Sterling decided that he would commission Paul Pollock to design a sculpture with a similar motif. He sent Pollock a photo of the mural that Mia created, and left the rest to the artist. Sterling thought that this would be a perfect addition to Gabby's new home. It would be his house warming gift to her.

Carmel by the sea is a much more quaint, yet sophisticated beach city, compared to Todos Santos. Both of these communities attract many artists.

This short diversion would be a welcome quiet retreat after several days with Alex Blair. Sterling intentionally planned on driving alone through the Big Sur, with its seaside cliffs and views, and narrow stretch of highway .

This would give him the needed time to reflect on how he would deal with the news that Gabby's attacker was searching for her.

Gabby and Maggie
Todos Santos, Mexico October, 2010

Moving Day! Exciting, except for the minor fact that I have nothing to move, accept one suitcase of clothes.

"Actually, Gabby, this is ideal. You have a clean slate, and whatever you choose to do with it is totally up to you." Maggie said encouragingly.

The past ten days, Maggie and Gabby formed a comforting bond of friendship. Their age difference did not seem an obstacle.

Both women learned that their love of literature, the arts, music and theater was so strong that it opened doors to hidden attics. Each of them started to confide some of their secrets, and what they discovered, was like a scalpel that removed infectious ulcers, it left open discussions, and space for healing to occur.

Gabby was particularly impressed at how creative Maggie was. She seemed to have a natural gift to see beyond the ordinary and find the unique; very similar to Molly.

This was not limited only to her script writing. It was also true with her interior designs. Several prominent people hired her to decorate their homes.

The theater in Todos Santos and Cabo San Lucas were both successful. They performed several of Maggie's original one act plays, and she also directed other drama presentations as well. The only part of Maggie's life that was incomplete was her love life.

"I hope that now, you will believe that Sterling has only been a good friend to me, Gabby. It took me many years, after I was kidnapped and forced to be a sex slave, to feel self worth.

Sterling arranged for me to finish college. He encouraged me to write. And, when I directed my first original play, here in Todos Santos, it was like a miracle. Hearing people's applause made me feel that my life was actually worth living again."

Maggie's voice was animated with joy.

"I admire how well you have adjusted. But, what about this Blake Santiago that you were with at the club the other night? You must know Maggie, that when he looks into your eyes, there is no denying that the man is in love with you." Gabby said without hesitating.

Maggie, then opened up to me that Blake Santiago, a former professional soccer player for the Mexican National American football team, played In 1999 in the IFAF World Cup competition . Mexico lost to Japan and took second place; Blake had a knee injury that ended his career.

Since high school, Blake wrote music lyrics. When he was told that he would never play soccer again, some friends, who he used to play in a band with, were just now being discovered. Since their lead guitar player left, the band was looking for a replacement.

Blake started traveling with Las Magis Rocos throughout Mexico, Brazil, Puerto Ricco, and for a short time they were the opening act in America for Santana and Molotov. They became known as a Mexican rock band that features a mixture of Spanish and English rap lyrics.

At Todos Santos, during an impromptu jam session with, Buck Miller, a former guitarist for Peter James Millson, was where Maggie first saw Blake.

The music Buck played resembled classic old rock. Best advice he gave to Blake, was to keep dreaming, like the Stones say, "lose your dreams, lose your mind."

Buck convinced Blake to find his own music style. He decided to stay awhile in this small fishing village. Being introduced, to Maggie Mendoza by Buck's wife, probably had a huge impact on that decision.

Blake and Maggie soon began dating, although Maggie was very reluctant and apprehensive.

"You just can't understand Gabby. I may look like normal on the exterior, but inside, every day I struggle with relationships, and not only romantic ones. You, Mia, Eleanor, and Sterling are the only ones I feel comfortable with. I exclusively only date Blake, because he is patient, and quite honestly my safety net.

What I mean, is that with Blake I have an escort to any function, and since everyone knows we are dating, I avoid having to deal with new men.

But, marriage or even cohabitation, that is as likely to happen as being abducted by aliens. I really haven't even had sex for nine years, and neither do I want it." Maggie confessed.

It was then that I understood her fear. It also has been about that long since I was with a man intimately.

After the rape, there was no desire for sex; even with Sterling. That was one of the primary reasons I chose not to see him any longer.

Without the sex holding us together, it seemed useless to continue the relationship.

"Believe me, Maggie I can understand how you feel. There is an emptiness that hurts, but to fill that void may be even more painful. But, without taking chances, we have allowed our enemy to control us." I was really trying hard to believe my own words.

Then, a few days after our talk, while I was having a glass of wine, at the Hotel California bar, Blake came in. He was there to meet Maggie before their dinner date. She texted, letting him know that she would be about thirty minutes late.

Since, I had met Blake several times, at his own nightclub, called *The Maggie Mariposa*, I asked him to join me.

"Maggie told me that you found a beach house near Sterling's home. Congratulations! That is a beautiful area." Blake said.

" I was very lucky that it was available. I suppose I didn't even realize that Sterling was in that division. He is gone so often that I am sure we will never see each other."

I really didn't want anyone to think that the reason I bought the house was due to the proximity to Sterling…especially Sterling.

During our time together and after several glasses of wine, I asked Blake why he stopped touring with the band.

" I tried to convince Maggie to go with me. The tour was going to be about six months. We were finally getting noticed. Our agent was fairly confident that the next gig, our manager would book, we would be the headliners, instead of just the openers.

Maggie didn't want people to think she was a Roadie, or a Groupie . I couldn't change her mind. Six months away from her, was just too long. So…I cashed out, and decided to open my own club right here in Todos Santos." Blake explained.

"And you named your club after Maggie. But what does Mariposa mean? I know it means butterfly, but is there any other significance?" I asked, genuinely curious.

"Are you familiar with a poem called, " La Bella Mariposa"? It is written by an anonymous poet, but what impressed me was the poet celebrated the life of a butterfly.

He saw it as much more than a mere insect. In the poem the butterfly is compared to a young woman whose greatest desire is to be free and soar through the sky. Both the lady and the butterfly struggle through hard times, yet now they both have grown into beautiful creatures, with no fear.

They both learn how to explore their world. This is what I wanted for Maggie." Blake explained.

"Have you ever told Maggie about La Bella Mariposa, Blake?"

I asked, fascinated how much this man loved Maggie, and what he sacrificed to be with her.

Is this how Jake felt when he had to leave me after he lost his leg in Vietnam? Is this what Caden is now experiencing leaving Kaitlyn, just to have a chance with me again? Maggie was just a few steps behind where I have already walked.

"I was hoping, Gabby, that I wouldn't need to tell her. I was hoping that she would realize it herself. I am still hopeful, that in time that will happen."

Blake was talking to me, but I really didn't even need to be there. I could tell that he would wait a lifetime for Maggie if necessary. It would be up to me to prevent that from happening.

There is nobody alive that knows better than I, how difficult it is when revisiting your destiny.

CHAPTER 45

Ever has it been that love knows not its own depth until the hour of separation.

Kahlil Gibran

Gabby and Maggie
October, 2010
Todos Santos, Mexico

It was amazing how Maggie was able to furnish my two bedroom house in one week. Even the accessories were carefully thought out. Every plant, flower, art work, and candle reflected exactly my personal taste.

But, the most exciting "reveal" was totally unexpected. I just came home from a short visit to the local Mercado. Maggie had stopped by with some homemade tamales for dinner.

Before I could even get totally through my front door, Maggie grabbed the shopping bags and put them in the kitchen. Like an excited child who just discovered a new toy Maggie's exuberance was uncontrollable.

"You have got to see this Gabby! It is out of this world!" Maggie said, leading me to the terrace.

Beneath the natural backdrop of the abundant shade trees, placed precisely in the center of the tiled patio, was a wired sculpture, approximately six feet in height in the shape of a faerie with dragonfly wings.

She was suspended with one foot up and one foot down, as if she was doing a pirouette. On her head was a jeweled crown, with

Swarovski crystal, emeralds, diamonds, and sapphires.

But, what immediately caught my attention, was the realistic dandelion with a yellow flower, white puff, and green stem.

I had never seen anything so surreal as this statue. At the bronze base, with an elaborate scroll design, were only the initials: To GG from SP. What was left unsaid was the real mystery .

Did I ever share with Sterling my phantom girl and her dandelion gift? And…even if I did why would he capture that image for me so artistically?

In almost every part of the world, the dragonfly represents an altering of self perspective, and self realization. It is the symbolic source for mental and emotional changes that lead to a new meaning of life.

This magnificent creation took my breath away. I could not take my eyes off of it.

"I cannot wait to show this to Mia. She is going to be blown away!" Maggie said, as impressed as I was.

Maggie and I stood there for several minutes, without saying another word, in awe.

"My friend, Gabby…there are plenty of messages transmitting from this figurine. Are you thinking the same thing I am about the significance of the dandelion ? Good luck at trying to make sense of all of this." Maggie pointed out.

Knowing Sterling as I do, he would never explain what any of this meant. He may even find it amusing to watch me attempt to understand his motive.

Once during a visit to the Musee de Louvre, in Paris, I was admiring the Venus de Milo and asked Sterling to explain why it was so impressive to the world. His answer was,

"Art never needs to be justified. Once it is dissected it is no longer art, it is a carcass."

But, this…this breathtaking statue is so much more complex than any other gift I have ever received. Even Jake's journals, that provoke much soul searching, seem to have direction. I am not even certain how to approach a discussion about this gift.

What I was hoping for, was an impromptu visit from Sterling. I was not even sure if he was home yet.

On the other hand, why should I expect Sterling to check in with me? We live separate lives, and when he wants to include me he will. Friendships with the male species is really complicated.

One evening, when Maggie stopped by the house to drop off some sample window fabric, I decided to ask her how she was able to maintain her friendship with the opposite sex.

"Well, it does help if you are never romantically involved or attracted to each other. I have never had many male friendships, but, those I have had, are entirely different than female friends.

In almost all cases, I listen more than I talk. When they have "lady" problems, then they ask for my advice, or we only talk about general topics." Maggie said introspectively.

"Do you think of Blake as a friend or a lover?"

I asked, with the intention of convincing Maggie to admit her attraction to Blake. I was determined to show Maggie that Blake deserved a chance.

"Blake is a friend that I love to be with. But, I am not in love with him. I am not sure if I will ever be in love romantically with anyone.

But, you Gabby, also need to reexamine your feelings for Sterling. It isn't easy to know where he draws the line with you.

Since I have known him, and it has been nearly nine years, you are the only woman that he would ever do all this for. I have seen him with other ladies, and now, I have seen the two of you together. He may not even know how much he loves you."

Maggie finally expressed her own observations .

"What you see, Maggie is a man who is incapable of intimacy. And, for many years that worked well for me. But, now that I have a chance to recapture even a small part of the past I must try. Don't loose Blake because of your own inhibitions ."

Now was the time to tell Maggie about Jake and I . Hopefully by knowing how much we loved each other, even beyond the grave, she would finally understand why she must not let Blake go.

After listening, and crying with me, Maggie finally understood that when we are young, anything and everything we do is drawn from an intense desire, so strong that our desire clings to the favorable outcome until it is no longer plausible.

" There are libraries filled with fiction and nonfiction love tragedies. Do not allow yourself, Maggie to be the understudy to any of those tragic heroines. It took Jake the last months of his life before he truly understood what love was. I am still struggling with that same question. Do not make those same mistakes." I pleaded with her.

How much really penetrated through the steel armor that shields her heart, is impossible to know. I was fairly confident, however, that I gave her something to definitely reflect upon.

It had been several days since I felt the need to turn to Jake, like I always do, when nothing seems to make sense.

Today I was ready to read the journal entry titled, "My Final Thoughts". What I immediately noticed was that these pages were typed, not in Jake's own handwriting, like all the previous ones.

Forgive me Gabby for dictating these final last messages, but I know that my time is nearing the end. If you begin to notice that I am contradicting myself or that some things I say even seem more confusing than normal, it is because of the morphine. Okay…so being in control is what I want to tell you, today.

This is probably the most important thing to remember. I never wanted to control you or our future. But that is exactly what happened. The day our lives changed was not in the Cambodia Jungle. It was that last trip home in December.

There was still time to marry you, go to Canada, and live. I regret not making that choice every day. But, I have never regretted loving you. So, because I love you, this final journal is all about making the right choices.

I have had a long time to think about Caden Cassidy. Since he was the one you turned to after us, I had to know how he was able to successfully woo you.

I was able to examine and research his lifestyle quite sufficiently, up to now. I probably know Caden Cassidy better than you do. Did you know that he was born in Inchydoney, Ireland? The same village that I sent you on our recreated honeymoon? To be honest, that was pure coincidence. Only discovered much later, and I did not want that to prevent you from being focused on us. But, now that your trip is over, I thought you might find this fascinating.

And, his friendly Aunt Selena that introduced you later to Alex Blair…that was really Caden's mother. I am sure that by now he has discovered this mystery. Beginning to sound like a real life soap opera, isn't it?

His life changing moment was when he walked out on you. Unlike me, he never gave you closure. Nor, did he fight to get you back. You need to ask yourself and perhaps even him, if he ever enters your life again.., why? And, was he ever really ready for that commitment to you?

I also know about Sterling Powers. That relationship I understand much better. Perhaps because it is why I stayed with Isabella. She cared for my physical needs, as Sterling provided you with an emotional cleansing.

It is what I would call a platonic sexual arrangement . By this time all you really wanted was to block further pain; anesthesia applied successfully to the heart accomplished this.

Sterling Powers was the perfect anecdote for a loveless life. But you just might ask yourself Gabby, why Sterling? While you are at it, ask yourself, what are you afraid of?

It might surprise you, that Sterling and you both share the same fears. I know this, because all of us, lost someone we loved, and couldn't live without. But, you Gabby, can take that fear and pain and reverse it; use it to your benefit.

Now, I know that this sounds like I no longer believe that we will reunite. That is not true. Review all the notes on Parallelism, Gabby. Whatever *choice you make in this life, will not prevent our afterlife together. I can only hope that you are reading this before you have made any critical choices.*

There will never be a time that I will not be with you. But, Gabby you must fulfill your own destiny now. You will know when and who this will be with.

Refer back to the red string with the bell, if you have any doubts. Until we meet again, sweet Gabby, I will always be loving you.

Jake

This was the last page in the journal. I was now on my own, yet never alone. Jake was right about choices. Caden was right about choices. It never was between these two men, it was always my fear that the wrong choice would be unbearable. In truth , not having any choice is what destroys your future.

CHAPTER 46

No man is rich enough to buy back his past.
  Oscar Wilde

Sterling Powers
October, 2010
Todos Santos, Mexico

Since his return from California , Sterling was intentionally avoiding Gabby. He knew that eventually he would need to tell her that he met Alex at Pebble Beach.

But, before that, his priority was to arrange secret service agents to watch over her. This had to be done without her knowledge.

Sterling feared that if Gabby found out that her rapist was trying to stalk her, she would become a recluse. He also realized that choosing not to divulge this information, was taking a risk.

It was a risk, nevertheless, that Sterling was willing to take. The house warming gift was intended to encourage her to be optimistic about the future.

Maggie noticed that the beach house flag was hanging out on the deck. Sterling, adopted this tradition from Queen Elizabeth, of Great Britain. Whenever the queen is in residence, the Union Jack is displayed. Sterling liked that idea, but made a slight adjustment.

When his flag was flying, it was not only an indication that he was at Todos Santos, it also invited people to visit.

Rather than showing up uninvited, Maggie wisely chose to telephone first. She was anxious to hear how the fund raiser went, and to let him know Gabby's reaction to his gift.

"Welcome home, Sterling. Did you enjoy your golf junket at

Pebble Beach?"

Maggie asked cheerfully. She would be able to deduct from the tone of his voice whether she wanted to visit.

"The good news is that our team won first place, and we each brought home two hundred twenty five thousand dollars for our charities.

Eleanor told me that you were able to get Gabby into the beach house at Pescadero. That means that we will be neighbors . How far is she from my house? "

Sterling was both relieved that Gabby was in her own home, and that she was nearby him. He would insist that she install the same security system that he has. The service could link Gabby's with his, giving him the ability to assure her safety.

"Yes, we were lucky that Casa Carmela was just listed a few days earlier, and it was ready to sell. It is maybe three miles from you. I think you can wave to each other from your balconies." Maggie said.

"Did Gabby tell you that she received any surprises lately?" Sterling asked anxiously.

"Absolutely! Where in this world did you find that masterpiece? She is thrilled with it. But, we both have a lot of questions to ask you about that statue. Since it is her gift, I will allow her that privilege." Maggie said, slightly pouting.

" The two of you ladies are so much alike that I really need reinforcements to assist me, when we are all together. Next time we go out, you will need to ask Blake to join us. At least then I will feel that I have an ally." Sterling said playfully.

"If you are planning a dinner and club engagement it better be soon. I believe that now that Gabby is settled in her casa, she is planning on Caden Cassidy visiting her in the next few days." Maggie wasn't sure how Sterling would react to this news, but she felt it would be better he heard it from her.

"She did mention that to me before I left for Pebble Beach. Well, then it will be a party of five for our next dinner engagement. I am looking forward to meeting the gentleman Gabriella Girard, tormented for the past forty three years."

There was something in Sterling's response that had a sweet and sour tone. Maggie was curious to see how that meeting would turn out. She always had her own suspicions about Sterling's true feeling for Gabby.

Caden and Kaitlyn Cassidy   Gabby Girard

When Caden finally moved to Huntington Beach he left almost everything he owned in Savannah , with the exception of his George Harrison album, a few clothes, and the emerald ring that Selena had given him on December 31, 1967.

The night he finally told Kaitlyn that he was leaving Savannah and did not know when, or even if, he would ever return , was an ugly confrontation.

Perhaps it was a coincidence, but he chose garbage day, which was also their "sex" night to break the news to her.

Just as Kaitlyn was preparing to remove her bra and panties, Caden said,

"Tonight is not a good time for this. It would be better if you get dressed and we have a talk. I will wait for you in the kitchen."

He didn't even look back to see her reaction.

It took Kaitlyn at least five minutes to finally appear.

"Is this something about your health? Did the doctor diagnose you with some illness? Or are you going to tell me you have some sexually transmitted disease, that you got from some whore you've been humping behind my back?

There was no doubt that Kaitlyn was irritated. And, Caden knew at this moment there was no easy way to tell her.

"Well, I guess you should be happy to know that I have no STD's, and I have no bad news from the doctor."

Caden took a deep breath before continuing.

"And, I haven't cheated on you…well, at least not physically."

Caden once again paused. This time he stood up and tried to find the right words to make it less painful.

"What exactly do you mean, not physically? Have you been watching those porn movies again? Or do you have someone that you have phone sex with? I mean…really Caden, just admit whatever you have done, we will get over it, and move on. I will even go with you to therapy to help you…"

Caden could no longer here his wife's attempt to understand.

"I have never loved you Kaitlyn. It is not your fault. I am totally to blame. For forty three years I have tried to convince myself that I had no choice but to move on with my life. And, I did the very best. But, now…now, I at last I have been given the opportunity to truly be in love again…"

Kaitlyn patiently listened, quietly during her husband's entire diatribe, but then , she rose from the table and slapped Caden across the face.

Caden was stunned. During their entire marriage, neither of them had ever been violent, until this moment.

"You, son of a bitch! You wait until I am sixty years old to tell me you NEVER LOVED ME…Just because YOU couldn't be with the woman YOU LOVED? Well, Fuck You Caden Cassidy.

When I am through with you, that other woman won't want to ever see you again…You will be lucky if you can find a hole to live in!

How can you be willing to sacrifice everything for a mid life crises? Why can't you just go out and buy a corvette convertible like every other bastard who isn't happy with their marriage?"

Kaitlyn was about to throw a pan from the stove in Caden's direction, when he grabbed her by the wrists and forced her to sit down.

"Now, Kaitlyn, I understand that this is a shock to you. I am so very sorry that I had to tell you this way. But, you need to be reasonable and hear me out.

Any violent action that you take right now, will only make things worse and it will not change my mind."

Caden finally released the grip on Kaitlyn's wrists, when he was satisfied that she would not retaliate.

" Are you ready to listen to me now?" Caden asked.

By this time Kaitlyn was crying and trembling. Caden handed her a box of tissue and waited a few moments for her to calm down.

"I have already made arrangements with my attorney to have *The Molly* transferred to your name. Devon can take care of the daily business, he knows exactly what to do. You may want to consider giving him a little bonus, but that will be your decision. The house, car, and bank accounts will be entirely yours.

The life insurance will still go to you and the boys. If we went through a nasty divorce, you know that the best you would get is half of all this. I am leaving it all to you."

Caden gave Kaitlyn a few minutes to digest everything that he just said.

"Why Caden? Why are you doing all of this now?" This was all Kaitlyn could say.

" My dear Kaitlyn…You would never be able to understand. I have been living with this pain for so many years, that I do not even know how to explain it. All I can say is that I am not ever going to let this chance pass me by again."

Caden felt like he had just survived an atomic bomb and he wasn't certain how much was left of him. However, the worst was now over. He would be ready to leave for California in three days.

Thankfully, money was not an issue. When Salina was diagnosed with brain cancer, she had very little time left.

This news about her being his mother was not surprising. It actually now made sense as to why their bond over the years was so strong. Not that he didn't love Claudia, because he did, it was just that he always felt that Selena was more than just his aunt.

Caden was grateful that he could bring Selena back to his home. And, Selena was grateful that she could spend the final months of her life with her only child.

On her deathbed, like her stepmother before her, she had saved a small fortune in a safe deposit box in Washington DC. When she gave Caden the key, she reminded him to use those funds to acquire something that he has always wanted, regardless how extravagant it might be.

"Caden, I want you to understand that all the Cassidy men before you have been plagued with some unknown curse that has destroyed their lives. I want that curse to end now. You are to use that money to set you free." Selena said her final words with conviction.

Once Gabby finally left Alex and agreed to meet with him, he knew that the money from Selena would finally free him.

For ten years Caden never opened the safe deposit box. But, once he did, he knew that now, he could leave Kaitlyn everything, and begin his new life with no more regrets.

When Caden finally received the call from Gabby that he had been waiting for, there were no more doubts.

"Hey, Caden...Buenes Diaz from Todos Santos. How is your Spanish?" Gabby asked excited to tell him her news.

"My Spanish is limited, but I make up for it with my French tongue, baby." Caden said instantly.

"I am counting on that promise. How soon can you get here? You will need to fly into Las Cabos Airport. It is located about twenty four miles from Cabos San Lucas, and then another hour to Todos Santos."

Gabby, at last was allowing herself to finally look forward to seeing Caden once more.

"I will call the airlines as soon as we hang up and text you all the details. Are you sure you will recognize me after all these years?" Caden asked.

"You are kidding, right? I would recognize you if you were dressed like a clown." Gabby said laughing.

"Okay, then. I guess we are finally going to do this. I will get on it right away…Oh, and Gabby?" Caden wanted to make certain that she didn't hang up.

"Yes. I am still here."

"Gabby… I love you! And, I can't wait to hold you in my arms." Caden finally said what he had been holding back for months.

"I want all of that too, baby. Now, get on that phone and make it happen. See you soon."

Gabby was the first to hang up. She hoped that Caden did not notice that she didn't respond with "I love you too."

It wasn't that she didn't love him…once, it was just that, now there was just so much they had to clear up. Or, at least, acknowledge.

It only took Caden three hours to make reservations for a direct flight from San Diego on Wednesday afternoon. That was only three days from now. Gabby was both excited and nervous.

Forty three years is a lifetime. How would she feel making love to him now? She certainly is no longer that innocent, naïve girl he fell in love with. But, on the other hand, it has been years since she had sexual intercourse with anyone.

The few times, after the rape, when she and Alex tried, she made him stop because it made her physically ill. After a few of those times, thankfully, Alex stopped trying.

There was no doubt in her mind, that Alex was being sexually active with others, but Gabby felt more relief than remorse. Yet, for some odd reason, the thought of being with Caden was not repulsive. It was almost exciting.

Sterling generously offered Gabby the town car service, with a driver, to pick up Caden from the airport. What Gabby didn't know, was that the driver was also a security agent.

Caden packed all his belongings in two suitcases and he had one carryon bag. The flight from San Diego to Cabo was only slightly longer than two hours. When the plane landed he asked the flight attendant to allow him to change his clothes and be the last one to deplane.

Once he explained why he needed that time, and that he was meeting an ex lover after forty three years, everybody, including the pilot was excited to see Gabby's reaction.

Once at the airport, Gabby and the driver walked to the luggage area to wait for Caden. As all the passengers went through customs first, the wait was about forty five minutes.

But, after everybody seemed to pass through the gates, Gabby began to be concerned when she couldn't see Caden.

Then, finally the flight crew came forward, and following behind them was a person fully dressed, from head to toe as a clown, carrying a bunch of inflated heart balloons.

It took Gabby a few seconds to realize what Caden had done. That is when she rushed up to him. He lifted her off the ground and when they kissed everyone, including the limo driver were cheering and some of the flight attendants were in tears.

When Caden finally released her, Gabby said,

"I can't believe you were able to pull this off in an airport. I am so glad you are finally here."

Gabby was happier at that moment than she had been for the last nine years. Whatever would happen in the future, could not compare to how complete she felt at this moment.

CHAPTER 47

Revenge, the sweetest morsel to the mouth that ever was cooked in hell.
Walter Scott

Murray Jackson
March, 2010-
October, 2010

Murray was admitted to the Savannah County Hospital, after the police picked him up from The Molly Pub, with multiple lacerations to the face, three teeth missing, two ribs broken, and a severe concussion.

After three days, he was transported to the local jail where he was being held until Kentucky enforcement agents could extradite him back to Lexington, where he was being charged with carjacking and rape.

When Murray's APB (All Points Bulletin) was transmitted to nearby states for robbing a liquor store in Columbus, Ohio, an attentive detective, in Louisville, matched a composite sketch of a man, who nine years earlier was accused of raping the wife of a prominent surgeon and owner of an elite horse breeding ranch in Lexington.

Sargent Brady, was on call the night that Gabriella Blair was found raped at the abandoned garage about ten miles outside of town, on Halloween night 2001.

Although the two men involved in the crime escaped, Mrs. Blair was able to describe in detail to the police sketch artist, what the man who raped her looked like. They also obtained the DNA from the hospital rape kit.

Now that Murray Robinson was being escorted back to Lexington, Detective Brady was certain that there would be enough evidence to prosecute this scum bag. All he needed now, was Mrs. Blair to identify Murray in a police lineup.

Unfortunately, after several weeks of attempting to contact Mrs. Blair, he was told that she was out of the country indefinitely, and would not be available, any time in the near future. Brady had no choice but to let Murray loose.

" You better be damn glad that I don't sue you Mother Fuckers for keeping me in this hell hole, without any evidence. The guy that should be arrested is Caden Cassidy, owner of The Molly Pub in Savannah . That pecker nearly killed me."

Murray was yelling loudly as he was going through the release protocol.

" Don't you piece of shit think you got away with this crime yet. Sick rats like you are easy to follow. Next time the cheese we put out for you, will have enough arsenic, that a trial won't be even necessary. Now get the fuck out of here, prick."

Brady was used to guys like Murray. He was sure that It wouldn't be long before they met again, and next time he would make sure Murray would be going to the Big House.

As soon as Murray was back on the streets, he hooked up with a few Spicks, that turned him on to mighty fine coke. But, coke ain't cheap. The Spicks told him how he could make enough to finance his habit and have as much pussy that he wanted.

"We even provide you with a plane ticket to San Diego. Today is your lucky day, Bro. We just lost a couple of Coyotajes who couldn't follow simple directions. So its all yours Man." The recruiter said.

This was the break that Murray was waiting for. Ever since, his brother, Calhoun split from him, he has been looking for jobs like this where the money is good and the work is easy.

The icing on this gig came when he learned that the fucking

asshole, Caden Cassidy was living in Southern California. Murray would show him, that he messed with the wrong Mother Fucker, when he took on Murray Jackson.

But, what really made Murray get a hard on, was when he was told that Gabby was unavailable to testify against him.

" That bitch wants me as much as I want her. That's why she left town. Once I find that Gabby, I'm gonna finish what we started, and then start all over again."

Murray started masturbating, closing his eyes and thinking of how Gabby will feel once he is inside of her again.

Then a few days ago, one of the Spicks told him that they have an amiga who cleans La Mansion in Ensenada. She told him that some American lady, was staying there for a few months and her name was Gabby Girard.

This Spick knew that Murray was searching for his property, and he gave him the address where his bitch was living.

Fuck, I was only a few days late. Gabby just left for Cabo San Lucas. But that's okay, because in a few weeks, I am going there to deliver some coke before my next Coyotaje run. My guys over there, already know that whoever finds my bitch will be rewarded with some of the purest coke on the black market.

I can still taste her pussy. Just thinking about how I will try all my new sex toys on her makes me sweat.

That basement in my house has been designed with handcuffs mounted on the beams to hold her up while I bang her. Then there are those whips for her ass. They are guaranteed to make her scream for more. Yeah, it's the perfect setup.

But, first I need a plan to get that Caden bastard to be there when I am ready to abduct Gabby. I will make him watch how I fuck her, and then I'll put a bullet in his head.

I will hurt you mother fucker, just give me the right time. When you think you are safe...happy! Oh, yeah just when you feel invincible that's when I will turn your dreams to shit, and when I stick my dick dripping *with your girls juices, into your mouth...only then will the debt be paid. That's when you will hear **BANG! BANG!***

CHAPTER 48

And I'd choose you;
In a hundred lifetimes,
In a hundred worlds,
In any version of reality,
I'd find you and,
I'd choose you.
The Chaos of Stars
Kiersten White

Gabby and Caden
October 2010
Todos Santos, Mexico

The ride home from the airport felt comfortable. Like I was picking up an old friend that I hadn't seen for a very long time.

We held hands, made out like teenagers, without going too far, but just far enough to know that there was still something strong, enduring, and very much alive.

My head on Caden's chest, his fingers stroking the strands of my hair, my hand rubbing the inside of his thigh, all this became very natural, very easy. Maybe too easy.

"Where have you been all these years, Gabby? I mean REALLY, where have you been internally?" Caden asked quietly.

That question brought me back to reality. For these past few minutes together when no words were needed, and just touching was enough, I was that eighteen year old Gabby, crazy in love again.

But, now, the ugly head of reality surfaced, just enough to remind me, of the critical issues, doubts, and questions, that must eventually be addressed.

"That is a very insightful observation, you want me to answer, Caden. I guess the best way to explain where I am now, is to understand where I have been.

Try to imagine my life as a chess game. At different times in my life I have been all of the pieces. Early on, soon after you left me, I was a pawn, who could never move backwards, only forward, but without much direction.

Then I met Alex, who would be the King; the whole chess world revolves around him, and in life this is also true. Now my identity metamorphosed into a rook.

Marriage to Alex meant that I was now only permitted to move in very specific lines, or boundaries. Everything in my life had a monetary value. Until, of course, I discovered that I could be a knight.

This was my awakening; my epiphany . Like in chess, the knight makes spiritual leaps into uncharted territories. Only a knight or pawn can initiate this first move. For once, I felt that I had more power than even the Queen.

After many difficult choices, some I controlled, and many I did not, I transformed into the bishop. Now there were only two paths available. One toward the intellect, the other toward the heart. So, as you may have noticed, I am still deciding what my next move will be." This I said with conviction.

"Wow! I had totally forgotten how amazing you are. How are you able to make these analogies? God, I have missed you all these years."

Caden was laughing and kissing Gabby at the same time. She was his oxygen; only she could resuscitate years of obliteration.

This is where he belonged. He now knew that he could never lose her again.

"I suppose I could ask you the same question Caden. What has kept you busy the last forty two years of your life, while I was moving around the chess board?" Gabby said, trying to lighten the tension.

Caden wanted to tell her that until today his life was an empty vacuum, with no purpose, and no direction. But, that was not totally true. Perhaps the unexpected, unsolicited, outcome was not desirable, but honestly, his life was fairly successful.

The Molly was his opus. It replaced his dream to be an architect. People in the community respected him. The Pub was now as popular as that iconic bar in Boston, named after the popular television series *Cheers*. And, just like that friendly watering hole, every regular customer was treated like family.

He, and Kaitlyn must have raised their twin boys well. Both graduated from college, started their own surf and fishing store at Huntington Beach, California, where they were now living *Their Dream*.

In spite of feeling that his marriage was incomplete, he never allowed that to interfere in his daily life. That is, until Gabby stepped back in. That made all the difference in the world.

"Well, to be perfectly honest, almost everything was quintessential . When I left Georgetown there was nothing that I wanted to remember, especially you, Gabby.

Savannah was my safety net. I was fairly confident that you would never come home.

Although, later, I hoped that I was wrong. *The Molly* was designed with you in mind. God, I wish you could see how much of you is in that place. But, then it just became a daily reminder of what I had lost.

Remind me to tell you the story of *Abbey Road*, and the day I met George Harrison. I am not as good at illustrating my feelings as you are Gabby, but I can tell you with a strong conviction that I would rather experience a tidal wave than ever be separated from you again."

Caden was determined to make Gabby understand how critical

this trip was for both of them.

This was not as clear for Gabby. It was not that she disagreed with giving their relationship a chance, to nurture once again, but Caden needed to understand that they were no longer the same two people who were in love, years ago.

One condition that she would need to make him understand, is that she was not ready for a sexual relationship. This would be difficult for Caden to accept, since that was the core at one time that held them together.

Gabby needed to know, now that they were both so much older, that sex was not the only attraction.

The guest room, located on the main floor, but on the opposite side from her master bedroom is where, at least initially, Caden would sleep.

Allowing him to share her intimate space, was not something Gabby was immediately ready to relinquish.

The decision to go directly to the beach house from the airport would allow both of them some needed privacy. There would be plenty of opportunities later for Caden to meet Sterling and Maggie.

Once the driver, helped unload the luggage from the car, they were now finally alone. Before any misunderstandings would occur, they would need to talk.

"Find a place out on the balcony, and I will bring a plate of chips, guacamole, and tostadas that my friend Maggie prepared for us."

Gabby did not give Caden any opportunity to get close enough to her, as she disappeared into the kitchen.

When she was certain he was outside, Gabby walked to the French Doors and without stepping outside asked Caden,

"I have Sangria, Margaritas, beer, or just about any other alcoholic beverage, as long as it isn't too complicated." Gabby waited for Caden to respond.

But, he was admiring the dragonfly faerie statue that Sterling had given her.

Sounding preoccupied, he walked around the artwork, and said, without looking at her,

"Beer, will be fine…or anything that is easy for you."

Then, as if he appeared to come out of his trance, he added,

"Do you need help with anything?" But, by that time Gabby was out of sight.

Caden took a seat in the leather bucket patio chair, pondering how to politely ask who SP was? It really was an innocent question. After all, that wire garden statue is the focal point on the patio, only being second to the ocean view.

And, since whoever it was that gave this to Gabby made sure his initials were obvious, she must be used to having people enquire about it.

"So, what do you think about this ocean view, Caden? Isn't it just spectacular. And, because the balcony wraps around the house, we can see both the sunrise and sunset."

This was one of the features that convinced Gabby to buy the property.

Caden stood up when he saw her approaching and reached for the tray that appeared quite heavy.

"Thanks…I was hoping that I could make it this far without causing a mess. Didn't realize how heavy it was until, you took over." Gabby said relieved.

"Glad to know that I can still be some help to you." Caden said, trying not to sound irritated.

But, when their eyes met, Gabby could sense a slight feeling of tension as she took her seat and handed Caden his bottle of Dos Equis.

She then poured a glass of Shiraz Casa Grande for herself. It was one of the white wines that she brought back from the Ensenada Wine festival.

She particularly liked the taste of black fruit, cinnamon, hazelnut, and semisweet chocolate. Gabby had brought an extra glass for

Caden if he decided to try it.

She was going to suggest a toast, but then again what exactly would be appropriate . Then Caden broke the silence when he raised his beer bottle, looked directly at Gabby with those familiar, cornflower blue eyes, the color blue that is impossible to match,

"To second chances"

He then tapped her wine glass, reached for her empty hand and kissed it, never taking his eyes off of her.

Keeping my composure was going to be difficult. I could feel the fire and ice streaming through my veins, with such intensity that if there was lightning and thunder, it would be silenced. I then raised my glass in response,

"May the best day of our past be the worst day of our future" Gabby clicked her glass with Caden's beer.

"Touché, Gabby. I never realized that you knew any Irish toasts?"

And, Gabby was not about to reveal that this quote was one that Jake included in his journal, for her, while she was visiting Inchydoney, Ireland. Especially now that she knew that was where Caden was born.

It was just the right response to eliminate the tension. Until, Caden brought up Sterling's elusive gift.

"This wire faerie statue is quite impressive, Gabby. Whoever SP is, must also be impressed by you. I can't imagine that there is more than one of these anywhere else in the world."

Caden waited for her response. He felt that whatever was in the past he could live with, but if there was any competition for her affection, he needed to know now.

Gabby took a few more sips of her wine, trying rationally to decide how to explain Sterling to Caden. There was no easy exit to this door he just opened.

"Alright, Caden I am going to be perfectly honest with you. We cannot ever hope to renew our relationship if there are lies. But, this affair is complicated. You will need to accept what I reveal without questioning, because honestly I don't have answers."

Gabby was trying to assess Caden's reaction, but there was none. She decided that there was no easy way to explain this.

"Sterling Powers and I were lovers for twelve years, while I was married to Alex. It was only a sexual relationship. I mean, no love, just physical satisfaction for us both. That ended on Halloween night 2001.

I was with Sterling that evening, until I picked up my car from a local garage and was kidnapped. One of the men raped me, and probably would have killed me, if Sterling had not found out where I was. He saved my life, and nearly died that night.

I only saw him a few times after that, until seven months ago, when I called him from Tybee Beach and asked him to help me leave until I could decide what to do with my life.

We now have a platonic relationship . The statue was a house warming gift. But, you need to understand Caden, that since the rape, I have not been sexually active. If you want to go back to Kaitlyn or California I will understand." A great relief took over my inner being.

There was still details about Jake that I needed to confess, if Caden decided to stay. But, the most immediate issues were now in the open.

Caden, got up, walked over to me and kneeled down so that he could look directly in my eyes closely. With both his hands, he held my face and we kissed for what seemed like hours.

"Gabby, you must know by now that what I feel for you, has never has been limited to only sexual desires. We will work this out together and at your pace.

All I ask is that you don't shut me out of your life. I could never take that again. If you no longer love me, like you did, I will stay in Todos Santos just to be near you. Let's just take this each day at a time. Is that agreeable with you?"

He wanted to tell her about his confrontation with Murray, and how he came close to killing him several months ago. But, that would just add more pain to that nightmare.

Caden, instead wiped the tears that were now flowing uncontrollably from her eyes. For Gabby It was the first time in many years that these were tears of joy and not grief, but she could not share this with Caden now.

You pierce my soul. I am half agony, half hope. Tell me not that I am too late, that such precious feelings are gone forever. I offer myself to you again with a heart even more your own, that when you almost broke it,(forty three years ago).

Dare not say that man forgets sooner than women, that his love has an earlier death. I have loved none but you. (Jane Austin)

CHAPTER 49

Sometimes our light goes out, but is blown into a flame by another human being. Each of us owes deepest thanks to those who have rekindled this light.

Albert Schweitzer

Caden and Gabby
October, 2010
Todos Santos, Mexico

Caden and I spent the next several days walking on the beach alone, holding hands, watching sunsets and sunrises, sometimes not speaking for hours, but never having sex.

Other times, we would stay inside all day talking about anything and everything. The past, present, future were all discussed, lamented, and projected. Yet, sex was avoided like the plague.

Cooking dinner together became a ritual. Caden proudly shared his recipe for his Irish version of Shepherd Pie, and I made the only thing I knew I wouldn't burn, fettuccine with fresh shrimp.

Most of the other days we played it safe and Caden grilled everything from rib eye steaks to cedar plank salmon. My only contribution was a fresh green tossed salad.

"I guess you were lucky to marry someone who had a cook, or maybe I should say, he was the lucky one." Caden laughed at his own cleverness.

Teasingly, I stabbed him with my fork, and we playfully started fencing with our eating utensils. When I lost my "dagger "I used my white napkin as a symbol to surrender.

"I thought that you would remember that I was never really very good at any domestic chores. Cooking is only one of my limitations. Soon you will realize how fortunate you were that we never married." Gabby said jokingly.

Caden looked up, reached across the table and lightly put his one finger on her lips.

"Not marrying you Gabby was the MOST unfortunate choice in my life. I was young, restless, proud, and insanely immature. I have replayed that moment many times in my head." Caden said remorsefully.

Choices. I recalled that was what Jake wanted to tell me in his final journal. He almost made the exact same claim that Caden just made.

What was it that Jake said I should ask Caden? Gabby tried intensely to recall what he wrote. *Yes…I now remember…Ask Caden why he never tried to find out what really happened that New Year's Eve night? And, was he ever really ready for a lifetime commitment.*

Gabby admitted that she needed to know the answers to those questions.

But, there would be time, *time to awaken the sleeping giant, time to make excuses, time to build that mental wall that prevents the sea from revealing an unbearable pain, and time to ponder what Pythagoras really meant about time being the soul of the universe.*

It was ironic how his past actions are on my mind and yet, it is me giving advice that,

" Continuing to dwell on the past will never move us toward the future Caden."

It was too late. I said these words even while I had unanswered questions myself.

Now was the best time to just change the subject and move on.

"Maggie and Blake have invited us to join them for dinner at *The Hotel California*. Then you can meet the lovely Eleanor Rigby." I waited for his reaction.

" Don't you find it just a little odd that Eleanor Rigby lives in The Hotel California? I mean, you must remember the lyrics to that song by The Eagles?"

Now Caden was honestly curious about this coincidence.

" Well, who did you expect to live there? Maybe Witchy Woman? " I was quite pleased at my response.

"Okay…you win Gabby. I guess that is why I am here. I never know what to expect with you."

It was a relief that we were moving to another subject.

"After dinner, we will all go to Blake's club for drinks and entertainment . Just make sure that you get plenty of rest before we go. Nightclubs and bars have no official closing time here. We will probably be up into the early morning hours."

Before she gave Caden a chance to object to any of her plans, Gabby carefully sliced a small piece of her steak and tempted Caden to take a bite.

"You do realize Gabby that this is what Eve did to Adam in the Garden of Eden with her apple." Nevertheless, Caden took the steak that she offered.

When Gabby spoke to Maggie, later that night on the phone, Gabby told her that she and Caden were looking forward to meeting for drinks and dinner.

Maggie, wisely suggested that neither Sterling nor Caden know in advance, that they would be finally meeting each other also.

"This will make the introductions more natural. They won't have time to think in advanced any preconceived opinions." Maggie added.

Gabby agreed that this was the best approach to take. She had not seen Sterling since his return from Pebble Beach, to even thank him for the breathtaking sculpture.

And, although she had been perfectly honest with Caden about her relationship with Sterling, this was a very complicated puzzle that she wanted to avoid turning into the Devils Triangle.

For the next three days, Gabby made sure that Caden was relaxing comfortably. They slept late some mornings, always in their separate bedrooms, and whoever was up first, would prepare the coffee. It was beginning to feel like Caden was a very close roommate.

Caden was not on the same mind wave with Gabby. The last few days were pleasant, but he needed to convince her to let him back into her physical life.

During the months before he left Kaitlyn, it seemed more difficult for his cock to get hard. And, when he was able to get the head of his penis to tingle, the swollen member would drip uncontrollably before Kaitlyn was ready. He didn't want that same thing to happen with Gabby.

Each morning, when she would stroll into the kitchen, wearing nothing but a cotton night shirt that barely covered her well shaped bottom, Caden had to control his desire to take her right there.

Sometimes, while pouring her coffee, she would stand directly in front of the sunlight revealing her breasts and naked vagina.

Caden, discretely moved one hand into his boxers, stroking his prick, until he could no longer take the pressure. That is when he would take long, morning hikes up the mountains.

When he returned, Gabby was already dressed, making it much easier to cope. Caden knew that Gabby had been without intercourse for many years, but there was so much more that they could do to express their mutual love.

Maybe this evening, after a few drinks, he could at least convince her to let him into her bedroom.

As Gabby predicted, Blake and Caden immediately became friends. Like with Maggie, the age difference was not an issue. They both owned and operated a popular pub; both had a common taste for music, and both loved women that were mysteriously elusive.

When Gabby introduced Caden to Eleanor Rigby, he did not feel that familiar warmth from the elderly woman.

Typically , Eleanor's demeanor was like receiving a jovial greeting card for no expected occasion. There was always something about

Eleanor that made Gabby feel genuinely uplifted after a visit.

So, when she appeared rather cold, but polite to Caden, it seemed out of character.

"Nice to meet you, Mr. Cassidy. I understand that you will be visiting our small town for a short time?"

Eleanor seemed to emphasize, short time.

"Actually, Eleanor, Caden has not yet decided just how long he will be remaining in Todos Santos. He is also a business owner, like you."

Gabby was trying to find a common bond between them that would ease the tension.

Eleanor picked up four menus, ignoring Gabby's comment, and took them both, silently , to a nice table next to the water fountain in the patio, where Maggie and Blake were already sitting.

"Well , Mr. Cassidy, then as a business owner I am sure you cannot be away from your business for very long. " Eleanor said, while distributing the menus.

"But, please enjoy your stay, and visit us again." That was Eleanor's final comment.

"Am I the only one that sensed that Eleanor was saying goodbye to me more than hello?" Caden said while reviewing the menu.

"Don't take it personal." Maggie added.

"Eleanor sometimes just has bad days. This must be one of them."

After the introductions to everyone, dinner went smoothly. When Maggie suggested that Gabby join her in the restroom, she told her that Sterling would meet them at the club.

"God, I hope that this isn't going to be a mistake Maggie. Caden knows now about Sterling, and Sterling knows about Caden. So, why do I have this uneasy feeling that I am in the direct route to the eye of a tornado ?"Gabby said, on the way back to the table.

"You knew Gabby, that once Caden arrived here this was impossible to avoid. Just remain calm. We are all civilized adults, this should not be a problem."

Maggie assured Gabby with a reassuring smile, and her hand steady on her shoulder for support.

For just a very brief second, like when you turn your head too quickly, it was Molly talking to me. A light touch of her hand was all it took. It was what she knew how to do best when I got rattled.

It was after ten, when we finished dinner, and decided to take a short walk to *The Mariposa*. A full moon was out, making it very pleasant.

Blake had reserved for us a table with five chairs, nearest to the stage. After about five minutes , I noticed Sterling standing near the bar. He looked taller than usual.

Instinctively, I walked over to meet him. It had been several weeks since we had talked.

If it wasn't for Maggie, I really would not even known for sure, that he was back from California . Then Maggie had made these plans, and now that we were all here, I was beginning to get a little nervous.

Sterling bent down slightly, so that he could put his arms around me.

Because of the loud music, I whispered in his ear,

"Your housewarming gift is exceptionally beautiful. Everyday I see it, I think of you. One day, we must talk about it together. Thank you."

My first instinct was to give him a grateful kiss on the cheek. But, then I remembered that when we were intimately together, his unspoken rule was no kissing.

Instead, she took Sterling's hand and guided him to the table where everyone was seated.

Sterling had not said one word to her. But, there was no doubt that he was impressed with the emerald green sheath dress, with the cut out, crisscross back that exposed her tan waist.

He also could not help but notice that her hair was partially braided in the front,forming a halo crown. The remainder of her dark tresses continued to cascade right above her waist.

Gabby appeared radiant this evening. It was not until Sterling noticed the slightly grey haired gentleman, with his long hair pulled back into a ponytail, that he realized why.

She was still holding his hand when Caden rose and said,

" Hello Mr. Sterling. It is a pleasure to finally meet you. I am Caden Cassidy."

Sterling shook his hand, pulled a chair to the table and sat next to Gabby, who was in the middle with Caden on the other side of her.

"Welcome, Mr. Cassidy to Todos Santos. Gabby has told me how long it has been since the two of you have met. Is forty two years correct?"

Sterling wanted there to be no doubt, in this man's mind, that Gabby and he were close enough to share everything.

"This must be a remarkable reunion."

He added, trying to sound genuinely polite.

For some unknown reason, Sterling could not identify why, but the hairs on the back of his neck were standing uncomfortably upright. The last time he felt this uneasy was when he met Alex Blair.

Because of this strange feeling, he restrained himself the remainder of the evening to conversation that was considered safe, general topics. Sterling did not like feeling out of control.

Thankfully after several rounds of drinks the mood was cautiously friendly.

"I understand that you and Gabby met at Georgetown as students, in 1967. Those were exciting years. Would I recognize any of your building designs at Savannah ?"

Sterling, once again was taking the offensive position. He wanted to know more about this intruder. But, what he really wanted to know was how Caden managed to keep Gabby still interested after all these years.

Sterling had no way of knowing that the questions he was asking were leading Caden to a very unpleasant past that he was not prepared to currently discuss with a complete stranger. It was like Sterling throwing fresh salt on old wounds.

"Gabby and I actually attended Savannah High School together. We even graduated in the same class."

Caden finally stretched his arm around her shoulder, displaying for the first time his obvious affection.

"Unfortunately, for me, she was preoccupied during those years. So, when I finally had the opportunity to meet her again at Georgetown, it was fate."

Caden kissed Gabby's hand, but avoided providing Sterling with any information about the architect fiasco, and why he left Georgetown without a degree.

"Caden owns a very successful Pub, *The Molly* , in Savannah . Very much as popular as your *Maggie Mariposa*, Blake."

Gabby was making every effort to shift the attention away from Sterling.

This was not the time or place she wanted to go into a detailed explanation about her relationship with Caden. All Sterling knew, at the moment , was that he was going to stay with her, at least for awhile.

Perhaps this uneasiness might have something to do with me sitting, sandwiched between, the first man that taught me to feel self confident sexually, and the other man, who introduced me to an entire new world of erotica. Somewhere , there has to be a suitable balance between them.

Unlike Savannah, most bars in Mexico remain open until there are no longer customers. Gabby knew that this would be a very long night.

"I have regular customers here that come in at ten in the evening and stay until the sunrise. We fix them huevos rancheros for breakfast, a hangover Bloody Mary, a house specialty, and then send them on their way until the next day when it starts all over once again." Blake explained to Caden.

"And I was told that this was a sleepy town that retired each night at ten."

Caden said, directing his comment to Gabby.

"The majority of Todos Santos does not live Blake's lifestyle. He is an exception to everything." Gabby smiled.

" But then Maggie likes that unpredictable natural quality, don't you Maggie?"

Gabby managed to make Maggie blush. Keeping her true feelings incognito, was a game Maggie played expertly. Soon that game would be a past memory.

By two AM the group of five decided to move their party to Gabby's residence. Nobody but Maggie and Caden had ever visited her new home.

"Of course we can all go to my beach house. I only suggested Sterling's because it is so much larger." Gabby explained.

What Maggie had no way of knowing, was that it was always going to be at Gabby's house.

Privately, Gabby pulled Blake aside, and asked reluctantly,

"Are you certain that you want to do this tonight? Maybe it would be better if the two of you were alone." She, added.

Earlier, that afternoon, when Blake delivered a sheet cake, to Gabby's house, with his picture on the front and the words, *Marry Me Please, Maggie!* She knew that he was determined that tonight was the right time.

"I am hoping that with you and Sterling here, and everything that you have told her, I will have at least a chance to make Maggie my wife." Blake was not going to let anything stop him tonight.

"How do you know what I told Maggie, Blake?"

Gabby was hoping that she was able to convince Maggie, but felt a little uncomfortable knowing that Blake also knew about Jake and Caden.

"Oh No...Maggie never revealed what you told her, but a few days ago, for the very first time in three years, we woke up together in the same bed. It was magic, Gabby for us both. That is when I knew that I didn't want to spend another night without her."

With this confession, Gabby took the cake, and prayed that at least one of them would find their happily ever after.

Once they all arrived, at Gabby's house, It was not a surprise that everyone raved over the faerie statue. Sterling mentioned how pleased he was that it fit perfectly on the balcony.

Because the early morning had a nice ocean breeze the guests all found a comfortable place on the inviting terrace. Maggie had strung an assortment of mini lights, that included mercury glass mushrooms, multicolor glass finials, and pierced metal stars, on the two largest Ahuehuete trees.

When Gabby first saw this it reminded her of an entrance to a secret garden. Soon it would be the place where Maggie would renew her faith in love.

Gabby excused herself briefly to brew some fresh coffee . She then added Kahului and tequila. Maggie insisted on helping, but Sterling convinced her to find some pleasant mood music, and he would help carry out the beverages.

Alone in the kitchen, Sterling asked directly If Gabby and Caden were now a couple.

"If that is what you really want Gabby, I will understand. But, I am going to fly to Catemaco , Veracruz in a few days for another spiritual cleansing. If you want to join me, alone of course, it might be what you need now."

Sterling felt that Gabby needed to experience at least once this ritual, before she made a commitment to Caden.

"If you are asking me if we have had sex, the answer is no. We are however, growing closer every day. I do not know if I can actually go through with intercourse , but Caden is making that fear slowly disappear. I think I love him, but I am also confused.

Did you know that Blake is going to ask Maggie to marry him in a few moments? Let's just focus on that for now."

Sterling had to convince Gabby to go with him to Veracruz . He would be able to tell her about Alex, and give the security team time to wire her house.

"Alright. We will wait until Monday, when you come into the office. Just remember Gabby how vulnerable you are right now." Sterling conceded but was not giving up.

Blake took the cake from Sterling, placed it on the glass table and asked Maggie to help serve the dessert to the guests.

She opened the top of the box and said, "This cake is so large Blake, it could feed the entire town."

Then she suddenly became silent. Her eyes filled with tears as she read the words *Marry Me Maggie!* Scrolled in purple icing, her favorite color.

Before she could answer him, Blake was on his knee, holding an exquisite pear shaped solitaire diamond, surrounded by smaller ones.

"Maggie…You are the center of my universe. I love you now and forever. Please say yes, Maggie?"

Blake waited patiently for what seemed like forever.

Then Maggie looked directly at me, for affirmation. I blew her a kiss, and nodded my head yes. Then Maggie, bent down on her knees also. Blake slipped the ring on her finger and they embraced, kissing passionately.

Sterling started clapping, and put his arms around the young couple. Caden congratulated his new friend, and Maggie, but never took his eyes off of Gabby.

"I need to call my Madre and Papa…they will be so happy. And Gabby…you must be my Maid of Honor…please Gabby, please!"

Maggie could not stop her excitement. Until Blake reminded us all that it was already three in the morning.

Everyone began to exit together. But, while Caden carried the remainder of the cake to Blake's car, Sterling reminded me to be at his office by ten on Monday. Before I could say a word, he was waving adios.

Once inside the house, Caden began helping to clear the plates and coffee cups off the balcony.

Then Gabby, without any warning began to kiss Caden. First gently, softly with her tongue searching for the right rhythm . When he respond with a powerful thrust he made Gabby's lips quiver. Then, her pelvis began to gyrate against his bulging pants.

It had been years since he felt this alive. Without hesitating, her hands unzipped his pants. Caden managed to release both breasts from her plunging neckline. First, he squeezed gently each nipple.

"My God Gabby, I want my mouth to taste your breasts until they are as hard as my cock."

Caden continued to nibble and lick famished from so many years without her. Gabby said nothing.

I tell her everything that I am going to do with her. But when I begin to remove her dress, she stops me.

Instead, she moves my hand inside her thigh. When I realize that she isn't wearing panties, my fingers begin to explore her wet inviting vagina. All I really want at this moment is for my tongue to return deep inside of her where it has always belonged.

But, before I am able to move any further, Gabby, releases my swelling penis. She then removes the rest of my clothing. I am completely naked, while she remains fully dressed, with only her breasts exposed, like an erotic portrait.

Using her tongue to lick me from the neck down , she reaches my penis . On her knees, I feel her inhale my cock. Her tongue is so long, so soft.

I guide her head with my hands, and fingers through her hair, moaning in complete pleasure. Once her hands reach around my buttocks, Gabby begins to squeeze them, using the same pace as her mouth. I can feel my self getting ready to come, and I yell for her to stop.

That is when, still wearing that green gown, Gabby and I lie on the leather couch, with her wet pussy on my stomach.

Without a word she mounts me guiding my penis into her vagina until it is sucked in like her mouth swallowed my cock. Her dress feels like clouds, as she moves her hips in a circular motion penetrating deep, I can feel her contractions claiming me. With her breasts in my mouth, we climax together like a well tuned instrument.

Her body and mine joined together, neither of us move. My ejection has somehow remained stiff inside although the semen droplets were proof of my orgasm.

Gabby leads me into her bedroom. I am sore, but cannot not get enough of her. I am tired but cannot sleep. I want to close my eyes while holding Gabby close, but I never want to awaken without her again.

That is when her head moves down once more to my cock, while her pussy is in my mouth. Together we have oral sex. I can taste my leftover semen mingled with her sweet juices.

Finally, after we can do no more, I notice the bloody sheets beneath us.

"Gabby, are you alright? Certainly you have gone through menopause already, haven't you?" I asked worried that there was something wrong.

We are both too old for all of this sex, but it felt better than any other time in my life.

"I am like a well seasoned virgin, Caden. Remember, it has been seven years since I had intercourse. You are my first, and this is the proof." Gabby says.

We move into my bedroom, and return to the bed. Our naked bodies fit perfectly into a comfortable slumber.

It is not until Sunday afternoon that Gabby wakes up and sees Caden lying next to her.

How did this happen? Not only once but many times, If I remember correctly.

Caden begins moving his hand to feel Gabby, but she is sitting up with a robe around her.

"Hey, there stranger. Remember me? Come over here and let me help you recall what a great time we had. You are one hell of a lover, Gabby!"

Caden took her hand and let her feel how hard he was. It was almost like when he was eighteen again.

Gabby pulled her hand away.

"I don't remember all that we did Caden, and I know that you won't believe this, but I really did not know I was with you. I mean…it was like I was dreaming!" Gabby was still totally confused.

" I know what you mean, baby. It was so unreal that I still do not know how many times we had sex. I mean, you kept wanting more, and I was somehow able to keep giving you more.

We must have gone through at least five different positions. Some I didn't even knew existed. But, my favorite was when we ate each other at the same time…I mean that was surrealistic!"

" STOP Caden! You don't understand what I am saying. I mean that I really don't remember having SEX WITH YOU at all last night. Whatever happened, was a terrible mistake."

Gabby somehow needed to understand why this happened. Was it really possible that she could have amnesia?

CHAPTER 50

This is only a record of broken and apparently unrelated memories, some of them as distinct and sequent as brilliant beads upon a thread...
Ambrose Bierce

Gabby and Caden
October, 2010
Todos Santos, Mexico

After Caden actually realized what Gabby was telling him, he was torn between pain and anger.

"How can you expect me to believe Gabby that after, over twelve hours of the most gratifying sex I have ever experienced in my lifetime, that you tell me, not only that you do not remember it, you don't remember being with ME during that time.

I mean, really Gabby? Who the fuck were you fantasizing I was?" Caden could not accept any of this.

And, Gabby could not explain it even to herself. What was most disturbing now, was that Caden somehow blamed her for all of this.

"Do you really want to know what I think Gabby? Are you willing to listen? Okay, these problems we are having, it has never just been about us. It has always been about the three of us. Jake, you and me." Caden finally knew that this was true.

"You need to let him go Gabby. You forgave Jake for leaving you, but you could never forgive me. Fuck it, Gabby...Jake is dead. He sent you around the world trying to convince you that he was still alive. He gave you journals!" Caden picked one up from the bedside,

" He still is trying to manipulate you from the grave. But he is

FUCKING DEAD. But, I am not! And, I have loved you longer and harder than he ever could. Let me in, Gabby. What else must I do to prove this to you?"

Gabby could not look directly into those crystal blue eyes. It was impossible for her to respond. He was right. But, there was something very wrong.

"I need to find out Caden what happened last night. Until then, I can arrange for you to stay at The Hotel California or with Blake Santiago. There is also the option of leaving. Whatever you decide.

I am going to Veracruz with Sterling for a few days. There is a Shaman that hopefully will be able to sort out all of this. When I return, we can decide together what our next move will be."

Gabby amazed even herself at how calm she was after all that just had happened.

"And, now, you tell me after this mind blowing sex we had, you are leaving me here and going with an ex lover? Oh, Hell No! Gabby."

How many insults does she really think I am going to take before retaliating? I may be in love with her but I'm no Fucking idiot.

"Calm down Caden. First of all you can't tell me what to do. This is my house and you are my guest." Gabby was pacing back and forth trying to make sense.

"And…I explained to you my relationship with Sterling, even though you had no right to know. This is all very complicated. You either trust me or you don't. That part is simple. Either way, I am going to Veracruz."

He should consider this an ultimatum. In the past I have lived my life the way other men have expected me to. Not any more.

Eventually , Caden decided to stay with Blake, who was happy to have a roommate. He would let this drama play out to the final scene, and then no further excuses. Everybody has there limits.

" Man, your timing is perfect. I need help at the club, now that Maggie and I are formally engaged. We can take a ride over to Cabo and maybe do a little fishing, and by the time Gabby gets home everything will be cool.

Trust me Caden. If Maggie Mendoza finally agreed to marry me, Gabby will also come around." Blake sounded more optimistic than Caden felt.

Before Caden left, Gabby decided to give him the Christmas card that she found at the art gallery.

" I have a peace offering to give you . I thought you might remember this." She handed him the photograph and waited for his reaction.

"Unbelievable. Where did you find this? Just look how young we were then. Our whole lives ahead of us. That trip to New York with you, nothing ever compared to it, with anything else in my life." Caden placed the photo safely in his laptop carrier.

Gabby walked over and put her arms around Caden's neck.

"We will find someway to work this out. After all we are here together after forty two years, in the same city, again. Anything is possible Caden."

We kissed, like we were saying goodbye forever. It was the closure we never had before, and it made me shiver.

Caden then walked over to the door, and without saying another word, turned his head slightly, smiled nervously , and then he was gone.

I could swear that for those few minutes that we held each other, we were back in our Georgetown apartment on New Year's Eve, that pivotal moment when our lives changed forever. *Choices!*

Before, I met with Sterling the next morning, I decided to do some research on amnesia. I may not find the cure but at least I could understand maybe the cause.

The first source that I found on the internet was a book, "The Drama of the Gifted Child: The Search of the True Self" by Alice Miller.

The following passage immediately drew my attention: "Without realizing that the past is constantly determining their present actions, (gifted children) avoid learning anything about their history.

They continue to live in their repressed childhood situation ignoring the fact that it no longer exists , continuing to avoid dangers that although once real, have not been real for a long time."

This may have been directed as a children's study, but I could have been one of those clinical subjects that Mrs. Miller used to develop her theory.

Although, this observation was very accurate it did not give me any further insights on amnesia, specifically sexually related amnesia.

After further scanning through Google, an entire plethora of sites popped up.

In November 2009, Foxsexpert published an article that recognized how the most incredible sex can lead to sex amnesia. Since 1956 TGA, transient global amnesia known as "recurrent coital amnesia" , is triggered by sex. Luckily this is traced to a stressful emotional event. Now I finally was beginning to make some progress.

Certainly in the past nine years, if not my entire life, I have been a candidate for this phenomenon.

This report went on to say that TGA is typically triggered after climax. BINGO! *There it was. Clearly stated. Sexual amnesia is caused by a sudden lack of blood flowing to the brain, resulting in memory disruptions .*

What seemed to be lacking was an explanation as to when this amnesia begins.

I was full cognizant when Caden put his arms around me and we kissed. We also both willingly engaged, sometimes for a lengthy period of time, at kissing, from the time he arrived at Todos Santos.

But, sometime, after his initial kiss last night, it led to many hours of exceptional sex, without my intentional consent.

Under no circumstance would I have agreed to any form of sex with Caden until I felt that our unresolved Issues had been addressed . And, has this ever happened before to me? Is there anything that I can now do to prevent this from happening again?

As reluctant as I was to tell Sterling what happened, I also questioned if this ever happened when I was with him. More importantly, did he know any local sex therapist that he could refer me to?

Sleep for now was the best solution. There was nothing left to do but wait until tomorrow. In my bed, there was a sense of sadness.

I truly wanted so much to be with Caden once again, but maybe he was right about Jake. I would need to decide what to do with those journals. It maybe time for the journals to retire or given to another lost soul.

I could no longer dwell on Caden, Jake, Alex or even Sterling tonight. As I prepared for bed, I made certain to take one of my last Ambien sleeping pills. If it worked properly, by the morning, I should at least be able to concentrate.

Passing from reality to the dream world, I was visited by several wise owls that had messages for me from the master sages.

First, Bhagavad Gita, means Song of the Lord, when translated from Hinduism, offered me the insight that *never the spirit was born, the spirit shall cease to be never. Never was time, it was not, End and Beginnings are dreams!*

"That is a very astute observation Gabby. One that I may have pondered on during one of my earlier lives."

My muse had returned. This time fully grown from the young child that greeted me many years ago.

Trying to determine where I was, looking out the train window , I recognized the familiar sign stating Platform 67. This was when I realized, that this time, I was actually in the train, whereas, in the past dreams, I was waiting for the train. Did this mean that I finally knew where I was going?

"Not exactly, Gabby. But, it is definitely progress. I mean you did take the initiative to at least board this particular train."

"How were you able to hear my thoughts? Are you able to do this all the

time? I find that gift both annoying and fascinating." I said aloud to my traveling companion.

"Actually Gabby, you have this same ability. Unfortunately, however, you do not tend to pay very good attention to what is being said…especially to yourself." The lady sounded a bit frustrated.

That was when the second owl interrupted and said that it was time to receive my second message. This time it came in the form of a talking note:

" If a man could pass through paradise in a dream, and have a flower presented to him as a pledge that his soul had really been there, and if he found that flower in his hand when he awake-Aye, what then? (Samuel Taylor Coleridge).

Could the dandelion that both Maggie and I received in our dreams validate this assumption?

"There you go again Gabby, second doubting yourself. The dandelion is your connection to this dream world. The voices that provide you with answers are your dreams crossing into reality." The lady smiled, satisfied that we were finally making progress.

Just as I was about to ask my Dream companion if she knew where this train was going, and if she was traveling with me the entire way, my final owl appeared.

"Watch the messages written on the billboards, Gabby."

I followed , this final owl's directions, when I could feel the train beginning to move slowly, I read each message aloud:

"We are such stuff as dreams are made on; and our little life is rounded with sleep (Shakespeare)"

"Gabby, we find who we really are in our dreams."

"Your true meaning in life Gabby, will never be found in your waking hours; the answers are here, in your dreams."

I noticed the young lady across from me, standing up. The remainder of the train appeared empty.

"Where are you going, my traveling partner? Please don't leave me yet? I have so many unanswered questions." The more I pleaded, the faster she faded away.

Once again I was alone realizing that if my dream was only an illusion, then my life is also no more than that illusion.

Chapter 51

The belief in a supernatural source of evil, is not necessary; men alone are quite capable of every wickedness."
  Joseph Conrad
  Gabby and Sterling
  October, 2010
  Catemaco, Mexico.

"No Gabby. You never had amnesia when we had sex. Maybe it was just not mind blowing enough for you!"

Sterling could not stop laughing when Gabby explained what happened with her and Caden.

"This is not a joke, Sterling. Having sex without remembering, or even consenting, is a serious issue. I only told you because I was hoping that you could help me. Not mock me." Gabby's was beyond herself.

She really didn't even want him to know about this, but she wasn't sure who to confide in. If she told Maggie, it might make her fear that the same thing could happen to her.

Gabby didn't want to be responsible for causing any doubts in Maggie's mind, that might lead her to canceling her plans to marry Blake.

"You are right, Gabby. Forgive me? But, I can understand why Caden is upset. And, by the way, I am not very fond of him."

Sterling could not really pinpoint the reason why he disliked Caden, but he knew that he was not good for Gabby.

"This really has nothing to do with Caden…well, what I mean is that he didn't do anything wrong. I just need to find out why it happened, so it doesn't happen again…EVER!"

Gabby sounded desperate and felt out of control.

"Okay. Calm down." Sterling walked over and held her in his arms, reassuring her that they would work this out.

"Not far from Catemaco, in Veracruz, there is a sex therapist that I sent Maggie when she was having trouble adjusting to a normal life. I will call her. Okay…?" He waited to get a positive reaction from Gabby.

She nodded her head, relieved that she was at least making progress.

"Thank you. Now tell me about this witch doctor. Do you really think that he can solve my other problems? And, what can I expect to happen?"

Gabby was anxious to get everything back to normal, even if it meant using an unorthodox process.

"Before we discuss that ritual I need to tell you what happened at Pebble Beach.

Sterling decided that he could no longer keep this from Gabby. It might not be the best time, with all these other revelations, but it would at least be out in the open. The news about Murray, the rapist, would still need to be concealed.

Now that Caden wasn't in the beach house, and Gabby would be with him at Veracruz, it would make it easier to install the surveillance equipment.

By the time they both arrived home from Catemaco, Gabby would be safer than the President of the United States.

When Sterling had explained all the details about his uncomfortable predicament with Alex Blair, Gabby said,

"It sounds like a very awkward golfing situation. But at least now you have met two of my former lovers in person. And, Alex with another woman in public is not anything new. He just seems not to be concerned about hiding his affairs anymore."

The next time she and Alex conference call, Gabby was going to propose that divorce is now eminent. It is the twenty first century, both of his parents are deceased, and it is time to close the casket on a marriage that had died many years ago.

Alex never, during these past months denied Gabby any financial funding. She was confident that they could come to a final arrangement that would be agreeable to both of them.

If she continues to live her life out, here in Todos Santos, Gabby would be taken care of for the remainder of her life. There would be no need to depend on anyone else again.

Sterling interrupted her thought process when he asked,

" Can you be ready to leave tomorrow for Veracruz? It is a about a four hour flight from Cabo to Catemaco. Our Shaman, will not see us until the next morning.

Overnight we will be staying at The Reserva Ecologica Nanciyiga. It is a self contained property that has wooden rooms with mosquitos nets. I remember how much you hate camping, Gabby, but in this case we have no choice. It is the closest location to where the ritual will take place. I was at least able to get us a private bathroom."

Sterling had played with the idea of not telling Gabby about the rustic accommodations, but rejected that idea. He needed to make certain that she would be prepared for what will happen.

"Can you at least tell me how long we will need to stay there?"

Gabby never camped before in her life, and at the age of sixty one, although physically fit, the thought of "roughing" it was undesirable.

"The ritual will take a few hours, but the recovery could last forty eight hours. When we have completed the treatment, it has been arranged for us to be transported to La Finca resort, which is much better than the camp, but not a five star hotel. We should be ready to return to Cabo by Saturday."

To be perfectly honest, Sterling was not certain what the Shaman would perform this time on both him and Gabby. He was told that once they arrived their needs would be assessed accordingly.

The private flight the next morning was uneventful and rather somber. Neither Gabby or Sterling were in the mood for small talk. Both were mentally preparing for the unknown.

The night before they departed, Gabby researched Catemaco, which is referred to as the community of "brujos" translated to mean, witches or sorcerers. These magical practices can be traced back to the pre Hispanic era, but survived because of the remote location and the energy that is emitted by the lake.

There were some disturbing references attributed to one sorcerer, known as Alejandro Garcia, who claims that all one needs to kill a man is "a black cloth doll, a thread, a human bone and a toad."

Apparently , once the Prince of Darkness, the Devil, has approved your request, all that is needed is to slash the throat of the doll, shove the bone down the toads throat, sew up the toads mouth, take it to the nearest graveyard and chant the proper words. According to Garcia, the person will die in thirty days.

What the hell have I agreed to do? Is this finally the beginning of my end? How did I allow Sterling to convince me to participate in this insanity? The answers to those questions were now less than forty eight hours away.

Just as Sterling explained, when the aircraft landed, we were taken to the Ecological camp where we would spend the night. Although I had no appetite, Sterling insisted that we eat dinner.

"It will be your last meal until you recover from the cleansing, Gabby. There is no breakfast in the morning. By 6:00 am, we will be on the road to the Temazcal. I suggest that after dinner we both retire immediately."

Sterling did not exaggerate about the rustic rooms. We were only separated by a sheer curtain, but each bed was enclosed with a mosquito net.

I had not decided yet, if that net was a comforting accessory or a frightening one. It soon was obvious that the net was needed, as I could see in the dark the flying insects trying to find some way in. The risk of malaria in this region, required these precautions.

If I survived the next few days in this environment I promised to never complain about my life again.

When Sterling woke me the following day, I was surprised that I actually slept. The early morning sun was just rising when we boarded an old Jeep for the ride up the mountains, where the ritual would begin.

The unpaved dirt road continued through the jungle for about forty five minutes, when a coral pink archway came into view. As we passed through it another larger coral building was visible. At a short distance several temazcal huts were being maintained by Shaman assistants, whose job was to keep the center coals hot.

We were then greeted by a young woman who introduced herself as Naomi. A welcome drink of hibiscus water was served to us in gourd cups.

Soon Sterling and I were taken inside the coral building and instructed to remove all of our outer clothing, and as much of our undergarments as we wanted.

I removed everything but my panties, and Sterling was completely naked. Neither one of us objected. At one time, clothing was optional when we were together.

Naomi and Maya, her helper, began coating our bodies with various herb oils and aloe Vera to prevent being burnt. Large Palm and banana leaves were then positioned on our chests, thighs, and between our legs.

It was finally time to enter the temazcal hut. Rugs were spread on the ground where we were seated. Once we were comfortable the Shaman and his warriors entered. We were reminded that to enter the temazcal was to step inside Mother Earth.

It was emphasized that this was not to be a resistance test. If at any time we wanted to be released, that would be accommodated. The reason we're here, was solely to be cleansed.

A large cup filled with copal incense was given to Sterling first and then passed to me. We were told to make a silent request to the gods and throw the cup in the fire pit.

Finally, thick blankets covered the entrance from the outside, leaving the interior totally dark, with the exception of the glowing rocks.

Nothing was said verbally by anyone in the hut. But, the warriors began chanting, "U'pe, Ka'ape, ooxpe" and handed both of us separate vials containing DMT, or Dimethyltryptamine, known as a hallucinogenic drug that is more powerful than LSD.

This drug is a plant based mixture that is used by Shamans to allow their followers to "journey" into the realm of the dead, or allow those deceased to re-enter the world of the living.

After a few moments I could feel objects nearby floating and growing. But, then Jake appeared, as real as he was when he was alive. Walking with him was a young woman I did not recognize.

Together, I felt an overwhelming unconditional love moving in the air. Purple, blue, yellows, all images of love surrounding me and Sterling. There was an undetermined, outside force circling around us. The entities were so convincing, that verbal communication was not needed.

Both the male and female images brought with them art objects that were only visible briefly. One was a collection of faeries painted on an unframed canvas, and then next a rather large mural floated above our heads with images of Molly and I, splashing in the ocean, with a lighthouse at a distance. Then slowly they began to melt into puddles beneath our feet. Those puddles felt cold, in spite of the flames from the pit.

The supernatural objects of our endearments took over our bodies so that we were now one with them. At times the female became me and I was then floating above her head. Later, Sterling's body was inside of me and the male apparition became the female embodiment. This went on for what I imagined was years.

Although there were at times no body parts visible, I could feel a mouth on mine, or a head on my lap.

At last, the two apparitions removed themselves from our bodies. But before they departed, they returned for one final moment, just long enough to join my hand to Sterling's, and our bodies became one. Our hearts were beating together in the same body.

When he inhaled, I exhaled his air. When he closed his eyes, I opened them. I had never felt more at peace, as I had during this time.

And then they were gone.

CHAPTER 52

I just want to sleep. A coma would be nice. Or amnesia. Anything , just to get rid of this, these thoughts, whispers in my mind. Did he rape my head too.

Speak
   Laurie Halse Anderson

Murray Jackson
   October, 2010
Ensenada Mexico

All women should be like Kelly. She knows what a man wants and gives it up easy. There are no fucking games. No forcing her to spread her legs.

Murray and Kelly met in a strip club in Ensenada. On stage, Kelly was using the pole like Murray wanted her to use him. When he made it "rain" with dollars, at the end of her performance, Kelly jumped down and gave him a lap dance.

Whenever Murray was in town delivering his "load" to the Jefe, (bosses), the first place he came to, once he got paid, was The Pink Panther. As a matter of fact, the only reason he kept this route was so that he could hump Kelly, and buy Viagra over the counter.

Since he had that unfortunate run in with Caden Cassidy, a few months ago in Savannah , Murray restrained himself from using coke or meth, unless he could occasionally skim the shipment, or for special occasions.

Before that time, he never had any problem getting hard. Then one day, Kelly was giving him a blow job, and Murray realized he couldn't ejaculate.

Then it started taking longer to fuck Kelly. Man, he needed to get his pecker working by the time he grabbed Gabby. There was no back up plan. It was a no fault arrangement.

His pecker needed to be stiff, and stay stiff when he took Gabby back to his basement. If he couldn't deliver when the time came it would ruin everything.

Kelly would be his Mexican bitch, when he came in once a month, and Gabby would be his permanent bitch, in San Diego. When he was ready to tell Calhoun, his brother, then he would regret not coming out west with him.

"Hey, Poncho...Hola! You have something for me Amigo?It's been several weeks. Did your Bro find her?"

Murray was waiting patiently for Poncho to track down Gabby. He just missed her when she was in Ensenada by a few hours. But, now it actually might even be better.

Poncho pulled out a plastic bag, and threw it to Murray.

"This is what you get for your down payment, hombre! Once we get the rest of the dinero, you will get the key that opens that box." Poncho sat down next to him drinking his Corona.

Murray, pulled out the silk panties, and inhaled the pussy that he was now obsessed to make his. He would never forget how that Bitch smelled.

"You did good compadre! Where is she? And, how do I get there?" Murray was nearly foaming at the mouth.

"Well, Senor Murray, getting her out of the country, that might take a lot more cash. Gabby Blair is, let's just say, extremely close friends with a billionaire macho jefe, Sterling Powers.

They both live on the beach at Todos Santos, but not together. A few weeks ago, some other gringo showed up, and is now shacked up with her. His name is..., man, I don't remember.

But, anyway... for some strange reason, he moved out... maybe a lovers spat. That was when your Gabby broad got on a private plane with Sterling Powers and they are now in Veracruz."

Murray couldn't believe how that bitch moved around. Just when he gets close, she finds an escape door. The good news is, that other bastard is probably Caden Cassidy.

The plans now might just slightly change. Before he takes Gabby back to San Diego, he will set it up so that Caden will get front row seats to watch his girlfriend get her anus fitted with Maury's cock. Then he will have Poncho's hombres take Caden to the desert where it will be "hasta luego basura"(trash)

"The good news for you, Murray, is that they are due back home tomorrow. The bad news for you, Murray is that while she was gone, her beach house has been wired with so many surveillance cameras and alarms, that it will be more difficult than Scotland Yard to penetrate."

Poncho let out an annoying laugh that was so boisterous that Murray was sprayed with saliva.

Okay, so Gabby lives in a fortress. All he needs is a good disguise and a key to the front door. He can take over from there.

"Can your bro get me a key to her place, man?"

Murray wasn't going to let a few cameras keep him from bagging what belonged to him. He was an expert at transporting illegal aliens and drugs across the border. Gabby Blair would be a piece of cake. One that he could eat and have at the same time.

"That should be no problem. For a couple hundred US dollars, I can get you a key to almost anywhere."

Pablo always bumped the price up to assure that his cut was sufficient.

"Great. I'll have the money for you tomorrow before I leave." Maury was going to get a good night sleep tonight.

Caden Cassidy
October, 2010
Todos Santos, Mexico

It was difficult not calling Gabby these past few days, but Caden was going to let her have the space she needed. Once she came home, they would have a long, serious talk about moving out of Mexico.

Living this close to Sterling Powers, an ex lover would never work. He didn't care what Gabby wanted to call that relationship. When a man fucks a woman exclusively for those many years, you aren't going to convince anyone that it is now platonic.

Selena left him enough money that he and Gabby can live anywhere, during whatever time they might have left on earth. Anywhere that is, except Todos Santos.

" Maggie just texted me Caden. Gabby and Sterling will be home from Veracruz tomorrow early evening. But, you will need to take a few days before you have that heart to heart conversation. Maggie is staying with Gabby for a week while her house gets fumigated. I think that they are also going to be busy planning our wedding."

Blake updated Caden with the latest news he received.

"Well, then Blake, I guess you and I will be spending a few more days as roomies. Do you have anything exciting planned?"

Caden was finally understanding that time was really not on his side. As much as he wanted to get all of this out of the way, he really was limited on how much he could demand.

"You like futball? I guess in the US you call it soccer? Well, a group of us guys get together once a month and kick the ball around, and afterwards drink a few pitchers of beer at the cantina. It might help you get your mind off of all this for awhile."

Blake knew exactly what Caden was going through. Well... maybe less forty three years.

Murray Jackson
October 2010
Ensenada, Mexico

"The boss wants you to pick up some cargo tonight and take it to Sonora."

Janet, one of the messengers found Murray at his usual spot at The Pink Panther.

"Not tonight Janet. I have to deliver some kilo to a VIP client in Cabo. That's a sixteen hour drive from there, and only if I don't stop. There is no way that I can make that drop off and get to Sonora in time. Tell the Jefe that Murray ain't no pigeon. Only pigeons can make those kinds of trips."

Murray traded with Pablo his normal route from TJ to San Ynez for only one reason. He was on a tight time schedule to get into Todos Santos early enough to rest before picking up his own personal cargo and head home.

This truck would be a perfect vehicle to transport Gabby home to San Diego. There was plenty of room and it was soundproof. Even if she tried to escape it was impossible.

"Okay, Murray, but the boss man doesn't like it when you guys make switches without him knowing about it. So you better get all the deliveries there on time and get your ass back here for the next load."

Janet was a tight ass bitch. She was probably fucking the boss, but Maury didn't care, as long as she left him alone. The money for this gig was great. He wasn't crazy about all the miles he was hauling, but the payoff made it worth any discomfort.

Murray took out the old fashioned road map he kept in his back pocket. GPS was fine, but he always preferred to see the whole distance before he was on the road.

At the small bar table, while waiting for the next stripper to show up, he unfolded the worn out map and looked for Todos Santos.

Once he was able to find the small dot, he took out his sharpie and drew a heart with a penis right where the map showed the city.

In just forty eight hours Maury would be deep inside that pussy. Only thing more satisfying, will be forcing Caden Cassidy to watch

Maury sodomize his dream girl. Justice will finally be his!

CHAPTER 53

Whatever our souls are made of, his and mine are the same.
Wuthering Heights
  Emily Bronte,

Sterling and Gabby,
October, 2010
Catemaco, Mexico

Something without logic, or rational explanation traveled from the land of the dead, to join together, that which was shattered, with no destination.

Awakening from a deep slumber in an unknown room expecting nothing , my arms stretch to both sides, still weak, still without direction. Until...I feel a familiar touch, lightly with fingertips as gentle as a down feather.

I do not feel oppressed, nor do I feel unnatural. Yet, to open my eyes might defy or offend this new discovered peace.

Perhaps if I slowly move my leg toward his, it will just be enough to validate why this spiritual guide placed our bodies next to one another.

Sterling was the first one to slip his hand into Gabby's. He then took each of her fingers linking them to his. With his other hand, he started to caress the softness of her breasts; the firmness of her nipples.

Her eyes remained closed, until he moved his mouth closer to hers. He had never watched her sleep before. Never, in nine years, did he kiss her eyes, nose, cheeks, and lips, like he is doing now. Gently, he parts her lips with his, conscious only of her, without reason or purpose.

Once Gabby felt his virgin tongue exploring her mouth, she knew she wanted more. Those were the lips that spoke the words from his heart. The same lips that smile when she enters a room. And, the lips he prays with in private.

Gabby knew, with no doubts that she was now ready to invite Sterling into a temple that he explored but never allowed himself to appreciate.

His touch was never this light, his body never as determined to please, as it was at this moment. She could not prevent herself from trembling, not with fear, but delight.

Never in her life before, not even with Jake, did anyone totally complete her body, her mind and her soul. They were one. When she pleased him, she was pleased.

Her tongue fluttered instinctively, knowing what he needed. She could hear his body aching for her, and she would give him all that she had.

Gabby was lost inside of Sterling and she never again wanted to be removed from him.

When Sterling wrapped her into his emptiness, where those vacant, void places created a vacuum in his soul, she knew that here she would now be loved and safe.

For twelve years the two of them studied sexual movements, explored various positions and witnessed erotic exhibitions . But, never did they make love. Not until now.

"Where did you get that red ribbon, with the small brass bell on your wrist?"

Gabby had never seen Sterling wear that simple bracelet in the past. Sterling looked down, confused.

"Years ago, on my mother's death bed, she gave me something very similar to this. But, I do not recall the bell attached."

Gabby also recalled the same bracelet that was in Jake's journal. She used it as a book mark, rather than wearing it.

"She told me that it would lead me to the person that I belonged with. At that time, she knew that I would never stop mourning Gisselle. Neither did I, until today. But none of this explains why I am wearing it now. It isn't even the same one that she gave me."

Sterling was about to remove it, when Gabby stopped him.

"No, Sterling don't take it off. That red bracelet is the same one in Jake's journal. Or at least it looks like the same one. He also told me the same story your mom did."

Gabby was now anxious to get home and see if the red string was still in the journal.

"I will leave it on for you. But just know that I don't need a talisman to know how I feel. Whoever you are and wherever you came from, Gabby, I cannot let you go. Not ever. Does that sound too controlling? Because I don't want you to be frightened."

Gabby, for the first time, was at a loss for words.

On the bed, with her elbows together, Gabby inched her way back to his chest, and began nibbling on his nipples, until she looked up into his pewter eyes, and said,

" I am whatever and whoever you want me to be; your forever fantasy, your most intimate desire."

Gabby could no longer hold back. With her legs straddling his chest, she guided his hand into her wet, white flame. The penetration was slow, and it felt like volcanic molt, gloriously hot, melting, exquisite .

Their eyes were open, watching each other ; dancing partners, moving to a sound only they knew. Together at the edge of the cliff, he clung to her round buttocks , while bringing his hips closer to meet her. Gabby screamed his name as he lifted her with his cock still inside and together they came in unison.

Sterling continued to hold her naked body as close to him as possible, wanting to always remember this moment. The moment when their joined hearts and bodies together learned what love could offer.

Gabby did not know how she was going to explain all of this to Caden. He would never understand. Even during their most intimate time together, Gabby now knew that there was only one man that she was fated to be with, and that was Sterling Powers.

When her cell phone rang, Gabby was relieved to hear Maggie's voice. Although there was no way to avoid Caden, this moment was not the right time.

"Hola, Chica! How is your camping trip going?"

Maggie sounded as she was still glowing from her engagement surprise last week.

"Everything is marvelous!" Gabby said, while Sterling playfully distracted her, by playing with her hair.

"Can't wait to tell you everything. We will be home tomorrow afternoon." Gabby said .

"Does that mean you don't need to see the sex doctor?"

Maggie was hoping that Gabby's cleansing took care of her amnesia problem.

"Thankfully, no, I won't need to see her. Pretty sure that will never happen again." Sterling was winking and making silly faces trying to get her to laugh.

"Sounds like a very well worth trip. But, I really called because I need a place to shack up for a week, while the pest controllers fumigate my place.

By the way, Blake says he is keeping Caden busy and entertained. I was afraid to ask Blake for details, but thought you would be glad to hear that."

Maggie did not want to add that Caden was still annoyed about her traveling with Sterling.

"No problem. You can stay as long as you want. It will be like an extended sleepover. Looking forward to seeing you soon, Maggie."

When Gabby heard the phone click, she moved back to be closer to Sterling.

"This sounds perfect. Maggie can stay at your place, and you can stay with me. We will just continue what we started here. And, then eventually you can move…"

Gabby stopped Sterling from finishing his sentence.

"Did you forget just one small detail? Caden is expecting to move back in with me when I return home. He just left his wife, business, and crossed the border to be with me again. I owe him an explanation."

Gabby knew that there was no other way.

"WE owe him an explanation Gabby. I don't want you to face this on your own. We will do this together. But, you are right. No plans about moving in together until Caden is told. Have you also considered asking Alex for a divorce? I can't imagine him objecting, to that, not now."

Sterling was anxious to spend the rest of his life with Gabby, and he didn't want any further obstacles in their way.

"Yes, I was actually thinking about that exact subject before we came here. I will call Alex in a few days and get everything started. I am hoping there will be no need for an attorney, if we are both amicable." This was all now beginning to seem real.

After a late dinner, Gabby and Sterling returned to their room for the most restful sleep either of them had ever experienced. Sterling felt like they had never been apart, and yet everything was new, exciting.

They both, realized that they had been given a rare gift, their own destiny revealed at last; always so very close but now there were no doubts.

When their private plane landed at two that afternoon, on October 31, neither of them realized the date. At the Cabo airport, Sterling decided to send Gabby in the town car to Todos Santos by herself. He wanted to talk to the security officers about the surveillance installation, in private.

When he got home, he would call Gabby and tell her how to use the security code when entering the front door.

Since Maggie was already there, he knew that she could also give Gabby a quick tutorial on the necessity for security protection.

"I will be home in a few hours, after this important business meeting. Let me know later tonight when you want to meet with Caden. I can make myself available at any time, once you arrange it."

Sterling took one final long kiss, before he sent Gabby into an unknown tsunami.

When the driver realized that it was The Day of the Dead, October 31, he knew that the traffic would delay their trip back to Todos Santos.

"What is going on out their Miguel? The streets are packed and people are dressed in weird skeleton costumes?"

Just as Gabby said this, she realized why, It was October 31! For nine years, Gabby avoided leaving her house, even in the daytime on this day. And now...now she was in the center of all the festivities, without any recourse.

"Today is the Day of the Dead, Senora Gabby. Everywhere in Mexico, even in small villages like Todos Santos, people are celebrating. Here we believe that the gates of heaven are opened at midnight and all the deceased children are allowed to reunite with their families for twenty four hours. On November 2, the spirits of the adults come down to enjoy the festivals."

All that Gabby could remember about October 31 is that it was the gates of hell that released her attacker.

" In Todos Santos, you will find alters with mounds of flowers, and bakeries that offer *pan de muerto, or bread of the dead.* Senora Gabby, this is a major holiday to us.

During these three days, we do not only celebrate, we also go to the cemetery and clean tombs, listen to music and pray."

All that Gabby wanted was to get back to her home and wait for Sterling. He was the only one that could understand how disturbing this holiday was to her.

What would be a ninety minute drive home, resulted in two and a half hours. Gabby put her dark glasses on and tried to escape from this nightmare.

Murray Jackson
October 29-31
Todos Santos, Mexico

Murray had arrived at Cabo San Lucas two days ago, October 29. After delivering his load as promised, Pablo's brother, Jaime reviewed with him on the map how to get to Todos Santo.

"There is a place downtown, called The Hotel California that is located just a few blocks from where Caden Cassidy is staying. He is bunking up with Blake Santiago.

He owns the Maggie Mariposa, a popular bar and night club in town. And, a few days before October 31, the Day of the Dead, everything will be busy.

Not sure what you plan to do with all this information. Don't know if I want to know, but here it is, along with the keys to the rental car and the contact cells for the Nuestro La Familia drug cartel. They can advise you on what to do next.

Oh… and here is the key to Gabby Blair's beach house. The rest of this history you make on your own." Jaime handed him all the details in a sealed envelope.

" Oh, and make sure that you burn all of this when you are done with it. These gauchos are bad asses. If they even think that they can be linked to any of this shit, you will be the one buried in an unmarked grave in the desert. And, by the way, they're fucking killing machines. When they're done with you, it will look like a barracuda chewed you up and spit you out."

Murray just shook his head, and exchanged the envelope with the money he owed.

"Those guevos don't threaten me. I've been in this business since they were sucking on their mommy's titties. All I need them to do is dispose of Caden's body when I'm done with it."

Such perfect timing to celebrate his and Gabby's first meeting. Like their anniversary, only this time, it will be even better. This time he will also have his revenge

Murray, finished his beer, thought twice about having one last fuck with the senorita that promised him fifteen minutes of fun, for half price today.

It would be a good way to test his pecker before he got the real prize, but the Viagra seemed to be working fine lately. All he wanted to do right now, is get checked into that Hotel California and case out the town.

The ninety mile drive was traffic free, once he got away from the crowded streets of Cabo.

From what Murray could tell, most of the land looked like desert. He was thankful it was late October and not fucking hot, like it has been.

It was so hot, that a few months ago, when he was transporting some wet backs in the semi, one of the elderly women died of a heartache. He didn't get paid for that one, and then needed to find a place to bury her. What a fucking nightmare that was.

Murray must have been daydreaming, speeding, or both because the sign he just passed said it is 5km to Todos Santos. He was here. The first thing Murray noticed, when he got to the front desk was a post card of the Hotel California, with writing underneath it.

Where do the eagles nest?
Along a dusty, remote, lonely empty road.
Where the Tin Man and The Straw Man share "colitis",
Welcome to the Hotel California in Todos Santos!
(Gabriella Girard Blair)

Murray, picked up the complimentary post card and read it again. Holy shit…Gabby is personally welcoming me to this shit hole! He stuffed the card in his pants pocket. Maybe later he would masturbate on it.

"Buenos Diaz, Senor, and welcome to The Hotel California!"

Eleanor Rigby was anxious to have a customer. It had been a slow month, and the revenue was low. Even now during the Day of the Dead celebrations, many people went to Cabo, where everything was more elaborate.

"How many nights are you wanting to spend with us? We have a special rate during this season, two nights for the price of one."

She was hoping that this would be appealing to an obvious drifter.

"The price ain't an issue, and I am not sure yet how long I will need the room, but I want one in the back...away from any other people and noises."

Murray wanted his privacy just in case he needed to bring Gabby here for some reason. According to this postcard she must like the hotel.

Eleanor Rigby smiled to herself...*no problemo, there isn't another living soul in this old hotel, accept me.*

" Here is your key, and a map of our city. Oh, and there are a few coupons on the back from local establishments that you may want to use."

Eleanor took the money, paid in full for three nights, and the registration card. Murray had listed San Diego as his residency, but Eleanor thought he had a southern accent. Oh, well, she didn't really care if he was from Transylvania, he was a paying customer.

Murray walked up the long sweeping staircase, and located his room, number 999, at the end of the hallway. He couldn't wait to tell Calhoun that he stayed at The Hotel California, in Mexico, AND, in room 999! At last, Murray felt that he was better than his brother.

Inside the room, there was a double bed, television, small desk, and a large window with a view of the alley. But, that was fine. Murray was here for a purpose and he didn't need any view to take his mind off that purpose.

Before he started to undress, he noticed on the back of the map he was holding, there was an advertisement for The Maggie Mariposa.

Murray wondered if there were any good stripteasers in that club. If so, he might stroll over there to check out the merchandise.

But then he remembered what Jaime said about Caden staying with the owner. Better not be too visible around here. *Don't want to blow my cover.* Instead, he found the guavas contact in his pocket and punched in the numbers.

"Hola, es Ricardo, como se llama."

"No habla Espanol" Murray said, realizing for the first time that there may be a language barrier.

"Okay... H-E-L-L-O mother fucker!"

Ricardo hated when gringos came into this country wanting his help, but then expecting him to speak their language. If the money wasn't good he would tell them to go screw themselves.

"Good you speak English! Jaime told me that you would be able to dispose of...ah, some unwanted garbage for me."

Murray remembered Jaime telling him to be cautious. Just in case the phones were tapped, he wasn't going to take any chances.

"That all depends on how much you are willing to pay for that removal, and how difficult it will be to transport."

Ricardo liked that Jaime's friend spoke the same "language" when it came to a job.

After about thirty minutes, explaining his plan, they agreed on a price, day, and time. If all went as planned, Caden would be worm food, and Gabby would be his sex slave. Life is Good!

CHAPTER 54

Death must be so beautiful. To lie in the soft brown earth, with the grasses waving above ones head, and listen to silence. To have no yesterday, and no tomorrow. To forget time, to forget life, to be at peace.

Oscar Wild

Gabby and Caden
October 31, 2010
Todos Santos, Mexico

Gabby was greeted with hugs and kisses from Maggie, as soon as she walked through the door.

"Tell me…Tell me…Tell me everything. Do not leave one detail out. How was the whole cleansing experience? Does it really work to remove everything negative? I'm thinking of going before the wedding, just to guarantee that I won't screw up Blake's life forever."

Whenever Maggie would get excited, Gabby would say she reminded her of Betty Boop . That famous cartoon character created by Max Fleischer in 1930.

"Who is Betty Boop?" Maggie would ask confused.

Once Gabby showed her pictures of the famous animated character, Maggie liked the comparison.

"Hold on Betty Boop! There is nothing wrong with you that Blake Stantiago can't repair. Honestly Maggie, all you should be thinking about now is what your wedding dress is going to look like and who you are going to invite."

Gabby wanted to reassure Maggie that her life was finally going to be as beautiful and wonderful as she deserved.

"You are right, Gabby. There are just times, like now, October 31, when I still flashback to the past. I know why, but I want to get passed it. But, anyway, now tell me what happened at Catemaco."

Gabby wanted to tell Maggie that she knew EXACTLY how she felt today. But, there is no reason to intensify the problem with both of them reminiscing.

Instead, Gabby went into as many details as she could comfortably share with Maggie, about Catemaco . Even as she was describing how surrealistic that first moment was with Sterling, and how majestic it was, there was a part of her that tried to make her feel that she did not deserve such happiness.

"Oh, but you deserve it Gabby. You and Sterling both deserve to be happy. But, now how are you going to tell Caden? I mean, that man has been in love you for over four decades."

Maggie did not wish to be Gabby when she finally had to tell Caden.

"It is probably the most difficult meeting I will ever have, but at least it will be closure. That was the one thing that we never were able to have in the past."

Even as Gabby was saying these words she hoped that when the time came she would not lose her courage. The sooner this would happen, the better. No need to prolong the drama, but tomorrow would be soon enough.

The Hotel California:
October 31, 2010

Maury had just returned from his tour of the city. A full moon was predicted to be out this evening, which he always thought was a good omen.

Ricardo told him that Blake left for the club at nine o'clock every evening. The last few nights he was alone. If Maury wanted to nab Caden, tonight would work well with Ricardo.

The original plan was going to take Caden to Gabby's house, rape her in front of him, and then let Ricardo get rid of the body.

Then Ricardo told him it was too risky moving people around. He decided to put a tracker on Caden's phone. Once Ricardo knew that Caden was on his way to see Gabby, he would call Maury. The rest would be up to him.

Ricardo wasn't into watching kinky sex. He would return for whatever was left to dispose of. That was the deal.

At ten o'clock , Blake called Caden from the club to tell him that Gabby was home. Ricardo had a tracer on both Caden and Blake's phone. When that call came through, it was the signal Ricardo was waiting for.

Now it was all up to Murray. He grabbed his gun, knife, and chlorine to knock out Gabby if necessary, oh...and the duct tape.

The beach house was less than twenty minutes from down town. Murray would make it there in plenty of time before Caden.

Gabby's house was easy to find with the GPS. Once he parked the rental car, he walked up to the front door with his backpack of paraphernalia, and positioned himself directly behind the large shrub that hid him perfectly. When Caden arrived, they would both surprise Gabby together.

Sterling decided to check in with Gabby at about nine o'clock. But, it was Maggie that picked up Gabby's phone. She had just set her ring tone to "Faith" by George Michael, to alert her whenever Sterling would call.

Since Maggie also knew this, she decided to take Sterling by surprise, instead of letting the phone go to automatic messenger.

"Hello, Babe. Where have you been hiding all night." Maggie said in a disguised voice.

"You're not Gabby." Sterling said playfully.

"I am so glad that you can tell the difference, after spending all that time exclusively with the lady that you just left hours ago."

Sterling was not sure how much Gabby had shared with Maggie, but he was going to take no chances.

"I just wanted to make sure that she knew I was home, I mean just in case she wanted..." He paused, not sure how he wanted to relay that message.

"Just in case she wanted to hear your voice? Or maybe, stop by and visit? Or maybe share your bed?"

Maggie loved that she could tease Sterling. He was always the one doing practical jokes with her, or teasing her, sometimes relentlessly. Now it was her turn.

Sterling, by this time, could tell that Maggie was having fun at his expense.

"What exactly did Gabby tell you? No...I don't even want know. Just tell her that I will meet her in the morning for breakfast at Mama's Casa. She knows the time."

But, before he hung up, Maggie added,

" Seriously, Sterling she was exhausted. I told her to go to bed and I would answer any calls for her. If you stop by the club tonight, give my baby a kiss from me." Maggie said.

"If I stop by Maggie I will tell Blake you sent him a kiss, but honey, you will have to do the delivery yourself." Sterling said, feeling back in control.

As soon as that strange conversation was over, Maggie checked the time in the kitchen. It was already ten 'o'clock.

She grabbed a glass of water, walked back to the guest room and decided that Gabby had the right idea to retire early.

She closed the guest bedroom door, just in case Sterling decided to come over and surprise Gabby. Maggie wanted to make sure that they had their own privacy.

Sterling thought that it would be better to get a drink at The Hotel California first and then call Blake before going to The Mariposa. He wanted to avoid any confrontation with Caden Cassidy.

On the way into the bar, some hotel guest, wearing shades, at nine o'clock at night, and a black hoodie, nearly knocked him over.

"Hey, Buddy, slow down and takes those glasses off before you run into the wrong guy."

Sterling thought he heard the dude tell him to fuck off, but before he could turn around the asshole was out the door.

Eleanor Rigby was standing behind the check in desk watching the close confrontation.

"Since when do you rent rooms to scum bags, Ellie."

Sterling said before heading for the bar.

"Sorry Sterling, but business has been really slow lately and that stranger just checked in for a three days stay yesterday. He also paid in full. If I didn't really need the money I would tell him to leave. He makes my skin crawl. But, bills need to be paid."

Sterling sympathized with Eleanor, but he knew that the lack of customers was only a temporary dilemma. Next month, with the holiday season, this place will be sold out.

At the bar, Sterling realized that there was something else about that moron in the lobby that bothered him. He couldn't figure it out, but he thought that he recognized him from somewhere.

But, with all the people he comes across during the charities and foundation it could have been anyone.

After a few drinks, and talking with a couple of the locals about the surfing competition last weekend, Sterling checked his watch. It was ten thirty. If Caden Cassidy was not at the club with Blake, then Sterling would stop by to see how he and Maggie were doing after the engagement party.

It would also give him an opportunity to get some insight on what he thought about Caden, since Blake had now spent several days with him.

When Blake's cell phone rang directly to messenger, Sterling decided on calling the private direct line to the club. Stephanie, the bartender answered the phone.

"Hey, Sterling, how's it going. Heard you took a little trip to Catemaco for a few days? Glad to hear you're back."

The music in the background was pounding, and it was obvious that the club was busy tonight.

"Don't bother Blake if he's not close by. Do you know, Caden Cassidy? That, gentleman who has been staying with Blake... is there tonight?" Sterling asked directly.

"Let me take a look around...hold on just a sec."

Stephanie put down the receiver briefly. Sterling was on hold for five minutes according to the counter on his cell. Just when he was going to disconnect, Stephanie returned.

"Sorry Sterling I took so long, but there are a hell of a lot of people here tonight. Probably because of The Day of the Dead celebration.

You would think we were giving away free shit. But, anyways, no, that dude isn't coming in tonight and Blake says to stroll on over. He has a booth reserved for you."

Stephanie sounded rushed and out of breath. Sterling had totally forgotten about the date. He should have insisted that Gabby stay with him tonight.

But, since Maggie said Gabby was sleeping, he could only hope that it meant she found her own way to avoid the nightmare that haunted her.

He also would remember to give Stephanie a good tip when he got there later.

The Mariposa was definitely jumping tonight. Probably because most were staying in the surfers compound. They definitely were not all locals.

Most looked like tourists, but when he saw Eleanor earlier tonight, she was complaining about only have one guest in the hotel.

This crowd was great for business, but Blake was counting on Caden coming with him tonight.

Since he owned a pub his help would have been priceless. But, then when Blake called Maggie and she told him that Gabby and Sterling were home, that was all Caden needed to hear.

"Did Maggie tell you why Gabby didn't call me? Or why her

phone is going to auto messenger when I call her?"

Blake tried to calm Caden down. In retrospect, he probably never should have told him that Gabby was back.

Because the band was playing and this crowd was kicking, he couldn't stay on the line for long, but he thought he heard Caden say that he was going over to talk to Gabby.

Blake didn't even know if Caden remembered him saying that Maggie was staying there for the week.

When Blake finally saw Sterling walk over from the bar, it was almost eleven o'clock.

"The band is about to take a break. When that happens we need to talk. Wait for me at the booth with the reserved sign on it."Blake said, before he noticed Stephanie calling him over to the bar.

When he was through extinguishing any fire, that always seems to start at the bar, he needed to tell Sterling that Caden knew they were home. Maybe even more important, when he last spoke to him, it was obvious that he was pretty agitated .

Murray's Celebration Party!

Ten thirty , Murray finally heard Caden's car engine turn off. Something was up his ass, because It only took him a few seconds to rush up to the door.

Before Caden could knock, ring the door bell, or take out a key Murray had his mouth and arms taped. Murray was so fast that Caden had no idea what happened.

"Remember me, mother fucker. I am your worst nightmare all the way from Savannah . I am about to put on a show for you that you will never forget, dick head."

When Caden realized Murray's voice he tried to use his legs to knock him down, but then everything went dark.

Murray left Caden slumped in the bushes and walked to the back of the house that faced the ocean. That was when he noticed the French Doors were left ajar.

Before Caden came, Murray had cut the wires to the surveillance cameras and re wired them to show everything idle, with no disturbances . One of the only worthwhile tricks he ever learned from his brother.

Now that he could go through the back door, he wouldn't need to worry about any alarm when he brought Caden through the front door.

Someone was kind enough to leave a kitchen light on for him.

The chloroform that Pedro gave him for this job was much easier to get in Mexico. It should work for at least fifteen minutes. Plenty of time to set up the stage and get Gabby out here.

Both the bedroom doors were closed with no sound coming from either one. Kind of like that dumb kids story about the Lion or the Tiger.

The one to his right had double doors. A good sign that this is where his pussy was. He slightly cracked the door open, and there she was, fast asleep.

Murray quietly approached the bed, then without any resistance he was able to tape first her mouth, and then grab Gabby's wrists and tie both of them together in front of her.

The moment that she was able to open her eyes and her blurry vision focused on Murray she began to resist with her legs, twisting her body as far as possible from this disgusting creature from hell.

"Now Gabby, don't be this way. You knew I was coming back for you. It's been longer than I expected.'"

While Murray was talking his fingers began to feel her wet pussy. The same vagina that only hours ago was safe in the loins of the man she loved.

Mother Mary of God, hear my prayers. Give me the strength to hear not the sounds of silence but your answers. The celestial whispers that will deliver me to my Christ. Protect my unworthy soul from this damnation, I pray in the name of the father…"

Gabby could no longer say the words in her head. They were being interrupted by Murray carrying her limp body into the living room.

He sat her on the kitchen chair and stared at her with his yellow eyes. He is *"the fiend from hell" that has been reincarnated to avenge Cain, Adam's son who kills his brother. And, I am the chosen one to bleed for all those innocent tormented souls.*

Murray positioned Gabby to sit straddling on the wooden chair so that when the time is right, Murray said,

"That's a good girl. Now I can fuck you in the ass and finish what we started nine years ago. But first, I have a surprise for you."

Murray opens the front door and makes Caden, who is barely coherent, sit in front of her at her feet. Murray took out his switchblade knife that Calhoun gave him for his thirteenth birthday, and held it to Caden's neck.

"Now that we are all here, we can begin this party. This is not only a celebration for Gabby to feel my dick in her ass in a few minutes, but, unfortunately for you Caden, it's a going away party. When I am done fucking your bitch, your next. And then, my friend Ricardo will be here to dispose of you."

Murray was so busy giving Gabby and Caden the details that he never heard Maggie come in.

"Whoever the hell you are, take that tape off both their mouths and arms or I will blow your head off." Maggie had the 45 caliber hand gun pointed directly at Murray's head.

Murray took his knife and started laughing.

"Sweetie. Have you ever shot anyone in your life before? Well, let me tell you. From where you are standing if you don't have me in your perfect range, when that bullet hits the wall, I will slit this assholes throat so fast...."

"I said, MOTHER FUCKER, cut their hands loose." Maggie demanded once again.

"Do you have any idea what I am capable of doing?" Murray said, now getting pissed at the interruption.

Before Maggie could pull the trigger, Murray plunged the knife

….once, twice, three times, into Caden's chest.

Then, at least four bullets from Maggie's gun went through Murray's heart, as his body fell on top of Caden's.

With both hands on the revolver, Maggie shot him once more close up, and then pushed his body as far away as she could. Now, Murray's blood was mingling with Caden's.

Still shaking, Maggie quickly removed the tape from Gabby's hands and mouth.

"My God, I am so sorry Gabby. I had no idea that he would stab Caden before I shot him. Oh , my God…Gabby."

Immediately, Gabby and Maggie pulled Murray off of Caden, removed the tape from his mouth and binding on his hands.

Gabby knelt down begging Caden to hold on. In her arms he whispered in Gabby's ear,

"We almost made it, didn't we, Gabby? I have always loved you, my Abby with a G. Never forget that. Promise me Gabby, that you won't forget what we once had…" Gabby's tears touched Caden's lips as he took his last breath.

When The police, ambulance, Sterling and Blake all arrived at the same time, Gabby was soaked in blood, cradling Caden's body.

Sterling immediately rushed to her, past the officers. When he tried to release her arms from Caden's shoulders, Gabby wouldn't let him go.

"Gabby," Sterling whispered gently. "Gabby, he is gone, baby. There is nothing left that we can do."

For that one moment, it was like Jake and Caden were in the same body. She was clinging to Jake as he was pulling away, at eighteen years old, and now it was Caden's lifeless body being ripped away.

When Sterling at last was able to release her grip on Caden, he tried to help her stand, but Gabby's legs no longer could support her body.

She was a waxed candle melting from inside. Sterling lifted her up and carried her to his car. When they arrived at his house, it was as if she was in a coma. Gabby said nothing.

After Sterling laid her in his bed, she stared into empty spaces. Nowhere, and nothing mattered.

When the doctor arrived, he examined Gabby and gave her a sedative injection.

"Gabriella has suffered an emotional breakdown. How long this will last is difficult to predict. What I have given her is a strong dose of medication. She could sleep for forty eight hours.

If she does not wake by then, you will need to admit her to the hospital in Cabo. I am not skilled enough to go any further."

The doctor left a few more oral sedatives, and general observation instructions, before he left.

Sterling remained by Gabby's side in a vigil for two days. On the third day he was making arrangements to transport her to Cabo, when she finally woke up.

"Thank God, Gabby. I have been crazy worried about you. What do you remember? Anything? If not that's fine. It will take time."

Sterling kissed her hand, afraid to move too close and frighten her.

"He's dead, isn't he?" Gabby was looking at her hands as if they were stained with blood.

There is a luxury in self reproach. When we blame ourselves, we feel no one else has the right to blame us. It is the confession not the priest that gives us absolution.(Oscar Wilde) Like Lady Macbeth, I cannot ever remove that stain from my soul.

"Yes Gabby, Caden is dead. But you must know that it wasn't you that killed him. It was Murray, and If Maggie had not shot him, you all may have been dead."

Sterling was determined that Gabby not blame herself for something out of her control.

Caden's death was traumatic for Gabby, but what was nearly as terrible for her, was never being able to explain to him what she learned about their relationship.

She will never be able to tell him now, that she was in love with him on that New Year's Eve in 1967. When Selena questioned her, about that love, Gabby hesitated. But, now she knew that she and Caden could have been happily married.

The only consolation to this tragedy is Caden died without ever knowing that she is, and has been in love with Sterling since they met twelve years ago.

CHAPTER 55

Your visions will become clear only when you can look into your own heart. Who looks outside dreams; who looks inside awakes.
Carl Jung

Gabby, Sterling, and Maggie
January, 2011
Mexico

Gabby never did return to her beach house. Sterling arranged for all of her personal belongings to be moved to his house. The garden statue, with the enchanting dragonfly fairy, blowing on the dandelion, was transported to the entrance of the new Humanities School located in Ensenada with an extended satellite campus located in Todos Santos.

Sterling commissioned a smaller version of the beloved statue to also be located in the lobby of The Gisselle Theatre in Cabo San Lucas. It was a visual inspiration for those who doubt that hope and faith exist.

Gabby dedicated the statue to Molly McGee, Caden Cassidy, and Jake Chevalier.

In her speech, on the day that the Gisselle Theater reopened, Gabby finally was able to give the eulogy to all three of the most important people in her life.

The red ribbon, with the brass bell, that Gabby found in Jake's Journals, was no longer in the leather book. Sterling always wore the one that was on his wrist, that morning he and Gabby consummated their love in Catemaco. He bought her a matching one weeks later.

Although there was an investigation involving the killing of

Murray, originally from Savannah , Georgia, all charges were dropped against Maggie. Police were able to collaborate with certain informants that Murray had arranged a premeditated murder.

A few weeks after, Caden's body was returned to Savanna, to his ex wife, Kaitlyn Cassidy, who arranged for his burial. He was laid to rest near his, biological mother, Aunt Selena and his adopted mother, Claudia.

Blake Santiago, was the one to fulfill Caden's final request.

"The morning before Caden's death, he asked me to hold for him in the club's safe, this item for you, Gabby."

Blake revealed the most exquisite emerald cut diamond surrounded by exactly forty three emeralds.

He then retold the story Caden shared with him, about this ring.

"This was the ring Caden planned to give you on that New Year's Eve when he left you. He added an emerald for each year the two of you were separated. Caden was planning on giving it to you the night he died."

Gabby could no longer cry. There were no tears left. She had to give it to Caden's twin boys in California.

She would share with them their father's story and let them decide who should pass it on to the next generation.

The signed George Harrison Abby Lane album, with the letter G added, was donated to the Todos Santos theatre, in memory of Caden Cassidy.

On Maggie's wedding day, right before she walked down the aisle with her father, Gabby handed her Jake's Journals.

"It is time for me to pass these on Maggie. Since I never had a daughter, and never will, I am leaving you these many words of wisdom. Share them with whoever you believe will benefit from them."

Gabby handed the journals to the only person she knew could appreciate them.

"But, these are Jake's words. Are you sure you want me to have them?" Maggie knew how important these journals were to her best friend.

"There is no soul alive on this earth that I would give these to, but you. Now take that walk down the aisle and begin the most incredible journey in your life."

Gabby hugged Maggie and knew in her heart that Molly, Jake, and even Caden were all here tonight walking with her to the alter. Before she walked down the aisle where Blake was waiting, Maggie took off the mustard seed that she always wore.

"Gabby, this gift to you means more than anything except the ring on my finger." Maggie then placed the necklace around Gabby's neck. It was the final piece needed to bring their life back to normal once again.

December 31, 2012 Gabby and Sterling married in an intimate, candlelight ceremony at Laguna Beach, California. It was a time to bury the old, and celebrate the *dreams that come true that you never even knew you had.*

Two years later, Maggie was giving an interview for her first Broadway play, in New York, titled Destiny Revisited, by Maggie Santiago.

Before meeting with a reporter for her interview, a stage manager handed her an envelope.

"I know that *Break a Leg* is more appropriate for an actor, but I hope it is also good luck for the playwright. Look for me in the front row tonight, Maggie Mendoza Santiago, I will be your loudest fan."

Congressman Charlie Malone

Maggie could not believe that Charlie was really here.

How did you ever find me? And, you a Congressman. There would be time soon for answers and embraces.

"Can you perhaps Mrs Santiago share with your audience who inspired you to write this moving play?"

The reporter asked, preparing to write down every word.

"Well, let me tell you about this young girl, Gabriella Girard, who lived in Savanna, Georgia, once upon a time."

About the Author

Eleanor Tremayne

After twenty five years teaching literature high school and college students, Eleanor Tremayne has finally completed her literary opus. *Destiny Revisited* was released, July 1, 2017 and is sold at Amazon, Barnes and Nobles, and many other fine retailers and book stores internationally.

"Where the hell is Gabby?"

Destiny Revealed answers that question and so much more. Both novels address the complicated love triangle of Gabriella Girard, originally from Savannah, Georgia. It is a study that examines how the turbulent 1960's influenced a young girl's rite of passage.

Gabby is gifted. She is able to recite and remember powerful literary passages from Dante to James Joyce. She also struggles with relating classical literature to her decisions in life.

Olga Voneggerth, the heroin, in Eleanor Tremayne's third novel traces an eighteen year-old girl's frightening escape from St. Petersburg, Russia during the Bolshevik Revolution. Although the events are written as fiction, it is based on Eleanor's own Grandmother's exile. Olga, escapes a Bolshevik firing squad, survives a brutal Siberian Russian winter, before she is finally rescued by a Cossack soldier who helps determine her fate.

His orders are to deliver Olga to the last Prince of Khiva, Razek Bek Khadjieff. When the Prince meets Olga, for the first time, she is wearing a dead Cossack's pants, ragged peasant blouse, and has soot on her face. It is a face that Razak Bek falls in love with nevertheles. Their whirlwind love affair conquers the ravishes of war, leading them both to a comfortable life in Mexico, and eventually the United States.

This novel is a tribute to Eleanor's maternal grandmother who raised her, and lived to the age of ninety three years-old. It is a remarkable tale with layers of fascinating Russian history, Prima Ballerinas, and a dedicated photo journalist who is determined to deliver a one hundred year old diary to its rightful owner. *Seven Days in Lebanon* offers the reader a thrilling adventure.